# OUR NEW NORMAL

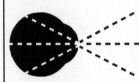

This Large Print Book carries the
Seal of Approval of N.A.V.H.

# OUR NEW NORMAL

## COLLEEN FAULKNER

**THORNDIKE PRESS**
A part of Gale, a Cengage Company

Copyright © 2019 by Colleen Faulkner.
Thorndike Press, a part of Gale, a Cengage Company.

Thorndike Press® Large Print Relationship Reads.
The text of this Large Print edition is unabridged.
Other aspects of the book may vary from the original edition.
Set in 16 pt. Plantin.

LIBRARY OF CONGRESS CIP DATA ON FILE.
CATALOGUING IN PUBLICATION FOR THIS BOOK
IS AVAILABLE FROM THE LIBRARY OF CONGRESS

ISBN-13: 978-1-4328-7335-6 (softcover alk. paper)

Published in 2020 by arrangement with Kensington Books, an imprint of Kensington Publishing Corp.

Printed in Mexico
Print Number: 01      Print Year: 2020

For my mother, Judith French,
who taught me how to be a daughter,
a wife, a mother, and a friend.
All I am, I owe to her.

# 1
## LIV

I stand at the upstairs bathroom door, glancing down the hallway to be sure no one is coming. I tap lightly. "Hazel?" I whisper because my husband's family's summer cottage is old and voices seem to carry for miles. Especially bad tidings. I think every argument Oscar and I ever had in this house was overheard by at least three family members and possibly our closest neighbors, half a mile away.

I wait, refusing to allow my mind to think of anything but what I'm making for dinner on the grill. Most of all, I don't think of my sixteen-year-old self on the other side of this door. "Hazel?" I repeat, a little louder.

*"Mom!"* She manages to express her anger, displeasure, and disappointment in every parenting mistake I've ever made in her tone with that one word. The door opens, but only a crack.

7

I see Hazel's eyes. My eyes gazing back at me.

"You look. I can't." Hazel pushes an object through the crack and slams the door.

I clutch the plastic stick that my daughter has just peed on. I can't bring myself to look at it. "Did you time it?"

I hear her push against the door and then her voice comes from the direction of my knees. She's sitting on the floor now, her back against the door, her knees drawn up. I know the position. Been there occasionally over the years when life seemed too overwhelming.

"Yes. I *timed* it, *Mom.* It wouldn't make much sense if I didn't. Ten minutes. Ten minutes are up. Twelve, now." She's on the verge of tears, but she isn't crying.

I close my eyes for a second. I take a breath, steeling myself.

*Please, please don't let it be positive,* I pray. If it's negative, I'll go to church more often. I'll donate more used clothing. I'll adopt a stray dog, a stray jackal even. Just please don't let it be positive.

I open my eyes. And stare at the positive sign in the window of the pregnancy test. It's bright blue, practically neon.

"Mom?" says Hazel.

"Pee on the other one," I tell her, feeling

8

light-headed. And angry. How could she have been so stupid — my straight-A-student daughter? "It's a two-pack. Get the other one out of the box," I order, no kindness or empathy in my voice. I'm pissed. And hurt. And scared to the tips of my toes.

"I'm pregnant," Hazel says miserably from the other side of the door. "It's positive, isn't it?"

I press my hand on the door and lean against it, my cheek to the painted white wood, still clutching the pregnancy test in the other hand. "Just do it, Hazel."

"Mom . . ." I hear her getting to her feet. "Peeing on another stick isn't going to make me *not* pregnant."

And she's right.

She hands me a second positive test eleven minutes later.

I push my way into the bathroom, and this time it's my turn to slam the door. "Hazel." It comes out as an exhalation. "How the hell could you get pregnant?"

"Do I have to explain it to you, Mom?"

She stands in front of me barefoot, in a tank and jean shorts, hands on her narrow hips. How will those teenage girl's hips bear the weight of a child?

I glare at her. "You know what I mean. It's the twenty-first century. You got 1505 on your first try on your SATs. You have my credit card." I'm practically poking her with the two pee sticks. "I don't even care about the sex, Hazel. No, I don't mean that. I *care*. You know how I feel about teens, *any* teenager, having sex. I wouldn't want your brother —"

"I don't think there's any fear of that," she quips, backing up to the sink, leaning on it with her hands behind her. She has her father's hair, a gorgeous dark auburn. My dark-brown eyes. Her father's freckles, but my nose.

"You know what I mean," I say, whisper-shouting at her. "You're too smart not to have used birth control."

"Apparently not," she deadpans.

I stand there staring at her, clutching not one but two positive pregnancy tests in my hand. She stares back, defiant. This is how she argues with me. She gets defensive in a smart-assy way, which makes me angry. Mostly because she probably learned it from me.

I close my eyes for a moment and exhale. "Oh, Hazel," I whisper. My voice cracks. "I'm so sorry, sweetheart."

She just stands there.

I open my eyes, drop the plastic sticks into the trash can, and walk to the sink. She slides over a couple of inches to let me get to the faucet. I pump soap into my palm and lather my hands. The smell of peaches wafts from the foaming bubbles.

"I can't believe I'm going to have a baby," she murmurs. "I'm going to be a mom."

I turn the faucet on with the back of a sudsy hand. "Not necessarily. You have options."

She moves away from me as if she's afraid I'm going to slap her. "Mom, I would never have an abortion. This is Tyler's baby." She cradles her abdomen as if the baby is a full-term eight-pounder, not a lima bean.

Tyler. *That little jackass.* I could hardly stand the sight of him *before* I knew he'd knocked up my daughter. He's the epitome of a lazy, goalless, sulky teenaged boy. A one-dimensional cartoon character. I've always believed there was a good reason why stereotypes exist.

I rinse my hands. "I didn't suggest you have an abortion." Truthfully, if she'd said she wanted one, I'm not sure how I'd respond. It doesn't matter because that's clearly not what she's thinking. "How late are you?"

When she doesn't answer me, I say, "How many missed periods?"

"Jeez, Mom," she huffs. "Three."

11

*"Three?"* I don't shout at her, but only because I don't want anyone beyond these bathroom walls to hear me. Three months, that means it's a hell of a lot bigger than a lima bean.

"I figure I'm between thirteen and fourteen weeks by the way they count it. First day of my last period," she adds in a whisper.

"More than three months," I whisper under my breath. I close my eyes for a second and then open them. "Hazel, I wasn't suggesting you have an abortion. I was talking about adoption."

She stares at me as if I *have* just slapped her. "Give away our baby?"

I turn off the water and reach for the white towel with a loon embroidered on the hem. A leftover from the days when my mother-in-law was still living. Six years later and we've still got loon towels . . . and loon throw pillows, and loon bottle openers. Oscar and his siblings affectionately call the cottage the loony bin . . . for more reasons than one.

I lean against the sink, taking great care in drying my hands. I feel slightly nauseated. How could this happen? How could Hazel be pregnant? This wasn't supposed to happen to her. It wasn't supposed to happen to me.

How could this happen now, *to me?*

I moan inwardly. Of course, I know this isn't about me, it's about Hazel. I know it rationally. Logically. But it *feels* like it's about me. Because . . . I groan. "Hazel, you should consider the possibility of putting the baby up for adoption," I say softly. "It would be the best thing for you and the baby."

Now she looks as if I slapped her *and* her unborn child. "How could you, of all people, say such a thing?" She strides toward the door, her long legs slender and tanned. "I'm not going to put my baby up *for adoption.* Tyler and I are going to have this baby and get married and —"

"Get *married?*" I know I should be more empathetic. Undoubtedly she's in shock. Teenagers don't always make the connection between sex and the possible end result. Not even smart ones. And she's got to be scared.

But I can't help myself. I take the trash bag out of the can and tie up the white corners to take outside to the Dumpster, as if I can alter anything by hiding the evidence. "You're not being realistic. You and Tyler are not *getting married,* Hazel. You've been dating him for less than a year. You . . . you're sixteen years old."

"I'm going to be seventeen soon," she corrects me.

"You're going into the eleventh grade," I counter. "You can't even drive alone until next week. You . . . you have a whole life to live before you get married. College, a job." I open one hand, almost pleading. "What about wanting to be a physician? You're going to make an amazing doc." *And you don't need an albatross like Tyler around your neck.* I think it, but I find enough self-control not to say it.

"Tyler loves me." She yanks open the bathroom door. "We're going to have this baby and get married and, and we'll — we'll figure the rest out."

I follow her into the hall, carrying the trash bag. "I have to tell your father," I call after her, still trying to keep my voice down.

"I don't care who you tell," she flings back, making a beeline for her room.

I stand there in the hallway, my arms at my sides, the trash bag dangling from my finger. "Hazel, honey. We need to talk about this. We need to —"

She slams her bedroom door behind her.

". . . Make a plan," I finish under my breath. And then I go downstairs to tell my husband that his sixteen-year-old daughter has a bun in the oven.

Downstairs, I find our eighteen-year-old, Sean, sitting on the couch playing a video game on the massive TV in the family room. He's wearing a headset with a microphone. He's oblivious to the world around him: me, the family crisis that is bubbling up around him, and global warming. I tap his bare foot with mine. "Where's your dad?"

He glances at me for a split second and then his gaze is fixed on the game again. Zombies stagger across the screen, practically life-sized.

"Your dad," I repeat louder.

"Outside." He doesn't take his eyes off the game on the ginormous TV Oscar and his brother insisted we have here at the cottage.

Out of the corner of my eye, I see blood spatter across the screen and I wonder for the millionth time if I should have limited Sean's video game time when he was younger. Would he have more friends? Be less awkward in social situations? Would he have had his first date yet? But it's kind of late to worry about it now, isn't it? And he *is* headed to college to pursue a bachelor of science degree in *interactive media and game development*. It took me a while to learn

15

how to say that. I didn't even know such a thing existed until he came home from school last year telling me he wanted to design video games for a living.

I leave him to his zombies and go out the back door onto the deck where I drop the trash bag into the Dumpster on the side of the house. If only destroying the evidence *would* destroy the reality of the situation.

I gaze out at the breathtaking beauty of my surroundings: blue sky, blue-green water, bright warm sun. The kind of beauty that you feel in your chest.

The house was built on a bluff overlooking a cove, one of many in mid-coast Maine. Oscar's grandfather built the house, raised his children here. A lobster fisherman turned merchant. Eventually they moved to a bigger house, inland, one that wasn't so cold in the winter, but the family kept the property as a summer place and a reminder of their past. Now Oscar and his brother and sister share it. We're all assigned different weeks and weekends in the summer. This was one of our weekends, but we basically have an open-house policy with first come, first serve on beds. Oscar's sister and her family were supposed to be coming tonight, but they canceled at the last minute this morning, which turns out could be a good thing, considering the calamity at hand.

I walk across the deck, taking in the beauty of the sky and the cove below, water so blue it hurts my eyes. I spot my big bear of a husband down the grass slope in one of the colored Adirondack chairs we had all given each other one Christmas. He's sitting in his red chair, which he always sits in, even when no one else is here. Which I think is sweet. He's reading. It's his favorite thing to do when we come to the cottage.

I walk slowly across the lawn, a hundred thoughts bombarding me at once. Hazel is going to have a baby. My baby is going to have a baby. And what is she going to do? *What are we going to do?*

What am I going to do? Again, I fully realize that this is not about me, but right now it feels a little bit like it is. Because for once, just *once,* I want something in our family to be about me. These next few months, they were *supposed* to be about me.

I officially begin my job in two weeks. My first contract for my newly formed business. The project I've been dreaming of for years. Literally my dream job. I'm finally going to be a part of the world again, after years of breast-feeding and diapers and toddler playdates and volunteering at elementary school book sales and the junior prom. Which my son did not attend because he chickened out asking "this girl he works with" at the store where he sells TVs and cell phone cases.

I haven't worked in almost sixteen years. After Hazel was born, my design job in Portland got to be too much. Even though they let me work mostly at home, juggling my job, and the house, and the kids. Even the occasional commute was too long; child care was too complicated. And Oscar's job was shift work with ten- and twelve-hour days. It was too crazy trying to work around his schedule and mine, so at Oscar's insistence, I became a stay-at-home mom. I hadn't liked my job all that much, but I found that I missed it. I missed getting dressed for work the one day a week, even if it was in jeans and my "good" Blundstone boots. I missed talking to adults about adult things. Oscar and I talked about me going back to work when Sean started kindergarten, but by then Oscar decided he liked the energy in the emergency department at the local hospital and I realized pretty quickly that there was no way he could work those crazy hours and care for the children. So . . . I stayed home and made peanut-butter-and-honey sandwiches.

I halt a few feet behind Oscar and just stand there for a minute trying to find my balance, emotionally.

His curly auburn hair is thinning but he's in denial. When he asks me if it's thinner and I tell him maybe a little, he argues it isn't. He spends a lot of time in front of the mirror combing his hair in one direction and the other, trying to camouflage the area where you see skin.

I've been telling him for two years, since he started going bald, that I don't care if his thick head of hair isn't so thick anymore or if his hairline is receding. If he can accept me with my little wrinkles around my mouth, my thickening middle, I can accept his receding hairline. He argues that I don't understand because he's older than I am. By five years, though we graduated at the same time from the University of Maine, because it took him a little while to "find himself."

I look over my shoulder at the house, sensing someone's watching me. I spot Hazel in her window. She's waiting to see if her father spontaneously combusts when I tell him. She's daddy's little girl and she's right if she thinks he's going to be upset that she's been having sex. Oscar isn't a prude. He knows what teenagers do; he knows what

19

he did as a teenager with Ally Kemp in her grandmother's basement. He just isn't going to like having his own daughter's sexuality thrown in his face.

And a part of me hates the idea that I have to tell him that Hazel's pregnant. Because he's going to be angry and hurt and disappointed. I don't want to hurt him. And a part of me resents being the one who has to do it. Shouldn't Hazel be the one to do it? Of course, I didn't give her that option, did I? Couldn't, because I know my daughter. It would be Christmas before she broached the subject.

How am I going to tell him? How am I going to break his heart? In my mind, Hazel is still the daughter I knew an hour ago, but what if Oscar doesn't see her that way?

I walk to the Adirondack chair beside his and plop down.

Our dog, a black-and-white Bernese mountain dog, who's really not our dog at all but Oscar's, lifts his head and looks at me, then lowers his head to his paws again. Oscar named him Willie Nelson. That's what we call him, not Willie and not Nelson. Willie Nelson. A crazy name for a dog, but the kids thought it was funny and I gave in because I don't have to worry about anyone grabbing the wrong Willie Nelson's medical records at the vet's office.

Oscar closes his book, one finger inside to hold his place. He's a big guy, six-four, not heavy, but sturdy. With big hands. Right now, I want to reach out and take his hand. Feel his warmth, but I don't because things have been weird between us lately. We don't hold hands like we used to.

"Can you guess what Eleanor Roosevelt, Mahatma Gandhi, and Hitler all have in common?" Oscar asks.

It's a game we play all the time, more often when we're here at the cottage. He's an avid reader of nonfiction and he likes to share what he learns with me. He's been reading books on World War II for more than a year now. The facts are interesting, but I liked his Genghis Khan phase better.

My first impulse is to blurt out, "Your daughter's pregnant!" Instead, I just say, "What?"

"All three were nominated for a Nobel Peace Prize."

Ordinarily I'd find that little tidbit fascinating, but I'm still trying to wrap my head around the idea that in about twenty-six weeks, my daughter is going to push a baby out of her vagina.

I must have a good poker face because Oscar doesn't seem to notice that I feel like my life is imploding. Actually, shattering is a more accurate description. I can feel bits of me separating from my body and floating away without gravity to keep me together.

"Nineteen thirty-nine." He folds the dust jacket of the hardback book into the pages to save his place. He sets the book down and reaches for his beer bottle in a koozie. "Three months before he invaded Poland and started World War II. A guy in the Swedish parliament nominated him, calling him the 'prince of peace on earth.' He was being facetious, trying to get people's attention around the world, I guess. He withdrew the nomination, but . . ." Oscar shrugs. "I guess it was too late. Hitler already had incredible momentum."

He's wearing an old New England Patriots T-shirt and shorts and is barefoot. He appears so relaxed. This place is his escape from the world and the critical, sometimes dying, patients he cares for as an emergency department physician's assistant.

Suddenly I have second thoughts about telling him about Hazel. We have to go home tomorrow night; he works Monday. Maybe I should wait, give it another day, give Hazel some time to think. Give myself time to fully wrap my head around the situation.

But that's never how Oscar and I have done things. We don't lie to each other, and we don't withhold information, not to protect our children, not even to protect each other. It's something that's always been good about our marriage. It was one of the things my friend Amelia felt was a problem in theirs; her divorce just became final, and after eighteen years of marriage, she's suddenly single. It's not as if I think not telling Oscar that our daughter is pregnant until after he's had dinner is going to end our marriage, but it's the principle of the thing.

And I need him. I need him to see that Hazel cannot keep this baby. He knows her. He knows she's not mature enough to be a mother and he knows that dipshit Tyler well enough to know that he's not going to be any help on the parenting end. Oscar will agree that the baby should be put up for adoption and maybe he and I, together, can convince Hazel.

Oscar sips his beer. He's a Shipyard enthusiast and no fancy flavors; he's a local guy, local beer. "Some people think Hitler was nominated as a way to provoke the Nazis —"

"Hazel's pregnant," I blurt. I lower my face to my hands. Suddenly I'm fighting tears.

23

"I'm sorry?" He says it as if he didn't hear my fast-food order.

"Hazel's pregnant," I repeat. Then I lower my hands and look at him. "About three months. Pregnant." I repeat the word.

His suntanned face turns visibly paler. I see him clench his hand into a fist.

And then we're both quiet for a moment. Which surprises me because it wouldn't have surprised me if he'd shouted, "Pregnant?" loud enough for Sean to hear, even wearing his headphones.

I look at him. Wait. When he doesn't say anything after a minute or two, I go on. "She says she wants to have the baby. She and Tyler are going to," I make air quotes, " 'get married, have the baby, and then figure out the rest.' " I laugh, but there's no humor in my voice. "I think it's a terrible idea. Even to contemplate."

When he finally speaks, his voice sounds strange. As if it's someone else's and not my husband's. "I don't know if this is your decision to make."

"Oscar . . ." I turn in the chair so my whole body is facing him, our knees touching. "Tyler is not going to marry her. We wouldn't want him to even if he agreed to it. He's lazy, emotionally detached, and . . ." I exhale. "There's no question in my mind

24

that Tyler will not be around for the birth of this baby. He might not even be around after she tells him she's pregnant." I search my husband's face. He's not meeting my gaze. "Hazel *cannot* take care of a baby. She's just going into the eleventh grade! She wants to be a physician. She wants to see Greece. She wants to buy a new Nissan Cube. She'll never get to do those things if she has a baby at seventeen years old."

His eyes tear up and a lump rises in my throat.

"I don't think any decisions have to be made today," he says. "We have time, right?"

I reach out and squeeze his hand.

"Tell me what you're thinking," I say softly. "You don't really think she can take care of a baby, do you? She can't remember to feed the dog."

Willie Nelson opens one eye as if to confirm that he's missed more than one meal due to our daughter's lack of responsibility.

Oscar sets down his book in the grass and stares out at the water. I stare at him.

"I guess there's no need for me to ask if you're sure?"

"Three missed periods, two positive home pregnancy tests."

He strokes his short red beard that's

sprinkled with gray with his thumb and index finger. "Abortion isn't a solution here, Liv, and you know it. Not for her. And maybe she will be able to take care of a baby." He hesitates. "But . . . if she can't handle it, we can take the baby for a while." He looks at me. "We're not too old to be parents, Liv. Technically you're still young enough to have a baby. We could do it."

I sit back in the chair, crossing my arms over my chest. This was not what I was expecting. Certainly not what I wanted.

"I mean it," he says, almost seeming excited by the prospect of dirty diapers and fevers of a hundred and four again. "After Hazel has the baby, she can go back to school. She can go on to college. We can take care of the baby until she's old enough, until she's ready."

"And what if she comes to the conclusion that she doesn't want to be a mother?"

He shrugs. "Then we keep the baby. We do whatever we have to legally to —"

"Oscar," I interrupt, feeling my ire rising. "We're not equipped to have a baby any more than Hazel is. You're fifty years old."

"Forty-nine," he corrects me.

"You know what I mean." What I want to say is that when he's talking about *us* keeping this baby, raising this baby, what he means is *me*. Because I'm the one who has raised our two children. Yes, he's been a good provider, financially. And yes, he's always been big on trips to the beach and to the movies and our annual trip to New York City. But Oscar has never been the kind of father who packed lunches, made sure homework was done, or waited outside a pizza place for two hours to pick up one of his children. He's never cleaned up a one-thousand-and-twenty-two-piece LEGO starship off the back porch. He's never cleaned up puke from a car seat and he's never sat up all night with a barfing child with a fever.

"Liv, we can do this," he says, taking my hand in his. He looks into my eyes.

"Oscar, I start work on the Anselin house in two weeks. And I'm preparing a bid for another restoration. And I have no idea what I'm doing with either house. I'm going to be working forty or fifty hours a week. How am I going to take care of a baby?"

"We'll find day care. My sister can help. She was just telling me the other day that she's got empty nest syndrome."

I feel the warmth of his hand holding mine. I hear the desperation in his voice. He wants this baby. He wants me to want this baby and I feel terrible. Because I don't.

I love my children. I have never regretted for a moment having them. But I-do-not-want-another-baby. I'm forty-four and premenopausal. I want to sleep at night. I want to enjoy a glass of wine alone with my husband for dinner occasionally. And I want to work. I want something of my own now, damn it.

And I feel like an awful person even admitting this to myself.

"Day care?" I say. "You didn't want *our* children in day care. That's why I quit my job. To stay home with them."

"Different times."

"Oscar —"

"Liv, this baby will be a part of us. A part of our daughter." He takes my other hand. "How could you give away a part of us? Of our family?"

"I'm not talking about giving the baby away on a street corner in Portland." I pull my hands from his and wrap my arms around my waist. I hug myself, wishing Oscar would hug me and promise me everything was going to be okay. But he doesn't. And it isn't. I know that in my heart of hearts. Nothing is ever going to be okay again. At least not in the way things were going to be okay an hour ago when the re-

28

ality of Hazel's pregnancy wasn't our reality.

Oscar is watching me. "I can't believe you'd even suggest adoption after what you went through."

"Not every kid is like me. Look at the Andersons." Our neighbors who adopted two girls from China. "They've never had a minute's problem with them. Grace is going to Stanford."

"Grace's acceptance to Stanford isn't a reflection of her emotional state."

"No, it isn't," I admit. "I'm just trying to think about what would be best for the baby."

"Right." He gets up from his chair and Willie Nelson immediately leaps to his feet, too. "Liv, I'm not saying this is the perfect situation, but we have to do what's best. For all of us. Hazel wants to keep her baby." He opens his arms wide. "This isn't 1952. We can't send her off to live with relatives so no one knows she's pregnant, take her baby away from her, and put it up for adoption."

"I know that, I just . . ."

I just what? I wanted him to agree with me? I wanted him to be on my side, for *once*? Because it seems as if he always sides with the kids. Sean wants big bucks for some kind of software camp, I say no, Oscar says yes. Hazel accuses me of judging her, I say I'm being honest, and then Oscar comes back and tells me I'm being too hard on her. The same goes for my parents. I think they should start considering a move to a house with less maintenance, maybe even to a retirement community. Oscar agrees with them; he thinks they're fine where they are. My mother criticizes something I've said, done, and when I tell Oscar about it, he doesn't see anything wrong with her comment. It never used to be like this, but I can't pinpoint when things changed. It seems like decades ago, but it was probably only a couple of years.

"Oh, Liv." Oscar stands there, looking at me, his hands at his sides. "Sean know?"

I shake my head, getting up. "I don't think so. I don't even think she's told Tyler yet. She's in her room."

"Should I go talk to her?"

I look up at him feeling so sad, so . . . defeated. "You can try, I guess. She might not be ready to talk to you yet. She's going to feel awful about disappointing you."

"Right." He runs his hand through his hair. "You want me to start the grill?"

I look down at the grass, my arms crossed across my chest. Again I wish he would hug me. I wish he wanted to. "Um . . . sure. Yes. Thank you."

Oscar picks up his book and he and Willie Nelson head back toward the house, leaving me to stand alone at the edge of a cliff.

# 2
## HAZEL

I lie on my bed staring at the ceiling fan, holding my phone over my head. I glance at the cracked screen.

**WHERE ARE YOU? TEXT ME BACK!** I text for, like, the tenth time. All in caps because I *am* shouting. At least inside. I'm not a shouter — that's my dad. He hollers when he's called us for dinner three times and my brother and I still haven't come downstairs, and the taco fixings are getting cold. He hollers when we leave wet towels on the bathroom floor. Also, when you back into his car with your mom's. Which Sean said was totally Dad's fault. He never parks behind her car.

I drop my phone beside me on the bed and close my eyes, trying not to cry.

I can't believe I'm pregnant. I can't believe I'm goddamned pregnant.

Dad says I shouldn't say *goddamned* because it offends people. Well, I'm offended, goddamn it. How could God let this happen? It was just the one time.

Just that one time when Ty forgot to buy condoms. Or maybe he didn't have the money to buy them. I told him "No glove, no love," but he was so sweet and I'd had a couple of beers and . . .

Oh, God, will my baby be born with fetal alcohol syndrome? I feel a sudden sense of panic, the kind that twists in your belly. We watched a movie in health class last year about fetal alcohol syndrome. It's a horrible thing to do to a baby.

I grab my phone and Google search "can my baby get fetal alcohol syndrome if I drank alcohol when the baby was conceived?"

I scroll quickly through the hits and settle on one. *Fetal alcohol syndrome and fetal alcohol spectrum disorders only occur in babies born to mothers who drink alcohol during pregnancy.*

I hold the phone to my chest. My boobs hurt.

Okay, so if I don't have any more beer, any more anything alcoholic, my baby should be okay. No learning or intellectual disabilities. No pinched face or little head. No coordination issues. No heart problems or kidney —

My phone dings, notifying me of a text, and I lift it up, thinking it has to be Tyler. The jerk finally checked his phone. He's supposed to be at his uncle's, kayaking on Sebago Lake, but a person doesn't kayak all day long. At least not Tyler. He's not exactly athletic. Not into being uncomfortable in any way even for fun. Mostly he likes to sit on his mom's couch and play video games. Not the kind like my brother plays, though. Ty's into deer hunting and racing cars on a TV screen that takes up half of his mom and stepdad's little living room.

And getting me pregnant.

The text isn't from Tyler. It's the manager at the drugstore where I work asking me if I can come in two hours early Monday. I don't answer. I'm kind of in the middle of a crisis here.

I keep thinking about the TV show *16 and Pregnant* that Mom and I used to watch when I was a freshman in high school. I always thought those girls were such idiots to get pregnant. They seemed like idiots about everything else. I always wondered if the show was for real or if it was scripted, like did the producers tell the pregnant girl to throw the plate of spaghetti at her baby daddy? Did they tell the baby daddy to make it look like he went out with some other girl, even though you find out in the next episode that he was just getting a ride home because he didn't have money for gas?

I don't think I'm like the girls on the show, even if I was dumb enough to get pregnant.

I understand why it's essential that I get a good education. I understand that how I treat others influences how I'm treated. I know that if people my age don't start protecting the planet, we're all going to die. If someone doesn't blow up the earth with nukes first. So, I get good grades in school and I try to be nice to people even when they're not nice to me. And I use my brain. I can figure stuff out. Like I have common sense. When I hear something or read it, I can say, "Does this make sense?" and respond accordingly. My dad taught me that when I was little. Or maybe it was my mom.

I'm smart.

Too smart to be going into the eleventh grade and knocked up by my boyfriend who *isn't* smart.

We're not really all that much alike, Tyler and I. We don't even like the same things. I know that, but opposites attract, right?

I like to read; he doesn't. I like to watch stuff on TV like *Game of Thrones,* even though I've seen every season ten times. Tyler likes stuff like *Sharknado 3,* which is the stupidest movie you could ever imagine. A tornado made of sharks? Really? I told him that a wind tunnel that starts over the Pacific Ocean and hits California is technically a cyclone. That went right over his head. But he's cute and he likes me and . . . And I love him. He's my first boyfriend. Aren't you supposed to love your first boyfriend?

I close my eyes, mostly because the ceiling fan is starting to make me feel dizzy and a little nauseous. I'm dreading the conversation with Mom about Tyler. She doesn't like him. She thinks he's a loser. Which maybe he . . . could be if he doesn't get his crap together. But she doesn't see the possibilities I see in him. I've been helping him bring up his grades. He passed this year because of me and I didn't let him cheat. I don't even think it's his fault, the school thing. His parents are weird. They don't ask him about his grades. They don't talk about him going to college, even community college. They want him to go to work with his dad at his uncle's auto repair shop. His dad says stuff like if being an auto mechanic is good enough for him, it's good enough for Tyler Junior. Tyler Junior likes driving cars but he doesn't really like fixing them. Probably because he's terrible at it. I'd be a better auto mechanic than he would.

But I don't want to be an auto mechanic. I want to be a doctor in family practice. If I become a doctor, I'll have more education than Mom or Dad. It might make Dad feel weird if I outranked him. But maybe not. Maybe he'd be proud of me.

A bang on my bedroom door startles me. "Dinner in fifteen!" my brother hollers. His voice fades as he keeps going, toward his room, probably. "And the kitchen trash is full. Your turn to take it out."

I want to holler something at him like, "I'm having a little bit of a breakdown here. Couldn't you take out the trash?" But I don't want to tell him I'm preggers. He's going to call me an idiot. And that's going to be the nicest thing he says to me. Mom and Dad don't like Tyler but Sean hates him. He calls him stuff like Pea Brain and Little Dick. He calls him Little Dick because Tyler used to have an old GMC Sierra pickup that had a really loud muffler and Sean says only guys with little teeny-tiny dicks make their trucks louder. The engine went out in it so he doesn't have it anymore. I don't know if Tyler's dick is little or not because he's the only person I've ever had sex with.

"Trash!" Sean yells, banging on my door

again as he goes past in the other direction. "Dinner!"

I sit up. I feel sick, but I don't know if it's the baby that's the size of a lemon in my belly making me sick, or the idea of going down to dinner and having Dad look at me the way I know he's going to look at me. Because I'm sure Mom already told him. She loves to give people bad news. And she tells Dad everything. Even stuff I'd rather she didn't, like when I had a crush on his friend's son in the sixth grade and when I got my first period. Both times Dad felt compelled to say something that embarrassed me so bad I think I'm still emotionally scarred from it.

I look at my closed door where my green rain slicker is hanging, next to another slicker that belongs to one of my cousins. We share the bedroom. This is my grandparents' house. Dad's side. Was before they died. My dad and his brother and sister share it. This is the girls' room. My aunt gave us our own room when my oldest cousin started growing boobs. She said we were too old to sleep in the "dorm room," which is where Sean sleeps. I kind of miss the dorm room.

I look at the door again. I don't want to go down to dinner. I just want to sit here on my bed for the next twenty-six weeks or so until I have this baby.

*What am I going to do with a baby?*

I get up, fighting tears. If I go downstairs looking like I've been crying, Mom will jump to all kinds of conclusions. She'll think she's won. She'll think she can give my baby away, but she can't. This is one thing she can't do to me. There are laws against that.

I tuck my phone into my back pocket and leave my bedroom. I go downstairs and the back way into the kitchen, hoping to avoid everyone. I wonder if that's possible for the next twenty-six weeks.

I can't believe Tyler still hasn't called me back. I told him I had something really important to tell him. Something bad.

I go into the kitchen from the laundry room and step on the pedal that opens the lid of the trash can. Mom and Dad are standing at the counter talking about fixing the hinge on the back door. Like this family doesn't have bigger problems right now.

I stare into the trash can. Lying right on top is one of those plastic clamshell thingies that berries come in. I yank it out and throw it into the recycling bin. I put it right next to the trash can so it would be easy to sort. I put a recycling bin here and at home and at Gran and Granddad's. Could I make it any easier for them?

I dig into the trash, knowing full well that there's more recycling in there.

Sure enough, I come up with a cardboard tube from a roll of paper towels. At home, we mostly use cloth wipe thingies I bought on Etsy. When they're dirty they go into a basket and then into the wash. It's easy and it's way better for the environment. Some people argue about the water used in washing the cloth towels, but I've done the research. And I don't use soap; I use household vinegar to wash them. Dad sneaks a roll of paper towels into the house once in a while. I just pretend I don't see it.

I throw the paper towel roll into the recycling bin hard and all of a sudden I feel like I'm going to cry. "Recycling in the trash again," I holler in a general announcement.

I know Sean isn't listening. I'm sure he's got his umbilical cord connected to the TV. I think my brother is on the autism spectrum. He's so weird. And awkward. And his obsession with video games is beyond normal even for guys his age. I used to say I think we should have him tested. His mature response was usually to stick his tongue out at me. At least then he responded to me, even if just as a taunt. This last year, his senior year in high school, I don't think he knew I was alive. Which makes me sad because when we were little, he was my best friend.

When we were little, we played together all the time. Sure, we played DUPLOs because that was his thing, but he played chef with me, too, and vet's office. When we got into elementary school, we raced our bicycles in the driveway, did homework together, and sometimes he and his friends even sat next to me in the school cafeteria. It wasn't until I started growing boobs in middle school that things got weird. Or maybe it was when he started growing man balls. There was no big fight between Sean and me, he just . . . drifted away. Mom says that happens sometimes with siblings, especially when they're male and female. She says he'll drift back. I hope so. Because I miss him.

I sigh and dig into the bag again. Hit a pocket of something gross. Food. Food is supposed to go in the compost container on the counter. My fingers hit the ridge of something hard and I pull out an empty salsa jar. "Who cares about the planet?" I practically scream. "We're all going to die someday, right?"

Suddenly I realize the house has gotten really quiet. Mom and Dad have stopped

41

talking. I don't even hear the dog walking around, his nails scraping the hardwood floor. I look up to see my parents staring at me. Sean, too. He's standing at the counter with a bag of hamburger rolls in his hand. They're all looking at me.

I wonder if Sean knows.

"Recycling goes in the blue bin," I say, feeling like I could stomp my foot or do something else equally childish. "If you don't know by now what goes in recycling, flip it over and check out the symbol. Or just ask," I say, speaking slowly, as if they can't understand my words. Only with a nasty tone. Really nasty.

Sean looks at my parents as if I've just appeared, an extraterrestrial from a faraway galaxy. So maybe he doesn't know he's going to be an uncle.

Dad picks up a serving plate of corn on the cob. "Burgers are ready," he announces, avoiding eye contact with me. "Let's eat before everything gets cold."

And I want to die. Right here beside my recycling project from the seventh grade.

# 3
## LIV

I stand at the bathroom sink staring at myself in the mirror. Unlike most women my age, I still wear my brown hair long — well, just past my shoulders. I just haven't been able to get into the *sensible* haircut prevalent here in the Northeast. What Oscar and I jokingly refer to as the L.L.Bean haircut. I do wear my share of L.L.Bean clothing, but not the hair. Never the hair.

I tip my head back, smoothing my not-as-shiny-as-they-used-to-be locks over the crown. My roots need touching up. My hair used to be a darker brown, but with the graying and the constant upkeep, I've let it go a little lighter. I think the new color is a little gentler on my aging skin.

I let go of my hair and reach for a head-band to push it all back so I can wash my face. I can't believe I'm thinking about my hair. I've got bigger problems than that. *We've* got bigger problems. Oscar and I.

I stare at my reflection while I pump face soap into my palm, then I rub it all over. It's not a bad face for a forty-four-year-old woman. I'm developing laugh lines around my mouth and there's some discoloration under my eyes, but nothing drugstore concealer won't fix. I wonder if I need to talk to my dermatologist about Retin-A. The laugh lines are definitely worse. And what's with my droopy eyes? I can barely see my lids anymore.

I meet my gaze again, still rubbing the soap on my face. My best feature is still my eyes. Brown, with flecks that look green sometimes. I always wonder where they came from — if it was my mother or my father. Birth mother or father. I sometimes wonder if they're still alive, if there's someone out there with my eyes.

I splash warm water on my face to rinse and reach for the hand towel to blot, not rub. My girlfriend Amelia tells me I'm being too rough with my skin. She watches YouTube videos on skin care and makeup for forty-plus-year-old women. She insists I should be watching them, too, but I don't see any need when she relates the information to me.

I glance out the bathroom door. Oscar is stretched out on the bed on his back in nothing but a pair of boxer briefs. He's reading. His briefs look faded and baggy; he needs new ones.

"Are we going to talk about this?" I reach for my moisturizer. When he doesn't respond, I look at him again.

My husband of two decades continues to stare at the book. I can't tell if he heard me or not. Or if he's really reading or just holding the book up to avoid me.

"Hon?"

He doesn't even try to hide his sigh of impatience. He keeps his eyes on the book.

"I thought we were going to let this season."

*Let this season.*

I used to like this phrase he brought to our marriage from his Quaker upbringing. It means to think about it, but also to just let it sit and . . . season like a marinade. But over the years, I feel as if it's come to mean that Oscar is just going to ignore the subject. Which is not going to work this time. By my calculations, our daughter will give birth the first week of March.

"Oscar?"

Again, the sigh, which is now bordering on a groan. He lowers his book to his bare chest and there's a silence that stretches between us that happens more often than it used to. And it makes me sad. We were best friends for so long. We could talk about anything. Everything. I stand there rubbing moisturizer into my face, wondering how this happened. How we drifted apart. Only *drift* isn't quite the right word. It's been sort of a lurching process. Sometimes we lurch away from each other, then lurch back, but each time it seems as if it's farther to return to the place we once were. Amelia says it's an inevitable stage of the institution of marriage, but is it? Does it have to be?

He closes his eyes. "She wants to keep her baby," he says softly. "It's the natural thing, Liv. For a woman to want to keep her baby." He still won't look at me.

I grab my glasses and slip them on; I can't see a damned thing without my contacts. I flip off the light and walk into the bedroom in a baggy T-shirt and panties. I can't remember the last time I got into bed in something cute or even bordering on sexy. My oversized shirt has a loon on it. It came from the communal bottom drawer of the dresser here in the master bedroom. Next week Oscar's sister will probably be wearing it to bed.

"Right, but . . ." I sit down on the edge of the bed, rubbing the leftover moisturizer into the backs of my hands. "That doesn't mean that's what's best for the baby. Or Hazel." I wait for his response. And wait. I watch him stare at the ceiling as if he's a seventeen-year-old boy and his mother has asked him a question. And I hate feeling this way. As if I'm his mother.

His gaze shifts and he finally meets mine. "I think what we said . . . about letting it go for a couple of days is a good idea. It's still so fresh. She still hasn't even talked to Tyler yet."

"So you did talk to her?" I get up and walk around to my side of the bed. There are two prints of loons above the old maple bed that was once his parents' bed. They're black-and-white aquatic birds that have the most beautiful, haunting song. One print is of a male, the other a female. Loons mate for life. In the evening, we hear our loons in our little cove calling to each other. It's how they communicate, how they let each other know where they are on the bay. I wonder if as they get older they call less often to each other.

I sit down on my side of the bed and swing my feet over to sit beside him on top of the cotton quilt. He's staring at the ceiling again, and even though we're right beside each other, close enough to touch, he doesn't reach out to me. I don't reach out to him. Sitting so close and not touching makes me feel alone. Like the female loon drifting alone on the water, far from her mate.

"Oscar —"

"Yes, I spoke with her, Liv. Before I came to bed." He's looking at me now. "I just stuck my head in her bedroom door to say good night. Didn't you?"

"What did you say to her?"

"I told her that I loved her." He takes his time with each word. As if it's painful to talk with me. "And that . . . we'd figure this out."

"And what did she say?"

"She said she loved me, too."

I want to cover his hand, resting on the bed between us, with mine, but I don't do it. "You said she hadn't talked to Tyler. How do you know that if —"

He interrupts. "I just asked her if she'd heard from him. We didn't talk about the pregnancy. I could tell she'd been crying and I just asked . . . you know, if they'd talked."

"And they still haven't?" I ask.

"She thinks maybe his phone died and he doesn't have his charger. Or he broke his screen again."

I roll onto my side, propping myself up on

my elbow so I'm facing him. He's still handsome, even with his slightly receding hairline and gray temples. It was his blue eyes I fell in love with the day I first spotted him in the UMaine student center. It took another two weeks of us semi-stalking each other for me to finally get up the nerve to ask him to hand me a napkin. I was so madly in love with him at that point, even before he'd spoken to me, that I probably would have married him on the spot if he'd asked. Or at least gone back to his apartment for a quickie before my world history class. In those days, we couldn't keep our hands off each other. Now we're lying here half naked with nothing to stop us from having sex and the spark isn't there. It just isn't and I don't know where the hell it went. What's maybe even worse is that the desire to comfort each other isn't there, either.

"Oscar," I sigh. "I think we need to —"

My cell on my nightstand rings. It seems as if my life is full of interruptions. It's the sound of a loon, signaling it's a call from my parents' house. Our son's idea of a joke because he insists my parents are both crazy. At least loony. Eighteen-year-old-boy humor.

I roll over and grab the phone because it's never a good thing when my parents call after nine p.m. They're usually in bed by seven thirty, eight at the latest, because that way they can be up and bright-eyed and bushy-tailed when they wake me at five thirty a.m. to tell me there's a purple finch in their bird feeder.

I lift my phone to my ear. "Hello?"

"I told her to leave it until you came over. She wouldn't listen," my father says. "She never listens to a thing I say. I think she needs her head examined."

"Dad, what happened?"

"Your mother fell off the zucchini."

"Zucchini?" I say. I know he doesn't mean zucchini. Occasionally he says the wrong word. Early-stage dementia. And I know it's not helpful to repeat the incorrect words he says, but sometimes I can't help myself. It's a little unsettling when your father tells you someone fell off a zucchini.

"Not zucchini," my dad mutters. "I didn't say zucchini. How the hell would she fall off a squash?"

I don't make any comment on either subject. If I do, it will only take me longer to get to the bottom of what's going on.

"She fell off the ladder." Now my dad gets snippy with me. "Your mother fell off the *tarnal* stepladder."

I ignore his creative curse; he has a whole

basket of them. He can't remember the word *ladder,* but he can come up with the word *tarnal.* "Mom was on a *ladder*?" I get out of bed. "Dad. What was she doing on a ladder?" I want to shout, "How did she manage to get out of her wheelchair onto a ladder?" but I control myself.

"Lightbulb. I got the bleeding stopped."

"She was *bleeding*?" I say. "What do you mean? Where was she bleeding?"

"I'm a doctor, Liv. You think I don't know how to stop a head wound from bleeding?"

Technically he *was* a doctor, but he's long retired. And he was an ophthalmologist. He didn't deal with a lot of bleeding head wounds. "How much blood was there?" I ask calmly. Because I'm always the calm one. I've always had to be. My sister, Beth, gets to be the hysterical one, Oscar the emotional one.

"A good bit. I used those napkin things on the roll," he says, struggling for the word and gets angrier by the second because he can't think of it. "The . . . the . . ."

"Paper towels," I say softly, my heart breaking for him.

"Those. It's just above her eyebrow, but I wonder if she needs to go to the hospital. To have her head examined!" He shouts

51

these last words, apparently for my mother's benefit.

"Dad, is she okay? Is she fully conscious?" As I speak, I pick my shorts up off the chair, then decide against them. If I'm going to spend the night in the emergency department, I don't want to do it in a pair of old khaki shorts that I spilled mustard on. I dig into the bag on the floor beside the dresser to look for the jeans I'm sure I packed.

"She's conscious, all right. Won't stop yapping. Yap, yap, yap," he repeats. Also for my mother's benefit.

I cut my eyes at Oscar. He's sitting on the edge of the bed, trying to figure out what's going on. "Mom fell off a ladder. Changing a lightbulb," I tell him.

"What's she doing on a ladder?" Oscar asks.

I step into the jeans, and say into the phone, "I'm on my way. Put Mom on the phone."

There's a pause. I hear my mother's and father's voices, though I can't make out what they're saying. Jeans zipped and buttoned, I put the phone on speaker and set it on the dresser.

"I can go," Oscar offers.

I close my eyes for a moment, pulling my T-shirt off over my head, flashing my bare

52

breasts at my husband.

"Come on, Liv. Let me do this," he says.

"You went last time."

"Last two times," is his comeback, trying to make a joke, but only halfheartedly. "I don't mind. I might get her seen faster."

I put on my bra. I can still hear them talking. "Mom? Dad?" I lean over my phone, speaking into it. "Hello?"

From the depths of my bag, I come up with a three-quarter-sleeve white T-shirt. As I pull it on, my phone goes silent. "Mom? Dad?" I look at Oscar. "They hung up."

"I'll go, Liv. You should stay here with the kids. With Hazel."

"No, you should be here. You're better with her anyway." I redial. They're number four on my speed dial. Oscar is first, then Sean, then Hazel, then my parents.

The call goes through.

"Your father hung up on you." It's my mother.

"I didn't hang up!" my father shouts. "Dropped the swiving phone."

"Are you okay?" I ask Mom. I want to ask her why she was on a ladder changing a lightbulb. At nine thirty at night. A part of me wants to ask why she had to do it this weekend when I was away. It's only a forty-minute drive from here to their house, but

53

it's the principle of the thing. Couldn't they have behaved themselves just for the weekend? Just so I could get away and stay away.

Then I feel guilty. My mother hurt herself and I'm worried about my own inconvenience. I press the heel of my hand into my forehead. What's happening to me? Why am I becoming such a bitch?

"Mom," I say in a gentler tone.

"I'm fine. I don't need to go to the hospital. You don't need to come home."

I slide on my flip-flops, debating whether or not I should take the time to put on a little makeup or risk frightening the ED doc. "Dad says you were bleeding pretty heavily."

"I'm fine. I called your sister. She says I'm fine."

I stand there, hoping maybe I just got dressed for no reason. I ought to know by now to get the whole story before I leap into action. A couple of weeks ago my father called me from his cell phone to tell me that my mother had left him in the car while she had gone into the grocery store in "one of those battery wheel things" and that she'd never come back out. I tried her cell, got no answer, and then I drove to our local Hannaford. Neither Mom, Dad, nor their twelve-year-old Honda was there. I found them at home. Mom was doing a puzzle. Dad was watching his bird feeder from the window. Turns out they had been to the grocery store, but according to my mother, she'd been inside only long enough to get rye bread and the orange sherbet that was on sale. She had no idea what my father was talking about and she didn't even know he knew where his cell phone was and that he must have called from the backyard because they'd been back from the grocery store since before lunch.

"Beth came over and had a look? Good," I say with a sigh, stepping back out of my flip-flops.

"No."

"No?" I step back into them.

"No," my mother repeats. "She said I didn't need to go to the hospital, not if it stopped bleeding. Well . . . it has for the most part. Dribbling a little. I told your father I needed a paper towel and he tore one in four quarters and gave one small piece to me. You know how he doesn't like to waste anything."

I cut my eyes at Oscar. He's standing by the bathroom door. "I'll come have a look, Mom," I say into the phone.

"There's really no need."

"I'm going to bed," my father shouts.

"Good night, Beth!"

"He doesn't really think you're Beth," my mother says gently into the phone. "He's just being difficult for difficulty's sake."

"It's okay," I murmur, knowing she's covering for him. "Why don't you sit down, watch something on TV, and I'll be there in forty-five minutes."

"Fine. I'll work on my puzzle. Can't watch TV. Your father disconnected it again, trying to unplug the lamp. He thinks my mother's lamp is running up the electric bill."

She hangs up and I just stand there, holding the phone. My parents have been in the same house for forty-five years. I can't imagine them living anywhere else. And yet, I'm not sure how much longer they can stay there. Not alone.

"Come on, hon. Let me go," Oscar says, walking toward me. "Let me do this for you."

"It's fine." I shake my head.

Oscar stops. Stands there in his baggy underwear. "We can't ask her to abort her baby," he says.

It takes me a second to switch gears. Crises. "I didn't suggest that. I never said that," I answer quietly, my heart aching for Hazel. For Oscar. For us. For the child that

56

will be of my body, one step removed.

He reaches for my hand and catches my fingers. "We could do this," he whispers, choking up.

"We'll talk about it later. I have to go." I turn away, pulling my hand from his. "I'll text you when I get there and see what's going on."

"You can't just call your sister and get her to go over for you?" he calls after me.

I throw him a look over my shoulder.

"Liv, I think you need to be here with Hazel tomorrow. With us."

"I'll be back," I tell him, opening our bedroom door.

For a second I think he's going to follow me. Half hope he does.

He doesn't.

"Take these." I hand my mother two over-the-counter pain relievers and sit down on the edge of her bed. I pass her the glass of water and watch her drink.

"All this fuss."

"Three stitches," I point out, taking the glass from her when she's done. I set it on her nightstand beside the Amish romance paperback she's reading. She's obsessed with them; I'd never known such a thing existed until a few months ago when she started getting them automatically delivered to the house. She says they're her escape.

"I didn't need to go to the hospital. Could have used Steri-Strips." She fusses with the hair over one ear; she went with the sensible New England haircut when I was in middle school. "Your father will have kittens when he sees this bill. He thinks the electric bill is high?" She snorts. "Wait until he sees this one."

I smile. My mother and I have always had an interesting relationship. I love her, and I know she loves me, but we've often been at odds. Growing up, she was so pragmatic. Too pragmatic. She could plan a birthday party and get me to every soccer or softball practice, but she never had time to talk to me about my childhood and then teenage woes. She was never interested in listening to what I had to say. Dad was always my buddy, my partner in crime, the one who would listen to me boohoo over the B I got in spelling, the girlfriend who didn't invite me to her birthday party, or the guy who asked someone else to the prom that I was sure he was going to ask me to. I think my rapport with my mother is better now, though. I admire her so much, the way she's dealt with my father's declining health. Her own. Her grace in growing older. I'm beginning to see her in a different light.

She was diagnosed with degenerative joint disease almost ten years ago. A year ago, she started using a wheelchair on her "bad days." Now her bad days come more often. But her mind is fine, better than fine. She could beat me at Trivial Pursuit any day of the week. And she deals with my father if not with patience, then with aplomb.

"Your father in bed?" asks Mom, lying back on her pillow. They stopped sleeping in the same room years ago. My father snores and my mother likes to stay up late reading. He says the light from the iPad screen bothers him. She says his foghorn bothers her.

"He's sound asleep." I glance at her digital clock beside her bed. It's 2:10. I debate whether I sleep here on the couch, drive back to the cottage, or just go home. We only live ten minutes away. I know I should go back to be at the cottage when Hazel wakes up, but a part of me wants just to go home and hide under my duvet. Let Oscar handle it. Oscar who wants to be a father again and make up for all of his mistakes.

It's as if he thinks he can get a redo. He thinks he can make up for all the holidays he missed when he was on call and couldn't get home. And it wasn't just Christmas and birthdays he missed, or the gift buying for his son and daughter. He missed school plays, and soccer games, and parent-teacher conferences. He missed Sean's first tooth and the first time Hazel rode her bike without training wheels. He missed reading Curious George books over and over again and making snowmen in our front yard. He missed the events and I think now he misses the memories.

But can a parent really have a redo? Even with another child? He'll still never have the relationship with Hazel and Sean that I do.

I close my eyes for a moment. That's unfair. And unkind. But probably mostly true. I open my eyes. "Soooo" — I draw out the vowel — "no sign of Beth?"

"What's wrong, Liv?"

"You called her, and she didn't want to come?"

"She was on a date." My mother lowers her voice as if there's someone else in the room to overhear us. "A nice banker. Or stockbroker." She waves her hand as if she can make him either one with her invisible magic wand.

"She couldn't come check on her eighty-one-year-old mother who fell off a ladder because she had a *date*? Was she in another state?"

My mother exhales. While she's usually able to be patient with my dad, the same rules don't apply to me. Her expectations of me have always been high, and I feel as if I've always fallen short. "Tell me what's wrong. I can see it in your face." She lies there and waits, her hands folded neatly. Such beautiful hands once, before arthritis gnarled them. My mother was always so beautiful, the kind of beauty that makes a young, awkward daughter feel ugly in her presence.

I rise from the bed and walk away. There are baby pictures of me and of Beth wearing the same froufrou pink dress, hanging on the wall flanking my dad's old maple dresser. Beth is giggling in her photo, chubby hands raised. My face is solemn, my hands on my lap. Beth always teases me when she sees the images. She calls it my baby resting bitch face.

"Olivia?" Mom drawls out my name.

I exhale, debating. I wasn't going to tell her tonight. I'm not even sure I have the right to tell her at all. Shouldn't Hazel be the one? If she's old enough to have sex, isn't she old enough to tell her grandmother that she had unprotected sex, which is going to make her a great-grandmother?

I wrap my arms around my waist, hugging

61

myself. Wishing I had hugged Oscar before I left the house. We used to kiss each other hello and good-bye. We still do sometimes, but I wish I had kissed him good-bye tonight. I wish I had told him I loved him.

I turn around. "Hazel's pregnant." I'm surprised by the emotion that rises in my throat, practically choking me.

My mother gasps.

"She told us today. I think she should consider adoption." I shake my head, beginning to pace. "But she's dead set against it."

"She wants an abortion?" my mother asks.

I shake my head and again emotion bubbles up, this time threatening to strangle my words. "She . . . she wants to keep the baby. She and Tyler."

"Well." My mother crosses her arms. Settled back in a pile of pillows, she looks almost like a queen in her white robe and nightgown. Images of the elderly Queen Victoria come to mind. "I can't imagine he'd have enough energy to get up in the middle of the night to tend to a little one."

"Exactly my point." I walk toward the bed, excited by the thought of having someone on my side. "Oscar is opposed to the idea, but, Mom, I think we need to consider . . ." I rephrase. "I think Hazel and Tyler need to think about putting the baby up for adoption. She's just going into the eleventh grade. She can't take care of a baby."

My mother frowns. "She can't put her baby up for adoption. You'll just have to raise it. You and Oscar."

My heart sinks. *Et tu, Brute?*

"Mom." All I can manage is a sigh. I feel like I'm going to burst into tears, collapse on the floor, scream my head off. I feel like I'm on the edge of a great precipice and if I stumble off the edge, I don't know that I can find my way back up the cliff. I'm tired and I'm worried about my parents and I'm half paralyzed with fear for my sweet, beautiful daughter. What will her life be now? She and Tyler are going to marry and raise a baby? The idea of her marrying Tyler is almost more frightening than the idea of her being a mother.

"It's the way we used to do it, you know," my mother goes on, unaware of how close I am to the abyss. "My aunt Lulu on my dad's side had a baby out of wedlock, and her parents just took the baby in and she became Lulu's youngest sister. Lulu ended up marrying a nice plumber or electrician or something." She does the wave thing again.

I press the heel of my hand to my forehead. I can feel a killer headache coming on. I wish I'd stopped for a cup of coffee somewhere on the way home from the hospital. The only coffee my parents have here is caffeine-free instant.

I wish I'd let Oscar come instead of me. He would have had enough sense not to bring up the pregnancy with my mother.

I wish I'd followed up on my sex talks with Hazel. I suspected she and Tyler were having sex. But I've been so focused on getting my business off the ground that I didn't do my job as a mother. I didn't protect her. I didn't protect my cub.

Tears fill my eyes and I turn away so Mom can't see them.

"I'm surprised you'd even consider adoption," she continues. "After all the trouble we had with you."

I find her choice of words interesting. My little sister, Beth, my parents' biological daughter, a "surprise" baby, was ousted from nursery school for biting. She failed the fourth grade. She was expelled from two high schools, and as an adult has flitted from job to job, man to man, financial crisis to financial crisis. And good old Bernice and Ed have bailed her out. Every . . . single . . . time.

I wasn't *trouble.* I was just a little girl who was confused about why her birth mother would give her away.

"What does Oscar say?"

I sniff and turn back to her. "He thinks Hazel can do it. Raise the baby. And if not . . ." I exhale, too tired to even think about it now. "He thinks we should keep the baby," I say softly.

Mom slides down in her bed and closes her eyes. "You married well, Liv. He's a good man."

"He is," I whisper.

A silence hangs between us.

"You staying overnight?" she eventually asks, eyes remaining closed. "Clean sheets on the bed in the spare room."

"I think I'll go back to the cottage. So I can be there when Hazel gets up." I cross the room to her bed and lean down and kiss her cheek. It's leathery, yet still soft. "Good night. I'll call you in the morning."

"Good night."

I turn off her bedside lamp and walk toward the light in the hallway. Closing the door behind me, I go down the hall to Dad's room. He's easy to find: I just go in the direction of the snoring.

He's fallen asleep with the light on, his iPad on his chest. Asleep, he looks like his old self: the aquiline nose, broad forehead, cleft chin. He has a five o'clock shadow and his white hair is shaggy. He needs a cut. He used to go to a barbershop down the street, but he caused a ruckus a couple of times over whose turn it was that Mom told him they closed. So far, he hasn't noticed when he walks by that the place is, indeed, still open for business. I cut his hair now.

I gently lift his hand and pull his tablet out from beneath it. It comes on when I touch the screen. He's playing Candy Crush. Sean loaded it on his iPad for him, thinking it might be good for his brain. I'm surprised how much Dad likes it. It was sweet of Sean, smart of him to think of it.

I close the cover and set it beside the bed. Then I just stand there for a moment, sad. Sad that a man of such great intellect is now struggling to follow the rules of Candy Crush. Sad for what he's lost, for what I've lost, too. What we've all lost.

My parents were always partners. They adored each other. While my mother never worked outside the home, she didn't just cook and clean for Dad and my sister and me. Over the years, she worked on some amazing volunteer projects at the hospital, the library, the schools. She had friends, she lunched, she took free courses at the local community college. And she adored my father. As a kid, I remember her waiting on a call from him saying he was on the way home from his office, and no matter what we were doing, she'd run into the bathroom and check her makeup and tidy her hair. She always greeted him at the door with a smile on her face and often a cocktail in her hand for him. My dad loves a cocktail. And he was as happy to see her at the door as she was to see him. They always fell right into conversation, enthralled with each other even after years of marriage.

I sometimes wonder why they adopted me. I know they did it because Mom couldn't have children, or so she was told, but I wonder why they felt the need. Was it just because it was expected of them? Because I always felt as if I was a little bit of an intrusion in their lives, a third wheel. They didn't need me to fulfill their marriage. They always had each other.

Sometimes I'm jealous now of that relationship they had then. I don't know that Oscar and I ever had it. We certainly don't now.

I set Dad's iPad on the nightstand and lean down to kiss his cheeks. He opens his mouth and exhales in a loud snore. It makes me smile. "Good night," I whisper, turning out his light.

And then I head into darkness, back to the cottage.

# 4
# HAZEL

I've been lying on my bed all morning trying to count how many times the ceiling fan goes around in one minute. I even used the stopwatch on my phone. It's not going that well because, even on the slowest speed, I can't really tell when it makes a full spin because it's already on the next one.

Waiting for Tyler to call me back. Avoiding Mom and Dad and my weirdo brother.

I don't know if Sean knows. I don't know if Mom or Dad told him or not. But he keeps looking at me every time I walk through the living room where he's camped out in front of the TV, shooting zombies.

If he does know, I wish he'd just come out and say whatever dumbass thing he's going to say and be done with it. Or better yet, stop looking at me like that and just ask me if I picked out my car yet. He and I have this running game that I know is stupid, but it's fun, and it's a way to talk to the weirdo.

We pretend that zombies have taken over the world, like in *The Walking Dead,* this TV show we used to watch together before he got too cool to hang out with me much. So, in our game, we're making plans as to what we would do if zombies really do take over. We play a round until we get bored and then we start a new one with new parameters. Sometimes Mom and Dad haven't been eaten yet. Sometimes they're alive and we even have to haul Gran and Granddad around. In this round of the game, our family is all long gone, turned into zombies and stumbling around Rockland or somewhere eating stray dogs and cats. Sean and I have decided we're going to Key West because it's too freakin' cold here in Maine. And in the Keys, we can pick an island and better defend ourselves. We're taking two cars down, just to play it safe, so I'm supposed to pick mine. He keeps saying he wants a motorcycle — like he thinks he's Norman Reedus or something. Like he could ever look cool on a motorcycle. Or drive one. He's backed into Dad's car twice already.

I'm thinking about stealing a Toyota Land Cruiser. Well, it's not really stealing because in the zombie apocalypse there will be cars abandoned everywhere, just parked on streets and in garages. Our neighbors have a green Land Cruiser. I could take his. Because Sean and I are the ones controlling the game, I can just say the Petersons are all dead and I can take their car.

I pick up my phone, just to make sure the ringer is on. I know it is. I've already checked. Ten times. Maybe twenty.

This is killing me, not being able to talk to Tyler. He's going to freak out. I didn't even tell him I was late. It just seemed too weird to talk to him about my period. When I'm on, I don't tell him. I just say I don't want to have sex with him because he's being a dickwad. Which can almost always be true at any given moment.

Guess we're going to have to talk about it now.

*I cannot believe I'm pregnant.*

*I cannot believe I'm pregnant.*

*I cannot believe I'm pregnant.*

That thought just keeps going through my head over and over again. I'm devastated. You hear people throw that word around. Kids in my Algebra 2 class were *devastated* because they failed because Mrs. Binner is a mean, fat cow. Tyler's dad is *devastated* that it doesn't look like some guy is going to win the Coca-Cola 600 NASCAR race. *Devastation* means ruin. It means something is destroyed. I'm devastated because my life

71

as I thought it was going to be is ruined. It's destroyed. It will never be what I thought it was going to be. What I hoped it was going to be.

I throw myself back on the bed on my favorite quilt. I've been carrying it around since I was a baby. I pull it over my head and breathe in the weird smell of old cotton and the eco-friendly lavender fabric softener Mom buys. When I was little, Mom said I used to scream when she took my quilt I called Blankie away from me to wash it when it got too gross. And then I'd stand in front of the washing machine when we had a front loader and watch it go around and around. And then I would want it while it was still wet, and I'd scream when she put it in the dryer.

I wonder if I should get my baby a blanket he can still be sticking in his overnight bag when he's sixteen. If I do get him one, and I already know he's a boy, I'm going to be smart about it. Smarter than Mom was. I'm going to get him something new so it doesn't start out being ratty like mine did. My quilt was from way back when my mom was in college. Somebody her mom knew made it.

It's hot under Blankie so I throw it off and check my phone again. Jeez and crackers. Where is he? I'd call his house, but I don't want to risk having to talk to his mom. She always asks me weird questions like where I get my nail polish and if my dad had any dead patients this week. Tyler's parents are weirdos. Not like Sean is a weirdo. Not smart weird like he is. Just weird weird. They eat too much McDonald's. That's my theory. That stuff is so bad for you, full of carcinogens like TBHQ, dimethylpolysiloxane, and L-cysteine, an amino acid made from DUCK FEATHERS. I keep telling Tyler it will kill him. It's a wonder any of his sperm could even swim, he's so full of trans fats and who knows what else.

"Come on, Tyler. Come on," I whisper. "Call me, please." The last words come out sounding so pitiful.

And then, freakishly, my phone rings. Tyler's name pops up on the screen, and I sit up, grabbing it with both hands.

"Tyler?" I practically holler.

"Hey." He sounds like he's far away.

"Where have you been?" I ask, afraid I'm going to start crying. Which I know I can't because Tyler's not like Dad when Mom cries. Not that she cries much, but when she does, Dad gets all sweet and talks quiet to her, hugging her and stuff. Tyler gets angry with me and makes excuses to get away from me when I cry.

So, I'm not going to cry. "Why didn't you call me?" I ask, stalling really because I've been going over in my head what I'm going to say, how I'm going to say it, but now . . . I don't know if I should just blurt it out.

"What?" Tyler says. "I can't really hear you."

The connection is bad. Not scratchy like landlines can be after a big snow, but it's like I can only hear some of the sounds in his words, so I have to guess what he's saying. "I said, 'Why didn't you call me?' " I say louder. As if I'm talking to Granddad when he can't find his hearing aids. "I need to talk to you about something important." I get out of bed and start to pace. All of a sudden I feel like I have to pee. Like I *really* have to pee. I'm so scared to tell him. But I have to. I know that. I mean, it's his baby. And how are we going to make plans if he doesn't know? "It's really important. Tyler, it's —"

"I can't hear you. You'll be home tonight, yeah?" I decipher.

"Yes, but —"

"I'll talk to you then. I have to —"

I lose the next few words and then his voice cuts back in again.

74

"Tyler, this is serious. I need to tell you that —" I hold my phone tight with both hands. I'm trying not to cry.

"Talk to you later," I hear Tyler say.

Then he's gone.

I look at the phone screen. I debate whether or not just to text the asshole. But that's not right. We need to talk. We need to talk about our life together with our baby. About how we're going to do it. On *16 and Pregnant,* sometimes the teenagers move in with their parents. I'm not dumb enough to think that's going to happen. There's no room for me in Tyler's parents' house. Tyler already shares his bedroom with his step-brother. And Mom and Dad would never let Tyler live with us. I wouldn't want him to anyway. That would just be too crazy, living with the guy I had sex with, and my dad.

I sit down on the end of my bed, holding my phone, trying not to cry. Crying anyway. Then I call Katy. My best friend. I wasn't going to tell her until I told Tyler because that's only right. Right?

Katy answers. "Hey. I thought you were at the cottage."

I slide off the bed, to the floor, the footboard against my back, pulling my knees up to my chest. "Katy," I whisper. I don't even try not to cry now. "You're not going to believe this."

# 5
## LIV

I drag the garbage can to the refrigerator. We're packing up to go home. I haven't seen anyone for an hour. Hazel is hiding in her room from the reality of her pregnancy. Sean is hiding from the world inside a virtual combat game. And Oscar is somewhere, hiding from me.

I yank open the refrigerator door. Something stinks inside. It's been smelling for at least two weeks. I smelled it two weekends ago when we were here on a Friday night for family game night with Oscar's siblings and their families. I kept thinking someone else would go on this expedition: Oscar; Marie, his sister; his brother, Joe; somebody's kid. Marie's twins are just a little older than Sean; you would think that eighteen-year-olds would be able to suss out the stench. But even Joe's twelve-year-old, the youngest of the cousins, is old enough to smell something in the refrigerator that stinks like Limburger gone bad in a fourteen-year-old boy's gym bag.

I crouch and my knees crack. I bounce a couple of times. I don't work out, but I watch what I eat, not hard to do with my chief of food police, Hazel, and I do yoga as many mornings a week as I can manage. I like to hike; Oscar and I used to hike together. First with the kids and then, when they got older and whined that they wanted to stay home on a Saturday morning, we would go alone. I'd always looked forward to our Saturday morning hikes; it was a way to connect without the noise of the pile of bills on the kitchen table and the kids' latest needs. But Oscar's put on a few pounds and doesn't seem as open to doing things like that anymore. Whether it's me or just the fact that he's older and more tired, I don't know. I'm hoping with the new job I'll be more active, get more exercise just being on the job site.

I reach for the nearest thing: a carton of free-range eggs. I open it. No eggs are broken, but I take a sniff anyway. They're fine. I scoot them to the left. Next is a glass container of something unidentifiable from the outside.

When I got home from my parents' this morning, I climbed into bed with Oscar, my clothes on. I drifted off to sleep. I'd hoped we could talk when we got up, but I slept until after eight. When I woke up, he was gone. Downstairs, the coffeemaker was on and he'd left a mug out for me. I found him out back in his chair, just sitting there with a cup of coffee in his hand, his book on his lap, staring at the water below. The tide was coming in, crashing on the rocks. Willie Nelson was sprawled at his feet. We exchanged a few words about my mom's trip to the ED and then I tried to broach the subject of our daughter and her predicament. *Our* predicament.

He wasn't receptive. He mumbled something about a man wanting to have a cup of caffeine without having to settle the unrest in the Middle East and I left him to his coffee, his dog, the Nazis.

I find shriveled green beans in the glass container. They're not the source of the stench, but they're certainly beyond edible. I set them on the floor and lower myself to my knees because my calves are starting to cramp.

As I dig in for another treat, I hear Sean's footsteps. Funny how a mother knows the sound and rhythm of the footsteps of everyone in her home. He comes up behind me, reaches over my head, and grabs a bottle of fat water — my children's name for an unsweetened, carbonated water. I glance up at him. He's gotten tall in the last year. I wouldn't say he's handsome because he hasn't put on the weight yet that his almost-six-foot frame needs. He's still gangly and awkward and his acne is just beginning to clear up since his latest visit to the dermatologist. But he's got nice eyes, his father's blue eyes, and his father's hair. It was Oscar's dark-auburn hair and the eyes that made me swoon so many years ago.

"Hey," I say, glancing over my shoulder at him.

He's got his enormous noise-canceling headphones wrapped around his neck. A nice change from last year when he wore them over his ears all the time, so he never heard when anyone spoke to him.

"Hey," he echoes.

"See your sister?" I ask.

"Nope. Probably upstairs talking to Tyler." He cracks open the bottle. "The douche."

I eye him, but I don't comment on the name-calling because if I do, my son will just wander back to his army buddies on the big screen. A mother takes any conversation she can get from a son who's about to fly from the nest.

"What a loser. To get your sixteen-year-old girlfriend pregnant. Didn't he take health class in the ninth grade?" He screws up his face and takes a sip of water. "Probably flunked the class. Douche," he repeats.

I want to agree, but that doesn't seem like good parenting. "So . . . she's talked to him? Talking to him?"

"I don't know." He grimaces. "She wouldn't tell me. She barely speaks to me."

"I wasn't asking if she told you she'd spoken to him." I gaze into the refrigerator, planning my next attack. "I just wondered if . . . maybe you overheard a conversation?" Sean was a great spy when he was young. So good that eventually I had to have a talk with him about not being a tattletale.

"I say we don't tell him at all. This is a big enough shit show without putting Tyler Taylor into the mix." Again, the grimace. "And *his parents*?" He takes another sip. "Anyone who would name their kid Tyler Taylor? You think they're going to have any reasonable input?"

I can't help myself. I laugh. Because he has a point. And then I want to hug him. Sean's still coming out of his shell, but I like the person I see emerging.

I change the subject. "Seen your dad?"

"I think he's washing his car."

81

I grab a suspicious-looking wad of tinfoil. Not from our house. Has to be Marie's or Joe's. We don't use commercial wraps, at least not in Hazel's presence. We have squares of fabric covered with beeswax that we use to cover containers and wrap leftover food. My daughter intends to save the world, one roll of plastic wrap at a time. We give her a hard time about it, but we're actually starting to get used to it, the recycling, the glass rather than plastic containers, buying food in bulk and bringing it home in our own glass mason jars. And I'm so proud of her, proud of her for not just talking about how to change things, how to change the world, but because she's going to do it.

Which is maybe why I'm so sad about this pregnancy. Because no matter what happens, I know this will change her. I just hope it won't break her spirit.

I glance up at Sean. "Order your books for your classes?"

"Check."

"Give notice at work?"

He shrugs. "They knew I was going to school, I just told them my last day. Mr. Jenkins was nice about it. He said to just let him know whenever I want to work, like if I'm home for the weekend or Christmas or whatever. He said they could always use me to fill in for somebody who's called out or whatever."

"That was nice of him." I open the ball of foil slowly, waiting to be bombarded by the stench I'm still smelling. Nope. A petrified dinner roll. I toss it in the compost bin. "You hear back from Richard?" His new roommate, assigned to him by the college. Sean won't know anyone at school. Surprisingly, he seems okay with that.

"Yeah. He e-mailed me last night. His mom has some kind of list. Something about us not bringing two refrigerators? I gave him your e-mail. Told him to tell her to e-mail you. Richard and I are going to decide what equipment to bring. Who's bringing the TV, the Nintendo Switch, stuff like that."

I laugh. The school did a good job of assigning roommates. Richard is in the same major, but they put them on a floor with some math and science nerds. At orientation last month the parents and students all had lunch together and the boys on his floor all sat and talked together. I tried not to look their way too often, but when I did, Sean seemed to be attempting to engage. "Good. You guys going to meet?"

"I think so. Portland this week."

I'm so excited that Sean is reaching out to his roommate-to-be like this. He's struggled socially his whole life. He has a few good friends now, but they're all pretty much like him. Gamer nerds. I'm hoping college will not just introduce him to an academic world but to a social one, too.

"He, um . . ." Sean taps the trash can with his bare foot. "His sister and some friends of hers are coming."

I almost don't catch that because he's swallowing water as he says it.

"Other people will be there, too," he mumbles.

I keep my gaze fixed on a glass bowl that is definitely the leftover nacho cheese from family game night two weeks ago. I don't want to spook Sean. "Like . . . a party?"

"Outdoor concert or something." He walks away. "What time we leaving?"

I'm thinking an hour, but I say, "Soon." I don't want him getting involved in a game with someone in Germany and have us all sitting around waiting for someone to use up his last life so we can go home.

It's happened.

I dig in the refrigerator for another five minutes. I find an apple with a bite out of it, some floppy celery, and a bottle of BBQ sauce missing the lid. But no Limburger. I surrender, empty the food in the compost bin, and load it in the dishwasher. As I bag the trash, I see Oscar through the window. He is washing his car. I have no idea why. He never does it here, always at home. I carry out the trash bag and drop it in the Dumpster, which I roll out onto the edge of the driveway, so we don't forget to put it on the curb when we leave. There's always a discussion about whose turn it is when we leave because we have a long driveway that snakes back to the house that sits right on the water.

I watch Oscar for a minute, debating whether to go talk to him or let it go for now. We've got two cars here, so we aren't going to be able to talk together on the ride home. Unless we let Sean take one of the cars home and make Hazel ride with him. We do that sometimes. But there's always a discussion as to who has to take the dog because he's almost always wet on the ride home. Willie Nelson loves to swim in the bay and it seems as if he always sneaks off to jump in, right before we go. And something tells me Oscar isn't going to go for it, sending the kids home in my car, even if I agree the dog can ride with us in his car. Because he doesn't want to talk to me. Because he's still *seasoning* the issue of our

85

daughter's pregnancy.

I walk out into the driveway.

Oscar is standing there barefoot, holding the hose on his Subaru, watching the water hit the side panel. His hair is a brighter red in the sunlight, as is his beard. Willie Nelson is lying in the stream of water running down the driveway, lapping it up.

"He's drinking the soapy water," I say.

Oscar glances in the direction of the dog, but then returns his attention to the spray of water.

I hook my thumbs in the back pockets of my jean shorts. I'm wearing my Graceland Tour thirtieth anniversary sweatshirt the kids gave me for Christmas. My dad took me to see Paul Simon on tour. Boston, June 1987; Mom stayed home with my little sister. He was that kind of dad. I know every word to every song. And my kids do, too.

"I don't know if Hazel talked to Tyler or not."

He glances at me, then back at the car. Doesn't say anything.

"Oscar." My voice catches in my throat and for a minute I think I'm going to start crying. I fight it because I don't do well expressing myself once I start crying. I don't like crying. I don't like the way it makes me feel out of control. And vulnerable. "I need to talk about this with you. I can't *let it season* any longer." I don't say it in an accusatory way. I say it in a scared, I-need-my-husband kind of way.

He stands there with the hose, still staring at the point where the water is hitting the car.

I take a step toward him. "Oscar . . ."

"What, Liv? What?" He says it loudly, not exactly shouting at me, but certainly not in a tone we usually speak to each other with. Which shocks me a little. Oscar can lose his temper over lights left on in an empty room or the freezer being left open a crack so his ice cream melts and runs onto the kitchen floor. But he doesn't lose his temper on big things. Important things.

"What do you want me to say?" he asks . . . no, demands. "You already know what I think."

"No. I don't know —" I start to speak over the sound of the water, but he turns it off at the spray handle and suddenly it sounds like I'm shouting, too. "I don't," I say, lowering my voice, "know what you're thinking today. I know what we both said yesterday, but . . . but we were in shock. Now . . . we've had some time to think."

"I'm not going to change my mind." He shakes his head stubbornly. "I'm not giving

87

in to you, Liv. Not this time."

"I'm not asking you to *give in,*" I say, prickling. "When do I ever ask you to *give in?* About what we're having on our pizza? Sure. But not when we're talking about something like this."

"You're right." He starts curling up the hose on the pavement at his feet. "Because you're always right. I never give in. You never ask me to." *Sarcasm.*

"Oscar, that's not fair." Tears spring to my eyes and I take a step closer. Now I'm standing in the water the dog is lying in. "You and I need to talk about this. Think it through." I take a breath, exhale. "It's not that I don't want our grandchild, but . . ." I look down and then back up at him. "I can't do another baby. I *cannot* stay home with another baby with the diapers and feedings and the endless crying while you saunter off to work every day and be a part of the world. I did it once for you, I cannot do it again."

"*Saunter off to work?*" He runs his hand over his mouth. "What the hell are you talking about?"

"Please keep your voice down." I glance back at the house. Hazel has enough to deal with right now; she doesn't need to worry about her parents fighting.

He takes a step toward me, the green hose still in his hand. "I don't know what we're talking about here, Liv."

"We're talking about the fact that I finally have a job again. A good job, a job I've dreamed of for a long time, and you're not going to convince me to give it up and stay home with kids again."

He stares at me for a moment, then he knits his brow, shaking his head. "Are we talking about when you left Lauder and Jones *sixteen years ago?*"

I look down at the black asphalt of the driveway. This was not the conversation I came out here to have with him. But we're here now. And ordinarily I'd just let it go. But I'm tired of letting things go, even for the sake of my family. "Yes, I'm talking about sixteen years ago. When I left my job to be a full-time mother and wife," I add, raising my voice to match his fervor. "You knew I didn't want to quit my job. You knew I didn't want to be home all day with the kids. I wasn't suited to that." I open my arms wide to him. "You knew I wasn't."

"Nope. Nope." He throws down the hose. "Not acceptable. You cannot be pissed at me sixteen years after the fact when you didn't say anything then. When you agreed to it *then.*"

"Oscar, I agreed to it because — because —" I look away. I agreed to it why? I can't even remember. Because I wanted to make him happy. Because I'm an adopted child who always wants to make everyone happy. Who wants everyone to love her.

"Have you been angry with me about this for all these years?" Suddenly he sounds hurt, not angry.

When I don't answer him, he says my name.

I look up at him. Tears are running down my cheeks. "I *cannot* be the mother to another infant, Oscar. I can't do it. I will *not* stay home and take care of another baby. For once, I'm going to do something I want to do. Something that's good for me. I'm going to do this renovation, and then another and another and another after that if anyone will hire me."

We're both silent for a few seconds. He's the one who crosses the imaginary line we've drawn in the driveway.

Oscar exhales audibly. "I'm not asking you to give up your job, Liv." He looks down at me. "I'm not asking you to give up your business and stay home. We'll hire someone. My sister can help. You heard her the other night, she says she'd have another baby in a second if Sai would agree to it. She's going to be lost when the twins go back to college. I'm not asking you to be a stay-at-home mom," he says, lowering his voice until it's a rumble of emotion. "I'm just asking you not to give our grandbaby away."

I stand there shaking my head slowly. I know that Oscar means what he's saying right now. But I also know him well enough to know how this will go down. I know me. Hazel and Tyler will keep their baby. Tyler will abandon them before the baby is three months old. Hazel won't be able to handle the baby and high school and, before we know it, she'll be going to soccer games and I'll be home making bottles.

"We need to get home. I have to go see Mom and Dad," I say, unable to look up at him. "Leave here in a half hour?"

He stands there looking at me and then leans over and picks up the hose. *"Ayuh."*

I hesitate a few heartbeats and then I turn around and walk away. As I go, I feel the distance between us doubling exponentially with every step I take.

# 6
## HAZEL

"So . . . you had a good time kayaking with your uncle?" I ask Tyler.

He doesn't answer.

It's Monday afternoon and we're sitting side by side on the swings behind the church that's a few blocks from my house. I didn't get to talk to him in school today, things were crazy, first day and all. So we agreed to meet here.

I live in a little town called Judith that's not too far from Rockland. We live just outside the city limits in a house that used to have farmland around it. The house is one of those cool ones with the barn attached. I guess it was a mess when Mom and Dad moved in when I was a baby, but Mom redid the whole thing. That's how she ended up starting her business. Because she did a fantastic job on our house and people told her she should do it for other people.

Tyler lives a few miles away; he doesn't

have his own car anymore since his truck engine blew up so he's always borrowing someone's. Sometimes his mom's, sometimes his dad's, or a friend's. He borrows his grandfather's truck sometimes, too, but then his grandfather forgets he gave Tyler permission and Tyler gets in trouble for *stealing* the truck again.

I look over at Tyler. He's spinning around and around on his swing, shortening the chain until his sneakers are barely touching the ground. I'm just sitting there watching him, trying not to think about what an idiot he looks like right now. His girlfriend is trying to tell him we're going to have a baby and he's playing on the swing like we're in the fifth grade? Which isn't fair because he doesn't know that I'm trying to tell him I'm knocked up.

"No, you didn't have a good time? Yes, you did?" I close my eyes and have to stifle a groan. God, I sound like my mother.

"It was fine." He picks up his feet and the swing spins in the opposite direction. His feet hit me in the leg and I push myself out of his reach. "Saw this badass Bayliner on Sebago Lake. One thirty-five hp Mercruiser. I bet it goes forty-five miles an hour. I think I'm going to buy one."

Like he has any money to buy a boat. And

if he did, he needs to be saving for college — or a baby — not a boat he can dick around on the lake with his friends in. But I don't say any of that because I don't want to piss him off. We need to talk, seriously talk, and I know that's not the way to get him to talk to me. Instead, I just nod and wait for his swing to unwind completely. "Tyler, I need to talk to you." I stare at my flip-flops. "To tell you something."

He comes to a stop and reaches over and tugs on the sleeve of my Earth Day T-shirt. "Okay. Tell me."

All of a sudden, I'm scared. I don't want to tell him. I mean, obviously I have to tell him, but . . . I look up at the sky. The sun is setting over the trees in the west. Maybe I should wait until I see a doctor or something. Maybe the pee tests came from a bad batch. That has to happen sometimes, right? This girl I knew in my English class last year thought she was pregnant and she just had a stomach virus.

Except that I don't feel sick, just stupid. And I know I am pregnant. And I know I need to tell Tyler. I can't stall any longer. I told Mom I'd be home in a little while. Told her I was meeting him. She didn't ask a single question, she just said, "Okay," in a really quiet, sad voice that made me sad.

Then she kissed my temple as she walked by me, carrying a basket of dirty clothes, which was really nice. It made me think about when I was little and how she used to kiss me and snuggle me when I was sad and it always made me feel better.

"Tyler —" Before I can get out the next word, he's spinning in the swing again. I reach out and grab the chain and stop him. *"Tyler."*

"What?"

I wait until the swing unwinds. Until he's looking at me. "I'm pregnant."

"What?" His second "what" has an entirely different tone.

I just sit there staring at my feet that are dusty in my flip-flops. My toenail polish is chipped. Katy and I need a mani-pedi night. "I'm going to have a baby." I punch him in the arm, only half playfully. "That night you didn't have a condom. Now we're going to have a baby."

He's quiet long enough that I look up at him. He's just sitting there, staring at me.

"Shit," he finally says.

"Yeah, shit," I repeat, returning my gaze to my teal toenails.

Then he's quiet for so long that I look up at him again. "You going to say something?"

"Yeah, I . . ." He looks at me. "You're

sure. Like, you're not just . . . you know."

He sounds uncomfortable even talking about my period, which I realize is kind of weird because he doesn't have a problem taking my panties off.

"Late or whatever," he mumbles.

"I took a pregnancy test. Two. You pee on a stick and it recognizes a hormone that kicks in when there's a baby." I whisper the last words because I'm still having a hard time connecting the fact that me being pregnant means I'm actually going to have a baby. Like a screaming baby with poopy diapers. Me. I'm going to be someone's mother.

He chews on his bottom lip. "You . . . you want to keep or . . . or do you think maybe you should get —"

I interrupt him before he can go any further. "I'm not getting an abortion." I hesitate and then go on. "I'd never judge a girl who made that choice, but . . . I'm not doing that. I'm just not and we're not going to talk about it because I know it's your baby, too, but it's my body and — and no, Tyler."

"You wanna have a baby?" Now he sounds scared.

*No, I don't want to have an effin baby.* That's what I want to scream at him. But I

96

don't because what would be the point? It would just freak Tyler out. Instead, I shrug. "Doesn't matter what I want. I'm having a baby." I think about it for a minute. "I guess I could have a miscarriage or something. It happens sometimes. When the baby's not right. Chromosome issues like Triploidy or Trisomy 13. We talked about them in the genetics chapter in biology class. Some genetic disorders are incompatible with life. A baby can't live and a lot of times the body just miscarries on its own." I shake my head. "But I don't think I'm going to get that lucky."

"Shit, Hazel." He reaches between us and takes my hand.

It feels good. Like maybe things really could be okay. I know this isn't the best situation, but I think Tyler can come through here. This will be his chance to show everyone he's more than what people think he is. With me helping him, he can do it. I'm sure he can. And for once, Mom won't be right.

We're quiet again.

"You tell your parents?" he asks me after a while.

I nod. The sun is setting fast and the breeze is picking up, making it cooler. We're two miles from the ocean here, but I can smell it. I love the salty smell of the ocean.

Tyler sometimes talks about moving somewhere, like going to Montana where a cousin of his lives. I could never live that far from the ocean. Where I couldn't smell it.

"Shit," Tyler says again.

"Yeah," I agree.

"So . . . what . . . what's gonna happen?" He gets up out of the swing and walks away.

Like he doesn't even give his pregnant girlfriend his hand to help her out of the swing. Not that I need help, but could he at least wait for me?

I watch him go, then follow him. "What's going to *happen*? I'm going to get really fat and then, sometime in March, I'm going to push a baby out of my V, Tyler. And you're going to be there when I do it because you put it in there." I poke him in the shoulder as I catch up with him. Then I take his hand. He squeezes mine and we walk toward the parking lot where his dad's truck is parked all crooked in a handicapped parking place. Nobody is at the church, so it doesn't matter.

"And then we have to figure out how we're going to finish school and take care of a baby. You graduate in June, so the next year won't be as bad, depending on what you do," I go on. "I thought maybe you could get a job and go to the community college at night. It takes a lot of money to care for a baby. Did you know diapers are, like, twelve dollars a pack? I looked it up on Amazon. And you have to have butt wipes and bath stuff and T-shirts and sleepers and, and a lot of other . . . *stuff,*" I finish because I'm freaking myself out just thinking about it.

We reach his dad's truck and he leans against the driver's door. He and his dad are supposed to be repainting the truck so it's an ugly matte-gray color right now.

"How do you know all this?" Tyler asks.

"The prices? I told you. Amazon. Pacifiers are, like, seven bucks apiece. The ones the kids will keep in their mouth. I know what you need because I take care of the Dorseys' kids sometimes. Down the street." I point in the general direction of our houses. "Lilly was only, like, six months old when I started watching her. I know about babies."

He lets go of my hand and reaches through the open window of the truck to get the pack of cigarettes off the dash.

"We're not going to be able to afford those when we have the baby," I point out.

He lights up. He knows I hate that he smokes. It makes his breath stink and it's so bad for you. Cancer linked to tobacco use makes up forty percent of all cancer diagnoses and three in ten cancer deaths are directly related to tobacco use. Like, how can you be so stupid?

Not that I have a right to be calling anyone stupid. I'm the one who's three months pregnant.

I watch him light up. He watches me watching him.

"I gotta go," he says as he exhales a big puff of stinky smoke. "Gotta clean up the dog shit in the backyard. If I don't, Mom says she's turning my phone off again."

I step out of the way of the smoke. Second-hand smoke is no joke with a fetus: low birth weight, premature birth, learning and behavior issues in a child. I lean against the truck, crossing my arms over my chest. My hands fall flat across my abdomen. I wonder what it will be like when the baby starts to grow. When my belly gets big. "You're going to have to tell your parents," I say.

He takes another drag, digging up gravel with the toe of his sneaker and sending the little pieces skittering across the parking lot. "My stepdad is going to freakin' kill me."

I'm afraid he means his stepdad is going to hit him. He does that sometimes. Mostly when he's had too much beer. Or when he and Tyler's mom are really fighting. He's not a bad guy, I don't think. Just a bad parent. And his mom is a bad parent for letting her husband hit her son. If Dad ever hit Sean or me, I think my mom would take him out. When she does something she thinks she's justified in doing, she always says no jury of her peers would convict her. I think that's what she'd say as she hit Dad back with the lid of her Le Creuset pot.

I look up at Tyler. "You can wait a little while." I brush his arm with my fingertips. Sometimes I feel bad that he has such a shitty home life and I have such a good one. "Maybe we'll get lucky and I'll have a miscarriage or something." I sort of laugh even though I don't think it's funny.

He sucks on the cigarette so hard that his cheeks sink in. He's a good-looking guy: tall with light-brown hair and pretty, dark eyes. His hair is shaggy, though, and needs to be cut by someone other than his mom. I resist the temptation to reach up and brush his hair out of his eyes. I'm not exactly feeling romantic right now. Considering that's how I got myself in the situation to begin with.

"I gotta go." He takes one last drag on the cigarette, throws it on the ground, and grinds it out with his sneaker. "Want a ride home?" He's already getting in the truck.

"Nah," I say. "I'll walk." I want to walk so I can think. I've got so many thoughts flying around in my head that I feel over-whelmed. Like I can barely catch my breath. I need to get my thoughts together to sit down and talk to Mom and Dad. Mom is so pissed at me. And Dad is . . . he's just really sad. And disappointed. I hate that I've disappointed my parents.

"See you in school tomorrow, maybe?"

"See you tomorrow," I echo.

I watch him pull out. He doesn't look back as he peels out of the driveway, throwing gravel from the tires of the truck. I reach down, pick up his cigarette butt, tuck it into my pocket, and head home.

# 7
## LIV

I'm leaning against the kitchen counter, spacing out, when the Instant Pot sings its little song, letting me know the chicken curry is done. I check the time on the microwave. Oscar texted me twenty minutes ago. He'll be home any minute. I glance at the electric rice cooker plugged in beside the Instant Pot. Only six minutes left until the rice is done. I pick up my phone and text Sean and Hazel. Group text.

Dinner in 15

I get a K from Sean. Nothing from Hazel.

I set my phone down. Hazel went to meet Tyler somewhere after school. She wasn't gone very long. My daughter didn't disclose any information on the exchange that took place, but I have a feeling they finally talked about her pregnancy. She looked as if she'd been crying when she got home. I asked her if she was okay. She didn't answer, just made a beeline for the stairs.

I pick up my phone again to text Hazel. A couple of weeks ago she had an argument with a friend and was upset. She wouldn't talk to me about it, but I discovered, purely by accident, that she was willing to *text* me about it. As I hold my phone in my hand, a part of me wants to fight the inclination. Kids need to know how to interact verbally, face-to-face, blah, blah, blah. But right now, Hazel's well-being is more important to me than improving her communication skills.

I text Did you get my text about dinner? Then I backspace. I know very well she got it. And she maintains you don't have to answer every single text someone sends you. She has several additional criticisms about my texting skills. I need to cut down on the emoticons, for one.

I think for a minute and then text:
Talk to Tyler?

Then I add about the pregnancy. No sense pussyfooting around here. I hesitate, then hit "send."

I set down my phone and get wide, shallow bowls from the overhead cabinet. Two blue, two green. I run my finger along the rim of one of them, feeling the cool smoothness of the pottery. They're made by a local potter. All handmade and fired locally. My dish cabinet is filled with handmade dishes

Oscar and I have collected over the years. A couple actually made by Oscar. He has his own wheel out in the barn that's connected to the house, which we use as a combination garage, tool shed, and general storage area. As I study the bowls on the black soapstone counter, I try to remember when he last started up his wheel.

My phone dings and I pick it up.

talked to him, my daughter has responded. She also says proper punctuation and spelling isn't required, depending on the message and the intended audience. She has a lot of rules, my daughter. A lot of criticisms, particularly of me. Never Oscar. Just me. But I suppose it's often that way with mothers and their teenage daughters. Oscar says it's because the two of us, Hazel and I, are so alike. I don't see it. I just think she likes him better.

I stand there for a minute, phone in my hand. Then I text And?

*Backspace.*

Instead, I text You okay?

I stare at the screen, waiting for her response.

I smile when the little bubbles appear. She's texting back. I hear Oscar pull into the driveway and the garage door go up. Willie Nelson, who's been lying in the kitchen, in any spot I'm trying to get to, jumps up and saunters out of the kitchen in search of his best friend.

okay. he was pretty upset, Hazel replies.

I read the text a second time and then hold my phone in both hands trying to think of how to best respond. I want to say, "He's upset? Probably not as upset as the rest of us because he has no idea how this is going to change your life forever."

I do not write that. Instead, I say, Did you talk about any kind of plan? Proper punctuation included.

I wait.

Plan? I'm going 2 have the baby that's the plan

No, plan as in how he's going to financially support his child. Who's going to watch the baby so you can both finish school.

Again, I delete the whole thing. Instead, I text, There's plenty of time. We can talk about it when you're ready.

I wait for the bubbles. Then for the text to come through. I hear Oscar enter the mudroom from the garage. He'll reach our big country-style kitchen in a second.

K is all I get from Hazel this time.

Willie Nelson chuffs as Oscar comes through the door.

The rice cooker sings its song.

"Good timing," I say to Oscar. I go to him, lay my hand on his chest, and give him a kiss on the lips. He seems surprised. I get a half-pucker. "Hey," I murmur, smiling up at him.

"Hey," he responds, trying to make his way around me and the dog to set his lunch bag on the counter. "He been out?"

"Yes." I walk back to the counter to take the lid off the Instant Pot and stir the curry. "Hazel told Tyler. She says he's pretty upset."

Oscar goes to the refrigerator and removes a bottle of beer. He uses an opener from a drawer and pops it open. "I have time for a shower?"

"Dinner's ready. Kids will be down in a couple of minutes."

"That a yes or a no?"

I turn around to face him, a wooden spoon in my hand. "Are you picking a fight with me, thirty seconds into the house?"

He sips his beer. His face is expressionless. "I had a bad day at work. I'd like to get a shower. Can you hold dinner a few minutes?"

"I can." I turn back to the curry. "Can we talk with Hazel about the pregnancy at dinner?"

"You think that's a good idea? In front of Sean?"

"I don't know, Oscar." My voice raises a note. "That's why I'm asking you."

He takes another sip of beer. "I think we should talk to her privately. Sean doesn't need to be involved."

"He already knows."

Oscar exhales. He's wearing dark-green scrubs. The new ED colors. He looks good in the green. Green has always been his color, with his red hair. He's still handsome, my Oscar, even with his hair thinning and the extra weight around his middle. If we were strangers, if I met him somewhere, I'd think he was good-looking. I'd be physically attracted to him.

"That's not the point, Liv. The point is . . ." He groans, raises his free hand, and lets it fall. He takes another sip of beer and then gestures with the bottle. "I don't know what the point is."

I put the wooden spoon down and walk over to him, put one arm on his shoulder, and rest my cheek against his chest. He smells faintly of rubbing alcohol and the body wash he uses. He kisses the top of my head, but doesn't hug me. Again, I feel that distance between us. Even resting my head against him.

"I'll be down in ten," he tells me.

I let him go. He walks out of the kitchen as Hazel walks in.

"Hey, Dad."

"Hey, Daisy."

He's called her Daisy since she was a baby. I have no idea why. He has no idea. Or we've forgotten, he's been doing it so long.

He turns around, backing out of the kitchen, beer still in hand. "How was your day at school? Anything exciting happen?"

"Katy broke up with Luke again. I think they're done this time." She chews on her lower lip, thinking. "Oh, and Mr. Mercer got called into the principal's office for something. We think it's because he was flirting with Mrs. Cortez. Her room's across the hall."

"Oh, dear," Oscar says. "They're married, I take it. To other people?"

"No." Our daughter wrinkles her freckled nose. "Divorced. But it doesn't matter, Dad. No fraternization at work. Eww."

He smirks, clearly amused by his daughter, turns, and heads out of the room.

"Want me to set the table?" Hazel asks me.

I'm surprised by her offer. She's at that age right now where she always does what I ask, but rarely volunteers. "Sure. Thanks. We just need napkins and spoons. I folded a fresh batch." I indicate the pile of clean cotton napkins on the edge of the counter. "You can put the rest of them away while you're at it." I hear a car and look through the window over the sink to see my sister flying up the driveway in her new car. She gets a new one every two years. One of the advantages of not having children, she once told me.

"Aunt Beth is here," I say. I want to be annoyed with her because the visit is unannounced. But they're always unannounced. And no matter how crazy Beth makes me, I'm always happy to see her. She's all the things I'll never be and I adore her for that, even in the times when I almost hate her for it.

"Oh, good." Hazel grabs some napkins. "She can stay for dinner. I'll set a place for her."

I take another bowl from the cabinet. With Beth here, that means talking about the baby over dinner won't be happening. I dig through a drawer, looking for a ladle. Maybe it's just as well. Maybe Oscar's right. Sean shouldn't be included in these conversations. I doubt he wants to be.

Willie Nelson chuffs a warning that some-

110

one is coming through the barn and the door flies open. My sister does everything at time and a half. *"Bonjour!"* she greets us.

"Aunt Beth." Hazel leans in for a kiss on the cheek and gets a big hug.

"What's for dinner?" Beth walks through the dining area and into the kitchen, plopping her handbag and a box wine on the counter.

"Chicken curry."

"Mm, I brought the wine. It's red. Does red go with curry?" She brushes her lips across my cheek. She smells terrific, of expensive perfume. She has a new boyfriend who took her to London for a long weekend a few weeks ago. To say I was jealous would be an understatement.

Ordinarily I wouldn't have wine on a Monday night. I usually reserve my alcohol consumption for the weekends. Mostly because of the calories. Tonight, I could use a glass of wine. I could probably drink the whole box. "Of course red wine goes with curry," I say, having no idea if that's true or not.

"You want a glass, yeah?"

"A big one," I say, wondering if I should pull a bread boule out of the freezer. I wasn't planning on having a fifth for dinner. It doesn't do any good to invite her because she's just as likely to not show up as to show up. Beth goes where the wind blows her. But she drops in all the time, here and at the cottage. And when she does, she lights up the room. She's totally undependable, but the life of every party. She gives good gifts, too.

"Bad day?" Beth takes two stemless wine-glasses from a glass-front cupboard I reglazed myself. "Think O wants some?" She calls Oscar O.

"He's got a beer." I hold out my hand, waiting for her to pour wine in one of the glasses from the black plastic spigot.

"You guys fighting?" She pushes the glass into my hand. Beth is a beauty: tall, athletic body, though she never works out, with my dad's blue eyes and my mother's killer cheekbones. She drinks like a fish, or an alcoholic, and never gains an ounce. She's thirty-four and could pass at a frat party for twenty.

I take a sip of the wine. It's not bad for box wine. A cabernet.

"Big fight?" Beth asks, pouring herself a glass, filling it nearly to the rim. "Like throwing stuff at each other big?"

I hesitate. Beth's obviously not talked to Mom and heard our news.

"She's upset about the pregnancy," Hazel

says, taking five spoons from a drawer and sliding it shut with her hip.

Beth's head snaps around to look at me. "Christ on a crutch, you're *pregnant,* Liv? At your age?" She shakes her head, taking a gulp of wine. "I didn't even know that was possible. Have you lost your f—"

"Not Mom. Me. I'm pregnant," Hazel interrupts. She carries the spoons to the table on the other side of the counter. "Mom pregnant? Why would you even *say* that?" She wrinkles her nose. "Gross."

"You're *pregnant?*" Beth demands, setting her glass down so hard that wine sloshes over the rim of the glass and onto the soapstone. She walks into the dining area. "You have got to be kidding me. How could someone as smart as you are be that stupid?" She's practically shouting. "Damn it, Hazel. We talked about this. I told you if you needed condoms, just to tell me."

The fact that Beth talked to my daughter about condoms is news to me. And it smarts a little. And makes me feel guilty because obviously I should have been the one talking to her about condoms. Not that I have never talked to her about sex and birth control. I've talked to her about my feelings on teenage sex and given her the "Don't do it, but if you do, be sure you're doing it

113

safely." But clearly I wasn't paying attention to her relationship with Tyler. Clearly I didn't do my job as Hazel's mother. I didn't protect her. But it still galls me that Beth talked to Hazel. That she apparently knew Hazel was having sex with Tyler and I didn't. And she talked to Hazel about it and didn't tell me.

"You get an appointment?" Beth demands, practically getting in Hazel's face. "She get an appointment?" She looks over her shoulder at me, then back at Hazel. "How many weeks are you? Still inside the window?"

Hazel looks like she's going to burst into tears.

"You may have to go to Boston. I know a clinic —"

"Beth," I interrupt, knowing where this is going. I inhale because this is hard for me to say. "Hazel's decision is to keep the baby."

Beth looks as if she's just taken a big bite of persimmon. "She's not *keeping the baby,*" she says to me. Then she looks at Hazel. "You're not keeping this baby. You're not ruining your life over that poor excuse for a boyfriend Ty—"

"I'm keeping the baby," Hazel interrupts. Her eyes tear up, but her jaw has a defiant set to it now. I know that look. Sean was always so easygoing, malleable, as a child.

But not Hazel. She had her own way of doing things, even as a baby, and when I crossed her, anyone crossed her, she got that look on her face. As if daring anyone to challenge her.

Beth just stands there staring at Hazel. Then she comes back into the kitchen, her bare feet silent on the twelve-inch barn-plank flooring Oscar and I put in ourselves. We bought the wood at a yard sale in New Hampshire. As I watch my sister's bare, tanned feet coming toward me, I remember the weekend Oscar and I bought the wood. It's funny how random memories like that can be. Mom and Dad had the kids; Hazel was probably only three at the time. Oscar and I stayed in a little B&B. It had two single beds and we slept together in one. Made love in the iron bed that Oscar's feet hung over and then slept in each other's arms. I can't decide if the memory brings me joy or sadness. Life was so easy then. I didn't think so at the time. I struggled being the mother of two small children. But I realize now how foolish I was not to have appreciated those years as much as I should have.

"You cannot let her have a baby," Beth retorts, half under her breath, at me.

I take another big gulp of wine. It's

115

already going to my head. I haven't eaten anything since eleven when I had an apple with some almond butter Hazel made last week. I take another drink. "She's decided."

"It's not up to her," Beth argues, grabbing her wineglass. It sloshes up one side, then dribbles over again. "You're her parent. Tell her she's getting an abortion."

Now I'm tearing up. "She's sixteen years old," I say, looking into my sister's gorgeous eyes. "I can't make that kind of decision for her."

"The hell you can't." She reaches into her bag. "I need a cigarette. Hazel. Outside."

Hazel meets my gaze. She's asking me to rescue her.

I should, but I don't. What was that saying my mother always used to say to me when I screwed up? You made this bed, now lie in it?

"You better not throw that cigarette butt into my herb garden," I warn my sister as the two of them head toward the back of the house.

Then I take another sip of wine.

# 8
## HAZEL

I lean against the metal table on the deck where we eat sometimes and watch Aunt Beth attempting, unsuccessfully, to light her cigarette. I'm trying not to cry. I totally expected Mom to scream and holler at me when she found out I was pregnant, and she didn't. And I never expected Aunt Beth to lose her shit with me. Not in a million years.

I look away. I can't believe Mom didn't come out here with us. That she threw me to my aunt wolf.

"I can't believe you were stupid enough to get *pregnant,*" Aunt Beth says angrily, flicking her disposable lighter over and over again. "I thought you wanted to be a doctor. I thought you were going to volunteer for Doctors Without Borders and fix cleft palates or some bullshit." She flicks it again; still no flame, just a spark. "Damn it!" She slams the lighter down on the table. As if that's going to make it work.

I just stare at her. I don't think I've ever seen her this angry. Well, maybe once with Mom. She blamed Mom when she hit Mom's car in our driveway. But Aunt Beth was pretty drunk that night. Mom was telling her she couldn't leave, and she got in her car anyway. They'd been fighting because Aunt Beth was supposed to take Granddad to the hospital for some kind of outpatient surgery and she hadn't shown up; that was what started it all. The bottle and a half of wine she drank just added to the whole evening. She didn't get too far that night. She didn't even make it out of the driveway before she plowed into Mom's car. Dad made her a bed on the couch in the living room. Nobody ever said anything about it again. Mom just got her car fixed and Aunt Beth paid the bill. So Aunt Beth's car insurance wouldn't sky-rocket. That's what Dad said. I guess she'd already had some accidents.

Aunt Beth tries to light her cigarette again. This time the lighter flares. The slam-it-on-the-table method worked.

"How far along? How many weeks?" she asks me, her tone still mean.

I cross my arms over my stomach. As if I could protect my baby from her meanness.

118

Because I don't want my baby to grow up in a mean world, with people who are mean to him. Even mean around him. "Doesn't matter. I told you, I'm not getting an abortion."

She takes a long drag on the cigarette. I take a step back to protect my baby from the carcinogenic fumes.

"About fourteen weeks," I say softly.

"Fourteen weeks!" She exhales, blowing smoke, looking at me like I'm the scum of the earth. I can't believe she's being so mean to me. She's just glaring at me now.

"Mom wants me to put it up for adoption." The minute the words are out of my mouth, I wish I could take them back. Mom says the best way to avoid an argument is not to engage. Then she told me I wasn't allowed to do that with her.

Aunt Beth cuts her eyes at me. She has the prettiest eyes I've ever seen. Pale blue like an alien's. She's gorgeous. Tall and skinny with long, beautiful blond hair.

*"Adoption?"* She laughs, a little like a crazy person. What's the word? *Manic?*

"That's interesting," Aunt Beth goes on, "considering the fact that Liv's been angry her whole life that she was adopted."

What Mom's *really* been upset her whole life about is the fact that her birth parents,

119

her mother, didn't want her and gave her up for adoption. She's not upset that Gran and Granddad adopted her. I'm surprised Aunt Beth doesn't know that. But this doesn't seem like the right time to point it out.

"What's your dad say?" she asks me.

"He agrees with me." I reach across the table to a big flowerpot of mixed herbs and snap off a piece of mint. I bring it to my nose and breathe deeply. I like the sweet, fresh smell. Mom always makes me peppermint tea when my stomach is upset. "He thinks I should keep the baby. We should," I amend. "Tyler and me."

She draws hard on the cigarette, shaking her head. "You and Tyler? Are you shitting me? That little jackass couldn't take care of a flea on Willie Nelson's ass."

"That's not very nice," I say. "Tyler loves me and I love him."

She eyeballs me. She looks like she's going to bust out laughing, but she doesn't. She just takes another drag on the cigarette, one step closer to some hideous cancer-related death. "You know it's just a glob of cells."

"He isn't and, Aunt Bethie, I'm not talking about this with you." I take on a stubborn tone. "You're not my parent. I don't have to talk about it with you. I don't have to talk about it with anyone if I don't want."

She walks over to this giant old cabinet that used to be in some rich person's dining room to hold dishes. Mom bought it at an estate sale and it stands against the side of the house, under the overhang of the roof. Mom filled it with potted plants. Aunt Beth pulls a little flowerpot full of dirt and cigarette butts out from behind a potted fern and drops ashes into it. She carries the improvised "ashtray" to the table.

"She's right, you know. Your mom."

I look at her.

"If you don't have an abortion, which I think is stupid, then you need to put the baby up for adoption. You need to give it to someone who wants a baby. Somebody who can take care of it."

"I'm not giving my baby to some stranger. I want my baby." I bring my hand to my flat belly where I know it's growing.

"You don't want a baby." She points at me with the burning cigarette. "What you want is some crazy effed-up idea of happily ever after with that asshole, Tyler. And . . . and you somehow think a baby is going to give you your own little family. You're going to have someone to love of your own." She opens her arms wide, mocking me.

I don't say anything.

"But you're not, Hazel. You're going to have nothing but sadness and misery and the worst of it will come knowing you brought a child into the world that you couldn't take care of. And not only are you going to be sad and miserable, but you're going to subject a child to that." She puts her cigarette to her lips and inhales. "Why do you think I didn't have children? Because I couldn't take care of a child," she blurts. "I can barely take care of myself."

I think she's right about that. I also think I'm more capable of being a responsible parent right now at sixteen than she is at however old she is. Thirty-something. But what's the point in saying that? It makes more sense just to show her. To show them all that I can do it. That I can love this baby and take care of him. That Tyler and I can do it together. I'm not saying it isn't going to be hard. I'm just saying I can do it.

I smell the mint I've crushed between my fingers again. "I'm not giving my baby away, Aunt Beth. You guys can't make me."

"The hell we can't!"

"Beth, that's enough."

I look up to see Mom standing at the back door. She looks pretty in the fading sunlight. Her hair is pulled back in a ponytail, but there are little wisps around her face. She's wearing a cool T-shirt with a mermaid on it that we bought last summer at this shop in Portland. I got one with an octopus. Same artist. A girl. I like female artists.

"Come on, Hazel," Mom says, her voice so soft that it makes me tear up. "Inside. It's time for dinner."

I cross the deck, past Aunt Beth and through the doorway. I want to tell Mom thanks for saving me, but I don't because I'm afraid I'll start crying if I try to say anything. Instead, I give her the little sprig of mint I picked. I don't know why.

She takes it from me and lifts it to her nose to smell it. And smiles at me. Just a little smile. Kind of a sad one.

Then Mom looks away from me. "You, too, Beth," she says to her sister.

And then we all go in to have dinner and I try not to think about the little baby growing inside me.

# 9
## Liv

I glance at my phone. It's eleven ten. Hazel's late. And driving my car. This is her second day of unrestricted driving privileges, as mandated by the Pine Tree State and she's already broken curfew.

I sigh and glance at Oscar, asleep on the couch, a book on his chest. He's snoring. Loudly. I think he needs a CPAP machine. He says he just needs to lose twenty pounds.

I'm sitting across from him in an old leather chair we inherited from my parents, *inherited* meaning we stole it from their basement. It used to be in my dad's office back when he still had a medical practice. It's got to be forty years old. Soft, black, creased leather. I love the smell of it. The way it seems to surround me, reminding me of the days when he would take me to his office on a Saturday while he caught up on his charts. I'd sit in this chair for hours and read while he worked at his desk.

I've been running some numbers on the Anselin house project. Like ours, their early-nineteenth-century home is a farmhouse built in a style referred to as "continuous architecture." While our home just has a large barn attached, the Anselins have a kitchen, a shed, a carriage house, and a large barn, all attached to their farmhouse. The additions would have been built as the family became more prosperous, and the tradition of attaching the outbuildings was for convenience's sake. Less snow shoveling during our hard winters. Farmers could get to their stored firewood, their sleigh or carriage, and their animals without having to go outside.

I shift in my father's leather chair. I use the downstairs bedroom just off our family room as an office. I could be working in there at my desk, but I settled here earlier in the evening so I could be with Oscar. I was hoping we could talk about Hazel. Start coming up with a plan. How she's going to finish out the school year. What she's going to do with the baby while she's in class. How Baby Daddy is going to support his progeny and what that will look like financially. Didn't happen. After dinner, Oscar turned on the TV to watch Boston play the Orioles and read. Both at the same time. I tried several times to start a discussion, but he wasn't having it. I got one-syllable answers and eventually gave up.

I glance at my legal-sized notepad on my lap. The Anselins have already set a budget, but then they keep adding upgrades. I can't seem to get them to understand that details like granite countertops and radiant heating in the floors can add considerably to the final cost.

Oscar gasps. Snorts.

I glance at him over the top of my reading glasses. His. I couldn't find mine. His strength is stronger than mine anyway. Sadly, I see better in them. And he must have half a dozen pairs here and there in the house. "Oscar?" I pause. Wait. He doesn't move. "Hon?"

He groans.

"Hon," I say a little louder. "You should go to sleep."

"I was asleep," he mutters, his eyes still closed.

"Asleep upstairs in bed."

He rolls over on the couch, taking his book with him, presenting his back to me. His T-shirt rides up as he moves and those few extra pounds around his waist spill out of the back of his shorts.

My cell vibrates, and I pick it up, thinking

Hazel is texting me that she's on her way.

Still up? It's my bestie, Amelia.

I turn my phone so that it's horizontal the way Sean showed me. Easier to text with the larger keyboard. Waiting for Hazel. She's late. In my car. Prob wrapped around a tree

Prob not Amelia responds.

I smile despite the fact that I truly am concerned about Hazel. Amelia has a way about her. She's the kind of friend that can talk me off a ledge. Any ledge.

How was your date? I ask.

Good. Nice.

The bubbles appear. I wait.

Ok, she adds.

He look like his pic or was it another one taken ten years ago? I ask.

In bed?

Working, I text. Watching Oscar sleep on the couch. O's beat the Sox in ten innings.

My phone starts vibrating steadily. Amelia is calling.

"Hey," I say, getting up out of the chair, setting the notepad on the end table. "What's up?" I pad barefoot out of the living room, turning off the lights as I go.

"We need better pitching," Amelia says, referring to the Red Sox.

"Our pitching was better than theirs. Lucky double in the top of the ninth." I push the readers up on my head so I don't trip.

"He did look like his photo." Amelia sounds morose. "Even better in person. He's an attorney —"

"I thought you said no attorneys."

"He's an attorney," she repeats. "And I liked him. He was nice and smart. We had a good time. . . ."

"But?" I ask when I hear her hesitation.

"I don't know. I thought we were hitting it off, but then . . ." She sighs. "I don't think he was that into me."

The disappointment in her voice makes me sad. I don't know what to say.

I struggled to support her during her divorce. I think she gave up on Sam too soon. On their twenty-three-year marriage too soon. Too easily. I think they could have revived their marriage with some counseling, with some effort. Neither was willing to put in the effort. Now Sam's dating a CPA ten years younger than Amelia. His and Amelia's daughter, a sophomore at Providence College in Rhode Island, is having a fit, according to Amelia. Lizzie says her dad is doing things with the girlfriend's children he never did with her. The whole thing is an ugly, sad mess. The way divorce usually is.

"Did you make plans to meet again?" I

ask into the phone. "Dinner or something?" Amelia's formula for online dating is to exchange a few texts in the app and then meet for coffee or a drink, depending on how optimistic she's feeling. Then additional dates to follow if she and bachelor #18 connect. So far, she hasn't met the new love of her life, but she's hopeful and I'm trying to be encouraging.

I lean against the sink with my hips, peering out the double windows into the darkness, waiting for the headlights of my car. I hope she hasn't wrecked it. For the obvious reasons, but then also because I think I've decided to trade it in on a pickup. It makes more sense for the job. I'll be hauling samples of tile and hardwood and assorted supplies back and forth to the Anselins' house. And once the remodel is done, I've got a budget for decorating. I'm hoping to pick up some nice odds and ends like tables and chairs and armoires at estate sales to fill the space.

Amelia sighs and I hear her take a drink. I wonder if it's chardonnay or vodka. I decide not to ask. In the early days, after Sam left, I was worried about her. She was drinking too much, too much to the point of going into work late. Missing work. Not cool for a public school principal. Not cool for anyone.

Or healthy. Luckily, by the time I brought up the subject, she already knew she was skating on thin ice and was able to back it off to a safe place before she fell through. That doesn't mean I don't worry about her starting the whole cycle over again. Especially now that she's out in the world of online dating and it's not going as well as she had hoped.

Amelia takes another drink of the unidentified beverage. "He asked for my number."

"That's good, right?" I try to sound enthusiastic, but not too enthusiastic. Supportively enthusiastic, without blowing smoke up her skirt. "He wouldn't ask for your number if he wasn't planning on calling you. Asking you out."

"I don't know." Amelia groans. "I asked him for his, and he brushed over it. I wonder if he thought I had stalker potential." She takes on a desperate tone. "Do I come off as having stalker tendencies?"

I laugh. She sounds so serious. Which also makes me sad. "No, you do not seem like the stalker type."

"You're just saying that because you're my friend and you have to."

"If I thought you had stalking propensities, I'd be the first one to tell you and you know it."

"True," she agrees. "Hang on. I have to take my top off. Going to put you on speaker. This underwire bra is killing me."

I smile at her comment and glance out the window again as I see headlights coming up our road from the direction of Hazel's friend Katy's house. It passes. I check the time. She's now seventeen minutes late. I wonder how long I should let it go before I call her.

"Can you hear me, Liv?"

"I hear you. Lost you for a second."

"God, that feels better," Amelia says. "I think maybe I need to make a new rule for first dates. I'm getting quite a list of them. New rule: No underwire bra unless it's something more than a cup of coffee or a glass of wine. I want at least three courses in exchange for a lacy torture device that cost me sixty-two dollars."

I laugh.

"Who came up with the idea of an underwire bra, anyway?" she demands.

I hear sounds that suggests she's still undressing. Dressing.

"Had to be a man," she tells me.

"I'm sorry your date didn't go better." I'm genuinely disappointed for her. "But who knows, maybe he'll text or call."

"Right. And maybe hell will freeze over.

131

Enough of my pathetic life. Tell me what's going on in your house in crisis."

"Now I'm putting *you* on speaker so I can text my wayward daughter."

I text Hazel, On your way home?

"No change," I tell Amelia. "I'd say it's like a battlefield around here, but it's worse than that. Instead of lobbing grenades, we're all tiptoeing around each other, trying not to lose our shit. Hazel can't speak to me without a *mean voice.*"

"Eh. Try not to take it personally. It's probably the easiest way for Hazel to react right now. To be angry with you."

"It's not even Hazel. I mean, yes, she's angry just on general principle, but Oscar, he's . . ." I turn and lean against the kitchen sink, propping one elbow on the edge behind me and lifting the phone to speak directly into it again. "He's really angry with me, Meels. Angrier than . . ." Emotion tightens my throat. "Angrier than I can ever remember him being. And not pissed off, shouting anger. That would be fine. That I could handle."

"When has Oscar ever hollered at you?" she scoffs.

"I know. But you know what I mean." I exhale, trying to find the right words to explain without bursting into tears. "This is like a quiet . . . stewing anger."

"He's not talking to you?" she asks.

"He's talking to me. About making Sean's tuition payment. About not wanting to stop for zucchini on the way home from work. But he's not *talking* to me."

"Hmmm," she intones. "Is he in denial that his teenage daughter had sex with a cretin and is now going to give birth to a baby cretin?"

She makes me smile even when I don't want to. "No. He's not in denial. He just doesn't want to talk about it with me. He doesn't want to talk about *anything* with me." I try not to sound sullen, but I don't pull it off well.

"Are you having sex?"

I laugh though it's not funny. "I wish. At this point, I'd take a little angry sex."

Amelia laughs with me, but it's the kind of laughter you share with someone you love when you're feeling her pain.

I glance at the clock on the back of the stove. "Hazel hasn't called, and she hasn't texted. Think I should go looking for her?"

"You call her?"

"Don't want her answering the phone while she's driving. I texted her."

"So you *do* want her texting you while she's driving?" Amelia asks.

"She's probably dead. All this upset about a baby and it's not going to matter because they're both dead."

"They're not dead. She's running late. Teenagers do that." Amelia sounds as if she really means it and she's not saying it just to try to comfort me.

"She didn't call or text to tell me she was going to be late. She always tells me when she's going to be late. Used to. She didn't last night, either," I add. "Am I supposed to start grounding her now? At this point? I mean, I thought we were beyond that."

"You never grounded your kids," Amelia points out.

"No. I never needed to." I turn to watch out the window again, if not for Hazel, then for the police cars and the paramedics with their flashing red lights. "Apparently I needed to. Apparently I need to lock her up in her room and swallow the key," I add tartly. "I can't believe she didn't use protection, Meels. I can't believe I didn't make sure she was having safe sex." My voice catches in my throat. "I can't believe I didn't protect her."

"We can't guard them from everything," Amelia murmurs. Then, "You hear from Sean?" A not-so-subtle redirection of the conversation. "How's the new roommate

134

and their visit to Portland? I thought it was great that they decided to meet before school started."

"He texted me to say he arrived yesterday. Got a pic of a mountain of fries today. Guess he's good."

"Our little Sean, all grown up."

I sigh. "Growing up."

Light comes through the window, casting shadows in the dark kitchen. Headlights. I turn around to look out the kitchen window. I don't think I've ever in my life been so thankful to see my Toyota. "Gotta go. She's home."

"Go easy on her," Amelia says softly.

"Going upstairs," Oscar calls from the living room as I hang up. "Can you let Willie Nelson out before you come to bed?"

"Yes," I call back. "Hazel's just getting home. I'll be up soon."

He doesn't answer me.

I hear the garage door open and I try to come up with a plan as to how to handle the curfew issue. I debate whether to be nonchalant or give her hell when she comes in the door.

# 10
## HAZEL

I sit in Mom's car, my hands at ten and two, just like she taught me. It's dark inside the car, but the overhead garage light is on. I closed the automatic door so the light will go out soon.

I did a good job driving tonight. I thought I'd be nervous, driving alone, but it was fun and not even that intimidating. Easier than last night. Tyler never knows how to get anywhere, but I didn't make a single wrong turn.

I even drove across town to go see Gran and Granddad. I wasn't scared. But I'm scared now.

Of Mom. Of my whole frickin' life. What it's become. Becoming. I've got a doctor's appointment next week with an OB/GYN. A pelvic exam. *Christ's bones.* That's what Granddad would say. He's got the best swears.

Mom tried to make an appointment with

*her* doctor, but Katy told me who her friend Miranda went to when she was having problems with her period. Dr. Gallagher is a woman. And not as old as Granddad, like Mom's guy. I know me having a baby means a lot of people are going to see my V, but I feel like I have a right to be somewhat selective.

I glance in the direction of the door that leads from the garage area of our attached barn into the laundry room. Pretty clever design. It was all Mom. She planned it. Dad just wrote the checks. The people who hired her to do their house and barn came here for some kind of party last year. People Dad knows from the hospital. I think she's a doctor there and he's an administrator. They loved it so much that they convinced Mom to renovate theirs and now all of a sudden Mom has her own business.

I'm still staring at the back door. I don't want to go inside. Mom's waiting for me. I know she is. I can feel her just on the other side, waiting to pounce. Waiting to fire off questions too big for my immature brain to handle. At least too big to be decided tonight, for sure. Like . . . how am I going to pay for a baby? How is Tyler going to pay for a baby because "God knows she and Dad shouldn't be financially responsible for our screw-up." Am I going to breast-feed? What kind of diapers am I going to buy? Do I want birthday presents for myself, or do I want to get a head start and ask for a car seat now? Maybe my own car to put the car seat in? Tyler and I can't be stealing his grandfather's truck to take the baby to the pediatrician.

I lean forward and rest my forehead on the steering wheel, being careful not to honk the horn. One bark from Willie Nelson and the whole house will be awake. Dad will be down here in his droopy underwear with his butt crack showing, asking what the hell is going on. None of us need *that* image burned into our brains.

I groan and kind of bang my head on the steering wheel, still being careful.

Mom's right, of course. About all of it. I've got a lot of crap to figure out and not a lot of time. How *am* I going to pay for a baby? *Am* I going to breast-feed? I looked up the data on breast-fed babies versus bottle babies. It's pretty cut and dry. Their immune systems are better on breast milk. I didn't dare look up what kind of toxins we put in baby formula. It makes sense to breast-feed, but how am I going to do it and go to school? What if I can't do it?

I know I've got a lot to figure out. But

does Mom have to keep asking the same things?

I'm already thinking so much that I feel like my head is just going to explode. And it won't just be questions when I walk inside. Mom's going to look at me. Look at me with sad eyes that are somehow angry at the same time. I know she's not trying to be mean, but mean is mean, right?

I glance at the door again and the thought occurs that I don't *have* to go inside. I could just . . . sleep here. It's warm out so I won't get cold. I'm tired; I bet I'd fall asleep on the backseat in two minutes. I'm *so* tired. And my boobs hurt. Not that I've got much in the way of boobs, though I think they're getting bigger. That or Dad put my bra in the dryer again.

I could also open the garage door, back out, probably without hitting Dad's car, and go back to Katy's.

I stare at the assortment of bicycles, skis, and weird stuff I can't even identify hanging on the wall in front of the car. My purple bike is hanging there. We used to go biking, all four of us together. Two summers ago, we camped at Acadia National Park and we rode our bikes all over. We hiked, too. It was so much fun. Mom and Dad were still getting along then. They were holding hands and laughing at private jokes the way they used to when I was little.

I sigh. I don't guess I'll be biking anymore. Or hiking. Not carrying a baby and a big-ass diaper bag. Every mom I see in the drugstore where I work is always carrying a huge diaper bag. I can't figure out why they bring it in the store. If the baby crapped itself and had to be changed, couldn't you just go out to the car and *get* a diaper? And the diaper bags are always ugly, with giraffes or bunnies on it, like something a kid ought to be carrying. I'm not getting one of that kind. I think I'll just use my old backpack from middle school. And I'm not taking it in stores. He poops, he can just wait until we get to the car. I've decided the baby is a boy. I just know he is.

I take a deep breath. All of a sudden, I feel like I'm going to start crying and I have no idea why. I can think of lots of possibilities. Maybe because I have to go to school every day and pretty soon I'm going to get fat and everyone's going to know I was stupid enough to get pregnant? Because Tyler was supposed to meet me at Katy's and never came? Because he never texted me back until I texted him three times? Or maybe I feel like crying because my class schedule is totally screwed up. Katy and I are only in two classes together.

The overhead light goes out and I'm in darkness.

I touch my hand to my belly. I'm not fat yet. Then I put my hand on my boob. Definitely bigger. I reach for my bag on the seat. I have to go inside. I have to face Mom. Or try to sneak up the stairs without her hearing me. Maybe she'll be in her office working. Better yet, already in bed. Not much chance of that, *consarn* it. Another Granddad-ism.

I open the car door and the garage fills with light again. I'm half expecting Mom to snatch open the door before I get there, just to get a head start on her questions and sad eyes.

But she doesn't.

On the steps, I cautiously open the door to the laundry room. It's dark. The dryer is running and it smells like Mrs. Meyer's lavender detergent. No mom. No dog.

Maybe they did go to bed.

The lights are off in the kitchen, too. The only one on is the one over the stove that Mom turns on before she goes to bed. She's always the last one to go to bed. She walks around and checks the doors, turns on the stove light, and then goes upstairs. She used to check on me and Sean as she went past our rooms. She stopped that last year when something happened with Sean. I think she must have caught him jerking off or watching porn or something.

The thought makes me smile. I tried to ask my brother what happened, but he got all weird and I let it go. I thought maybe I'd ask him in a few years when he's loosened up a little.

I lock the laundry room door and creep toward the staircase. I make it all the way there, almost into the safety zone, and then I hear Mom's voice.

"Hazel?"

I debate running up the stairs and locking my bedroom door. Instead, I groan really loud so she can hear me and drop my bag on the bottom step. I see light now, coming from the back door off the living room that leads to the deck. Mom must be letting Willie Nelson out to pee.

I go to the open door. It's cool outside now. Bugs are buzzing around the lamp attached to the house beside the door. Mom is standing on the deck, her back to me, her hands on her hips. She's staring out into the dark. I'm guessing Willie Nelson is out there in the yard somewhere, chasing a rabbit probably.

I don't say anything.

Mom just stands there. Which is weird because usually she starts right in on me.

"I'm home," I say finally.

"Keys?"

I close my eyes and throw my head back and groan. I left them in the ignition. I keep doing that. "I'll go back out and get them," I say.

"I was worried about you." She sounds far away. And sad, but a different kind of sad than I've been hearing in her voice. This isn't disappointed Mom sad, this is *sad* sad. It makes me feel weird. And also sad for her, which I don't like. It's a lot easier being angry with her.

"I didn't have any problems driving. I went to Gran and Granddad's before I went to Katy's and I backed out of their driveway, too. I didn't turn around in the grass."

"You went to Gran's?" She turns around to face me. She's wearing jeans and an old, faded Life Is Good T-shirt. With no makeup and her hair back in a pony, she looks a lot younger than she is. She has her summer freckles on her face. I like them. "You didn't tell me you were going. Why did you go there?"

I lift one shoulder and let it fall. "I don't know. Just to say hi. To check on them. I thought you'd be happy I went. They're fine. Well, except that Granddad took a bunch of fish out of Mr. Linden's fishpond. I think they were expensive. Koi or something. He says he didn't, but Gran said she found one in the trash can."

Mom swears under her breath, but it's not a good swear like Granddad's. It's just the generic kind. "Why would he take Mr. Linden's fish?"

"Why does Granddad do any of the things he does? He's crazy."

"Don't say that about your grandfather."

I roll my eyes. "He has dementia, Mom. Or Alzheimer's, or whatever you want to call it."

"He hasn't been diagnosed," she counters.

I know the whole story about Gran taking Granddad to the neurologist's and them coming back and saying Granddad was fine for a guy his age. Mom had a fit. There was a whole thing. Mom saying she can't go to everyone's doctors' appointments with them. Mom grilling Gran about did she tell the neurologist this and did she tell him that.

I look at Mom. "Yeah, well, he needs a new neurologist."

She stands there for a minute just staring at me. I hear Willie Nelson loping around in the backyard, chuffing. He's definitely after

144

a rabbit. Luckily, he never catches them.

"You're late, Hazel," Mom says. "You didn't call me to tell me you were going to be late."

"Why do I have a curfew?"

"That's a separate discussion." She turns and calls the dog, then looks at me again. "It's disrespectful to let me sit there waiting for you."

I look up. There's a bug buzzing really loud around the light. I wonder what kind it is. "I was fine. I did fine. I don't know why you were worried."

"Hazel, you shouldn't be out this late."

"Why, Mom?" I wave my hand in front of my face, trying to shoo away a little bug that I'm afraid is going to fly into my mouth. "Why are you worried about me being out late? You think I'm going to get pregnant?"

I kind of laugh. I know I shouldn't say anything else. I'm already in trouble for having a *smart mouth.* But I can't help myself. "Because if that's what you're worried about, that's ridiculous, Mom. Because you can get pregnant anytime. It doesn't have to be after ten o'clock at night." Now I just sound mean. Meaner than Mom ever is. "You know what? You can get pregnant on a Wednesday afternoon when you're sup-

145

posed to be studying for an English exam."

Before she can respond, I turn around and walk back into the house. I keep thinking as I make it to the stairs to grab my bag, then up the stairs, that she's going to come after me. That she's going to demand an apology and maybe ground me or something. Maybe she's going to tie me to a chair and barrage me with questions about how the next eighty years of my life are going to unfold.

But she doesn't, and I can't decide if I'm relieved or not.

# 11
## LIV

"Dad." When he doesn't seem to hear me, I say, "*Dad,* just leave it. I'll get it."

He looks at me, his face without expression.

He was trying to carry two paper plates to the trash can and dropped them both. He opened his hands as if he had forgotten what he was doing, and they hit the floor with the kind of splat only paper plates, soggy with food from a barbecue, can make. My mother will have a fit if she sees potato salad all over her freshly washed kitchen floor. They have a cleaning woman, Lynette, who's an angel, who comes three times a week. Mom has her scrub the kitchen floor, on her hands and knees, three times a week. I think I mopped mine once since Easter.

Dad looks at the floor. I look at the floor. I think he's considering picking up the plates, but I know from experience that letting my father clean up anything will mean an even bigger mess. Which I don't care about because I understand his need for autonomy and I see it slipping away. But my mother does care and she's the one he lives with day in and day out.

He stands there motionless as I pick up the plates and take them to the trash can. He just stands there, so handsome with his full head of gray hair and brilliant blue eyes, looking so lost that it makes me want to cry. He's staring at the potato salad and what looks like splatters of mustard and ketchup on the floor. There's potato salad on the toe of his blue Nike sneaker.

I grab a kitchen towel off the counter and walk to him, taking care not to step in the mess on the floor. I lean down and clean off his shoe. "Good as new. Go on outside and enjoy yourself. You probably won't see Sean again for a while. He's going away to college."

He studies me as if trying to process the information. Or maybe he's trying to remember who Sean is. He's having a bad day today, which I think has put us all on edge. Maybe because he also seems to be having them more often.

I look up at him and smile. He doesn't make eye contact.

Something catches his attention on his

hand and he slowly raises it in front of his face. Then he puts it to his mouth. Potato salad. He licks it and turns away. "You coming outside? They're playing that game where they throw the things into holes on the wooden thing."

"Yup. Give me five minutes. I just want to put these few dishes in the sink to soak."

I watch him go. Mom has dressed him in a dark-salmon polo, khaki shorts, and sneakers. His hair has been cut in the last week and he shaved this morning. He looks as impeccable as he ever did in his suit or in his white lab coat. Mom makes sure of that. But he doesn't look like himself anymore. His face somehow looks different, but it's not from the natural process of aging. It's not his wrinkles. It's as if . . . as if his bones and muscles have shifted, as if the man he once was is now slightly out of focus. He doesn't move the way he used to; his motions are stilted. And I'm noticing changes in his gait. He no longer possesses the powerful stride I once knew.

I'm just turning back to the sink when he stops and turns around. "She's going to have a baby."

His statement takes me by surprise. I know whom he's talking about, of course. I press my lips together, surprised by the

149

emotion that wells up inside me. We've told him several times that Hazel is pregnant, but he hasn't acknowledged it. Or can't remember. Evidently he remembers now.

"She is, Dad."

"She's young."

I exhale the way you do when you're in pain and trying to focus on something else. "She'll be seventeen soon. The baby's due in March."

"Too young to have a baby." He's looking beyond me, maybe to something he sees outside the window? "Baby herself," he mumbles.

I draw the clean kitchen towel I'm holding back and forth between my hands. "I don't know if Mom told you, but . . ." I hesitate. "Dad, I think she should put the baby up for adoption. She doesn't want to. She has this idea in her head that she and her boyfriend are going to get married and be a family."

He's slow to respond. I wait because I can tell he's thinking.

"Doesn't usually happen that way," he says. Then he actually meets my gaze for a split second. I see my old dad, the way he used to be, sharp and smart and empathetic, somewhere in the depths of his eyes. I think they might be starting to change color, his eyes. I noticed it the other day when I was here unclogging the kitchen garbage disposal after he put his toothbrush down it. There's a hint of dark gray in his eyes now. Mom says it might be cataracts, but I don't think so.

"I know, Dad. That's what I keep trying to tell her." I take a step toward him. Suddenly he seems like the father I knew before the plaque in his brain began to damage his blood vessels and cause the cognitive changes. He even sounds more like himself. "But Oscar agrees with Hazel." I give a little laugh that's utterly devoid of humor. "Dad, Oscar thinks he and I can raise the baby if Hazel can't."

I hold his gaze, suddenly hopeful because I'm not alone in this. I should have known Dad would be on my side. He and I have always thought so much alike. I don't know why I didn't come to him sooner. Why I didn't try to bring him into the discussion two weeks ago when we found out. "Maybe you could talk to Hazel?" I ask. "About how adoption might be the best thing she can do for her baby and herself? Maybe tell her some of the things you told me when I was growing up? When I was sad because I thought my birth mother didn't want me?"

He nods ever so slowly.

151

I wait for his words of wisdom. Maybe a plan we can formulate together.

Then he says, "She's doing the right thing."

I'm taken aback by his words. "I'm sorry?"

"Keeping the baby. It'll be hard, but Hazel's smart. She'll manage." He turns away from me.

She'll *manage*? I want to say. But instead, I say, "Daddy . . . she's going into the *eleventh* grade. She just got her braces off in June. She works as a clerk in a drugstore, part-time." I gesture with the kitchen towel, pointing in the general direction of the backyard. "The baby's father works weekends for his uncle in an auto repair shop. How are they going to *manage*?"

"We don't give away our babies. Not in this family," he says, his back to me now as he makes his retreat. "You want a brownie? Bethy brought brownies from the bakery. The kind with the nuts and the coffee icing. She knows they're my favorite."

I watch him shuffle toward the French doors that lead out to the deck. When he opens the door, I hear Oscar and Beth laughing. I hear Hazel talking, to my mom, likely. The backyard is practically a Norman Rockwell painting. The sun is shining, my son is headed off on what will be one of the

152

greatest adventures of his life, and Mom is having a good day, a practically pain-free day. My family is out there together having a good time, enjoying one another's company.

And here I am alone in the kitchen, feeling as if I could fall into a puddle of tears on the floor.

And I know it's ridiculous. I'm a logical person. I shouldn't be this devastated. My daughter is pregnant. She doesn't have terminal cancer. None of us do. I've been happily married for twenty years. I have a home that's more than half paid for and a family that loves me. And even though my parents' illnesses are difficult, they've both led amazingly happy, productive lives. And yes, my sixteen-year-old is going to have a baby out of wedlock, but that's pretty much been happening since the beginning of time. And young women *do* figure it out. I keep trying to remind myself of that fact.

I have a cousin, Theresa, who's my age, who got pregnant when she was sixteen. She went to college, though it took her a few years longer than me. She met a nice guy and married and they had three children together. Every year we get a Christmas card with a photo of them from Seattle. They look happy.

But I know Theresa's life wasn't easy for a long time. And I wanted more for Hazel. Want more for her. For our first grandchild.

I take a shuddering breath, fighting the urge to break down in tears. I think I want to cry, not just for my daughter, but because I wanted more than this for myself. And I feel so guilty for that.

I don't cry because I'm not a crier. Or at least I try not to be. Instead, I sigh the way my dad used to and go back to the kitchen sink, the same sink I washed dishes in as a child. The feeling that the world as I know it is gone passes, and I grab a crocheted kitchen rag my mother uses to clean up my father's spills. I go to the place where I see the remnants of my father's dinner on the floor and squat to wipe it up.

The familiarity of the pattern of the hard maple wood flooring, of the motion of wiping it, feels good. I've always found comfort in this house, which I find interesting because when I was a teenager, I just wanted to get away from it. But maybe it was just my mother I wanted to escape from.

My parents bought this house on Wren Street three years before they adopted me. Dad's practice was doing well, and they were happy. At least as happy as a childless couple who desperately wants children could be.

Mom loves this house; she says she intends to die in this house. No one likes to think about their parents dying, but if that's what she wants, I hope I can make it happen. I hope I can be strong enough to see it through, to hold her hand and watch her pass. Of course, I also hope we'll have many, many more years with her. I want that for my kids. Hazel especially. While my mom always struggled to connect with me, she's never had any trouble making a connection with my kids, particularly with Hazel. She and Hazel have always been best buds, and now . . . now Hazel is going to need her Gran even more.

The potato salad and condiments wiped up, I go back to the sink, rinse out the cloth, and give the floor one more swipe, just to be sure it will pass Bernice's inspection, and then I return to the sink to finish what I was doing.

I squirt dish soap on the plate that held the raw burgers before they went onto the grill. Stare out onto the front lawn that's immaculately kept. It's our last dinner with my parents and my family here for a while. Tomorrow I'm taking Sean down to Massachusetts.

I let the water run, staring out the window

155

but not really seeing anything.

I assumed I'd be upset about Sean leaving, but I'm surprisingly composed. I think he's going to be okay. And here I thought he was the one I needed to worry about, not Hazel. I know he'll excel academically. And despite his social angst, I think . . . I'm hopeful that he'll find his way. He had a good time in Portland with his roommate last week. He seems excited now to go, rather than scared the way he was a few weeks ago.

And by tomorrow afternoon, one of my chicks will have flown the nest.

That feels good. Scary, but good.

Tomorrow I'm driving alone with Sean to a little town outside of Boston, Massachusetts, and back. Oscar couldn't take the day off. I wanted him to go with me, with us, but it will still be good to ride down with Sean. He and I don't get to spend much time together alone. Then Tuesday I'm meeting the demolition guys I hired to take down a wall in the Anselin house. I'm excited to get started on the job. Nervous because even though I know I've thought of everything, I know I haven't.

I hear the door open behind me and I glance over my shoulder. It's Oscar.

"Hey," I say, hoping I don't look like I've

come close to tears several times in the last ten minutes.

He glances at me. "Hey, babe." I get a lopsided grin. "More beer in the fridge?"

I nod and turn to lean against the sink. I watch him open Mom and Dad's refrigerator that's so clean it looks as if it could be on the sales floor of the local Lowe's. "How's everyone doing out there?"

Two amber bottles of beer in hand, he lets the door swing shut and grabs the opener magnetically attached to the side of the refrigerator. He pops the caps, somehow managing to catch them in his hand. He knows how to open a beer, I'll give him that. He can also resuscitate someone. A renaissance man if there ever was one. It's one of the reasons I fell in love with him. Fell hard. What seems like a million years ago.

"Everything's good. Your mom is grilling Hazel about her doctor's appointment right now. Beth and I beat Sean and Hazel twice at corn hole. Now they want best out of five."

I feel like he's avoiding eye contact with me. I surprise him and me both by walking over and kissing him on the mouth. I stroke his beard. It's getting a little scraggly, a little ZZ Top. I'm amazed no one in the emergency department has said anything to him about it.

"What's that for?" He sounds suspicious.

"Have to be *for* anything?" I kiss him again, playfully, but a little harder. He tastes like beer and dill pickles.

He makes a face, curling his upper lip, Elvis style. "You don't want to *talk,* do you?"

He means about Hazel. I *do* want to talk to him. But not about Hazel. Not right now, at least. I want to talk about us. About this distance between us even when we kiss. Once upon a time, he would have abandoned the beers, pushed me up against the counter, and copped a feel. Kissed me good and hard. A time not too long in the distance.

He takes another sip of his beer. "You coming outside? One of us can sit out a game and you can play."

I push the hair that's fallen from my ponytail out of my eyes. "I was thinking maybe we could squeeze in a little vacation. Go up to Bar Harbor, or, I don't know, Québec City?"

He takes a long pull on one of the beers. "Hon, I can't take any time off right now."

"A long weekend, then, even midweek." I shrug. "Depending on your schedule. Just you and me. Hazel can stay with Mom and Dad." I sound pathetic. Desperate, and I don't like it. I don't like the vulnerability I hear in my voice. I feel in my chest. "We could take a walk on the beach? Go hiking?"

"We can do that at the cottage for free. My sister said something about all of us going next weekend." He sips his beer, not making eye contact with me.

"I meant the two of us alone together. Away from all this." I gesture to the kitchen floor where I just cleaned up potato salad.

He glances at the floor. I can tell he has no idea what I'm talking about, but he doesn't question me.

"We could use some time alone, Oscar." I pause. "Don't you think?"

"*Ayuh,*" he says like a true Mainer. He turns away. "We can talk about it. It's beautiful outside. Come on out."

I watch him go and then return to my sink duties. Not two minutes later the door opens again. This time it's Sean. I watch him cut through the kitchen, headed to the bathroom off the laundry room.

I feel like a revolving door of emotions.

When he comes out of the bathroom, I've retaken my position leaning against the sink. Watching him. Smiling. He looks good today. Suntanned from our days at the cottage. And somehow more relaxed. He had a good time in Portland with his roommate.

"You hiding in here, Mom?"

I frown. "No, I'm not *hiding.*"

"Aunt Beth says you're hiding from us. And the world." He starts to turn away and then surprises me by turning back. "We leaving soon?"

I think for a second. "Another hour."

"I told Hazel we could go for a spin in my car. She might want to buy it. She says she and Tyler need a car for the little bambino. She's got to look at some kind of brackets in the seat for a car seat? She started going on about regulations set up by the National Highway Traffic Safety Administration." He shakes his head. "I don't know what she's talking about. I never do."

I can't help but smile. Hazel is a bit obsessed with safety regulations in the U.S. Her fixation seems to be somehow associated with her interest in additives in manufactured food and her whole green campaign in general. It all started back in the sixth or seventh grade when she did an experiment suggested by her science teacher where she tried not to eat anything with high fructose corn syrup in it. I don't mind her preoccupation with all of it most of the time. It's good for her, it's good for a family, and it's certainly good for the planet.

160

It's still annoying.

"That's not your car, that's my car," I repeat. "I bought that car from your grand-dad."

"She doesn't know that." He grins.

"You are *not* selling your sister my car."

"Mom, I'm not going to need it. Fresh-men can't have cars. Richard says he might bring his next year, though." He makes a face. "I think his parents are rich. They own some kind of company in Augusta. They said they'd pay for the parking. He thinks they think he'll come home more often if he has a car. I don't need my car."

"You don't need *my* car," I correct. "What about next summer? You'll need it to get to work."

"Might not. My advisor said there are a lot of summer internships in Boston." There's an excitement in his voice. "He says the school places a lot of people. I wouldn't get to actually create any game content, not the first summer at least, but I'd get to see how it works."

Not come home for the summer? I feel that lump in my throat again as my auto-nomic nervous system kicks in. I blink to hold back the tears. For a person who has never been a crier, this seems to be happen-ing a lot. This is not the time to talk about

161

this. I know it. Besides, why would he come home to nowhere Maine when he could spend the summer in Boston earning money, getting experience working in gaming, and hanging out with friends? I never lived at home again after the summer following my high school graduation. I couldn't wait to get far away from this house.

"You're not selling your sister my car," I repeat yet again. "I'm thinking about getting a pickup truck. I can trade my car and yours in and get at least fifty cents." I cross my arms over my chest, taking my stand. "I'm not providing baby daddy Tyler with a car, Sean."

My son looks down at me. He's already at least two inches taller than I am. And he looks more like his father every day with his head of auburn hair. His movements. He's even got the stubbly red beard growth going.

He exhales just the way Oscar does when he's frustrated with me. "Mom, you gotta stop," he says.

His tone startles me. He never speaks to me this way. With criticism in his voice. He rarely speaks to me at all, except when forced to by a barrage of questions, or if he wants to know where his favorite blue shorts are. The ones I've repaired the seat seam in at least three times.

I feel myself prickle. "Gotta stop what?"

"This thing with Hazel. You gotta —" He stops and starts again. "Let it go. I know it's not the best situation, but —"

*Not the best situation?* I want to interrupt. But I don't, only because I'm afraid if I do, he won't speak his mind again to me until he's at least forty. So I suck it up. I keep my mouth shut and listen. Try to really listen.

"Hazel's keeping the baby." He's softened his tone. "It's a dumb idea. It's going to be a disaster. I know that. Tyler won't even stick around long enough until she *has* the baby. Which means she's going to have to raise it by herself. But, Mom, she's already decided she's keeping it and there's nothing you can do about that."

He slides his hands into the front pockets of his shorts. He's not done saying what he wants to say. I can see it on his face. I keep quiet, torn between being so proud of who he's becoming and being angry that even if he agrees with me, he's not agreeing with me.

"It's not legal. You can't take her baby from her and just give it to someone, Mom."

He sounds like Oscar now.

"You gotta stop making yourself crazy.

163

Making *us* all crazy." Now he's on a roll. "No one even wants to be in the same room with you because you just start up again with the whole adoption thing. Face it. Hazel isn't putting her baby up for adoption. It doesn't matter if it's the right thing to do or not."

I stand there looking at him for a moment, my heart swelling with love for him. Taking over the sense of betrayal I feel because he doesn't understand that this isn't about taking sides. It isn't even about me getting my way. It's about the instinct a mother has for protecting her child. Her cub.

I smile at him. A proud mama smile. "I'm going to miss you so much, Sean."

"You coming outside? You need to get control of Granddad. He's talking about going up on the roof to check the seal around the chimney. Gran just keeps hollering at him and calling him old man."

"Can I have a hug?" I ask, opening my arms.

My son makes a face at me as if to say I've just made the most ridiculous request he's ever heard. "Nope," he says. "Because you're still going to want a hug tomorrow when you drop me off."

# 12
# HAZEL

Mom pulls into Tyler's parents' driveway, and I close my eyes, wishing I believed in God or Mother Earth or Allah. Wishing I believed in something other than science, so I could pray for a miracle. Like an earthquake that would open a big crevasse under Mom's new truck and we would fall into the heated rock mantle and be consumed by flames.

Of course, that's not how earthquakes work. Crevasses don't open up during an earthquake; they happen *after* an earthquake when there are landslides and lateral spreads. An earthquake happens when two chunks of the earth's crust slide past each other because of friction on the fault while the rest of the crust away from the edges is moving really slowly.

The minute we pull in, Tyler's dogs start barking. Hopefully they're locked up in their kennels out back, otherwise Dad is going to start in about not getting out of the truck before someone locks them up. Then we'll have to hear about the latest dog mauling he saw in the emergency department. I think he makes up these stories to suit his needs because he's always got a story about a dog mauling, a boating accident, or a kid being blinded by a Nerf dart.

I glance up as Mom parks behind Tyler's stepdad J.J.'s truck. Sitting in the backseat, I feel small. Like I did when I was little and my legs didn't hang over the edge of the seat yet. I cringe at what I see, even though I see it all the time.

The lawn needs mowing and there's a cement birdbath that got knocked over last winter that no one ever got around to standing back up again. There's junk all around the house, too: last year's Christmas tree with old-school tinsel still hanging off it, two tires, a recliner the dogs chewed up and Tyler's stepdad got pissed and threw out the door.

I know I shouldn't be embarrassed. I know not everyone lives in a nice house and has cars that are less than ten years old. I know how much money someone makes or how much education they have doesn't define whether or not they're good people. I know all those things. My mom taught me

166

those things. But Tyler knew we were coming. He should have mowed the grass. Maybe cleaned the junk off the front porch. The adult diaper boxes have been sitting there for weeks, and it rained the other night, so now they're soggy. No one wears diapers in Tyler's house that I know of, but his stepdad likes to collect boxes. He's always talking about getting the garage *in shape.* Tyler says he thinks if he collects enough cardboard boxes, the garage will magically come to life one night and everything will jump into the boxes and the boxes will slide into shelving J.J. is going to build. Like in that scene in that weird early Disney movie with Mickey Mouse.

Dad, who is in the front passenger seat, glances in the back at me. "You okay?" he asks. He looks tired. And like he doesn't want to be here anymore than I do.

This was Mom's idea, this *powwow,* as she called it. Which is probably a racist thing to say. We don't have a drop of Native American blood in our heritage, so I don't think we're allowed to use that word unless we're talking about going to an actual powwow. Which we did once when I was little and we were visiting a friend of Dad's in Delaware.

I can hear through the window the dogs

going ape shit. Dad's still looking at me.

"I'm fine," I tell him. "Fan-*tastic.*" I open the door, hoping I won't be the emergency department's next dog mauling.

"You think we should wait? The dogs?" Dad asks me.

"Nah." My feet hit the driveway. "We'd already be mauled if they weren't in their kennels."

"What?" he says.

I slam the door. The three of us meet at the hood of the truck. Mom just got it the other day. It's a black Ford F-150. Tyler said they run, like, forty K. I told him no way my mom would pay that. Plus, it's, like, five years old and has a hundred thousand miles on it. I was surprised Mom actually bought it. She'd been talking about doing it all summer, but I didn't think she'd really do it. I guess she's serious about going into business for herself. She talked about doing that for years. I never thought it would happen.

I kind of stand there for a minute, waiting for Tyler to come out of the house. I texted him twice on our way over, but he didn't answer. Phone's probably dead. He never remembers to charge it.

The house is old and could use some work. Just some paint and someone either putting the shutters back on or taking them completely off would make it look a lot better. It used to be Tyler's mom's great-aunt's or something. It's two stories with only two bedrooms and one bathroom. It's really small. It's not like our house is huge, not like my friend Katy's. But I can be alone in my house. Tyler has to share his bedroom with his stepbrother and their living room is really small so we hardly ever hang out there, except when everyone is gone, like right after school. Mostly we go to Tyler's friend Rob's house because his parents are never home.

I glance at Dad and Mom. Mom is clutching her handbag like someone is going to run by and snatch it. They both look as uncomfortable as I feel.

"Well," Mom says.

Well, *what?* I want to say. Instead, I just walk to the porch and go up the creaky steps. "Careful," I mumble, pointing to a soft spot in the floorboards that I step over. At the door, I hesitate and then knock. Before I can pull my hand away, the door flings open, and Cricket, Tyler's mom, is there in the doorway. She's short and skinny and she's always dyeing her thin, shoulder-length hair a different shade of black; today it looks blue. She's still wearing her uniform

169

from work. She's a checker at Shaw's grocery store. Still wearing her name tag that says Cricket, not Christine, which is her real name. I don't know why, but I'm embarrassed by the name tag. Then I feel bad again that I would be embarrassed. Cricket works a lot of hours, always picking up extra shifts; she's always wearing her weird polyester-jacket thing. And there's nothing wrong with working at a grocery store. But no one when they're my age says they want to be a cashier at a grocery store someday. And her feet always hurt and I know it's got to be boring because working at the drugstore just the ten hours a week I work is sooooo boring.

I know there's nothing wrong with what Cricket does to feed her family, but I also know I don't want my little boy to have to do that. I want more than a broken birdbath for him.

"Come in, come in!" Cricket throws her arms around me and hugs me hard. She smells like BBQ potato chips. I think she's addicted to them. Tyler says she eats two big bags a day. Which is crazy because she's so skinny. That many calories, you would think she'd be huge. And be full of cancer because of the ingredients in cheap chips. Her lips are always a little orange from the food dye in them. She kisses my cheek with her orange lips, which grosses me out. She usually hugs me when she sees me, but she doesn't usually kiss me. I don't know what's up with that.

I manage to escape her arms and duck into the house. Mom and Dad both get hugs. I don't look back to see if Cricket kisses them. I don't see Tyler in the living room. Just J.J. He's asleep in his new recliner that replaced the one the dogs ate. I hate to feed into stereotypes, but if you were casting a part in a play or a movie and you wanted an auto mechanic from Maine, J.J. is who you would pick. He's average height with brown hair and a little bit of beer belly, though not any more than my dad's got. But J.J.'s hands are permanently dirty, with black under his nails, and he always smells like gasoline to me, even just after he's taken a shower.

Mom says stereotypes fundamentally have a basis in truth. I guess this is what she means. J.J.'s also got bad teeth. I think he had a crack problem a long time ago when Cricket met him when Tyler was in elementary school. That was when they used to live closer to Portland. I guess Cricket told J.J. she wouldn't marry him if he didn't get himself straight. Good for her. Good for J.J.

for being strong enough to break an addiction. I've been reading about the opioid epidemic in the United States for a while. I know what a big deal it is for J.J. to get clean.

"Tyler upstairs?" I ask Cricket. I have to talk over the TV that's always on really loud. And I mean it's *always* on. I don't think they ever turn it off. Not even when they eat. They don't eat dinner in their kitchen like we do. They eat in front of the TV. Which is like a huge no in our house. We don't do cell phones at the table, either.

"Not home yet." Cricket gives me a quick smile that looks forced. "Not yet. Would anyone like ice tea?"

Mom and Dad are just standing there in the little foyer area where there are shoes piled up and chewed-up rawhide dog toys. A couple of the shoes are chewed up, too. J.J. takes in dogs people don't want, usually because they're too mean or too wild. He's got four right now. All mixed breeds, but they all look like they have some pit bull in them to me. J.J. told me that pit bulls aren't naturally dangerous dogs. That their owners make them that way. I get what he's saying, but whenever you hear about a dog eating its owner or a neighbor's little kid, it's always a pit bull. Thinking about that, I make up my mind that the dogs aren't go-

172

ing to be allowed around our baby. It's just not worth the risk. I don't like the dogs anyway. They jump up and sometimes they have fleas and ticks on them.

"Where is he?" I ask, realizing Cricket's Kia wasn't in the driveway. Which means he took her car. She doesn't let him take it very often because she says he never puts gas in it.

NASCAR is on their gigantic TV mounted to the wall, which I don't understand because they just race on weekends and it's a Thursday. Is there really such a thing as NASCAR reruns? I'm not really into guys driving a car around in circles burning fossil fuels but it's something Tyler and his stepdad can actually talk about, so I get why Tyler follows it.

"Tyler?" I ask because Cricket looks confused or startled or something.

"Oh. Said he had to borrow a schoolbook from Rob." She gives a wave as if it's nothing to worry about. "Said he'd be right back. Right back."

I purposely don't make eye contact with Mom because I know what she's thinking. That Tyler's not here because he doesn't want to talk about the baby. She thinks he doesn't want to talk about him and me and our baby. She's wrong, though. I know she's wrong because Tyler loves me. And he's going to love our baby. This is all just a lot for him to handle. He hasn't had the same stable environment I've always had. His real dad beat the crap out of him when he was little. And he beat up Cricket, too. J.J. smacks Tyler once in a while, but nothing like his real dad did. I bet that kind of thing can mess with your head. Especially when you realize you're going to be a dad.

Of course, I know very well Tyler isn't borrowing a *schoolbook* from Rob. I'm not that dumb. He was probably going over to smoke pot, which I told him he can't do anymore because we can't spend the money. He needs to save the money he makes at his uncle's garage for the baby.

"Ice tea?" Cricket asks Mom and Dad again. "Or beer. We got beer."

"Iced tea would be nice." Dad sounds stiff.

He trimmed his beard. It looks nice a little shorter, but I wonder why he thought he needed to do it to come here. Mom's been bugging him about it for weeks. He's met Tyler's parents before. I know he knows trimmed beards aren't required.

"Iced tea, thank you," Mom says.

"Sit down. Sit down." Cricket repeats things a lot. She grabs a paper plate off the end of the couch that has half a soggy sandwich on it. "J.J. They're here." She gives her husband a poke. When he doesn't move and he doesn't open his eyes, she gives him a hard nudge in the shoulder with her fist. Not quite a punch, but close. "J.J.!"

Tyler's stepfather jerks awake and the remote control to the TV falls out of his hand onto the stained green carpet. I don't know what kind of DNA is on the carpet and I don't want to know.

Dad picks the remote up as he walks by and hands it back. "Hey, J.J.," he says.

J.J. grunts something that isn't real words and wipes his mouth with the back of his greasy hand.

Mom takes a seat on the couch where the paper plate was a minute ago and Cricket goes into the kitchen.

"Want any help?" I call after Tyler's mom. I don't want to help with the iced tea but I want to stand here looking at the three of them even less.

"Got it," Cricket calls back. "Already made up. I get the kind in a can. Just add water. Just the water."

I stand there feeling stupid. J.J.'s fully awake now and he pulls the lever on the side of the chair and lowers his feet. He's wearing heavy boots and they smell like the rest of him. The faint scent of gasoline is starting to make me queasy. This morning I barfed before school. Mom said it happens sometimes. She said she barfed a lot when she was pregnant with me although she says that at almost eighteen weeks, I should be out of the barfing stage. That makes me feel better, though not at the moment when I'm sitting on the tile floor in the bathroom waiting to see if I'm going to barf again. I really haven't thrown up that many times, but when I do, it's always in the morning.

I pull my phone out of the back pocket of my jean shorts. I couldn't button them so I use a hair tie looped around the button to keep them closed.

You better get home, I text Tyler. I'm here with your mom and J.J. and my parents

I send it and wait. No bubbles. But I can see he's read it.

You're supposed to be here, I text.

I wait. Still nothing.

"Here we go," Cricket sings, carrying three glasses of tea. The glasses have pigs on them. Cricket has a thing for pigs. Like Dad's mom used to have for loons, I guess. Cricket wears sleep pants with pigs on them. And T-shirts. And socks.

I take a glass of iced tea, even though I don't want it. Cricket steps into the living room area and hands Mom and Dad their glasses. They both take sips of the tea. I don't because I know it's nasty; I've had it before. Artificial ingredients. Chemicals that could harm a developing fetus.

J.J. is staring at the TV. It's still loud. Maybe J.J. and Cricket have hearing loss. Chicken or the egg?

Cricket barely drops her butt onto the flowered velour couch beside Mom when she bounces up again. "Oh! I almost forgot! I wanted to show you, Olivia. I bought some baby clothes!"

No one calls my mom Olivia, even though that's her given name. Well, Gran sometimes. But not often.

I tip my glass, pretending to take a sip, and accidentally make eye contact with Mom. *Tyler coming?* she mouths.

I nod quickly, like *Of course.* But I'm not fooling her. I can see it in her eyes. And all of a sudden, I want to cry.

Cricket is back in the living room in a minute with several baby sleeper things on white plastic hangers. She's got a little football tucked under her arm. Of course there's no way my son is playing football. Doesn't she know the statistics on head injuries in the sport?

Cricket's all excited and shows the clothes to Mom, not me, which I think is weird.

One has race cars on it, one has pigs, and the other, footballs. She hands the football to Dad. Dad knows less than I know about football. We're baseball fans.

Mom makes some appropriate comment to Cricket about the ugly sleepers being cute. Even from where I'm standing, I can tell they're thin and made of some kind of fabric that's going to burst into flames if my baby gets too close to the sun. There are price tags hanging from them, so they're new, so I guess that's nice. But I'd rather buy something secondhand that's better quality. I like secondhand clothes and we have a cool shop in town. They have a whole wall of baby clothes.

I glance at J.J. He's watching the TV. I look at the TV. The cars are still going around the track. The race was in Las Vegas, apparently.

"Is Tyler coming?" Mom asks Cricket. She's set her glass on the floor next to her feet.

"He said he'd be right back." Cricket lays the sleepers on her lap and keeps brushing her hand over them like she's petting them.

Mom looks at Dad. I can tell she wants him to say something. He takes a big gulp of iced tea.

Mom looks at Cricket, then at J.J., who

still hasn't said a word to us, and then at Cricket again. Mom clears her throat. "My parents are expecting us for dinner," she says, which is a total lie. We're supposed to stop at Hannaford on the way home and pick up a rotisserie chicken for them because it's Thursday and Gran likes to get the special that includes potatoes and a veggie. But I support Mom on what she would call a little white lie because being here is beyond awkward. I can't believe Tyler isn't here. I feel like I'm going to cry again.

"I know this isn't the best situation," Mom says, her voice sounding so weird that I kind of feel sorry for her. I feel bad I screwed up like this. I feel bad that I've put my parents in this position.

"But I think we need to discuss how we're going to proceed," Mom goes on, folding her hands in her lap. "How we're . . . how Tyler and Hazel are going to share responsibilities for the baby and the . . . finances."

"I just think this is the cutest thing." Cricket holds up the pig sleeper. "J.J., can't you turn that down?" she calls in his direction. "I'm just so excited about buying baby clothes. Aren't you excited about buying baby clothes, Olivia?"

I carry my glass into the kitchen and pour it down the sink that's green. Like, the actual sink color is green, not white or black. This is the first green sink I ever saw. I hear Mom's voice, but not what she's saying. Then Cricket's voice. She's still going on about the cute clothes.

I lean against the sink and check my phone. Tyler hasn't texted me back. He isn't going to. And he's not coming, either. And Mom and Dad's talk with Cricket and J.J. is going to be a waste of time. I feel like going into the living room and shouting that over the roar of the cars driving in circles burning the earth's resources.

Instead, I just stand here and wait for this to be over.

# 13
## LIV

That *was certainly a disaster,* I think as I open the door to get into my truck.

I don't know exactly what my expectations were going into Tyler's parents' home, but I assumed we'd at least *talk* about Tyler and Hazel and their situation. Talk about how they, us as their families, were going to share the expenses of the baby and the child care.

We never got there.

First, there was the awkwardness of the fact that Tyler wasn't present. Which no one spoke of, making it more awkward. Then, every time I tried to move the conversation in the direction of the purpose of the meeting, above the *roar* of a prerecorded NASCAR race on a television the size of a refrigerator, Cricket changed the subject. With surprisingly great aplomb, I have to admit. I'd say something about coming up with a budget and she'd start talking about a baby walker or a high chair she was going

181

to buy, or worse, a high chair a friend of hers bought for her grandchildren. I tried several times to loop back around to the original thread and Cricket would head off down another rabbit hole involving baby blankets or hand-crocheted booties someone sells at the church fall festival.

The only thing we *did* determine in the hour we were there was that Hazel and Tyler would *not* be moving in together. I think Cricket had it in her head that maybe Tyler could come stay with Hazel at our house, at least "to help out right after the baby is born," but Oscar stepped in on that one and stated in a deep voice, "I'm not comfortable with that, Cricket. Sorry. Not gonna happen."

I could have kissed him when he said it.

Then Cricket admitted that while she'd love to have Hazel and the baby stay with them, there just wasn't enough room in their house for two more people, especially with a crib and high chair and changing table and all the other stuff a baby needs.

J.J. never said a word the entire time we were there. Not a single word. For that, I could have kissed him, too.

I close my door as Oscar climbs into the front of my truck with me. Hazel gets in the back. She hasn't said anything in at least twenty minutes. I didn't even hear her say good-bye to Tyler's parents. I glance at her in the rearview mirror as I back out. As I head toward town, I debate whether or not to hold off on what I want to say. I know I should. Hazel's obviously upset that Tyler wasn't there to participate in what she was hoping would be a productive discussion about his responsibility to her and the baby.

I knew coming into it that it was possible that this wouldn't be a good conversation. But I hoped it would be. I really did. Because Hazel has made it clear she isn't putting her baby up for adoption. So I wanted this to work out.

We're all quiet all the way to the grocery store.

"Want me to run in?" Oscar asks me when I pull into the Hannaford parking lot.

"Would you?" I say it gently, as if I appreciate the offer because I do.

"Chicken with two sides." He opens the door. "We need anything else?"

"We're having tacos at home," I say quietly. "We have all the ingredients."

"Hazel?" he says.

I see her in the rearview mirror. She shakes her head no.

Oscar closes the door and I just sit there with my hands on the steering wheel. I look at our daughter again in the mirror. Her face looks a little fuller than it did a month ago. She seems even more beautiful. How can that be?

She's staring at her phone.

"Did Tyler text you?" I ask. "Say what happened?"

She doesn't look up. *"What happened?"* Her tone is nasty. As if this is my fault.

"Why he wasn't there, Hazel." I try not to sound angry. But I am angry. And I'm tired of pretending I'm not. I've been doing it too long. For too many years. I'm always trying to keep everyone else happy. Placated. Never rocking the boat. And I'm sick to death of it. With Hazel, with Oscar, with my parents, with my sister.

Hazel doesn't say anything.

I sit there and wait for her to respond. A minute passes. Another. I let five minutes go by, but then I just can't keep my mouth shut. "Hazel, I know you don't want to hear this, but —"

"So don't say it," she snaps.

I rest my arm on the seat and turn around to face her. "You know why he wasn't there. He wasn't there because he has no intention of taking responsibility —"

"Mom, you don't —"

"He has no intention of taking any respon-

184

sibility for this baby," I say, talking over her. "You realize that, right, Hazel?" I study her beautiful face. She looks like she's on the verge of tears and it occurs to me that maybe I should back off. Let it go, at least for now. But I can't. From the beginning, I was opposed to Hazel dating Tyler at all. I knew he was no good for her. I kept my mouth shut then, and in retrospect, possibly to the detriment of my daughter. I'm not holding back anymore and I'm not apologizing for saying what I think. And fair is fair. If I'm going to be a part of this, if I'm going to be able to help my daughter become a mother, I have to be able to have my say.

"Hazel, Tyler has no intention of watching this baby so you can go back to school next year. He —"

"Cricket says she'll watch the baby," she flings at me, crossing her arms over her chest.

"Cricket works shift work. How's she going to —"

"Mom! This isn't your baby! I told you I would figure it out."

"Please keep your voice down. The window is open." I pause and then go on. "You told me," I say calmly, even though I don't feel calm, "that you and Tyler were going to figure things out. What I'm trying to say is that I think this is a pretty good indication that *you're* going to be figuring this out on your own because Tyler —"

"Mom! Can we not talk about this right now?" She drops her phone to her lap and covers her face with her hands.

"Honey, I'm not saying you can't do it. I'm not saying that I think you're . . . incapable. I'm just saying you need to understand that, in all likelihood, you're going to be on your own on this. And even if Tyler *does* stick around —"

"How can you say that!" She drops her hands. "Of course he's going to stick around. He just didn't want to talk to you guys! He didn't want to talk to you, Mom! That's why he wasn't there! Because Tyler didn't want to —"

The passenger-side door jerks open and Hazel goes silent as Oscar gets in. "I can hear you across the parking lot," he says, looking at me.

Hear *me*? I want to say, my feathers at once ruffling. I'm not shouting. Your daughter is the one who's shouting.

But I don't say it. I don't say anything.

Hazel's crying now, big, loud, pitiful sobs.

I bite my tongue and start the new truck that I was *so* happy with this morning when I called my insurance company to add it to

186

our policy. I'm angry that I didn't get to share my pleasure over it with my family. I know it's just a truck, a possession, but it represents this new chapter in my life that I'm so excited about. And anxious over. And I want to share it with my family. With Oscar. I know pregnant teenage daughter trumps Mom's new job, but I can't help thinking that just once in the last month it would have been nice to have had my new business been the topic of discussion. Oscar's focus.

Which makes me a terrible mother. A terrible wife. And a terrible person.

I drive to Mom and Dad's. When I pull into the driveway, Oscar says, "You going in?" without looking at me.

"Do you mind?" I turn to him, making an apologetic face. "Could you tell Mom I'll be by after dinner?"

He gets out of the truck, taking the bag and smell of rotisserie chicken with him.

I can't hear Hazel crying anymore, but she's sniffling. Her phone dings and I want to ask if it's Tyler finally, but I don't say anything.

Oscar's back in the truck in three or four minutes and we drive home in silence. The truck has barely rolled to a stop in our driveway when Hazel jumps out. I want to call out to her something sarcastic about doing dangerous things while carrying my grandchild, but I check myself. I'm not that kind of mother. Well, I guess I am, because I thought about that, but I don't *want* to be that mother.

The back door of the truck slams and Oscar unbuckles his seat belt. But he doesn't get out. He just sits there for a moment and then turns in the seat to face me. "What the hell was that all about? What did you say to her?"

I unbuckle myself slowly, trying to take care in the words I choose. "I just — Oscar —" I glance at him, at my handsome husband, who looks so angry with me now. "I told her that I thought Tyler not being there might be a good indication of how much she's going to be able to count on him in the next few months. When the baby is born."

He shakes his head, looking away from me.

"It's true!" I defend. "You know I'm right. Tyler wasn't there tonight because he doesn't care about Hazel and he doesn't care about his baby. It's that simple."

"To you, maybe. But we don't all have the convenience of living in your world of black and white. Tyler not being there doesn't necessarily mean he doesn't care about his baby. It doesn't mean he doesn't care about Hazel. I think it's more complicated than that."

I make a sound of derision. Complicated, Tyler is not. But I don't say it because even if it's true, I know it will come off sounding mean and judgmental.

"Liv, what's going on with you?" Oscar doesn't even attempt to hide his displeasure with me.

"What's going on with me? What's going on with me?" I sound like Cricket now. If she said pink pig pjs one more time, I was going to strangle her. But I don't answer him because I don't know what's going on with me. My sixteen-year-old daughter is knocked up? No, it's more than that and I know it. He knows it. A midlife crisis, maybe? Does that even happen to women?

"We've always been a team, Liv," he goes on. "You and I and the kids. We've always been here for each other. Supported each other."

"What makes you say I'm not being supportive?"

He looks at me with exaggerated disbelief.

"Just because I'm not buying pink pig pjs? You think I'm not being supportive?" I lean closer to him on the bench seat. "Oscar,

189

I've been nothing but supportive of Hazel for the last sixteen years and ten months. I gave birth to her, I fed her from my body, I clothed her, I taught her to tie her shoes, I made a papier-mâché solar system with her." Now I'm ticking off on my fingers. "I took her to flute lessons, math tutors, and soccer games galore. I threw birthday parties for her with a bouncy house in the backyard and a homemade princess three-tiered cake. I held her in my arms when the first boy she ever liked didn't like her. I showed her how to use a tampon! I didn't hand her the instructions like my mom did. I *showed* her. So, don't tell me —"

"Liv —" he interrupts.

"Don't tell me," I go on, louder, "that I'm not being supportive of our daughter. No, I don't think she should keep this baby. But she *is* keeping it. Which affects me, which means —"

"Liv!" he says even louder.

I drop my hands to the tops of my thighs and go silent. I stare out the windshield. The wind is blowing and there are leaves tumbling across the lawn. This morning, when I left early to go have a look at some old windows someone had set aside for me, I felt the first chill of fall.

"You're being selfish," Oscar tells me.

190

I look at him. *"Selfish?"*

He exhales. He's not making eye contact with me now. "I know you did all of those things for her. I know you do things for her every day. But, Liv, that's just being a parent. Those are the things we do for our children." He hesitates. "And I get that you thought you were going to start having less responsibility, now that she's older. But . . . you can't just step back and say you're done" — he raises both hands, palms out — "because she made a mistake."

"I'm not saying I'm done. I *will* help her, Oscar." I look at him, needing him to look at me. "But I'm not going to pretend I'm happy about this. And I'm going to tell Hazel what I think."

He shakes his head, still looking straight ahead. "I'm not saying you have to be happy about the baby. I'm just saying you have to accept it and move on." He finally turns to look at me. "You think I want our sixteen-year-old daughter to have a baby? You think I don't see this every day in the ED? You think I don't know what she's up against now?"

I just sit there. I don't know what to say. I'm hurt that Oscar would accuse me of being selfish. I'm hurt that he doesn't even seem to be trying to see my side of this situ-

191

ation. I'm hurt that after almost twenty-one years of marriage, he would allow something like this to come between us.

He thinks I'm selfish. I worked fifty hours in the last week between the Anselin house and the county offices where there was a screwup in the permits. I made dinner for our family and my parents six of the last seven days. I have vacuumed and washed dishes and folded everyone's laundry in our house. I also did my parents' laundry twice this week because Mom is having a bad week, hasn't felt up to it, and refuses to let Dad use her washing machine. I went to two doctors' appointments with my mom, one with my dad, and I took Hazel for lab work. I also grocery shopped for us and my parents. And remembered to send birthday cards, with gift certificates, to Oscar's sister's kids, away at college. This week I ordered new scrubs for Oscar, a pair of stretchy pants for Hazel, I crawled around on the floor for twenty minutes to locate my dad's dentures, I took the dog to the vet . . . the list seems endless.

But *I'm* being selfish.

The two of us just sit there in silence.

Oscar breaks first in this adult game of conversational chicken. He smooths his beard with his hand, seeming to contemplate what he wants to say, which isn't like him. I'm the one always weighing my words. He just says what comes to mind and no one thinks he's selfish or uncaring.

"Liv, I think you need to move past the fact that you don't want Hazel to have this baby, to accepting it. Accepting it as the new normal. Hazel's normal. Our normal."

*And this,* I think, *is this* our *new normal, Oscar? This distance. This lack of . . . the connection that we've always felt?* But I can't bring myself to say it. Because if I say it, it will be real.

Instead, I sigh, realizing I'm tired. Really tired. I probably only slept five hours last night and five the night before. I've been combing the Internet, looking for antique hardware for the Anselins' doors and cabinets. At rock bottom prices, of course.

"You're right," I say. "I need to move on. Hazel's going to have a baby. That's our new normal." I give a little laugh, resting my hand on the seat between us. "We're going to be grandparents."

He offers a half smile and for a second I think he's going to take my hand, or maybe even put his arm around me and hug me. I could really use a hug right now. Instead, he opens the door and gets out. "I've got to do a little reading. Saw something interesting in the ED today. Call me when dinner's ready?"

I just sit there, staring at him as he walks away. "Sure," I whisper.

# 14
## HAZEL

Katy squeals and flings herself onto her back on my grandmother's bed, kicking and beating her fists on the mattress. "Oh, jeez, no! Was it as awful as it sounds? She just . . . went all up in there?"

We're supposed to be making the bed, but mostly we're just goofing around. I flop down on my back beside her, giggling. I love my gran's bed. It's the most comfortable bed I've ever slept in. I slept in this bed with her when I spent the night until I was, like, twelve years old. I could sleep with Gran because Granddad has had his own bedroom for as long as I can remember. Gran always said it was so they didn't get a divorce. I loved snuggling in bed with her. She used to tell me the best stories.

"It wasn't that big a deal," I tell Katy. "I mean it was quick. You put your feet up in the stirrup thingies and . . . I don't know. She does her thing while you stare at a poster of a baby in a uterus that's taped on the ceiling. She took a scrape of skin cells with this long Q-tip-looking thing. The test is to check for abnormal cells on the cervix."

"Do pregnant sixteen-year-olds even get cervical cancer?" Katy looks at me, her freckled nose only inches from mine. She's a redhead like me, which is crazy because there are only three gingers in our entire high school, now that Sean is gone. The third is this girl Althea, but she's a total weirdo. Previous homeschooler. No further explanation needed.

"I don't know if they get cervical cancer. I would guess they do; otherwise, Dr. Gallagher wouldn't have said I needed the test, right?" I turn my head to stare at the ceiling, my hand going to my belly that's definitely a little round now. I keep waiting to feel the baby move. From what I've read online, with first pregnancies, you don't usually feel the baby until twenty-five weeks. I'm only twenty now. But women who have had babies before, who know what it feels like, say they can feel their baby at, like, thirteen or fourteen weeks. I really want to feel my baby. But I want to know it's for real and not my stomach grumbling. Which happens a lot.

I keep getting indigestion. I didn't even

know what that was until one night I started burping up burrito and felt like my throat and stomach were on fire. Mom gave me some coconut water, which made me feel a lot better, and then we agreed I'd lay off the spicy salsa and jalapeños next time. We both laughed about it. After I cried because I was pretty sure I was dying from esophageal cancer, which meant my baby would die, too.

"I decided not to look up the whole cervical-cancer thing," I admit to Katy. "I've got enough stuff to stress over right now."

Katy laughs. She came to help me do some things for my grandparents, but mostly she just wanted to hear about my OB appointment. My second with Dr. Gallagher. The first time I was so nervous and so upset that Dr. Gallagher said we could just hold off on the internal exam until my next visit. That first time, we just did the pee test and then a blood test to confirm I was preggers.

Yesterday, Mom went with me, even though I can drive myself now. She even offered to go into the exam room and hold my hand or whatever. She said she wouldn't look. I almost told her to come in. But then I felt like a baby because if I'm old enough to have sex on Tyler's parents' couch after school, I'm old enough for a pelvic exam with a female, board-certified obstetrician-gynecologist. That's what I told Mom. She laughed and agreed with me. But she said she'd still go in with me, which, as much as I hate to admit it, I thought was sweet of her.

"Jeez, Hazel. I still can't believe you're going to have a *baby*. I haven't even had sex." Katy rolls onto her side and lays her hand on my belly beside my hand.

I think for a minute. "You said you let Hunter York play with your tits that night you drank too much beer."

She does this really funny thing that sounds like a pig snort. "He was so drunk he didn't even remember it when I saw him in school the next day. It doesn't count as sex if the guy doesn't remember it happened. Besides, that's not sex. That's just goofing around."

I agree with her, but I don't say anything. I'm glad she didn't have sex with Hunter because this girl we know from U.S. History said she had sex with him, and then he never talked to her again. Except to copy her bio homework.

"I'm going to be Aunt Katy." She stares at her hand on my belly like she's still trying to wrap her head around the idea.

I'm wearing my yoga pants that Mom ordered for me. I didn't wear them for a couple of weeks after she bought them. Instead, I wore them unbuttoned and used the hair tie trick. But one morning when my fat jeans were still wet in the dryer, I tried on the yoga pants because I didn't want to be late. They're so comfortable that I wear them almost every day. Mom keeps offering to get me another pair, but I tell her no because you give Mom an inch and she takes miles. She'll order me half a dozen pairs of the same pants if I admit I like them.

"You and Tyler talk about names for the baby?" Katy asks.

I keep staring at the ceiling. Two summers ago, Mom and Sean and I painted the room. Dad was supposed to help us, but he ended up working late or taking an extra shift or something. Typical Dad. The ceiling is eggshell white, the walls celery green. I helped Gran pick out the color.

"Tyler wants to name him T.J. Like Tyler Junior."

"Eww." Katy takes her hand off my belly. She looks like she just bit into something nasty. "You didn't agree to that, did you?"

I shake my head. "I like Charles for a boy."

"Charles?" Katy makes a face.

"I want a classic name. Not something stupid that teenagers name their kids like . . . like Brayden."

Katy laughs. "Brayden is a pretty stupid name."

"Right. I like Charles Leonard after Dad. Dad's middle name is Leonard. Or maybe Charles Edward after Granddad. We can call him Charlie."

"I like Charlie. What if it's a girl, though?"

"It's a boy."

Katy gets up, goes to the blanket chest on the end of the bed, and starts taking the dirty pillowcases off the pillows we stacked there. "You think it's a boy, but you don't *know* it's a boy? You didn't get a test?"

"I could have had an ultrasound yesterday that would have shown his penis, but I opted not to." I sit up, leaning on my hands behind me. "It's supposed to be safe, but . . ." I make a face. "How do you know if it's *really* safe? Doctors gave pregnant women thalidomide for nausea and their babies were born with flippers instead of hands and feet."

Katy screws up her face. "What is *wrong* with you? How do you even know this stuff?"

"Google it," I tell her. "It's true. Late fifties, early sixties."

She closes her eyes, shaking her head. "We're talking about ultrasounds. It's just sound waves. How can that not be safe?" She adds the two pillowcases to the dirty linen pile near the door. "Tyler think it's a boy?"

I flop back on the bed, staring at the ceiling again. "I don't know what Tyler thinks."

Katy is quiet and just waits for me to say something else. It's one of the reasons she and I have been friends for so long. Because she doesn't feel like she has to talk every minute of every day. And also because she puts up with my weird obsessions with health and safety and doesn't make fun of me about it. Too much.

"Tyler's being weird," I tell her. I look at her. "Don't you think he's acting weird?"

"Like weirder than normal?" Katy picks up the fitted sheet from a pile on a chair near the door. "Get up, fatty."

"That's not funny." I climb out of the bed. "I got on the scale this morning. I've gained, like, eleven pounds since the end of school last year."

Katy moves to the opposite side of the bed and flaps the sheet open. The sheets are white. Gran only uses white sheets, which I always thought was cool when I was little. The sheets are colored at our house. Mostly whatever was on sale at L.L.Bean the last time we went to Freeport.

"Eleven pounds? How big is the baby?" Katy shakes the sheet again. "I thought it was, like, the size of a cupcake."

"Banana." I catch the end of the sheet. "The weight gain isn't from the baby. He only weighs, like, two pounds. The weight's from increased blood volume and stuff."

"And all the red licorice you've been eating."

I stick out my tongue at her and pull the sheet down over the mattress. "I'm serious about Tyler." I keep my eyes on the sheet. "You think he's . . ." I exhale. "He's busy after school all the time. Working and stuff. The last three days he hasn't wanted to hang out. And now since I'm not working at the drugstore anymore, I could actually hang out with him more."

She doesn't look at me, either. "You told him he had to work more hours. Save money for the baby."

"I don't think he's working so he can save money for the baby. He's talking about buying a truck from his cousin. He says he's got half the down payment." I move to the end of the bed to stretch the sheet over the last corner. "You think he doesn't like me anymore because I'm getting fat?"

Katy's hands fall to her sides and the way she looks at me worries me.

"Marissa said she saw him talking to Amanda." I chew on the cuticle on my thumb, watching her. I'm taking psychology and we've been talking about body language. Marissa's body language was weird when she was telling me she saw Amanda and Tyler together. "You think he likes Amanda? Because you know he used to. Before we started talking."

"He's going to have a baby with you." Katy grabs the top sheet and comes back to the bed.

She shakes it out, and I grab an edge. "You didn't answer the question," I say.

She exhales loudly. "No, I don't think he likes Amanda. She's got a big nose."

My phone in my back pocket vibrates. Mom bought me yoga pants with a back pocket because she knows I like to carry my phone that way. The pocket's kind of small and my phone falls out sometimes. But it works. I pull my phone out, hoping it's Tyler. I texted him right after school. Then again when Katy and I got here. He still hasn't texted me back.

What time will you be home?

It's Mom.

I groan. My fingers fly. Later

203

The bubbles pop up. Mom's getting good at texting. She finally uses both her thumbs to type. She was trying to hold it with one hand and text with one thumb or hold it in one hand and text with one finger.

Can you stop at the grocery store on your way home and get fresh basil? And milk and TP????

I thought it was a good deal, getting Sean's car, but now I see that the only reason Mom agreed to let me drive it was because she wanted me to buy groceries every day.

Running late, she adds. Be home by 6:30 7:00

I groan and text sure.

"Tyler?" Katy asks me as I push my phone back into my mini pocket.

"Mom." I pick up the sheet and smooth it over the bed. "She wants me to go to Hannaford."

"You girls want a snack?" Gran asks from the doorway, startling me. She's so quiet in her wheelchair. She sneaks up on me.

I glance at her in the doorway. She looks tired today, and she doesn't look like she brushed her hair. It's really short so if she doesn't brush it, it stands up weird on her head. I think she's tired because Granddad kept her up most of the night talking to people in his room. People who weren't there. I wonder if we can sue the neurologist he's seeing. "What have you got?" I ask.

"Apples and almond butter and those cookies you like from the bakery in Rockland."

I look at Katy because I'm starving. "Hungry?"

"Yup."

"Be there in a minute," I tell Gran. "We're almost done in here."

Gran wheels back down the hall.

"You don't think he likes Amanda?" I ask Katy.

"I don't think he likes Amanda. Tuck that in." She points and goes back for the duvet.

"Mom's still going on about how he's not going to help." I bite the cuticle on my thumb again, this time ripping off a chunk. It starts to bleed and I suck on it.

Katy doesn't say anything. She just starts spreading out the duvet, also white, on the bed.

"She's so mean." I look at Katy, who's busy with the bed. "I mean, she's not mean, but she . . . she brought up adoption again at the dinner table last night. Dad got up and took his plate into the living room."

Katy's still listening, but she doesn't say anything.

205

"I don't understand why she won't just shut up about it. I'm not giving up my baby."

"I'm not talking about this with you," Katy says finally. "I told you. I'd have been at Planned Parenthood fixing it the first time I missed my period. I'm not having a baby before I finish high school. I'm probably not having a baby ever."

I grab the edge of the duvet, pull on it, and then smooth it out. "I know you don't want me to have the baby, but . . . you haven't been mean about it. You're . . . you know . . . supporting me. Supporting my decision."

My phone vibrates again. This time it is Tyler and I smile. He's finally answering me. To say he can't meet me after school. Or tonight. But he adds a banana emoji. A stupid joke when we first started talking. I smile.

"Tyler coming over?"

"Here?" I look up at Katy. "He'll never come here again. Not after Granddad told him he needed to wash his face so he doesn't have so many zits." Not that Tyler came here much before the zit confrontation. A few weeks ago, Tyler stopped by and Granddad gave him shit about "giving me a baby," which was interesting because

206

Granddad hasn't said a word to me about being pregnant.

Katy tosses the pillows on the bed. "He meeting you at your house?"

I make a face at her as I arrange the pillows the way Gran likes them. "You kidding? Tyler didn't come to my house before, except to pick me up. Now he won't come at all. He says it's because Mom 'looks at him mean.' "

"Does she?" The bed made, Katy picks up the dirty sheets. I'll throw them in the washer before we go.

"Yeah, I guess." I make a face. "But she did that before she knew I was pregnant. And why does he care how she looks at him? She's always nice to him. She still invites him to dinner. When he used to come, he'd eat, like, three helpings of everything. He couldn't believe Mom cooked dinner every night."

"*Ayuh.* You said they don't eat dinner at Tyler's."

"Yes, they eat dinner," I say, getting snippy with her. Everyone's always criticizing Tyler and his family. "They just eat a lot of takeout and frozen fish sticks and Tater Tots. I think it's because Cricket works so much at the grocery store and she's too tired to cook when she gets home. And I like Tater

Tots," I add. "And so does my dad. If Mom's going to be gone, that's what my dad makes us for dinner."

Katy's eyebrows practically touch in the middle, but she doesn't say anything. A couple of times in the last weeks she's told me I'm being hormonal. She thinks I overreact. I told her maybe she'd overreact if she had a kid sitting on her bladder. I have to pee every five minutes. That could make a person overreact.

She walks out of the bedroom with the sheets in her arms. She knows the routine. She's been coming here for years with me.

"I don't know why you're making faces," I call after her. "My mom's been working so much lately, the next time you come over, she's not going to make you that homemade tortellini you like. The fish sticks are coming out of the freezer!"

# 15
## LIV

When my phone rings, I debate whether or not to answer it; I don't recognize the number on the screen on my dashboard. I'm headed east, a circa-1840 pine fireplace mantel in the bed of my truck. It needs to be stripped and painted, but it was a great online find, authentic to the mid-nineteenth-century date of the Anselin house. The only drawback was that I had to drive almost three hours to pick it up, all the way on the eastern edge of the New Hampshire state line near White Mountain National Forest. I also picked up a couple of ladder-back chairs, which with some repairs I can do myself will be gorgeous, and an amazing picture frame that if I don't use in their house, I'll use it on another project.

The minute I signed the contract with the Anselins and realized I really was going into business for myself restoring old homes, I started worrying about whether there would be a second contract. Or a third. So, I'm flying pretty high this afternoon because a woman I've been talking on and off with for weeks called to say she and her partner had decided they had chosen me, out of two other contenders, to restore their eighteenth-century Cape Cod.

The house is north of Judith, near Lincolnville, so it will be a little longer drive than the Anselin house is, but I can make it to Terri and Louise's in thirty-five minutes. Completely doable. And honestly, the way things have been at home, I don't think I'll even mind the drive. These days, I find myself postponing going home. When I'm working, when I'm standing in the middle of the room directing my demolition guys, I feel like I know what I'm doing. I feel like I know who I am. When I walk into my house, when I sit beside Oscar at the dinner table, across from Hazel, I don't even know who I am anymore. I'm feeling like a complete failure as a mother and as a wife. But I'm discovering I really do have a knack for the restoration of old houses. A passion.

The phone continues to ring, and I realize it's a local cell exchange. Local to home. Afraid it's my mom calling from a stranger's cell phone to tell me Dad lost her in the grocery store again, I touch a button on the steering wheel to answer. It only takes me two tries to connect. I'm still becoming familiar with my new vehicle. "Liv Ridgely speaking."

"Liv, hi, *er . . .* this is Maureen Gray?" She says it as if she's not quite sure. "I live down the street from your parents. On the corner. Cape, cedar shakes, red trim."

When she says her name I vaguely recognize it, but I'm relieved she offers the additional clue. I immediately get a picture of her in my mind: short, round, a little older than me, with the typical forty-plus New England woman's haircut and striking green eyes. "Right, hi, Maureen," I say, wondering why on earth she's calling me. She has a son younger than Sean but older than Hazel, so we've bumped into each other on occasion at school functions, but mostly I know her from waving to her as I turn the corner onto my parents' street.

"I hate to bother you, but . . . I was wondering. *Er . . .* is your dad by any chance *er . . .* missing?"

"Is he *missing*?"

"Yes, I . . . Liv, I think I just saw him turning onto Bluebird." She sounds flustered. "I hate to bother you but . . . Liv, he . . . *er, he wasn't wearing pants.*"

Of all the things I was anticipating she might say, *that* wasn't one of them. "He's naked?" I'm unable to keep the shock out of my voice. My father is usually a very modest man. Always has been. A white crewneck T-shirt, oxford shirt buttoned up to the collar, robe over a full set of pajamas.

"No," she says sweetly. "He was . . . *er* . . . wearing boxer shorts. Red plaid?"

She says it in a way that suggests I would know what pair of my dad's underwear she's referring to. I frown, knitting my brows. "You sure it was my dad?"

"Yes." Again, the sweet, now almost apologetic tone. "It was Dr. Cosset all right, *ayuh.*"

"Did you speak to him?"

"No." She sounds whiffy to me now. "I just saw him through my bedroom window; it looks out onto Wren Street. I was putting laundry away. Wednesday I do towels and sheets."

A detail I'm not sure why I need, considering the circumstances.

I push the heel of my hand to my forehead, squinting behind my Ray-Ban aviator sunglasses. A gift from Amelia when I got my business license. She said every contractor needed a pair. "How long ago was this?"

"Er . . . fifteen minutes ago, maybe?"

212

I want to ask her why it took her so long to call me, but then it occurs to me that maybe she called Mom first. "Did you speak with my mom?"

"No answer."

*Great,* I think. I'm two and a half hours from home and my father is walking through town half naked. The only bright side to this is that at least it's not too cold out, though it's certainly cold enough to be wearing pants and a jacket. "Was he wearing a coat?" I ask.

"Sorry?"

I shake my head, realizing it's a silly question. Whether he's wearing a coat or not doesn't matter. The lack of pants is the critical bit of information here. And the fact that he's gone for a walk alone. After he retired, he used to walk all the time: into town to get something at the grocery, to buy a newspaper, or have a cup of coffee. He used to sit in a coffee shop and talk with retired men his own age, but he got frustrated with them and stopped going two or three years ago. He said they never wanted to talk about anything except their prostate, or what they'd seen on Fox News.

"Thank you so much for calling me, Maureen," I say. "It was kind of you."

"You're certainly welcome. Dr. Cosset was

213

always such a gentleman. Have a good day," she sings.

The moment she disconnects, I dial Mom and Dad's house. It rings until I hear my voice on the answering system. I hang up and dial again. Three times is the charm. This time, Mom answers.

She sounds half asleep. "Hello?"

"Mom, where's Dad?"

"Liv?"

I glance at the speedometer and bump my speed up five miles an hour. "Maureen from down the street on the corner just called me to say that she saw a man, who she thought was Dad, walking down the street."

"He's not supposed to go out without me. I was lying down."

"Mom, Maureen said he wasn't wearing pants."

She's silent for a moment, then I hear, "Oh, dear."

It's not funny but I can't help myself. I crack a smile. "Yeah, that's a problem."

My mother sighs heavily. "He'll come back. He always does."

"He's left the house without his pants before?" I ask. It's the first time I've heard about it. Most times Dad tells on himself when he does something like this. I don't even have to wait for Mom to tell me.

214

"Usually he wears his pants," she quips.

I shake my head. Now my eighty-one-year-old mother has become a smartass. "Mom, could you check and see if he's home? Maybe the neighbor was mistaken? Maybe it wasn't Dad?"

"You want me to see if he's here?" She sounds annoyed with me.

I hate to ask, but I don't see any other choice here. "I think you better."

She groans as if it's a great imposition. "It will take me a minute to get out of bed and into my chair. I'll call you back," she tells me.

Ten minutes later, she calls. "He's not here," she says when I answer, and then she goes on without letting me get a word in. "I'm not surprised. He was a pip all morning and I didn't have the patience for it. You know what he did before seven a.m.? Before I was even out of bed? He mowed the neighbor's roses down with the lawnmower. And Jessop came out and yelled at him. Last time he was on the mower he knocked over Jessop's mailbox."

I hadn't heard about the mailbox, either, and I wonder what else the two of them have been keeping from me. When Dad first started suffering from memory loss three or four years ago, Mom covered for him. She

215

covered for him for almost a year before I finally realized my father was suffering from something more than absentmindedness due to aging.

"What was Dad doing on the lawn-mower?" I ask. "I thought Oscar disconnected the starter so he couldn't drive it anymore." We have a lawn service that comes now that my father is no longer able to care for it himself.

"Good question," Mom says. "I guess he hooked it back up again. He kept going out into the garage. He told me he was looking for a screw. Maybe to replace the one loose in his head."

Again I crack a smile in spite of myself.

"He went out several times," my mother continues. "He wasn't bothering anyone, so I let him look. Liv, I know you don't want to hear this. I know you think he's perfect, but I've had it with him."

It's on the tip of my tongue to inject that I don't think my father is perfect, that I never thought that, but she's wound up now, and no one is going to stop her, least of all me.

"It's day and night he's into something. I tell him to sit, why don't you. I tell him to play his game on his iPad. I offer to put the TV on for him. There are movies he could

216

watch on Netflix. And if he'd leave the remote alone and stop pushing buttons, he might find that he could enjoy a movie once in a while. Now he's mowed down Jessop's fancy roses and Jessop isn't happy with us. He —"

"Mom," I finally interrupt. "You said you were lying down. Are you having a bad day?"

"I was having a bad day before your father went AWOL. I had to take a painkiller and lie down."

Which meant she couldn't drive if she wanted to. Even if she wanted to go look for him. Which doesn't sound to me like she does right this moment. "Mom, I had to go to New Hampshire to pick up something for the house I'm remodeling. I'm still two hours away. Can you call Beth?"

"I hate to bother her, Liv. It's her day off and she likes to rest on her day off. Do something fun. Her job can be very stressful, you know, dealing with everyone else's stress."

She makes it sound as if my sister is a social worker or maybe a psychiatrist. She's actually a massage therapist who goes to people's homes to give massages.

"Mom." I try not to sound annoyed because I know she's got to be exhausted. Dad hasn't been sleeping much and he keeps her awake at night pacing and talking. Or he gets it in his head he wants to do something at two a.m. like start a pot of spaghetti sauce, one of his specialties when he had all of his faculties and still cooked for us. And this isn't about Beth right now or about my lifetime resentment of her. I know it's not Beth's fault that she was always our mother's favorite. That she was born of my mother's DNA and I wasn't. Actually I don't think Mom even liked her better because I was adopted and Beth wasn't. Mom just liked her better, pure and simple. No matter how many ways she screwed up, how many cars she wrecked, how many times she had to be bailed out financially. How irresponsible she was practically every day of her life. Mom gave her a pass at every turn. She held me up to a nearly impossible standard and those standards never applied to my sister.

But this isn't about that.

This is about Dad. And my mom. I sigh. "It's okay, Mom. I'll figure it out. Why don't you just lie back down? I'll find him."

"And exactly how are you going to do that, Olivia?" she responds, taking a little attitude with me. "You're in New Hampshire."

"I'm back in Maine now. I'll give someone

a call. I'm sure he's okay. Make sure the door is unlocked. Someone in town has probably spotted him by now and he's on his way home."

"Wish the police would spot him. Do him good to let him sit in the pokey overnight."

I laugh. I've never thought of my mother as funny, but she does say some funny things about my dad. "I don't think an elderly man with Alzheimer's is going to the pokey, Mom."

"I can't believe he mowed Jessop's roses," she says, talking over me. "Do you know what those are going to cost to replace? They're some fancy hybrid from England. Your father wants me to use the same Ziploc bag three times. Just wash it out! he tells me. Wash it out, Bernice. Thrift comes too late if it's at the bottom of your purse. That's what he tells me, but then he wants to buy the neighbor new roses?"

"I'll call you when I find him, Mom."

She hangs up. Without saying good-bye. Something that's annoyed me for . . . for as long as I can remember. Now it's starting to amuse me. I dial my sister. I get her voice mail. "You know what to do," says her recording. Then there's a loud beep. "Call me back," I say. "Dad's missing."

As I hang up, I try to decide who to call

219

next. If Beth doesn't pick up when I call her, the likeliness of hearing from her in the same day goes down significantly. Now who do I call? I speed up again, now going more than ten miles an hour over the speed limit. I can't call Oscar. (A) He doesn't pick up when he's at work and (B) he and I had an argument this morning. Over the lack of coffee creamer in the refrigerator. He was *really* angry with me. Disproportionally angry. I did recall him asking me to stop for some yesterday, but there was an issue with a load of lumber I'd ordered and I completely forgot. And I don't even drink it. Why am I stopping by on the way home from work for something he needs? Why couldn't he stop for vanilla-flavored artificial creamer with aspartame in it on *his* way home from work? Oscar has adapted well to our daughter's obsession over healthy foods in our house, but he drew the line on his fake-milk creamer. She poured it out once while going through the refrigerator, ejecting anything that didn't meet her quality standards, and he threatened that if she ever threw away his creamer again, he was going to string her up by her thumbs in the barn. They both laughed about it. Hazel also never touched his creamer again, though.

So not Oscar. Not after Creamergate.

Amelia? I could call Amelia. Either that, or call the police. The Judith police force consists of six guys, three cruisers, and an old church turned station house. I'm pretty sure the donut-eating, coffee-drinking stereotype began at the Judith police station. I know four of the six guys. One I dated briefly while in high school. It wouldn't be a big deal to call them. They help old ladies get into their houses when they lock themselves out. They return bicycles left in the park by absentminded middle schoolers. I know they wouldn't mind taking a spin through town looking for him. It shouldn't be hard to spot an eighty-five-year-old man in red plaid boxer shorts, with or without his L.L.Bean barn coat.

But who wants to call the cops on their dad? Especially if he's walking around town in boxer shorts?

I auto-dial Amelia. She's at work, but I call anyway, on the outside chance she's available. Voice mail. I don't leave a message.

I consider Oscar again.

If I can't get him on his cell, I can call the ED and leave a message for him to return my call. I could apologize for the creamer and ask him to take off early and look for Dad.

I think I'd rather call the police.

But I don't want to call the police any more than I want to call Oscar.

I groan out loud and reach for my cup of mint tea that was cold an hour ago. I know I'm being petty about the creamer, but he's not being very respectful of my time. When I started playing with the idea of going into the restoration business a year ago, he was supportive of the idea, but he never really seemed into it. Maybe he didn't think I could do it. And now that I actually have a client, he doesn't seem to understand that time I spend working, contributing to our children's college fund, takes away from time I could be spending picking up vanilla creamer for him. And making pasta. The other day he complained about boxed pasta. He probably meant it as an offhand compliment when he said he liked my fresh fettuccine noodles better, but I felt like it was a dig. I felt as if he was saying that since I started working again, I don't have time to make my family fresh pasta anymore.

My list of who to call has gotten pretty short. In fact, short of calling Maureen back and asking *her* to look for my dad, I can only think of one person.

I pass two more vehicles, get back into the right-hand lane, and auto-dial Hazel. She's in class so I know she won't pick up, but I'm hoping she'll call me back between classes.

She answers. "Mom? What's wrong?"

"Why aren't you in class?"

"Bathroom. I had to pee. *Again.*" Her voice is echoing. Sounds like she's actually in the bathroom. "What's wrong? Why are you calling me?"

"Your grandfather." I groan. "He's missing."

I hear her peeing. "Missing?" She's immediately alarmed.

"Well, not *missing,* missing. But your grandmother doesn't know where he is and the neighbor thinks she saw him headed into town in his boxer shorts sans pants."

"Did he have shoes on?"

I hear the toilet flush. "I don't know, Hazel. She was mostly concerned about him not wearing pants."

"Jeez," she mutters. "I don't ever want to get old. I start forgetting my pants, I want to be cryogenically frozen and brought back to life when we have the capability to reverse aging."

I shake my head at that one but don't respond to it. Definitely a conversation to

223

be saved for another day. "I went to New Hampshire this morning to get that mantel. I was telling you about it last night. So, I'm still two hours from home. I'm sorry for calling you while you're still at school, but didn't know who else to call, hon." I'm feeling a little out of sorts now. I'm so used to being in control of things. I know logically I can't be in control of my father's disease, but it still makes me uncomfortable realizing I can't stop these things from happening. And that they're probably going to start happening with more frequency. "Gran's not feeling well enough to be driving around looking for him."

"That's probably not a good idea anyway. If he doesn't have any pants on, she's going to be pissed," Hazel says. Now I hear water running. She must be washing her hands. "Gran's gonna lose it with him."

"Aunt Beth won't pick up," I continue. "Amelia must be in a meeting. Hazel, if I called the school office and said you had permission to leave early, would you mind going out and looking for him?"

"You call Dad?"

I feel myself stiffen. I know Hazel knows things have been tense between her father and me over the last two months, but I don't want to draw her into our . . . into whatever is going on with us. "I didn't want to bother him," I say.

"I'll call Dad."

"Don't," I say.

She hesitates and then says, "No problem, Mom. I'll find Granddad. You don't need to call the school office. I'll go to the nurse and tell her my baby hurts."

"You'll *what?*"

My daughter laughs. "It's a joke, Mom. Adults act crazy when they see a pregnant teenager in school. All I have to do is put my hand on my belly and every adult within a two-classroom radius asks me if I'm in labor. I can sign myself out. I'll just say I have an appointment. I'm pregnant. Everyone thinks I'm a loser now, anyway. No one cares if I leave school."

There's something in her tone that makes me think she's not joking about being a loser. I debate whether or not to say anything, but decide against it. Like the cryogenics, it's probably a conversation better left to discuss face-to-face. And right now, my dad is walking around town in plaid boxers, so we've got that to deal with. "Thank you, Hazel." My voice is suddenly full of emotion. "Thanks so much for doing this for me."

She's quiet for a moment. "You okay, Mom?"

I hear teenaged voices now: talking, laughing. She must be out in the hall.

I adjust my sunglasses. "Yeah, I'm fine. Just . . . worried about your granddad."

"His boxers, huh? That's pretty nuts. Okay, I'm going to get my stuff in my history class and then I'll go to the nurse's office. Do you know which way he was headed?"

"The neighbor thought toward town, but she wasn't sure."

"I'll find him, Mom."

"Call me when you do? Or if you don't," I add quickly. "It's getting dark so early now. If we need to call the police —"

"Mom, I don't think we need to call the police just yet."

Her tone makes me feel like she's the mother and I'm the daughter. "Call me?"

"*Ayuh,*" she says, imitating her father. "Be careful driving home. I don't want you to be one of those statistics for road fatalities on the billboards, Mom."

I smile as I hang up.

# 16
## HAZEL

I call Aunt Beth as I get into Sean's car, which is my car now even though no one is actually saying so. And I didn't even have to pay him for it. Which of course I wasn't going to do anyway. Dickwad.

"Hazel!" Aunt Beth says when she answers, sounding way too cheerful. The fake kind. "How's my favorite niece?"

I buckle up. "I'm your *only* niece."

I'm annoyed with her. I know Mom is a pain in the butt, but most of the time Aunt Beth isn't a very good sister. Mom worries too much about Granddad and Gran, but I feel like that's at least part Aunt Beth's fault because she doesn't worry enough about them. "You're supposed to answer the phone when Mom calls."

I adjust the rearview mirror, moving it one direction, then back into place. I know it's right where I want it because I drove to school this morning, but it's gotten to be a habit in the last few weeks since Mom and Dad started letting me drive to school. It's like . . . a pilot's checklist used before takeoff. I always check the position of the seat, too. I move it forward, then back.

Aunt Beth groans. "She's such a drag."

"I don't think anyone has used that phrase since the sixties, Aunt Beth." I bet she's been watching *Mad Men* again. She watches a lot of TV. "She needed you. Granddad ran away and he's naked."

*"Naked?"* she says.

"Well, not *naked,* but some neighbor called Mom and said he was walking around town in his boxer shorts. Gran doesn't know where he is but she's not feeling good, so I guess she won't go look for him."

My aunt laughs.

"It's not funny."

"It's not funny, I know, but" — she giggles — "my dad walking through town without pants, even if he is wearing boxers? That's funny."

"Mom went to New Hampshire so she can't go look for him. I'm coming to get you." I check the rearview mirror, then look to my left and then my right over my shoulder. Then in the rearview mirror again. "We have to find Granddad."

"What do you mean you're coming to get

me? What if I'm busy? What if I'm not home?"

I hear her take a drink of something.

"What if I'm on a date or something?"

I back slowly out of my parking space, which I pulled into perfectly, with an even amount of space on both sides. "You're not on a date, Aunt Beth."

"It's my day off," she argues. "I could be."

I look at the clock on the dashboard. It's two thirty-five in the afternoon. "You're not on a date," I repeat. Once I'm in a position to move forward, I brake and then shift the car into drive. I press down gently on the gas pedal. "Bet you're sitting in your ugly pink robe that's like a hundred years old, watching reruns of *Little Women: Atlanta* and drinking white wine out of a juice glass."

When she doesn't come up with a snappy answer right away, I know my guess is right. I'm afraid my aunt, besides being a TVholic, is an alcoholic. I've talked to Mom about it a couple of times, like if it's time to sit down with her as a family and have an intervention or something. The kind of thing where we all sit around in someone's living room, basically holding her captive, and telling her why we love her and why we don't want her to die of cirrhosis of the liver. Mom says we need to mind our own business on this one.

That there have been discussions and there's no point talking about it until Aunt Beth is ready to talk about it. The good thing is that she doesn't drink and drive. Although I know for a fact she drunk texts because a few months ago I heard her and Mom talking about it. Aunt Beth was boohooing over a big glass of red wine because Mom only drinks red, and Mom was telling her he wasn't the right guy for her anyway. Apparently, whatever she texted him while she was sitting home alone in her robe, drinking her boxed wine in the middle of the night, made him decide he didn't want to go out with her anymore.

"I'll be at your place in ten minutes," I tell my aunt. "I'm going to take a quick run through town, and maybe call Granddad's friend Mr. Dugan. Granddad used to walk over to his house to have coffee."

"Didn't he die?"

"I don't think so. I'd have heard about the funeral. You know how Gran loves a funeral." I ease to a stop before pulling out onto the road behind my high school. "See you in ten minutes."

"Hazel —"

"If you're not dressed, you're coming with me wearing that ugly robe," I warn her. I disconnect before she can say something

230

back. I call the Dugans' house. Some lady answers and says Mr. Dugan is napping. I get the idea maybe she's a nurse or something. When I pull up in front of Aunt Beth's town house, she's standing out front on the sidewalk talking to some guy with a black Lab on a leash. She's wearing sweats and a jean jacket, a ball cap, and big dark sunglasses. She's flirting with the guy with the dog. I beep the horn and she gives me a really dirty look. She takes her time walking to the car. She waves to the guy as she gets in.

"You smell like wine. Are you drunk?" I ask her.

She slams the car door. "No, I'm not *drunk.*" She nods in the direction of the guy with the dog, walking away. He looks kind of old for her. Like, older than my dad. "Jason Purdue. He just moved into town. Four doors down. Divorced."

"Seat belt. Think he's really divorced?"

She looks at me like that's a dumb question.

"Mikey?" I remind her. "He said he was divorced. Turned out he wasn't." I give her an exaggerated sad face. She was really upset when she found out that the guy she was dating, Mike the podiatrist, was still living with his wife. And daughters. And the

231

wife didn't know anything about a divorce. There was a lot of drama, as I remember. It involved Aunt Beth coming to our house in the pink robe and Dad having to go out for another box of wine. "Seat belt," I say again. "Granddad's got to be getting cold, walking around in his undies."

"His name wasn't *Mikey*. It was Michael." She puts on her seat belt. "And he was getting divorced. It was just that she was trying to take him to the cleaners. He didn't think he should have been paying a mortgage on two houses, just so she could be a slut."

I don't say anything, even though I remember the story differently. If I'm recalling the right guy, *he* was the slut. I pull away from the curb.

"You're being awfully judgey today," Aunt Beth remarks, "for a knocked-up sixteen-year-old."

"I'm almost seventeen. And that was mean." I glance at her. She doesn't have any makeup on and she looks tired.

"You're right. I'm sorry, sweetie." She reaches out and grabs my forearm.

I pull away. I like to keep two hands on the steering wheel at all times. We're coming back into Judith proper now. "I'll drive. You look for Granddad."

"How are things going with you?" she asks

232

me, gazing out the window.

"Awful."

"Awww, sweetie." She looks at me. "What's the matter? What's going on?"

"Oh, you mean besides this?" I take my right hand off the wheel just long enough to point to my baby belly that I can't hide anymore.

She glances back out the window. "Your mother?"

"Yes, no . . ." I huff. "Everyone. People aren't being very nice to me at school."

"Mean girls?"

I think about it for a minute. "No . . . they're not being mean, they're just . . ." I come to a stop sign. "Left or right?"

She points right, I signal, and turn, staying in my lane perfectly. "No one's inviting me to things anymore. I was never super popular or anything, but I used to get invited out for pizza, to a football game tailgate. Stuff."

"I thought you and Katy were best friends."

"I don't mean Katy. Other girls. Guys. People are nice to my face, but I think I make them feel uncomfortable. This makes them feel weird." I rub my hand across my belly before putting it back on the steering wheel. "And I get that. It makes me feel

233

weird and uncomfortable, too. But . . ." I shake my head. "I don't know. I didn't think kids would care. It's kind of lonely," I say softly.

"It's always the guiltiest people who are the judgiest," she says. "They want you to think they've never had sex, but they're the ones out doing it every night."

I make a face. "It's not about the sex. Lots of kids in my school are having sex. It's not a big deal. I just feel like . . . they don't like me because I got pregnant."

"Probably because you're a reminder that they could easily be in your shoes. Take a left at the end of the street. Maybe he walked to that little park near the library." Aunt Beth points in that general direction.

"And I'm fat," I tell her, making a pouty lip. "I've gained fifteen pounds and Mom had to give me a pair of her flannel pj bottoms last night because I'm too fat for mine."

"You don't look fat."

"Look at my face." I pinch my cheek between my thumb and pointer finger. "My face is fat and my hands and feet are swelling. We went hiking Sunday at Beachhill, me and Dad. Mom was working." I roll my eyes. "And my feet were all puffy when I got home. Like my sneakers were tight and left marks on my feet when I took them off."

She gives a wave. "That'll all be over in a few months, sweetie."

"Right. And then my boobs will be leaking milk and my V will be stretched out so bad —" I groan really loud in frustration.

"What about Tyler?" she asks, getting a nail file out of her bag.

"What about him?"

She starts filing her nails. "Is he being supportive?"

"Mom hasn't told you?"

"You're not the center of every conversation your mother and I have, Hazel."

I glance at her filing her nails. "Are you even looking for Granddad? You're supposed to be looking for him."

"How hard is it going to be to miss an old man in his underwear?" She says it sarcastically, but she drops the file back into her bag and looks out the window again.

"Tyler isn't being very supportive. He's not even being very nice to me." I signal as I come to a stop. A lady pushing a stroller with a little girl in it is waiting to cross the street. I wonder how old the girl is. I'm not good at that kind of thing. Two, maybe? Once the mom realizes I'm not a teenage driver who's going to plow into her, she starts crossing in front of me. She meets my gaze and smiles. I wonder if she'd smile at me if she knew I was in the eleventh grade and pregnant. I smile back.

"Tyler's being a total dickwad." I ease across the intersection after the lady with the stroller has reached the other sidewalk. "I hardly see him anymore. We only have one class together and now we have assigned seats, so we don't get to sit together. Then half the time at school he's eating with his shitty friends at lunch. He says he's working every day after school at his uncle's garage, but I was at Walgreens last week getting trick-or-treat candy and he pulled out of the parking lot as I was pulling in. Which means he wasn't at work." I'm quiet for another block. No sign of my granddad and now I'm starting to get worried. It was a pretty warm day for early October, but it's going to start getting cold soon. "I don't think Tyler loves me anymore." It sounds pathetic when it comes out.

We ride for another block in silence, then Aunt Beth says, "Pull over."

"What?"

"Pull over," she says again, pointing. "Right there. You won't even have to parallel park. A bus could park there."

"I know how to parallel park," I argue, feeling insulted. "I got a hundred percent on my driving test and the written exam."

"Bully for you. Pull over."

I ease into the spot in front of a pretty little white house with flowers in window boxes hanging off the front porch.

Aunt Beth turns in her seat, taking off her glasses. Her eyes look puffy and red. Like she's been crying. Not in the last five minutes, but like crying hard, a lot, for hours. She makes eye contact with me. "Hazel, you don't have to do this."

I put the car into park and shut off the engine. "I don't have to do what?"

"Have that baby." The expression on her face is making me feel like she thinks I'm going to be in the next *Alien* movie. One of those horror movies where a monster baby rips its way out of my belly.

I put both hands protectively around my swollen middle. I'm twenty-five weeks pregnant. My baby is the size of a cauliflower. It's a real baby, a baby I can feel kicking now, or moving, or whatever. "Yeah, I do have to have this baby, Aunt Beth. Nobody does abortions this far along. I'm not aborting my baby."

She holds up her hand, palm to me. "Save the drama for your mama." She puts her sunglasses in a case and tucks them into her bag. "Yes, you've got to pop this baby out of your V, but you don't have to keep this baby. You can put it up for adoption and —"

"I'm not giving up my baby." I look at her like she's crazy. "What kind of person gives away her baby?"

She stares me down, narrowing her tired-looking blue eyes. "A smart one, Hazel. A smart young woman like you who realizes she made a mistake and decides not to let it affect the rest of her life. I mean think about it. This wasn't a big mistake, I mean it *was* in a sense of the end result but — Exactly how did you get pregnant?" She holds up her hand, palm toward me. "Wait, let me guess. Ding-Dong didn't have a rubber?"

I feel my cheeks get hot and I look straight ahead, through the windshield. I still have my arms wrapped around my belly.

"Hazel," Aunt Beth says quieter. She tugs on the sleeve of my white North Face jacket that I can barely zip now. "Just because you said you wanted to keep this baby two months ago, doesn't mean you can't change your mind now."

I feel like I'm going to start crying. I keep staring straight ahead, watching cars go by us. People who I imagine don't feel like their lives are caving in around them. Smothering them.

"As much as you know I hate to admit it, your mother, my sister, is right on this one. And, Hazel" — she grabs my hand — "this isn't about not wanting to do what your mother wants you to do. We're not talking about buying the green prom dress because your mom thinks the blue one looks better on you. We're talking about something, *someone* who's going to affect you for the rest of your life. Someone who is going to *ruin* the rest of your life. Because you're being stubborn. And stupid."

I swallow, blinking. I feel like telling Aunt Beth that she's not really in a position to be telling people what kind of life decisions they should be making. It's not like she's killing it in that department. But I can't find my voice because I'm trying too hard not to cry.

"Hazel, sweetie, it's not that I don't think, that *we* don't think you can raise a baby." She's not sounding so mean now. "We think you could if you had to, and I think you'd do a pretty damned good job." She gives a little laugh. "Better than I ever could."

She's quiet and I finally turn to look at her, hoping she doesn't notice that I'm tearing up.

"The thing is, even though you *could* raise this baby, you don't have to. Things are dif-

239

ferent now. Things aren't so rosy with Baby Daddy. And changing your mind doesn't have to be about your mom being right and you being wrong."

I look away, shaking my head. "That's not what it's about," I whisper.

"Are you sure?" she says softly. "Are you *absolutely* sure? Because having a baby when you're seventeen, it could screw up your whole life, sweetie. You get that, right? It's going to screw up all your dreams. Because you saying you're going to be a doctor and take your kids to Switzerland for Christmas, you know that's not going to happen if you become a mother at seventeen years old, right?"

"What happened to you thinking I could do anything?" I ask her, not daring to look at her again. "When I was growing up, it didn't matter what I said, what I did, you supported me."

"Truth? That was bullshit you tell a kid. It's what you're supposed to tell kids: You can be president of the United States, you can make the volleyball team, you can get an A on that stupid test you're so worried about. Only you're not a kid anymore. Are you?" She points at my belly. "That means you're not a kid anymore. And when you're not a kid anymore, when you're a grown-ass adult, you have to face the facts. And the facts are, you might as well kiss your dreams of being a doctor good-bye. Sure, maybe you'll make it through community college, if you're lucky, and learn to be a dental hygienist or something." She holds up her hand. "And I'm not saying that's a bad thing. But it's not what *you* want. And if you keep that baby, the fact is that you're going to be a single mom, working as a hygienist, and borrowing money from your parents to put gas in your car." She throws up her hands. "Do the math. You know that statistically, that's what's likely to happen."

"I want my baby," I whisper.

"Why? So you have someone to love? Someone who loves you? That's what teen-aged girls always say."

I tear up.

"Hazel, you've already got more people who love you than most will ever have."

I just sit there watching cars go by. I watch a couple walk by who are like my parents' age. They're walking two little white dogs. They're holding hands. They're also wearing coats. And my granddad might be out somewhere cold and maybe confused about how to get home. I turn the key in the ignition.

Aunt Beth stares out the window.

241

I pull out of the parking spot. "Where could he be?" I say, deciding the best thing to do is to just let the "you should give away your baby" conversation go. "Where would he go?" I grip the wheel. "Call Gran and see if she's heard anything. Then call Mom. Maybe some other neighbor has seen him."

We get lucky fifteen minutes later. Gran and Mom don't know anything, but while we're sitting behind a UPS truck delivering on Main Street, some lady Gran knows from her old gardening club knocks on the car window and tells us she just saw Granddad in the bookstore. Wearing a blanket around his waist.

I let Aunt Beth out at the next corner and she goes to the bookstore, which has recently been bought by people from Maryland. Turns out that's why they didn't call Gran when Granddad walked in wearing his brown barn coat, his hiking boots, and no pants. They didn't know who he was and he wouldn't tell them. When I walk into the bookstore, I find Aunt Beth sitting at a little table across from Granddad looking at her phone. He's drinking black coffee and looking at a hunting magazine, which is interesting because he's never hunted, as far as I know.

"Hey, Granddad." I'm a little out of

242

breath because I had to park a block away and ran most of the way here.

"Hello, Hazel." He doesn't look at me.

I glance around. "I didn't know they added a coffee shop to the bookstore. This is really cool."

"Want a caramel latte?" Beth asks. "I'm going to order one to go. Jeannie and Rob are the new owners. Coffee bar's got a good menu; they're doing pourovers. Beans are roasted down the road at that place, what's it called? On Route 1. Camden, maybe?" She's texting someone as she talks to me and I wonder if that guy gave her his number.

I look down at Granddad's legs under the table and see that he's definitely wearing a blanket around his waist. I see his bare calves above his Bean boots. He doesn't seem cold or hurt, or even scared. My first impulse is to ask him what the hell he was doing walking around town without his pants, scaring us half to death because we didn't know where he was. But I don't because I'm not his mother. Or his daughter.

"You call my mom?" I ask Aunt Beth.

She shakes her head. She's grinning at her phone screen.

"Gran?"

She's texting again, her fingers flying. She's a lot better texter than Mom is. "Not yet."

I groan really loud and then realize it's something my mother does when she doesn't like my answer. "You order the coffees, I'll call them." I raise my hand like I'm in school. "I'll be the adult here." I walk away, pulling my phone out of my yoga pants' pocket. "Because *somebody's* got to be," I mutter.

# 17
## LIV

When I try to pull into my parents' driveway, I have to wait for the pizza guy to back out. He waves at me as if he knows me as he slams on his brakes in the center of the street and shoots forward. I return the wave and pull in. I'm surprised not to see Beth's or Hazel's car in the driveway. I'm equally surprised to see Oscar's. Hazel called me about three forty-five to say she and Beth had found Dad. That he'd gone to the bookstore in town. I didn't get any more details other than that he was fine.

Now I'm concerned. It's only five o'clock. Oscar should still be at work. I hurry inside, afraid my dad has a medical issue. Or Mom. Or both. It's happened.

I walk into my parents' kitchen to find nothing out of the ordinary. Dad's sitting at the table playing Candy Crush on his iPad. Wearing pants. I hear the TV on in the other room. I suspect that's where Mom is.

"Hey, Dad," I say, trying to keep my concern out of my voice. I smell the pizza and glance over to see a box on the counter. "Everything okay?"

"Beth was here," he says, not looking up at me. "She left."

I nod, annoyed she didn't at least stay until I got here. Feeling guilty because I'm annoyed and I shouldn't be. Because my sister actually came through for once. Hazel said she helped her find Dad. Oscar and I were having a conversation the other night . . . well, a disagreement. He told me I'm never happy, no matter what anyone does. It was over something silly like how he loaded the dishwasher. I argued it wasn't true. It was just that the way he was loading it, the dirty surfaces facing away from the center, the whole load would have to be run a second time. In my mind, he was being passive-aggressive in his offer to "help" me clean up after dinner. He was saying he was going to do the dishes, but in reality, he was setting up the scenario of me coming downstairs in the morning to start to unload them, find them still dirty, and then I would have to take the time to rearrange the dishes and run them again.

But he wasn't really talking about the dishwasher; he was talking about my general dissatisfaction with him, with the kids, my parents, Beth. Was he right? Am I never satisfied? Can no one ever live up to my expectations?

I know I never live up to my own.

I glance down at my dad. "Where'd Beth go?"

He shrugs. The volume of the game is loud. I resist the impulse to reach over his shoulder and turn it down.

Am I *really* never satisfied?

For a moment, I chew on my lower lip and that thought. Then I ask, "Is Oscar here?"

My dad swipes candies across his iPad screen. "Little boys' room."

I glance in the direction of the powder room off the kitchen. The door's slightly ajar. The light's out. "Doesn't look like he's in there."

"My bathroom," he says. Something good must have happened in his game because there's a burst of sound.

"Ah."

That translates to Oscar will be a few minutes. And if he's got his phone with him, which I'm sure he does, he could be quite a while. Another disagreement we had this week. Not exactly a disagreement, but we both used *tone* with each other. I told him what time we were eating, then gave him a fifteen-minute warning. Then he parked himself in the bathroom and stayed half an hour. He told me he was reading the news while he did his business. There's no way he was reading the news on his phone for half an hour. Oscar listens to the NPR morning report while he showers and gets ready for work and that's a big enough dose for the day, he says. I think he gets a big enough helping of the reality of the world in the emergency department each day. He was playing a game on his phone in the bathroom. He's into online trivia games.

So he spent thirty-four minutes playing trivia in the bathroom and I served lukewarm mashed potatoes, broccoli amandine, and roasted chicken. Hazel and I started eating before he finally joined us. As I passed the bowl of garlic mashed potatoes, I asked him if he was watching porn in the bathroom. Hazel thought it was funny. I did, too. I was joking. Oscar got pissed. Which made me pissed because did that mean he *was* watching porn? While I was trying to make and serve him a nice dinner? It's not that I even care about the porn. Well, I do, but mostly because he doesn't seem to have all that much interest in having sex with me, but he wants to watch other people do it? But it wasn't about that. Again, it was about his disrespect of my time.

He's right. I never *am* satisfied, am I?

I take a breath, really not liking myself at this moment. I slide into the chair beside my dad. "So . . . what happened today? What made you decide to walk into town to the bookstore?"

I don't bring up the fact that he *knows* he's not supposed to leave the house without telling Mom where he's going because it's been a bone of contention with them. He argues he has a right to go to the mailbox without getting her permission and I see his point. But *her* point is that sometimes he bypasses the mailbox and goes to a neighbor's house or for a walk around the block and is gone an hour and she doesn't know where he is and she gets worried. He used to carry his cell phone, but it's sitting in the drawer now. It's hard to believe that two years ago he was still using an iPhone.

He keeps sliding candies, concentrating on the iPad screen.

"Dad?" I say gently, laying my hand on his arm. As I squeeze it, I realize that he's losing muscle tone. He was always a fit man, even into his seventies, but now he's thinner. Stringier. I wonder when that happened and why I didn't notice.

"I don't want to talk about that." He stops playing his game, but he doesn't look at me.

"You were gone a couple of hours." I rub his arm, feeling sad. I can feel myself losing him, losing the father I've known and loved my whole life. But I also feel sad for him because he knows he's losing himself, too. I know he knows. Somewhere in his mind, he feels himself slipping away and that thought makes me feel like I could cry.

"Mom said there's a problem with Jessop's roses?" I wait because he looks like he's thinking.

The pizza smells good and I realize I'm hungry. I wonder what kind it is. It's from a little pizza place in town called Mario's. Their logo looks something like one of the characters in the Mario Brothers video game, but I guess not so much like it that they're getting sued for copyright infringement.

Dad just sits there, staring at his iPad. I guess he's not going to answer me.

"Dad," I say a little louder. "Did you accidentally mow over Jessop's rosebushes?"

"How the hell would I do that?" he barks. "You can't *mow* rosebushes! They're three feet tall."

He has a point. I don't imagine he actually mowed them off at ground level; Mom

250

was probably exaggerating. But he *has* mowed some of the neighbor's landscaping before and done a pretty good job of it.

"How did you get the mower started?" I try to get him to make eye contact with me. "You told me it wouldn't start. Remember? But we agreed you wouldn't worry about it because you have that lawn service now?"

"You know how much we pay them a month?" he asks, finally meeting my gaze. "It's like being held up by bank robbers once a week! Bank robbers wearing those floppy hats. What? They think we're in the jungle? They look like zounderkites!"

That makes me chuckle. I'm going to have to look up the word *zounderkite.* The employees of the local lawn company we hired wear uniforms: khaki shorts, T-shirts with their logo on them, and khaki sun hats.

"I told Jessop not to plant those roses on my property. I don't like roses," Dad grumbles. "They're prickly."

There's a little bit of saliva in the corners of his mouth, which seems odd. Also, he didn't shave this morning. Not like him. I grab a napkin from the holder on the table and pass it to him. "Wipe your mouth, Dad."

He takes it and wipes his mouth with a big swipe, much like a child would.

251

"Dad, Jessop's roses aren't on your property. Your property line is marked by the lilac bushes. The ones you and I planted. Remember?"

"He didn't have to holler. Hells bells! It wasn't my fault."

"Jessop *hollered* at you?" I raise my eyebrows. Jessop and his wife, Lori, have been good neighbors to my parents. Both are retired schoolteachers, a little older than Oscar and me. They've lived next door for twenty-five years. They raised three children in their house and now it will soon be filled with the laughter of grandchildren. Their daughter just had their first grandson. "He hollered? Really, Dad? That doesn't sound like Jessop."

"I don't want to talk about it." Dad narrows his gaze, frowning. "I'm hungry. Bethie ordered pizza. It should have been here by now. I don't think I should have to pay for pizza that's delivered late. And cold," he adds. "Ought to be free."

"The pizza's already here. I'll get you some in a minute." I look up at him. "How did you get the lawnmower started, Dad?"

"Damn wire was detached. Don't know why it took me so long to figure it out. Reconnected it." He gestures upward with his hand. "Started right up."

I make a mental note to ask Oscar to disable the mower in a more permanent way. I wanted my father to sell it, or buy it from him. It's one of those nice zero-degree-turn mowers and only two years old. I'd love to replace our old lawn tractor. Our house is on an acre and a half and I mow about an acre. It would cut down on my mowing time. But Dad absolutely refused to sell it to me or anyone else. Even after he agreed that it was nice having the service do it because he knew he couldn't keep it up any longer. Not the way he liked it. He was always particular about his lawn. He and Jessop used to have some kind of competition going every summer about whose diagonal lines in the freshly cut lawn were the straightest.

"You were upset about Jessop, so you decided to go for a walk?" I ask. "And you forgot to tell Mom?"

"I didn't forget anything." He starts the game again. "She's not my mother. I don't have to have her permission to use the little boys' room."

"It's not about permission, Dad. It's about being respectful of other people in the house. She was worried about you. We all were." In the family room, the TV has gone to commercial. I expected Mom to come into the kitchen to say hello, but she's probably so annoyed with Dad that she doesn't want to be in the same room with him. Sometimes she just needs a break, which I understand. I can only imagine what it's like to be here all the time with him, especially on days when she's feeling bad and in pain. "You can't just walk out of the house without telling Mom."

"She wasn't worried about me. I think she wants a divorce."

That makes me smile. And I feel a tenderness toward him. My parents have always adored each other. Seeing them at odds like this is hard. "Dad, Mom doesn't want a divorce."

"She said she wants a divorce. That's why I went for a walk. So she could cool down. I don't want a divorce. Divorces are expensive. Once I pay out, I'll be living in a motel."

I hear Oscar's voice in the family room. I can't make out what he's saying above the volume of the TV. Mom's always complaining that Dad likes the TV too loud, but she likes it pretty loud, too. Oscar says he's going to start bringing earplugs when he comes over, for fear he's damaging his eardrums.

"So . . . what happened with your pants,

Dad?" I ask, unable to resist the question that's been burning in my mind since Maureen called me hours ago.

"What are you talking about?" He's annoyed with me again, now. Too many questions. He tells me all the time that I ask him too many questions. That we all do.

"When Beth and Hazel found you, you weren't wearing pants. You were just in your boxers."

"I'm wearing pants," he declares, the candies on his iPad exploding on the screen.

"Dad." I use that gentle tone again. "When Beth found you at the bookstore —"

"They have coffee now, you know," he interrupts. "Fancy coffees. The kind you girls like. Bethie bought one for Hazel." He motions with his hand in dismissal. "I just ordered it black. Free, the nice girl with the earring in her nose told me at the cash register. Black coffee is free to anyone seventy-five or older. I think that's nice. I'm sure if I start going every day they'll put the price up. God's bones, I'm not paying four-fifty for a cup of coffee."

"Dad, you were wearing a blanket around your waist when Beth and Hazel came to the bookstore to pick you up. A blanket someone gave you at the bookstore. And no pants."

He frowns and looks at me. "I was?" He thinks for a minute. "Was I wearing shoes?"

I nod. "Your Bean boots. And your coat. But no pants, Daddy. Just your undershorts."

His face colors and he looks down at his iPad. "I suppose Bethie told you that." He starts a new game of Candy Crush. "I know she's my daughter and I shouldn't say things like this, but, Liv, she's not always truthful. Remember when she had that accident with her mother's car and she told us someone ran into her in the parking lot? Come to find out, she was in Connecticut and she'd been drinking beer when she hit someone else in a parking lot. That one cost us a pretty penny. Lucky we didn't get sued."

What's interesting about this story, which is entirely accurate, is that it took place about five years ago. Not when my sister was sixteen when one would expect such shenanigans. I'm also fascinated that he can remember those details, but forget his pants.

I press my lips together. "Dad, you can't leave the house without telling Mom. It's not safe."

"I can take care of myself."

"Dad, you know you've been having some problems with your memory. We were afraid

256

you didn't know how to get home and we didn't know where you were."

"I know where the tarnation I live," he grumbles as Oscar walks into the kitchen. "Been living here nearly five decades."

I look up at Oscar. He's still in his scrubs; he looks tired. The skin beneath his eyes is puffy and the lines around his mouth defined. "Hey," I say, taking care with my tone.

"Hey," he answers. As he walks behind me, he draws his hand across my shoulder blades. "I ordered pizza. I hope that's okay. I didn't see anything in the refrigerator that would be easy to make them for dinner."

"Ah, yeah, sure." I rise from my chair. "I thought Beth ordered it."

"I got here forty-five minutes, maybe an hour, ago. She'd already gone home. Hazel was gone, too. She texted, said she'd see us later back at the house. Something about Beth needing to get home for a hot date."

I look up at him. I still think he's handsome, even with the little bit of chubbiness I see in his face. I have this impulse to lift up on my toes and kiss him. Somehow, over the last few months, we've gotten out of the habit of kissing hello and good-bye. I don't kiss him. I just stand there, close enough for us to touch, but not touching.

"Your mom's lying down on the couch."

257

Oscar hooks his thumb in the direction of the family room.

"She okay?"

He purses his lips and nods. "I told her to go ahead and increase the pain meds. Give her doc a call tomorrow. Maybe make an appointment to reevaluate. Just for bad days."

"He okay?" I nod my head in my dad's direction. He's staring intently at his game, sliding the candy pieces across the grid.

"Fine." Oscar goes over to the counter and lifts the lid off the pizza box. "Okay if I grab a slice for the road, Ed?" he asks as he takes one.

It's veggie: mushrooms, peppers, onions, black olives, and pieces of fried eggplant. My favorite. I wish Oscar had ordered one for us for dinner. I didn't take anything out of the freezer. We'll probably have omelets. Second time this week.

"You leaving?" I ask Oscar.

He nods.

I rest a hand on my hip. "You get off early?"

"Hazel called me about your dad." He shrugs. "Things were slow. I thought I'd come over and check on him. Find him a pair of pants." He cracks a smile.

I laugh and lay my hand on his chest. And

then I kiss him, not caring that he has a mouth full of pizza.

"Mm," Oscar says, kissing me back. "What's that for?"

It's my turn to shrug. "I can't just kiss you? There has to be a reason?"

He looks down at me, cocking one eyebrow.

"Thanks for leaving work early to check on them."

"You're welcome." He leans down and kisses me again and then, taking a bite of the pizza, calls over his shoulder, "Behave yourself, Ed. Keep your pants on."

I smile. Oscar and my dad have always had a good relationship. And Oscar has been able to get away with teasing him in a way we can't.

"*Ayuh,*" my father responds, raising one hand but not looking up.

"I'm right behind you," I tell Oscar as he walks toward the door. "I just want to say hi to Mom."

"She took her dose of painkiller a little early, so she might be sleepy."

"Should I be worried?" I ask him.

He stops in the doorway, taking a bite of the pizza. Chewing. "Nah, she'll be fine." He winks at me. "See you at home, sweetie."

*Sweetie.* I smile. He hasn't called me that

259

in ages. So maybe the creamer incident has blown over?

I turn to my dad as Oscar goes out the back door. Things seem pretty good between Oscar and me, good enough for me to want to get home to be with him. Maybe to talk. But not about Hazel and the baby. About something else, anything else. I want to tell him about my day and the mantelpiece in the bed of my pickup. I want to tell him I miss him, because I do. "You want your dinner now, Dad? I can get you a slice of pizza and your Sprite." He likes lemon-lime soda with pizza.

He shakes his head. "I'm winning. I'll get it myself."

"You said you were hungry. You were wondering where the pizza was."

"We don't eat until six. I don't know why your sister ordered it so early."

I don't tell him that he and Mom eat at five on the days they eat alone or that Oscar ordered the pizza. I walk down the hallway in the direction of the deafening sound of the local news. I find my mother lying on the couch, staring at the TV. Her Siamese cat is on her lap.

I lean down and kiss her cheek, something I don't do often.

"Whatever you've got to say, I don't want

to hear it." She holds up her hand to me as if fending me off.

"What?" I pull back, trying not to feel rejected by my mother.

"Liv, I don't want to hear it. First your sister, then your husband. This isn't a jail. I can't be responsible for your father every minute of the day. I can't do it. I won't do it." She crosses her arms over her chest, thrusting out her chin.

"First my sister and then Oscar *what*?" On the TV, someone is interviewing a park ranger from Lake Sebago. Apparently there's been an abundance of Canada geese on the state roads and visitors to the park are being warned to watch for them. And I suppose not run over them.

"The lecture. I don't want the lecture." Again, she holds up her hand to me that's tiny and shriveled.

"Oscar *lectured* you?" My hackles go up. "About Dad?"

"He most certainly did. He told me we got lucky this time. But that your father could have been seriously injured. Oscar said I needed to keep a better eye on him. That if he'd wandered out of town and into the woods, he could have died from exposure." She blows a raspberry, which might have been funny in other circumstances. It's not my mother's style to blow raspberries. She's a woman who wears pearls to the recycling center where she takes her booze bottles. I wonder if it's the higher dose of pain medication making her behave like this. She usually never has anything bad to say about Oscar, either. She adores Oscar. Always has. I can't remember a time when she adored me.

You would have thought that a woman who was told she was unable to bear children would have doted on the baby she adopted. You would think she would have spoiled the toddler who, at the time, she assumed would be her only child. But anyone who thought that would have been wrong. When I was growing up, my mother never acted as if she even liked me all that much. That's not to say that she mistreated me. She didn't. I always had the same clothes, the same toys, and later the same blue jeans and prom dress every other girl my age I knew had. I had braces, music lessons, weeks away at camp. I had all the things a woman of her socioeconomic means could provide a child. And I knew she loved me, but she never adored me. Not the way she adored my late-coming-to-the-scene sister. My mother didn't just love Beth, she adored her. Her face lit up when my sister walked into the room.

It was the same with Oscar. The first time I ever brought him to dinner to meet my parents, my mother laughed at his jokes, teased him, and asked him questions she'd never asked me like where he saw himself in five years. She complimented him on his sweater and the wine he chose. It was always that way from there on out. She wanted to know what Oscar was doing, when she and my dad would see him again. She always seemed happier to see Oscar than me. She always smiled at him in a way that she never smiled at me.

My mother says something, and I blink. "Sorry?"

"I said it's only going down into the forties at night," my mother quips. "I doubt he'd have frozen to death."

I set my jaw. I can't believe Oscar gave my mother crap about this thing with my dad. How dare he. And today of all days, when he knew Mom was having a bad day.

"I'm sorry, Mom. Oscar had no right to —"

"Oh, he's right," she interrupts sourly. "Ed's my responsibility. In sickness and in health. That's what I vowed before God. I know that. I just wanted to lie down for a few minutes. How did I know he was going to take off?" She lifts the patchwork quilt laying over her and draws it up to her chin. "Oscar says he can install some kind of alarms on the doors that will beep when your father opens them." She sighs heavily. "So, we'll put alarms on the doors. Then what? The windows? Next thing you know, you'll want me to chain him to the bed."

I stand there for a minute, staring at the TV. The temperature is expected to drop significantly over the weekend and they're calling for snow flurries on Sunday. I'm glad I got the cement pad poured in the Anselins' barn earlier in the week because freezing temperatures don't bode well for curing concrete.

"What are we going to do when he gets worse, Liv?" Her voice is suddenly full of emotion. "Because you and I both know it's going to get worse."

"I don't know what we're going to do, Mom." I use the same gentle tone I used with my dad. "We'll come up with a plan. But you don't need to worry about this tonight. Tonight, you should rest. Would you like some pizza?"

"Nope. Just going to lie here for a little while. Your father still in the kitchen?"

I look down at her. She looks old, and weary, but still so beautiful. My father

264

always said she was the most beautiful girl he'd ever met and that was why he married her. "He is. Playing Candy Crush."

"You may as well go home and make yourself some dinner." She shoos me away with her hand. "We'll have our pizza in here and watch *Family Feud*. It comes on at six. You father still likes if I put it on for him. He can always name a category or two that actually makes sense."

"You don't want me to stay?"

She makes a face of disgust. I feel as if she's angry with me. Why would she be angry with me? I was a state away when Dad took off. I didn't have anything to do with Oscar reprimanding her.

"Why would you stay?" she asks. "He won't go again tonight. I guarantee you that. I imagine he's worn out walking all the way into town to the bookstore. He bought a hunting magazine. I suppose he's going to take up moose hunting now."

I don't know how to respond to that so I just stand there for a minute, looking at the TV. I look back at her. "If you're sure you'll be okay, I guess I will go home." Go home and ask Oscar what the hell he was thinking, lecturing my mother on her responsibility to my father. About anything. I can't believe he'd do such a thing. It's so not like him.

"Good night, Liv." She glances up at me, then back at the TV. "Hazel's the one who found him. She was the one who was worried about him, not your sister. She's a good girl, that Hazel. I don't think you have to worry about her."

Don't have to worry about her? My sixteen-year-old daughter, who's pregnant? But I don't say it. My mother has enough problems right there in the kitchen playing Candy Crush. She doesn't need me to pile mine on top of her. "Call me before you go to bed?"

*"Ayuh."* Her gaze is fixed on the TV.

In the kitchen, I say good-bye to my dad, getting less response than from Mom, and then I head home. Five minutes from the house, I spot Oscar's car at the gas pumps at the Cumberland Farms mini-mart. I don't know what gets into me, but I wheel into the parking lot and pull up right behind him. He's leaning against his car, talking to a guy on the other side of the gas pump as they both fill their tanks.

I'm pretty sure I slam my truck door.

When Oscar sees me, he's startled. "Everything okay?"

The tall, slender man Oscar was talking to

has finished pumping his gas and is screwing on his gas tank lid. "Good to see you, doc."

Oscar glances at him. "You too." He returns his gaze to me, resting his hand on the nozzle still in his gas tank. "What's up? Everything okay?"

"*Okay?*" I ask, marching up to him. "Is everything *okay?*"

The guy hops into his car and closes the door. I'm guessing he's heard the same tone of voice from his own wife at some point and just wants to get out of Dodge.

"What did you say to my mother?" I demand.

"What?" Now he's got *tone.*

"What did you say to my mother?" I repeat. "About Dad? You upset her."

He twists his mouth one way and then the other the way he does when he's trying to decide whether or not to engage with me or back down. The gas pump clicks off and he yanks the nozzle from his gas tank and places it back in its cradle on the pump. "What did I say to her? I told her we got lucky. That the whole thing with your dad could have turned out much differently. I told her she was going to have to keep a closer eye on him." He shrugged. "Liv, if he'd gotten lost, or wandered into the woods —"

"How dare you," I interrupt. "How dare you speak to my mother that way." A young woman with a streak of snow-white hair falling over her cheek two gas pumps over looks in our direction. I don't care.

Oscar screws on the gas cap and slaps the cover closed. "Speak to her what way?" He's getting loud now.

I still don't care. "She's sick, Oscar."

"I know she's sick." He takes a step toward me. "That doesn't change the fact that things are going to have to be done to prevent your dad from wandering away like this. It's not the first time it's happened."

I shake my head. "What do you mean?" I shrug. "He's gone down to see Mr. Dugan to have a cup of coffee a couple of times without telling her."

"I'm not talking about him staying too long for coffee with Mr. Dugan. Two weeks ago, Bernice called me on a Saturday morning. She couldn't find your dad."

I screw up my face, wanting to accuse him of making this up. Of course, I know better. To my knowledge, Oscar has never lied to me or anyone else in his life. Not unless you count telling your children there's an Easter Bunny and a guy in a red suit who comes down your chimney to give gifts every December twenty-fifth. "Where was I?" I ask, spreading my arms wide.

"At the Anselins'. Where I think you spend more time than you spend at home."

"That's not fair, Oscar. It's not true and it's not fair. And how is me being at the Anselins' any different from you being at the hospital?!"

He cuts his eyes at me. I know it's on the tip of his tongue to say something along the lines of, "It's work. It's how I pay the bills." Lucky for him, he catches himself.

"Where was he?"

"What?"

"Dad. You said Mom called you two weeks ago. Dad was missing."

"He was down the street in someone's garage. Someone your parents don't know. Trying to start their lawnmower."

My heart suddenly feels heavy. I think about what Mom said about the fact this was only going to get worse with Dad. It's already worse, I just wasn't in the loop. But I don't say any of that because that's not what we're talking about. Right now, we're talking about Oscar and what he said to my mother.

"You had no right to tell my mother that it was her fault Dad got lost, walked away" — I make a sweeping gesture with my hand

— "whatever the hell it is that happened. They are not your parents. They're mine."

"Oh, Liv, we are not going there." He shakes his head slowly. He's so angry that his face is red. "I have been a son to your parents for as long as you can remember. I love Ed and Bernice like they were my mom and dad." He points at me. "And you damned well know it."

"It wasn't your place to say that to her."

"It wasn't my place to be honest?" He cocks his head. "Because someone needs to be. And who is that going to be? Your sister has no idea what's going on in that house." He's pointing again. "You know, but you're in denial."

"I am *not* in denial." I want to grab his pointing hand and fling it.

"All the signs are there, Liv. They're there and you know it: loss not just of memory but logical thinking, loss of muscle tone, confusion in doing ordinary things." He's ticking them off the fingers of one hand.

"The neurologist said —"

"I don't give a shit what the neurologist said! You know your dad. I know him and he's got dementia. And he's got no organic reason for it, no Parkinson's, no Huntington's disease, and he hasn't had a stroke." He's doing that counting thing again.

"It's not my mother's fault he walked away." My voice is beginning to waver. I feel like I'm going to burst into tears and I glance away. The girl who was watching us drives by in her car, still staring at us. Someone else has pulled into her spot at the pump and she's now looking at us with equal interest. She's wearing scrubs, which makes me wonder if Oscar knows her. I wouldn't want anyone carrying tales back to the hospital. I don't want Oscar to be the topic of discussion at the coffeepot in the morning.

"It's not her fault," I repeat, the fight gone out of me. A sense of guilt washes over me. I think Cricket is the trashy one, but here I am shouting at my husband in the Cumberland Farms parking lot.

"I didn't say it was her fault." He gentles his tone. "But he is her responsibility, Liv. And she's going to have to make changes. Changes to keep him safe. So he won't have to go to a care facility."

I cross my arms over my chest. All of a sudden, I'm cold. I'm wearing a new hoodie I bought from the bookstore when I dropped Sean off. But the temperature is beginning to fall and the wind has picked up. My coat's in the car, but I don't plan on standing at this gas pump arguing with my husband long enough to get my coat out of the cab of my truck.

"We're not sending my dad to a nursing home."

Oscar throws his hands up in the air, his tone hardening again. "No one said anything about a f—" He cuts himself off, looking away.

He's so angry with me. As angry as I am with him. And it hurts. It hurts me and I can tell by the look on his face that it hurts him.

When Oscar meets my gaze again, he says, "Liv, I'm not talking about a nursing home and you know it." His voice is calm now. Controlled. "I'm talking about doing some things to keep your dad safe. Just alarms on the doors will make a huge difference. Then at least your mom will know when he's left the house."

I'm still hugging myself. I look down at the blacktop. It's stained with oil or gas.

"I didn't mean to upset your mom, Liv" — his voice cracks — "I was worried when Hazel called me."

"She shouldn't have called you at work."

"You're right. She shouldn't have."

I look up at him, surprised he would agree with me about anything.

"*You* should have called me, Liv. You

272

should have been the one. I'm *your* hus-band."

There's emotion in his voice, anger for certain, but pain, too. I slowly lift my gaze and am surprised to see the pain in his face.

"What's going on here, Liv?" he says quietly. "With us. Since this thing with Hazel, I don't know what to say to you, what to do to make you happy."

My lower lip quivers.

"I know this isn't what you want for Hazel. But it's how things are."

Then he puts his arms out to me and as angry as I am with him right now, I go to him. I let him close me in his arms and I wrap mine around his waist.

He holds me tightly and kisses the top of my head. "I feel so far away from you," he says into my hair. "I wish I knew how to bring you back."

"I know," I whisper, squeezing my eyes shut to keep from crying. And I wish I knew how to bring myself back.

# 18
## HAZEL

"You wanna come over to my house?" I ask Tyler, chewing on the cuticle on my thumb. "We could work on your paper for history or something." I glance at him.

We're parked at a convenience store. He had to get cigarettes. I'm sitting beside him in the front seat of his new pickup truck. Well, new to him. It's thirteen years old, a Chevy Silverado. Blue, except for the passenger door, which must have been replaced because it's red. The truck needs a new exhaust system and muffler, but that's all stuff he can do at his uncle's when he gets the money for the parts. And it's why he got such a good deal on it.

Tyler came by for me about an hour ago, picked me up at the end of my driveway, and took me for a ride so I could check out the new truck. I'm sure I'll hear about that from Mom later. Luckily she was on the phone with Sean when I left. I waited until

274

I went out the door to text her and tell her I'd be home later. She texted me back, but I didn't read it because whatever she says, I'm sure it will piss me off.

"It's due in two days," I say when he doesn't respond. This is his second time taking history and we have the same teacher, just not the same class period. "You said you haven't started it."

The topic for our paper is completely open as long as it's related to Thanksgiving, which I think is a cool assignment. Mine is on why having turkey on Thanksgiving is a form of animal abuse. I totally eat turkey. Mom orders ours from a local farm every year: antibiotic and hormone-free and raised free range. But I still thought the topic was a good one. It makes you think about buying a grocery store turkey. Or really any poultry from a grocery store because the way most are raised is barbaric. Besides, I like riling people up with facts.

Tyler shrugs his shoulders. He's reading a text, but he got one of those things on his screen to keep his mom from seeing his texts so I can't see what he's reading or who is texting him.

He starts texting back. "I can turn it in late." He doesn't look at me.

"No, you can't." Now my thumb is bleeding. I suck on it. "It's due Wednesday. Then it's Turkey Day vacation. You lose ten points per day you're late. You'll fail if you don't turn it in before we get back Monday."

"I'll date it Wednesday. He said it has to be electronically submitted. He's doing that stupid plagiarism thingy now where he runs them all through a checker."

I want to say "because of people like you copying from Wikipedia." But I don't because we already had a fight today. It was stupid. I thought he said he'd see me at lunch at school. He said he told me he *wouldn't* see me because he had to take a makeup quiz. It was my fault I didn't listen. And my fault because I was being a total bitch.

"Ty," I groan because I don't think he's dumb. I really don't. But sometimes he says the dumbest things. "It'll be time-stamped when you submit it. Mr. Gaines will know you sent it Sunday night."

"Whatever," he mutters, continuing to text.

I look out the window at the car parked next to us. Some lady has just opened a can of Coke and is handing it to her kid in the backseat. I wonder if she knows there are thirty-nine grams of sugar in one can. That's almost ten teaspoons! I know that because

276

Dad was on a Coke kick for a while. He said he was trying to cut back on coffee at work because it was making him jittery. He wanted some caffeine, but not as much as he'd been consuming. His solution was Coca-Cola. I finally convinced him that while the coffee wasn't great for him, the soda was worse because of how much sugar was in it. He couldn't drink enough of that nasty creamer to get that much sugar in his coffee. What I really wanted to tell him was that he wouldn't be so dopey in the morning if he lost a few pounds and got some exercise. I wanted to talk to him about it, but Mom said it would probably be better to keep that to myself. She reminded me that he was in the medical profession. That he already knew the impediments of being overweight and he'd come to the conclusion to lose weight on his own eventually. I got the feeling she'd already tried to talk with him about it and it hadn't gone too well.

I look away from the little boy guzzling the Coke because I can't stand to even think about it. Excess sugar in kids' diets doesn't just cause tooth decay. It causes obesity, high blood pressure, high LDL, and low HDL. That's just a metabolic nightmare waiting to happen.

I look at Tyler. We've been sitting here for

at least ten minutes. "So . . . what do you want to do?" It comes out sounding whiny, even though I don't do it intentionally. I'm feeling sick to my stomach. I'm not sure if there are actual exhaust fumes leaking into the cab because the engine is running, or if I'm imagining them.

Exhaust fumes are full of poisons, and not just carbon monoxide. There's sulfur dioxide, nitrogen oxides, formaldehyde, and other crap I can't remember. I know because I looked it up when Tyler told me he was going to buy the pickup, but that it needed some work on the exhaust system. Also, on the heater. I'm wearing Dad's Columbia coat, zipped up, because I'm too fat to wear my own coat now. I'm thinking about getting my gloves out of the pockets.

I've got my window down a crack to lower the chances that Tyler's poisoning me and his baby right now with this great deal he got on a truck.

He doesn't answer.

"We could go to your house," I suggest. Which is really just code for *You wanna have sex?* I don't really want to have sex with him. It makes me feel like I'm going to pee on him because the baby's sitting right on my bladder, but whatever. Or maybe he'd be satisfied with a BJ. And at least if we were

278

sitting in his parents' living room we wouldn't be getting poisoned with carbon monoxide or freezing to death.

"Ty." I lay my hand on his arm.

"What?"

He kind of shakes me off. He doesn't hurt me, but it pisses me off.

Actually, I've been pissed at him all week. He didn't get me a birthday present. He said he was going to get me something when he got paid again. That everything he'd saved went into the down payment on the truck. But he didn't get me a birthday card from the dollar store, either. Or make me a freakin' origami pickup truck from a page of homework. When we first started talking, he made me a couple of origami things: a dog, a loon, a box he put some M&M's in. I still have them on a dresser in my bedroom. He wasn't great at making them; they're a little lopsided. But it was so sweet of him to try.

Tyler didn't even tell me happy birthday until Katy pulled him aside in the hall after lunch and told him he was an asshole and a dickwad. Which she and I laughed about later because really, she could have picked one or the other, right?

"Who are you texting?" I ask, looking at his phone in his hand.

"No one."

I point at his phone. "I see you texting."

He crams his phone into his Carhartt canvas coat pocket and throws the truck in reverse.

"Where are we going?"

He pulls out in front of a car and I hear a beep from behind us. I instantly lay my hand on my big belly. I'm beginning to wonder if I'm going to be able to let Tyler drive our baby around. A car seat provides a lot of protection. I've been doing a lot of research because that's what I want for Christmas. But even with the infant car seat with the highest safety rating, obviously, you don't want to get into an accident with your baby. Tyler's going to have to start driving more responsibly. Acting more responsibly if he thinks he's going to get to drive his son around.

"Guess I'll take you home," he mumbles. "My uncle said I can work for an hour or two tonight. After my cousins get off. I'll take you home."

I look at him. "I thought we were going to hang out."

"You said you want me to make money." His tone is mean. "You keep telling me you want me to buy diapers and shit."

I stare at him. He's trying to grow a

280

mustache, but right now it doesn't look great because it's sparse. It kind of looks like pubic hair above his upper lip. I feel like telling him so because he's being such a dickwad. "For our baby. Your baby. It's not fair to expect my parents to pay for everything."

"Why not? They're rich." He hits the gas pedal and races through a yellow light.

I look out the window. It's almost dark out even though it's only four o'clock. I love summers in Maine, but the winters are cold and dark and dreary. And it's already snowed twice this week and we're expecting snow on Thanksgiving.

"They're not rich," I say quietly. There's no way I'm getting into this conversation with him again, not when we just had it last week. All I asked him was if he wanted to talk to his parents about buying the baby's crib since my parents were getting the car seat and the good ones cost more than a crib. He got all pissy with me and said he wasn't asking his mom and stepdad to buy anything.

I stare out the window as he turns onto my road. I guess he really is going to take me home. Fine. I don't want to be with him if he doesn't want to be with me.

A lump comes up in my throat and not

the acid reflux kind. I feel like I could cry. I lean my cheek against the glass of the window and stare out. The wind is whistling over my head where it's coming through the crack, making me even colder. I'm glad Tyler is taking me home. I don't want to ride around with him in his stupid truck anyway. It's a death trap. He told me about the exhaust problem, but what about the squeaky brakes? I'm no car expert, but that sound has to mean something and I bet it doesn't mean everything is A-OK.

"You coming to Thanksgiving?" I ask him. "At the cottage. My aunt and uncle and their families will be there. And Aunt Beth is bringing Gran and Granddad. Unless Granddad's colitis is acting up again." That was what happened last year. Gran said it was because he ate a bunch of nuts the night before after she told him not to.

"Nah." Tyler doesn't look at me. "Going to Sebago. Uncle Benny's."

"I thought you said he wasn't talking to your mom because of what J.J. said about your uncle's ex-wife." I feel bad for Tyler. Every holiday, there's always a big fight with someone in his family. He says it's been that way as long as he can remember. Even when he was a little kid he remembered his family fighting. Like sometimes they hit each other.

One year, they drove to New Hampshire for Christmas dinner and turned around and came all the way back before they even got to eat.

He shrugs. "Mom's working till noon, then we're going."

"And J.J's going?" I only ask because on Fourth of July Ty's stepfather got drunk at some other relative of Cricket's and somebody called the cops and Cricket said she wasn't taking him to any family dinners anymore.

"I guess." His phone dings in his pocket. Another text. "I don't know," he says. "Why are you asking me all these questions?"

I cross my arms over my chest. "Just leave me at the end of my driveway."

"What?" He looks at me and makes a face. "No. It's cold. And getting dark," he adds, clearly pissed at me. "I don't care if your mom sees me. I don't care what she thinks."

I'm pretty sure I hear him say *bitch* under his breath. I'm not sure if he's saying my mom is a bitch or I am. Right this minute, it could be appropriate for either one of us. I still don't like it. But I don't call him on it. Instead, I say, "I don't care what she thinks, either. I'm saying let me off in the driveway because that's what I want you to do."

283

His phone dings again. Who the heck is texting him? His friend Rob lost his phone yesterday riding dirt bikes somewhere. He can't be texting him.

"Fine," he says, taking the curve just before our house a little too fast.

"Fine," I repeat, grabbing the seat, being all dramatic about it.

Tyler doesn't slam on the brakes, but probably mostly because his brakes are crappy and he can't. The truck is still rocking on its bad shocks when I unbuckle my seat belt and shove open the door.

I get out. I don't say anything. He doesn't say anything. I want to turn around and yell something at him. But I don't know what I want to say, so I just slam the door. I hear him tear off, the truck sliding on the snow that's blown onto the road.

Mom's in the dining room folding laundry on the table when I walk inside. I'm shivering, but I don't know if it's because I'm cold from the walk up the driveway or because I'm so upset. She looks at me as I stomp across the dining room, headed for the stairs.

"You okay?" she asks, one of my dad's scrubs tops in her hands.

Willie Nelson is lying on the floor between the kitchen and dining room area. He picks up his big head and stares at me.

"I have to pee," I say, like it's somehow Mom's fault. "Again!"

I stomp up the stairs, down the hall, and into the bathroom that I have all to myself now. I barely make it to the toilet and sit down hard, exhaling with relief as a bucket of pee runs out of me. My baby is now around the size of an eggplant, but he feels like an elephant when he's sitting on my bladder. As if he knows I'm thinking mean things about him, he rolls and I put my hand on my belly.

I still feel like I could cry. I finish peeing, pull up my old lady stretch pants, and go to the sink to wash my hands. When I look up, I hardly recognize myself in the mirror that Mom made from a big, old picture frame. My face is puffy, I've got a bunch of zits on my chin, and my hair is greasy because I was too tired to get up early enough this morning to take a shower. I used to be pretty. Now I'm ugly and fat and I'm never going to be pretty again.

Tears roll down my cheeks.

By the time I dry my hands, I'm full-out crying. I'm in big trouble, bigger than being pregnant, and I know it. Even though I've been pretending for weeks that I'm not.

But it's becoming pretty clear that I'm

pregnant and I'm alone because Tyler doesn't love me anymore.

I had sex with him because he said he loved me. I know I can't blame my getting pregnant on him because it's my fault, too. I realize that, but he *said* he loved me. He swore he'd always love me. And I made the decision to keep our baby because I knew we could do this together.

But what if there isn't a together anymore? I sure don't feel like we're together.

My back to the sink, I slide down to the floor, flopping my legs out straight because I can hardly cross them anymore, my belly is so big. It's like . . . like a basketball, it's so big. Like I have a basketball under the sweatshirt I stole from Dad's closet. Hugging my basketball belly with my arms, I sob.

I'm an idiot for not seeing it sooner.

Tyler doesn't love me anymore. I know he doesn't.

He hasn't said he doesn't love me, but he hasn't said he does in weeks. And he's been acting like such a jerk. And sneaking around. And I've heard from several people that he's talking to Amanda Peterson. That's probably who he was texting. Katy says he isn't, but what if she's trying to protect me? Or . . . or what if she's just wrong? If he

286

was going to cheat on me with someone, it would be Amanda Peterson for sure. She's got a reputation in school for stealing people's boyfriends. I know she liked him. Her and her friend Christina, both.

I cry louder. I can't make myself stop. I cry big, ugly, wet tears and my nose starts running.

A knock at the bathroom door startles me. I'm about to scream at Sean to take a freakin' hike. But then I remember he isn't here. I remember he'll never live here again, and even though he drove me crazy, I realize I miss him.

I suck in a big, loud sob. Because my brother is gone and we'll never live together again. I'll never be able to steal his no-show socks from the top drawer of his dresser, or lock him out of the bathroom while I sit on the floor reading a book with the shower running.

"Hazel?" It's Mom. "You okay?"

"Go away!"

I sob louder. I can't stop. I cry so hard I feel like I'm going to throw up. Sean said Tyler wouldn't be there for me when the baby was born. Mom said it. Aunt Beth said it.

And almost more than being afraid Tyler

287

doesn't love me anymore, I'm afraid they're right.

"Hazel, hon . . ." Mom says. "Is it okay if I come in?"

I'm crying so hard, I can't even holler again for her to go away. To go shop for tile or go build those people's house or go do whatever it is she's doing all the time when she's not here. Because she's never here anymore. She's never here when I get home from school. She's gone most Saturdays and now she's started going places on Sundays.

"Hazel, I'm coming in. Okay?" There's a pause and the bathroom door slowly opens.

I want to yell at her to leave me alone, but I can't. I don't. And the next thing I know, she's sitting beside me on the bathroom floor, hugging me.

I lean against her, still crying.

She holds me in her arms, rocking me, like she did when I was little. She just lets me cry for another minute or two and then she says, "Hazel, honey, what is it? Can you tell me what's wrong?"

"What . . . what's wrong?" I blubber.

Arm around my shoulder, she pulls me to her. "You and Tyler have another fight?"

I lean over, put my head on her boobs, and close my eyes and hold on to her. She smells so good, like the mom I remember when I was little. Like vanilla, and even though she smells a little bit like sawdust right now, she still smells like my mom.

And I cry harder.

"It's going to be all right," she soothes, rocking me rhythmically. She strokes my dirty hair.

"It's not," I sob. I lift my head off her shoulder to look at her. "How could I have been so stupid, Mom? I'm not stupid. I'm not the kid who does stupid things," I say, putting emphasis on each word. "I'm the one who turns her homework in early and researches running shoes before I buy a pair."

Mom almost looks like she's going to smile, but she doesn't. Maybe because she knows if she does, I'll freak out.

"How could I have gotten pregnant and ruined my life?" I go on. "And ruined some little baby's life and . . ." I hiccup. "How could I have been so stupid?" I say again. "People like me, we . . . we don't do stupid stuff like get pregnant. Not in the second decade of the twenty-first century, not with free access to contraception and our parents' credit cards." I drop my head to her chest, sobbing again.

"Oh, sweetie, you're not stupid," she whispers, pushing back my hair that's all sweaty now and probably snotty. "You just made a mistake, a tiny, little mistake."

"This isn't tiny," I wail, stroking my big belly that makes me feel like I've been kidnapped by an alien or something and now serve as a host body. "Look at it, Mom. Look at me. I'm enormous!"

She sort of laughs, but not like she thinks something is funny. It's the kind of sound you make when you decide you want to laugh instead of cry. "Come here," she says quietly and she helps me rearrange myself so I'm lying in her lap now. She's still stroking my hair.

"You made a mistake, but you're not stupid. We all make mistakes, especially when we're young."

"Not you. You never made mistakes. Granddad told me you were the best kid ever." I sniff and wipe my nose on Dad's sweatshirt I'm wearing. "He said you always did what you were supposed to. You got good grades, you never came home past curfew, and you never smarted back at him and Gran. And he said he wasn't just comparing you to Aunt Beth. He said you were a good kid, a good teenager."

Mom looks like she's going to say something. Then she reaches up and grabs a handful of tissues from a box on the sink and passes them to me.

I blow my nose.

"You want to tell me what's going on?"

I rest my cheek on her shoulder. "I'm fat and ugly."

"You're neither," she says.

"Tyler's not coming to Thanksgiving dinner."

"I'm sorry to hear that."

I know she's not, but it's still kind of nice of her to say it. "He got a truck, but there's something wrong with the exhaust on it. I don't think I should be riding with him."

"He bought a truck?" I can tell she's trying hard to be careful with her tone. Because what she really means is how does he have money to buy a truck when he's supposed to be saving money to help with the baby.

"Yeah, but I don't care about the stupid truck. I don't think he likes me anymore."

"What makes you say that?"

I roll over so I can look up at her. The floor is toasty warm because when Mom tiled it herself, she put this big heating-pad thing under it so the whole thing is heated. It's on a timer so it comes on every morning before I get up for my shower and then again late in the day so it's warm in the evening. "He never wants to do anything with me anymore. I hardly ever see him at school and when I do he's . . . I don't know. Weird."

She's still stroking my hair. "You talk to him about it?"

I meet her gaze. "Talk to *Tyler* about it?" I don't know why or how it's even possible, but I laugh. And then Mom laughs. And then we sit there on the bathroom floor for a long time talking about stuff, not Tyler stuff, just stuff like something Mom heard on NPR that she thought I'd be interested in and what kind of Christmas cookies we're going to make this year. And we stay there on the floor until Dad gets home and we hear him yell up the stairs.

"Liv? Hazel? You guys up there?"

Mom and I start laughing. I don't know why. But it feels good and it makes me feel like maybe everything will be okay.

# 19
## LIV

I turn the burner on under the pot of potatoes and reach for my glass of wine. I hear Oscar's brother, Joe, shouting, "Child! Child!" from the family room.

"Boy!" yells their sister.

"Boy child," hollers Joe and there's raucous laughter.

They're playing charades: Oscar, and his siblings and all of our children while I finish preparing our Thanksgiving dinner. Even my parents have joined in the game. Dad isn't actually *playing,* but I hear him chuckling, which means he's engaged. I feel as if he's better mentally when he's engaged with others. And my mother won the last round. She's having a good day, feeling decent. She arrived dressed in a skirt and sweater and knee-high boots and didn't need her wheelchair. I think she misses the old days when holidays were big in our house. She and Dad entertained often and they served many a cocktail in their home. While we didn't have many relatives, my parents had a lot of friends. No one who knew Ed and Bernice Cosset ever had to spend a Christmas or a Thanksgiving, or even a Saint Paddy's Day, alone.

The sound of the laughter makes me smile, but also thankful I'm not in the middle of it. After spending a fun couple of hours peeling potatoes, chopping veggies for stuffing, and making a homemade version of green bean casserole with different family members, I was relieved when Marie suggested they move to the family room and play a game while the turkey finished roasting. I genuinely enjoy cooking and I've been so busy working this week at the Anselin farm that being alone in the relative peace of the warm kitchen to gather my thoughts and catch my breath is nice.

I set the lid on the potato pot with one hand and sip my Malbec with the other.

"Mm, smells good in here."

I turn to see Oscar coming into the kitchen, a glass in each hand. "Marie likes the wine. Wants to know what box it came out of. And she needs a refill." He raises the stemmed wineglass high.

I smile and take it from him. Marie makes fun of my selections of wine. She buys bottles that cost forty dollars, but she can afford it; her husband, Sai, is a plastic surgeon. I see no reason to spend that much on wine, even if I had it. I doubt I'd be able to taste the difference between the eight-dollar bottle of wine and one costing five times that. The funny thing is that Marie admits my boxed wine is pretty damned good; she just can't bring herself to buy it.

"I'll get the wine," I tell Oscar.

"And your dad wants another Old Fashioned." He holds up the 1960s-style rocks glass that probably *is* from the 1960s. A remnant of Oscar's parents' possessions. Like my parents, they were seriously into their cocktails. Think *Mad Men* on a Friday night; that was the Ridgelys.

"Think it's okay?" He holds up the glass. "To make your dad another?"

"Sure. He's not driving the lawnmower home, right?"

We both laugh and Oscar surprises me by reaching out and catching my hand. "Hey, you look beautiful today." He pulls me toward him.

I know I frown, looking down at my jeans, V-neck sweater, and the old sheepskin boots I wear indoors in the winter. "I do?" But then I smile, looking up at him. "Thank you."

He takes Marie's wineglass from my hand and sets it on the counter. "You're welcome. I like you in that color blue." He wraps his arms around me and kisses me on the lips. I find myself closing my eyes. He tastes like Shipyard beer and the Oscar I knew of yore. His kiss is familiar, yet somehow excitingly unfamiliar. It's been that long.

I laugh when I open my eyes, feeling a little giddy. It's been some time since he's kissed me like that, in a way other than perfunctory. It's been more than a month since we had sex and, even then, there wasn't much in the way of kissing. Just right down to business. And while it was nice, I realize I miss the kissing. I miss the closeness I feel when we kiss. When we look into each other's eyes like this.

"Oh yeah?" I say, playfully. "You like this sweater that's a million years old?"

"I like *you* in this sweater that's a million years old."

Laughter drifts into the kitchen from the family room, but I feel insulated from what's going on in the other room. It's just Oscar and me here. And it's nice.

He kisses me again, this time longer. Tenderly, and when he finally takes his lips from mine, I actually feel breathless. A little dizzy.

"You drunk?" I ask, looking up at him, into his gorgeous eyes that I've missed.

He laughs. "Nope. I just . . ." He pulls me against his chest and I can feel his breath as his chest moves. "I miss you," he says in my ear.

"I've missed you," I whisper back, afraid to look up at him, fearing I'll tear up. It's been a hell of a fall.

"I miss *us,* Liv."

We just stand there in each other's arms and I try to enjoy his embrace, the scent of him, the sound of his breath, and not let my thoughts get away from me. Because the first thing that comes to my mind when he tells me he misses us, meaning the way we used to be, is to tell him that he's brought about this distance between us by taking sides with Hazel against me about the baby. But it's Thanksgiving, and time for family unity and not arguments. And I genuinely want a truce. I need one. At least for today. For the weekend while Sean is here and we can be a family. Before the intrusion of a crying baby and the stink of diapers in the trash.

"What's going on with the kids?" I ask, skirting the reason why it's been so long since we've held each other like this.

He takes a step back, but rests one hand

casually on my waist. "They're fine." He scratches his chin. He's had a few days off in a row so his red beard is unruly, like back in our college days. He wore a beard then, in the days when they weren't cool. "Your dad interrogated Sean for a while about his classes, but our son managed to get away relatively unscathed. He's playing charades."

"I'm surprised. Doesn't he go into withdrawal after a certain number of hours without killing zombies or racing cars?"

Oscar lifts one broad shoulder and lets it fall. "Marie unplugged the TV, so no video games."

We both grin. His sister is quite a character: opinionated, bossy, especially with her brothers. And their kids. She can be overwhelming at times, but her domineering ways can also be useful. Like when we need the boys to do something like reseed the lawn at the cottage or fix a leaky pipe. The boys, meaning her brothers.

"She told him and Lewis they were going to have to hang out with the family and pretend they like it if they want their TV privileges back."

"So, no football today? I thought Joe wanted to see the Ravens game."

A new round of charades has begun in the other room.

"House!"

"House," my dad repeats.

"School!"

"School," my dad says. Apparently he's playing now.

"Present!" Joe's daughter, twelve-year-old McKenzie, shrieks. "It's a present! A birthday present!"

Everyone laughs and I hear my father joining in. It's good to hear his laughter. He's been sullen for days. Another run-in with the neighbor. Dad wants to sell the house now. And move to Amsterdam. He went so far as to call a real estate agent, so then Mom was pissed at him because she had to send the woman away when she appeared on the front step, thinking she had a new client.

"A Christmas present!" Olivia calls. It sounds like she's jumping up and down.

"Those are doors and windows Dad's miming, nitwit," her fifteen-year-old sister, Emma, says.

"Mom! She called me a nitwit," Olivia whines. "No name calling, right?"

I meet Oscar's blue-eyed gaze and we smile, both remembering nostalgically the days when Sean and Hazel called each other names like nitwit and stinky butt. It's funny how in those moments, you don't realize how precious they'll become in your memory.

Oscar lets go of me and goes to the refrigerator for an orange and a jar of maraschino cherries. The makings of a proper Old Fashioned. "The game doesn't start until four thirty. We're recording it. We'll start it after dinner."

Everyone is staying tonight except my parents and Hazel. It was decided she would drive them home after dinner and spend the night with them. My mother doesn't see as well at night as she used to and there's an inch or two of snow in the forecast, so we agreed Hazel would ride to the cottage with us and drive my parents' car back to Judith. She and her friend Katy plan to meet Marie and me tomorrow in Rockland for lunch and a little Christmas shopping.

Hazel's original plan was that she would drop her grandparents off and go home to our house to sleep, but I nixed that. I don't want Tyler in her bed, in my house, on the planet right now. I'm fairly certain he's getting ready to break up with Hazel. He's been acting so weird, even weirder than usual. I think Hazel knows it's coming, too, but I haven't been able to bring myself to ask her about it. She sees the writing on the wall. I just don't think she wants to translate for her mother.

I look at Oscar. "I thought Marie unplugged the TV."

"Metaphorically," he explains.

"Ah." I slide a cutting board across the counter to Oscar and a knife. I'm tempted to ask him if he knows anything about what's going on with Hazel and The Shit, as I have come to acrimoniously call him. Instead, I err on the side of caution and say, "What's Hazel doing? I don't hear her in there."

"My sulky daughter?" He dumps a little super-fine sugar into my dad's glass and then a couple of dashes of bitters. "Sulking. I guess she thought Tyler was possibly coming today?" It's a question.

It feels like that's an invitation to jump into the Tyler conversation, but it seems like Oscar and I can't speak about Hazel and Tyler without getting snippy with each other, so, because he's offered an olive branch, and a couple of pretty nice kisses, I purposely keep my tone light. "He went to Sebago with his parents and stepbrother."

"Probably just as well. Your dad would give him crap about that mustache."

I laugh. There haven't been many sightings of Tyler lately. He's wisely been steering clear of us . . . and also the mother of his child, from what Hazel says. But we saw him at the pizza place in town the other night. We were sitting down to eat; he was picking up pizza. Hazel went over to talk to him at the counter. She said she invited him to join us. By the look on their faces, it didn't seem as if they were having a congenial conversation, but after my talk with Hazel in the bathroom the other day, I'm trying hard to see things from her perspective. And honestly, I'm just sick of the hostility, hers and mine.

I take Marie's wineglass to the end of the counter and fill it from the wine box. Oscar is muddling the bitters in my dad's glass with a little wooden stick that's been in the utensil drawer as long as I've been coming here to the cottage with Oscar.

"She feeling better?" I ask, setting the glass down so he can grab it on his way back to the family room.

Hazel was feeling nauseated earlier in the day. I have a feeling it was the nacho cheese with fresh jalapeños she was digging into when Marie put out snacks, but I've learned to keep my mouth shut about what she eats unless she asks me.

"She seems fine." He adds ice, then bourbon to the glass. "But I'm not asking. She almost took my head off this morning when

I asked her if she really wanted another chocolate chip pancake."

Again, our gazes meet and we both grin because we've both been there with Hazel multiple times over the last few months.

"Hey, Beth *is* coming, right? Your dad keeps saying she's in the bathroom."

I shrug. "She said she was. She's supposed to be bringing homemade cranberry sauce." She'd called me the previous night to confirm, but in the conversation, she mentioned she was on her way out on a date. I can't help wondering if the date turned into a sleepover and she's still asleep in some guy's bed.

He nods thoughtfully. "You want to bet on cans of sauce, or that she's a complete no-show? Five dollars."

I grimace. "I think my money is on a no-show."

"Fine," he says, pretending to be miffed. He points his finger at me. "But I get the no-show bet Christmas Day."

That makes me laugh and this time I'm the one who initiates a kiss. I've missed this banter that used to come so easily between us.

"Mmm," Oscar says against my lips, grabbing one of my butt cheeks. "How do you feel about running upstairs for a quickie?"

I giggle. I actually giggle.

It's something we would have done a long time ago. An afternoon quickie. Back when the kids were little, and we could tell them we were talking about Christmas gifts, locked in our bedroom. Back in the days when we had sex more often. When life seemed simpler. When our seventeen-year-old daughter wasn't going to become a mother herself.

"It's going to have to be pretty quick," I tease. Then I point at the timer on the stove. "Turkey."

Oscar arches a red eyebrow that's beginning to sprout a few gray hairs. "Seven minutes too quick for you?" He lets go of my butt and goes back to my dad's drink.

I eye him and move to the stove to check the potatoes.

There's a disagreement going on in the family room between Marie's twins, who also started college in September. Lewis and Alexa are arguing over whether or not Lewis's answer was close enough for a win. There are threats involving body parts being lobbed back and forth.

I reach for my wine. "Dinner in half an hour," I tell Oscar. "Sound the warning bell."

"We better wrap it up in there, anyway.

Before there's blood," he quips, adding the cherry and slice of orange to the Old Fashioned to finish it off. He picks up the glass, then grabs my hand. "Liv, I just wanted to tell you . . ." He hesitates, looking down at the drink. "I don't know. That I love you," he says quietly. "As much as I ever did. As much as I loved you when we got married. It's just that work and . . ." Letting go of my hand, he lifts his gaze to meet mine. "You know . . . stuff."

He means Hazel. He means our fundamental disagreement concerning our grandchild.

I want to say something, but I don't know what to say. Because I haven't changed my mind. Because I still think Oscar is wrong. Hazel is wrong. My parents, too. But I'm suddenly overwhelmed with emotion. With love for who Oscar has been to me all these years. With love for the life we've shared. Because I'm scared to death for my family. For my marriage.

I smile at Oscar and turn away, brushing my hand against his. On his way out of the kitchen, he passes Sean coming in.

"What time we eating?" our son asks. "I'm starving."

He's wearing a faded black T-shirt I gave him years ago that says, *No, I will not fix your computer.* It makes me smile because it's awfully casual for Sean for a holiday. Even just with the family, he was always the one in the oxford shirt and khakis. Sometimes he'd bust out a tie. I like this more casual side of him. He seems calmer, too. College life has definitely been good for him, though how I don't know. I get very few details from him when we talk.

"Half an hour," I tell him, poking the potatoes with a fork. They're almost done. "Want to mash for me? I need to pull the turkey out to check it in a minute."

"Sure." He takes a piece of cheese from an abandoned paper plate on the counter, then two crackers, and makes a sandwich with them.

"Who won?" I ask, indicating the family room with my chin.

He shrugs. "I wasn't really paying attention. I only played because Aunt Marie said we had to."

I hide my smile. At the refrigerator, I pull out two sticks of butter. "Catch," I say and hurl one across the kitchen.

Sean throws up his hands, catches one and then the other, and sets them on the counter. He gets the colander out from under the counter.

"You didn't *have* to play charades," I

point out.

He makes a face at me. "And risk the wrath of Aunt Marie? Mom, you don't cross Aunt Marie."

"You don't?"

He shakes his head as if I've said the most idiotic thing. Do my children really think I'm an idiot?

"Not if you can help it. She's like you. You're taking your life in your hands, you cross her."

"Like me?" I ask, feeling as if that comment came out of nowhere.

Sean turns his back to unwrap the sticks of butter on the counter. "You're kidding, right, Mom?"

"No." I look at him, genuinely confused. "You're afraid to *cross* me?"

He hesitates, obviously trying to decide what he wants to say. How much he wants to say.

I'm caught between being impressed that my quiet, shy, introverted son would speak up like this and being hurt by his accusation.

"Not just me." His back is still to me. "Hazel too."

"Have I been that terrible of a mother?"

He stands still for a moment. "I didn't say that," he says finally. "I just . . ." He exhales.

307

"No, Mom. You . . . you've always had to have your way. Dad always lets you have your way. We all do. You have to be in control of every situation. That's why you're so pissed about Hazel," he says quietly, almost more to himself than me.

I walk over to stand beside him. We're both facing the counter. "Sean," I say. "I thought you agreed with me on this thing with Hazel."

"I did, Mom. I do. But . . . you're still angry you didn't get your way and you're punishing all of us."

I open my arms wide. "How am I punishing you?"

He looks down at me; I think he's grown taller since he left for school. He's such a combination of Oscar and me. He has his father's red hair, but his face is narrow like mine, his hands and feet more delicate than Oscar's. And he has my hairline: a serious window's peak.

"You're punishing Dad. Hazel says all you do is fight."

"Since when do you talk to Hazel? I didn't know you guys have been talking on the phone."

He exhales impatiently. "We haven't. She doesn't want to talk to me. But we hung out for a little while last night. She actually said she missed me. She told me things suck at home. That you and Dad can't agree on what kind of pasta to make."

I'm immediately annoyed with my daughter for being a tattle-tale. I never allowed that when they were growing up. I'm even more annoyed because Oscar and I did have a disagreement a few nights ago on what kind of pasta to cook.

I look at Sean. I want to tell my son that he's not old enough to understand marriage. Relationships between a husband and wife. How complicated they are. How complicated they become over time.

I'm saved, or maybe Sean is, by the timer that goes off on the stove. "The turkey," I say, grabbing pot holders off the counter.

"You want me to mash the potatoes by hand or use the mixer thing?"

I open the oven and the air is hot on my face and smells strongly of roasted turkey. "Mashed by hand. The mixer does weird things with the starch if you're not careful."

I pull out the turkey and put the pan of stuffing that is technically dressing into the oven to reheat. Sean and I are both quiet for a couple of minutes while we concentrate on our tasks and try to figure out what to do with the awkwardness between us.

Finally I say, "So . . . school is good?"

309

He didn't arrive home until six last night and then there was a flurry of activity to get out the door. By the time we got here to the cottage, got the food unpacked, and figured out why there were no lights upstairs, Sean had settled in on the couch to play a video game with friends from school, via the Internet. Headphones on, a microphone to his mouth, he barely acknowledged me when I said good night on my way upstairs. I don't know how late he stayed up; apparently he and Hazel talked at some point last night. Then he slept in until I woke him at eleven when my parents arrived, eager to see their grandson after more than two months.

"It is." He moves to the stove.

"Care to elaborate?"

"I don't know. I like my classes. Richard is a cool roommate. We do a lot together." He dumps the hot potatoes into the colander, his back to me. "I met a girl," he says so quietly that I almost don't catch it.

"A girl?" I have to keep the excitement out of my voice.

"Yeah. She's in my programming foundations class." He's hovering over the steaming colander of potatoes. I can tell he's embarrassed, but also that he wants to share. "We've been um . . . studying to-gether."

"Ah." I make myself busy putting the green bean casserole in the oven. "She have a name?"

"Lucy."

I can't stand it. I turn to him, hot mitts on both hands, hands on my hips. "She your girlfriend?"

My son blushes and it's the sweetest thing I think I've ever seen.

"I don't know." He avoids eye contact with me as he carries the potato pot back to the stove. "Can I get back to you on that?"

I grin. "Sure can."

Marie and Joe's dogs burst into a cacophony of barks and race into the kitchen, headed for the back door. Willie Nelson, who has settled near the door between the dining area and the family room, lifts his head, but makes no attempt to get up.

"That must be Aunt Beth," Sean says, dropping a stick of butter into the potato pot. He looks as surprised as I am. "I'll go see if she needs any help."

"Tell her she owes me five bucks," I call after him.

# 20
## HAZEL

I sit on the living room floor, my back against the couch, and stare at my phone. Frank Sinatra is singing "White Christmas" on the Bluetooth speaker Mom and Dad gave to Gran and Granddad. Dad's playing a Pandora station through his phone, but I guess he's going to show Gran how to do it with her new iPhone she bought herself.

The reason I even know it's Frank Sinatra is because Gran and Granddad got into an argument earlier about who sang it better. Gran was on the Frank Sinatra side, but Granddad says Bing Crosby, and he wouldn't give in. Then, when he asked Gran to make him another Old Fashioned, this gross drink with bourbon in it, she told him to make his own damned drink. And Gran never swears. It was a pretty tense moment. Dad gets a point for the save when he offered to make Granddad his second Old Fashioned. Granddad is limited to two because of an incident after a third one on Thanksgiving Day at the cottage.

Gran is passing out Christmas presents now and the argument seems to have blown over. She even gave Granddad a gift: a pair of cargo pants. I'm not sure why she thought he needed pants with lots of pockets because what's he going to carry in them? He doesn't have car or house keys anymore, and now he's not allowed to carry his wallet with him because last week he left it in the yogurt cooler at Hannaford. Gran said strike three and he was out because the week before that, he put his wallet in their freezer and they didn't find it until Gran made herself a martini. And before *that,* he hid it under his mattress so the people who visit him in his room at night wouldn't steal it. Luckily, with the latest wallet incident, some nice lady found it nestled between boxes of Go-GURT and turned it in. Granddad tried to say she must have pickpocketed him, but Gran made him apologize to the lady and the poor guy at customer service who apparently Granddad also chewed out. Then she cried in the parking lot because he embarrassed her; Granddad told me the part about her crying when I was helping him clean up a box of Cheerios he spilled all over the floor and didn't want Gran to know.

Lately I've been going to their house after school every day just to give Gran a break. I think it's helping because she's been *having a good run* as she calls it. She's not using her wheelchair much and her hands don't hurt like they did. I think the fact that I got her to try a gluten-free, dairy-free diet might be helping.

Granddad seems to like getting a break from Gran, too. I know he frustrates Gran, but none of this is his fault. He doesn't want to be confused between an eggplant and an orange and I know he gets tired of Gran fussing with him. I don't mind going and Mom seems to appreciate it; she doesn't have time to check on them every day, and Aunt Beth is dating some new guy, and is too busy to even call sometimes. And it's not like I have anything else better to do. Besides Katy, I feel like I don't have many friends anymore. Everyone in school is nice to my face, but people are definitely avoiding me. Sometimes I want to holler, "You can't get pregnant sitting next to a pregnant girl at lunch!" but Katy says I'm being oversensitive. She also says they're avoiding me because I'm such a bitch all the time. She says I still get invited to parties and stuff. That I'm the one blowing people off.

I watch as my family's Christmas gift exchange goes on, happy to be here in the warm living room with the tree I put lights on and decorated and a fire in the fireplace. The house smells amazing: a combination of the wood burning, gingerbread from the cookies we made, and a scent I can't identify that smells like . . . a safe place.

Gran opens an iPhone case that Mom bought for her. Then Dad opens a bunch of Smartwool socks. Mom's next gift is a pair of silver earrings that look like calla lilies.

We've been coming to their house for Christmas Eve since I was born, and even though I used to complain about having to come, I find it calming this year. My life seems so out of control right now that I crave things that are routine. Anything that seems like the normalcy of my life before this alien started growing inside me. And *normal* is our Christmas Eve traditions at Gran and Granddad's. First, we have an early dinner: ham, macaroni and cheese, steamed broccoli, dinner rolls, and Mom's homemade applesauce. The menu is always the same. Then we go to church, which I think is a little hypocritical since Gran only goes on religious holidays and we don't go at all. But that's what we do. Then we come home for dessert and gifts. We used to go to midnight service, but Gran said she was too old for that, so now we go to the nine o'clock. But I remember being little and thinking it was so cool that Mom let Sean and me stay up so late on Christmas Eve.

I rub my hand on my belly where the skin is sore. I've got stretch marks and they hurt. No one told me they were going to hurt. Or that they'd be so ugly. They're big red lines that look like they could tear at any moment. Mom gave me some moisturizer to rub into them and she said most of them would go away. *Most* of them? WTF?

Still rubbing my belly, I wonder what kind of Christmas traditions Tyler and I will make for Charlie. After we're married, I mean. When we all live together as a family. I like the whole Christmas Eve thing here at Gran and Granddad's, so we'll definitely come here. But I'm seriously thinking about skipping the Santa thing. I feel like it's a bad idea to start lying to your kid when he's a baby. Besides, the whole idea of a man you don't know coming down your chimney to leave you tricycles and Hot Wheels tracks is just weird. How do you teach your kid to be careful around strangers, in case they're pervs, but then tell him it's okay to lure some guy in a fur coat into your living room with almond milk and peanut butter cookies?

My cell phone in my lap vibrates, and I look at it, hoping Tyler is texting me back. He said he was coming tonight. He promised. Since I won't see him tomorrow because he's doing something with his stepdad's family.

It's not Tyler. I've texted him three times and called him twice. Nothing.

It's Katy. I GOT IT! she's texted.

Gran's cat, Rama, climbs into my lap and starts to purr. He's a Siamese cat, named after the real-life king the musical *The King and I* is based on. The King of Siam, which is what we now call Thailand. I'm not into old musicals, but Gran is. All my knowledge of Rodgers and Hammerstein musicals has been forced on me. Gran likes to play the music loud while I clean and she tells me what to do and, against my will, I know a lot of the songs. Mom says she knows too many lyrics from *Oklahoma!* and *The Sound of Music,* too.

I want to text Katy back "Got what??" because I have no idea what she's talking about, but then I feel bad because she's been a really good friend to me since I got knocked up. And I haven't been a good friend to her. All we talk about is me. My problems with Mom. My problems with Tyler. The baby. She's been so patient with me. She doesn't just listen to me whine; she rubs my feet when they get swollen and lets me go to the bathroom before her because she knows I'll pee my pants if I wait too long.

Only the best kind of friend will do stuff for you like that, and I can't even listen when she tells me something. Katy likes this guy, Cal, who's in her English class and we've talked a little bit about him, but she could tell I wasn't really interested. I don't even know how their date went the other night. We were supposed to talk on the phone after, but I completely forgot to call her after I had a freak-out. I thought I was in labor and called Mom and made her come home from work even though she was meeting with some kind of inspector. Turns out it was something called Braxton Hicks contractions, which are like practice contractions. Guess I should have read that book about pregnancy and birth Mom gave me. I'm beginning to wonder if I'm suffering from some form of denial about having this baby. But how can I be in denial? I'm carrying this basketball/alien right in front of me every second of every day. It's hard to ignore.

Aunt Beth squeals when she unwraps a fancy wine bottle opener that's got a rechargeable battery. She yanks it out of the box.

I look down at my phone.

Yay, I text Katy. Then I wait, hoping she'll text me a clue so I can pretend I know what she wanted for Christmas. I'm sure we talked about it. I want a Britax ClickTight car seat. That's what I asked for. I'm secretly hoping for a new iPhone Plus, too, though. There's nothing wrong with my phone; I just really want the new one with better camera features. So I can take pictures of Charlie.

I hear a buzzing sound and look up to see Aunt Bethie making the metal corkscrew thingy go up and down inside her fancy bottle opener. No bottle; she's just running the corkscrew up and down and laughing. She's had a lot of wine today. Dad made her ride with us to church instead of driving herself.

My phone vibrates.

Not new. Dad vetoed that. But it only has 18 thou miles and it's red!!

Katy got a new car. The powers of deduction. I shake my head. She got a car for Christmas. I'm getting a car seat that I probably won't use because I'll be afraid to take my baby out of the house because something might happen to him.

I stare at the phone. Of course, Katy got a car. I try not to be jealous. But she gets everything she wants. I have a theory that her parents give her everything because she used to have a little sister who died of cancer. Parents do that kind of stuff. They try to make up for dead sisters by buying you a new pair of Ugg boots every year and cars that are practically new.

I look up to watch Sean unwrap a new sweater. The wrapping paper is fancy and there's red tissue paper folded just so inside a real gift box. Gran pays someone to wrap all her gifts. All of the gifts are wrapped in color-coordinated paper so it looks nice under her tree. There's always a theme, too: "down by the sea," with real seashells glued on the packages, or maybe "all that glitters" with, yup, a lot of glittery gift tags and bows and shiny foil paper. When I was little, it used to bug me that Gran was so particular about her gift presentation because I wasn't allowed to put my homemade gifts, wrapped in brown paper I decorated myself with paint and stickers, under her tree. My homemade disasters had to go under the "kids' tree" in the kitchen. When Charlie wraps a gift for me in a page of lion cubs from a kid's *National Geographic* magazine I'm going to let him put it under our family tree.

Sean holds up his sweater and everyone oohs and aahs.

Christmas takes forever with Mom's family because everyone has to watch while each gift is opened. We take turns by age, so Granddad opens something, then Gran, then Dad, then Mom, then Aunt Bethie, then Sean, then me. And then it starts all over again. But Gran gives good gifts so we don't complain too much.

There's a lot less organization involved with Christmas with Dad's family. Tomorrow we'll go to the cottage where Aunt Marie and Uncle Sai and their kids will be and once everyone is there tomorrow night, we'll get to rip open everything at once. Uncle Joe and his wife and their girls won't join us until the day after Christmas because they went to Aunt Petunia's parents' house. Her name isn't really Petunia, but that's what Dad and Uncle Joe have always called her. I think her real name is something weird like Millicent.

"Now, if you don't like the color, they have a blue and a red and a green," Gran tells Sean. "But I thought you might like black. Black's classic and it looks nice with your hair." It's an L.L.Bean sweater; Gran buys almost exclusively from L.L.Bean, at least for casual clothing. I got a similar one, in green. I can't wear it now because I'm too fat, but Gran said it would be nice to have something new to wear after the baby is born. We'll still have snow on the ground when the baby is born.

The idea of that makes me almost dizzy. It will still be winter when this kid is born. I can't believe I'm having a baby. . . . I'm thirty-one weeks. Which means that in nine weeks I have to push this big-headed basketball of an alien out my V.

I look at my phone that's vibrating again.

What time you going to cottage in the morning? Katy asks.

Want to come by and show you my new car. Only she hasn't spelled out *car,* she's used a red emoji of a car.

Not til 11. Which means 12 because nobody will be ready.

K.

Then the incoming text bubbles pop up again.

Tyler show up? she asks. She's added a poop emoji to the end of this one.

I don't want to answer her. Katy wasn't a Tyler fan before but now she pretty much hates him and she's not even trying to hide it anymore. Something happened between them a couple of weeks ago. I don't know what. Neither she or Tyler will tell me. But they aren't speaking except for her to call him a dickwad or for him to call her the C word under his breath when she walks away after she's said something to me in the hall at school. I wish the both of them would just stop because I feel like I'm stuck in the middle. If I take Tyler's side, Katy is mad. If I take Katy's side, Tyler's all pissy and makes excuses not to see me. At least when Katy's mad at me, she still texts me and stuff.

I push Gran's cat off my lap and get up without texting Katy back.

"Hazel. Your turn next," Granddad tells me, holding up a gift. The box is too small to be an iPhone Plus. Looks like jewelry.

"I've got one here for Tyler, too." Gran holds up an envelope that looks like a Christmas card with his name printed on it. "Gift cards for the movies. I hope that's okay. I thought you two could go together." She's still holding up the card as I walk by her. "Is he coming?"

"I have to pee," I say, not even trying not to sound grumpy.

"Go to the little girls' room. I'll hold it for you." Granddad sets down the little box

323

wrapped in pale-blue paper tied elaborately with white ribbon. I think the theme this year is White Christmas — why Gran keeps wanting to play the song over and over again. I'm not sure what the blue has to do with it, but it is pretty.

I look down at Granddad sitting on the end of the couch; he's wearing a shirt and bow tie with a red V-neck sweater over it. He's been on his good behavior all day because Gran's really mad at him. She was mad even before the song argument. Yesterday he got into a fight with a lady at a crafts store in town because he wanted to buy a socket wrench and she kept telling him they didn't carry wrenches. I guess he got confused. Apparently, a long time ago, the crafts store was a hardware store.

Gran said he got really angry and started talking loud about people not wanting to sell people things because of elder prejudice. I can't believe he thought they sold socket wrenches at a crafts store, but had enough of his marbles to know what elder prejudice was and to be able to argue the point.

Gran was furious. She'd left him in the car playing Candy Crush while she went into a store to pick up *one thing.* Then she had to hunt him down. She told me she was going to chain him to the car with a combination lock from now on. Which, of course, would be totally unsafe. But I didn't tell her that because I think she was kidding. At least I hope she was.

"I'll be right back," I announce to the room, bouncing up and down on my toes. "I really have to pee."

"Break time," Mom announces, getting up. She's been sitting on the floor at Dad's feet. They got into it yesterday about something, but there seems to be some sort of truce right now. Mom even brought Dad another beer without him asking. "Sean, could you get some more firewood? There should be more on the back porch," she says.

I hustle to the bathroom. I'm washing my hands when my phone on the counter starts vibrating. It's Tyler calling. I stare at the phone, trying not to panic. Tyler never calls me. He texts or we see each other. But we don't talk on the phone.

Either he's not coming or someone died.

I dry off my hands on my maternity jeans because I don't want to get in trouble for using Gran's pretty white hand towel with the green holly leaf embroidered on it. "You're not coming," I say into the phone as I walk out of the bathroom. I sound pathetic.

He doesn't say anything, but I know he's there.

"Ty, you said you would come." I'm not even whining. I'm genuinely disappointed he's not coming.

I wait. He *still* doesn't say anything. "Ty," I say, angry now.

"Nah, not coming," he finally grunts.

"Why not? You don't have to stay. But you have to at least stop by. Gran bought you a present. She got you a gift card for the movies. So we could go. We could go see the new Marvel movie. You like those stupid superhero movies."

At the end of the hall, I stop and lean against the wall. I can see into the living room. Sean is setting an armload of wood into the basket by the fireplace and Dad is stoking the fire. Mom and Aunt Beth have their heads together, laughing. Maybe because Gran gave Aunt Beth one of the bottle openers last year for Christmas. Might have been the same one. Granddad is just sitting in his chair, hands folded in his lap, in his bow tie, looking very Norman Rockwell there next to the tree.

"I said I'm not coming," Tyler says in my ear.

"Ty —" Suddenly I realize that his voice sounds weird. Almost like he's going to cry.

And I know something is wrong. Something bad. "Ty, it's okay," I say quickly. I stand in the doorway of the living room, hugging myself with one arm. Everyone is wandering around, talking, laughing. Except Granddad, who seems to be glued to that end of the couch. Christmas music is still playing on the Bluetooth speaker.

"You don't have to come," I say to Tyler, gripping my phone. "It's okay. It's boring anyway. We're going home soon. I'll just, I'll get your card. I can just tell Gran —"

"I want to break up with you," he blurts.

I get light-headed and my knees are wobbly. I feel like I'm going to faint.

No, like I'm going to just melt into the floor in a puddle and just . . . just evaporate. "Ty —" My voice cracks. "I can come over. We can talk. Where are you? I can come." The words come out in a rush and I sound so pitiful. I sound like an eleventh grader who got knocked up by her immature boyfriend, who should have known he was never going to stay with her. Who knew that no matter how much she loved him, he couldn't stay with her because he's not that guy. Never could have been.

"I gotta go," he says.

"No, Ty. Please . . . Ty, you can't break up with me." Tears start to run down my cheeks. "We're going to have a baby." My voice cracks.

That's when I realize everyone in my family is quiet and they're looking at me. Even Granddad is looking at me.

I'm so embarrassed. Because I'm crying. Because I just told my boyfriend he couldn't break up with me, even though I know he doesn't want me. Talk about pathetic.

I turn around and step into the hall, leaning against the wall so my family can't see me. I'm holding on to the phone like I just jumped off the *Titanic* and it's the only life jacket there is. "Tyler, please don't do this," I plead. "I love you."

"I gotta go," he tells me. "Gotta bring in the tree." His parents run late getting ready for Christmas.

"Ty, what did I do?" I beg. I can barely talk. "Please," I whisper, knowing even as I say it that nothing I can say is going to change his mind. That he probably wanted to break up with me weeks ago. Months ago. That this has been coming for a while. Maybe I even knew it was coming.

"So, um. Merry Christmas. And . . . and I guess I'll see you in school."

And that's it. Nothing about the baby. Nothing about making plans to take care of his son because of course he wants his son.

Even if he doesn't want me. Tyler just hangs up.

I slowly slide down to the floor, my back against the wall in the hallway. I'm still gripping the phone. "Ty?"

And then my mom comes around the corner from the living room and I look up at her. "Mom," I sob.

"Oh, Hazel," she says so quietly, I barely hear her.

"He broke up with me," I blubber as she reaches down, takes my phone, tucks it into the back pocket of her jeans, and then reaches out for me.

"Ty broke up with me. He doesn't care about me. He doesn't care about his b-baby." I can barely get the words out I'm crying so hard.

"Come on," Mom says, pulling on my hands. "Get off the floor. Let's go lay down on Gran's bed. You're tired and . . . oh, sweetie." She sounds like she's going to cry.

I let her help me to my feet, and when she wraps her arms around me, I start sobbing again. "What am I going to do? Tyler doesn't love me anymore. He — he doesn't love our baby."

"Shhhh," Mom soothes, holding me as close to her as she can with my big belly in the way. "It's going to be all right."

329

"No. It isn't," I moan, laying my head on her shoulder. "Mom, I'm going to have a baby."

She strokes my hair, not caring that I'm snotting all over her pretty sweater. Possibly in her hair. Definitely in mine. "It's going to be all right, Hazel," she soothes in the quietest, gentlest voice. "Things have a way of working out, sweetie. Even if they're not the way you think they will."

# 21
## LIV

"I can't believe I'm finally getting this done." Amelia pulls a long strip of wet wallpaper off the wall and drops it into the trash bin behind her in the middle of her bathroom. "It's been on my to-do list for . . . what? Two years?"

Standing on a step stool, I tuck the scoring tool into the back pocket of my jeans and grab the spray bottle of glue solvent and begin to spray it on the area I just scored. With Amelia two panels behind me, our timing is working well. I score and spray, and by the time she gets to the next section, the paper is loose.

"I've been telling you for months I'd help you." I give the next section of bamboo-print wallpaper a spritz.

Amelia groans. "But you're so busy."

"Not so busy I can't help you." I glance at her. "Do I give you the impression I'm so busy I don't have time for you?"

Amelia pauses, a long strip of paper in her hand. She looks cute today. She's dyed her hair a shade of light brown that's much closer to her natural color than her usual bottle blond and she's let it grow out a little so it's not quite so severe-looking. And she looks happy. Mostly because she is. She started dating a new guy just before Thanksgiving. The owner of a small local land survey company. And so far, so good.

She frowns. She's wearing a lighter foundation on her face and I like it. I always thought she went a little heavy-handed with the makeup, using a full-coverage formula. She thought she needed to use it to cover signs of aging. I think she looks younger with her freckles showing through.

"You are busy."

"Not too busy for you." I give the wallpaper another spritz. "What made you think that? You didn't ask for my help."

"Hit a nerve there, did I?"

Her tone makes me look at her again. "What?"

She arches one eyebrow. "Scraper? I've got a place that's stuck." She points at the wall.

I pull the three-inch-blade putty knife out of my other back pocket and hold it out to her. "Sorry. I just . . ." I shake my head.

"Mom. Oscar. They both —" I stare at the wall in front of me. Take a breath. Exhale. "Mom says they're not seeing enough of me. Hazel is going every day, but I want to start work on the new job the beginning of February and there are only so many hours in a day. And I can't be in two places at once. Don't they realize that?"

"The Anselin project is finally wrapping up?" Amelia gently pries up the edge of a piece of wallpaper, just the way I showed her, to keep from damaging the drywall behind it. The wallpaper is outdated and ugly to boot and I'm so glad she finally decided to strip it and paint the room. I even convinced her to give the vanity a new coat of paint and a granite top. A remnant that didn't cost her more than she would have paid for a faux-granite top in one of the big home improvement stores.

"Yup, we're wrapping it up. Well, not quite." I give the wall another squirt. "They want to remodel their master bath suite now. That wasn't part of the original quote. Or schedule."

"Ah." Amelia strips off another piece of wallpaper. "So, your mom wants you at her place?"

I shake my head. "I know she's over-whelmed. Dad has really good days, but

333

then . . ." I exhale. "Then he does something crazy or . . . says something that really hurts Mom's feelings."

"Something that hurts Bernice Cosset's feelings? I have a hard time believing that. That woman is a marble statue. What's he say that hurts her feelings?"

"Saturday night Dad walks out of his room all dressed up. Wearing his suit, shaved, hair slicked back." I chew on my lower lip, thinking back to my mom telling me the story. "When she asked him where he was going, he told her he had a date. With a pretty, young thing he met at a party."

"Your dad's going to parties where he meets women? Without your mom?"

I make a face. "Of course he isn't. Amelia, he drools now, if you don't tell him to wipe his mouth." Just saying that cuts me to the core. My father is fading before my very eyes. Fading fast. "He got angry when Mom told him he couldn't go out. He told her she wasn't his wife and she was holding him against his will and that he was calling 911."

"Liv, I'm so sorry." Amelia reaches for her mug of hot tea from the sink's counter and offers me mine.

I come down the ladder, accepting the tea. It's bitterly cold out today with blizzard-like conditions. Typical for mid-coast Maine in January. I hadn't intended to come to Amelia's today and start on this project. Oscar and I had made plans to do something together. We hadn't decided what yet, but I'd specifically told the Anselins that I would not be by today. That I was taking the Saturday off even if the electrician was coming back to do some work. He could do it on his own. Something I've struggled to get my clients to understand — that I don't have to be on-site at every moment work is being done.

Turns out I could have worked. Or gone to Massachusetts to see Sean or . . . just gone with Hazel to my parents' because, knowing he had plans with me, Oscar agreed to work for someone today. Which is out of character for him. He never agrees to cover anyone's shift on a weekend. Taking one for the team is for younger PAs.

Oscar did it just to avoid me. I know it. Thursday night we had a fight about whether or not the baby should have its own bedroom. He thought the baby should and wanted to clean out Sean's room and re-paint it. I said Hazel didn't get two rooms. That seventeen-year-olds who get pregnant don't get the luxury of having a nursery for their babies. When we had Sean, he slept in the room with us. We didn't have another bedroom. And when he got a little older, he slept in the living room. Or we did. It wasn't until we moved to the place we live now that Sean got his own bedroom. That Oscar and I got our own room. And we'd both earned a college education and worked for a living.

"We had to have Mom and Dad's house phone disconnected," I tell Amelia, going on with my sad tale. "They've had that number for more than fifty years. But Dad kept calling 911. He'd call if he couldn't find the bananas, if Mom told him to leave his snowy boots in the laundry room, if he couldn't figure out how to recharge his iPad."

Amelia smiles, then frowns. "Liv, I don't know what to say."

"Mom didn't want to disconnect the phone, but it was the only solution I could come up with. I told her Dad could be arrested for making unjustified calls to emergency services. That he could be charged with something legally." I take a sip of my chocolate mint tea. "She asked if they would put her in jail. She sounded hopeful." I eye Amelia over the rim of my mug.

She laughs. "She thinks, had you been

there, your dad wouldn't have made the calls?"

"No. Yes. I don't know. Maybe." I shrug. "She's frustrated."

"I know she is." Amelia sips her tea. "And Oscar? He's saying you don't have time for him?"

"Yes." I cross my arms over my chest, still holding on to the hot mug. "But what he means is that I'm not available when he wants me to be. That I'm not there at his beck and call anymore."

"Is that a little harsh?"

"No." I glance up at her. "Yes." I hesitate and then drop my head. "Maybe." I roll my eyes, à la Hazel. "I don't know what's going on. Everything he says, everything he does, annoys me. He does this thing with his fork when he eats. Like . . . he touches it to his teeth. He's been doing it as long as I've known him, but all of a sudden I can't stand the sound. I can't stand to sit at the kitchen table when he makes that sound."

"I thought you said you guys were getting along better after Thanksgiving."

I sip my tea. "We were, but then . . . I don't know. Things got crazy. Christmas. Tyler breaking up with Hazel."

"And they haven't gotten back together?"

"No. The week after Christmas they were

337

talking again, but then she found out he was texting with some other girl and —" I shake my head. "I think she's done with him. But then that caused a new set of problems because Oscar thinks we should talk to Ty's parents about financial responsibility after the baby is born. About how he's going to spend time with his child. How visitation with Cricket and B.J. is going to work."

"I think it's J.J.," Amelia says.

We both chuckle.

"Anyway," I go on. "My feeling is that the less contact we have with those people, the better off we'll be. Hazel and the baby."

"Where's Hazel fall on this?"

I cut my eyes at her. "Where do you think?"

"Ah, so you think Oscar is siding with her again."

"I don't think. I know he is." It comes out louder than I intended. Loud in the small room.

We're both quiet for a minute as we enjoy our tea.

It's Amelia who breaks the silence. "Look, Liv. I know I probably shouldn't be giving marriage advice. Considering the fact that I'm divorced, but . . . You and Oscar love

338

each other. This . . . this is a bump in the road."

I give a little snort. I'm pissed at Oscar today. Really pissed. Because he makes me out to be the bad guy, the one who doesn't want to work on our marriage, and then he's the one who cancels on our plans to take a shift for someone when he doesn't need to.

"A big bump in the road, I'll give you that." She nods. "But you two belong together, Liv. You need to stop being so combative and work it out."

I stare into my mug. "You think I'm being *combative*?"

She doesn't answer.

I look up. "Maybe I *am* being combative, but, Amelia — I'm overwhelmed."

"I bet Oscar is overwhelmed, too."

I groan and set down the mug. "You're probably right. This is my fault."

"I'm not saying it's your fault."

I start picking at a corner of wallpaper I've already scored and sprayed with stripping solution. "I feel like it's my fault," I say quietly. I move my head one way and then the other, stretching it. My neck is stiff because I fell asleep on the couch last night. Oscar didn't wake me and tell me to come to bed. I always wake him up. "I feel like it's all my fault."

Amelia starts peeling wallpaper beside me. "You're not responsible for Hazel having unprotected sex with a cretin."

I look at her. "No?"

"Nope." She drops a piece of dripping wallpaper into the trash can behind us. "But you *are* responsible for how you respond to it. And how you deal with the friction the pregnancy has caused in your marriage."

"Am I responsible for my dad trying to make popcorn on the stove and burning up Mom's favorite pot?"

"Nope. Not responsible for that, either."

We laugh and I feel a little better. And maybe a little more hopeful because, as long as I keep my sense of humor, there is hope, isn't there? Hope I can get through this. That my marriage can survive it.

# 22

## HAZEL

I stand in Dad's sweatshirt, a pair of wool socks, and my panties in the laundry room, waiting for my fat-girl jeans to dry. I'm just staring at the dryer, watching my jeans go around and around through the glass window. It's warm in the laundry room and it smells good, like the lavender detergent Mom uses.

My jeans thump every time they go around, a harder thump and then two little ones. Three syllables. Three beats.

*I hate him.*

*I hate him.*

*I hate him,* I say in my head.

Tyler. I'm so done with him. *So* over him. He's an idiot. Or maybe I am for ever going out with him in the first place. For thinking I saw potential in him. A future with him. For letting him stick his teeny-tiny dick in me. I didn't even like it. All that buildup, the big deal adults make about sex, and it

341

was a big flop as far as I'm concerned. I see blurbs on the front of women's magazines in line at the grocery store talking about women getting more out of sex with their man. Next boyfriend I have, I want to get something out of it. I want some of the fun it's supposed to be. Maybe when I'm lying around after the baby is born, I'll start reading up on good sex, just to be ready.

My jeans continue to thump as they go around and around.

*I hate him.*

*I hate him.*

*I hate him.*

Tyler's completely abandoned me. Abandoned our baby. But that's okay, I've decided, because Charlie and I will be better off without him. Tyler's going nowhere. He's going to be a nobody and he's never going to leave this town. And not because he couldn't be somebody, not because he couldn't leave. Because he doesn't want to. He's content to drive around in his piece-of-crap truck, poisoning himself with the exhaust while he poisons himself with nicotine and other carcinogens rolled up in white paper, and never dream about having something more. Something more to give to someone else. I bite hard on one of my cuticles. Someone like me. And our baby.

"Hazel!" Mom calls from the kitchen.

"Yeah?"

"Breakfast?"

"Nope. Running late!" I yell above the sound of the washer and dryer. Mom put in a load to wash a few minutes ago. She does wash every morning before she goes to work. Now she's renovating two houses. And some guy has called her about turning an old house into some kind of store right here in Judith, as part of a downtown revitalization program. She seems really excited about doing a commercial property.

I check the time on my phone. I don't want to be late because there's this guy who parks near me in the school parking lot. He's a senior. He always pulls in at the last possible minute, so if I'm there before he is, I can just sit in my car and pretend I'm fixing my hair or something and wait until he's getting out. Then we can walk into school together. We've done it twice this week.

His name's Jack. He's super cute and super nice. He asked me about the baby, but it didn't seem like a big deal to him to be walking into school with a pregnant girl. He treated me normal. And he smiled at me when we said good-bye.

"Hazel. Egg sammy?" Mom says. "To go. I can wrap it for you."

"Sure," I yell back, mostly because it's easier than saying no. If I don't want it, I'll toss it out the window on the way to school. Although I'm pretty hungry. I might eat it.

The dryer buzzes and I yank open the door. I pull on my jeans, hopping up and down because they're hot. "I'm leaving in five minutes. I don't want it if it's not ready in five minutes," I tell her, walking into the kitchen.

Mom's at the stove, cooking eggs. "Almost done. I'm making myself one to go, too. Could you pop the English muffins in the toaster?" She nods in the direction of the counter.

"Sure. Where's Dad?" He's usually sitting at the kitchen counter this time of the morning, reading one of his history books and chugging coffee.

"Running late. Still in the shower." She sets down the spatula, takes a travel mug out of the kitchen cabinet, and pours coffee. It's the big mug, so it must be for Dad.

"Your dad said you talked to Tyler. About sharing child care responsibilities. About Cricket watching the baby?" She doesn't look at me as she says it.

"I talked to Cricket because Tyler isn't speaking to me," I say, waggling my head with the Tyler part.

I cried for an hour last night about the fact that he doesn't even want to talk to me now, but I'm over it. I'm over him. He's going out with Amanda Peterson now. Who I liked until she stole my boyfriend. I kinda want to tell her to buy her own condoms. But then I'd have to speak to her and I'm not.

"And no, Mom, Cricket says she can't babysit. She says she has to respect her son's decision." I do the air quote thing. I really don't want to talk about this this morning. Mom always does this. She wants to start huge conversations first thing in the morning when I'm barely awake. And I need to get to school.

"Okay." She says it singsongy, which pisses me off. "So your plan now? I thought Cricket was going to watch the baby when you went back to school in the fall."

"I decided I don't want her watching Charlie anyway." I put four organic, whole-wheat English muffin halves in the toaster and push them down. "She'd probably let the dogs eat him."

"I don't think Tyler's mother is going to let a dog eat her grandchild," she says to me.

I watch her filling the ginormous coffee cup. Apparently Dad's back on his heavy

345

caffeine doses. "I don't need Tyler and Cricket, Mom. I'll just do the distance-learning thing my senior year. I'll take care of the baby and do my school stuff when he sleeps." I shrug. "I'm going to do it to finish out the year, anyway."

Distance learning is this program that allows students to do their schoolwork at home online and still graduate. It's free because the state has to give you an education through twelfth grade, even if you are so dumb you get pregnant in the eleventh. I read all about it on the Maine Department of Education Web site.

She sets down the coffeepot. She's still not looking at me. "You talk to your guidance counselor to get the details?" Her voice is getting tight.

She asked me about distance learning last week. And the week before. "No." I tighten my ponytail. First I was wearing my hair down, but then I decided to do the ponytail because that's how I always wear my hair. That or in a messy bun. I don't want Jack to think that I'm, like, doing my hair special for him or anything.

Mom goes back to the stove to flip the eggs. "You need to find out what kind of application process there is. You need to make sure you can even do it three-quarters of the way through the school year." Before I can answer, she goes on. "Because you've got five weeks, Hazel."

"I know," I groan.

"Maybe six until the baby is here." She's talking over me now. "And you can take a week off or whatever, but the more time you take off, the further —"

"Mom!" I interrupt, loud. "I told you, I've got this."

"Yes, you have told me that."

She puts cheese on two of the fried eggs, hers and Dad's, but not mine. Because she knows I won't eat it if there's cheese on it. I'm trying the no-dairy thing with Gran.

"But it doesn't look like you've got this because you're having a baby in a month and you don't know how you're going to finish the eleventh grade."

I rest my hands on my hips. "Nothing is ever good enough for you, is it?"

The English muffins pop up in the toaster. She turns to me, the spatula in her hand again. "What?"

"Nothing is ever good enough for you. Nothing I do is *ever* good enough." I hold my hands in the air. "I've never been *smart* enough, or *organized* enough, or *pretty* enough or . . . or *anything* enough." I'm almost shouting my last words. "God, I hate you!" I do shout that.

Before she can say anything, I turn around and stomp out of the kitchen. I grab my coat, my backpack, and my car keys from the laundry room.

"Hazel," Mom calls after me, sounding like she's going to cry.

I walk out and slam the door behind me.

# 23
## LIV

"Hazel?" I call after her, trying not to cry. I walk across the kitchen, stepping over the dog, watching my daughter march out of the room.

"Liv?" Oscar walks into the kitchen from the family room. "What's going on?"

I turn to him as the laundry room door slams. Hard. Hard enough to wake the dog.

"Honey?" He glances in the direction our daughter has just fled. "What was that all about?"

Tears slide down my cheeks and I wipe at them, feeling ridiculous. I'm the adult here. I'm supposed to be tough. Thick-skinned. A teenager's words shouldn't hurt me.

I want to go after Hazel and demand an apology. No one should speak to her mother that way. But I'm so hurt by her words that I can't move. And what would be the point? She just said she hated me. If she hates me, chasing her down and demanding an apology isn't going to make her hate me less. She'll hate me more.

My gaze strays to the kitchen counter and the half-made breakfast. She forgot her sandwich. She'll be hungry. She shouldn't be leaving the house without eating something. Not eight months pregnant.

I meet Oscar's gaze. "She hates me," I whisper.

He stands there for a minute, looking at me looking at him. He's dressed in scrubs for work, his hair and beard still damp from his shower. He opens his arms. I go to him.

"She doesn't hate you," he says into my hair.

"She just told me she hates me." I gesture lamely in the direction she went and press my face into his chest, breathing deeply, trying not to start bawling. I hear her pulling out of the driveway in her car. "She *acts* like she hates me. Now she's gone," I tell him. "In my car. I own it, I put the gas in it, I pay the insurance." I look up at him, sliding my hands upward to rest on his shoulders. "Should I be doing those things? Why should I provide her with a car if she hates me? She could ride the bus. It goes by here." I know I'm just babbling now.

He tightens his arms around me and I cling to him. My tears are going to leave a

350

damp spot on his scrubs.

"Because you're her mother and you love her," he says quietly.

I take a deep breath; he smells like body wash and the man I fell in love with a very long time ago. I look up at him, my head still on his shoulder. "What are we going to do, Oscar?"

He kisses my cheek. And his kiss is sweet and warm, and somehow being in his arms, I already feel a little better.

"What are we going to do about what?" he asks.

"Hazel. Since Tyler broke up with her, she hasn't been herself. She . . . she's not doing as well in school as she had been. Did she tell you that she failed a quiz in English the other day because she didn't read the homework assignment?"

"She did not." His tone is gentle, his voice reassuring. He's the calm to my storm. He's always been.

"Saturday night she came home at two in the morning. What's a girl eight months pregnant doing out at two in the morning? And she's done absolutely nothing about making arrangements to finish off the school year at home. Nothing. If she went into labor today, I guess she'd just flunk the year."

He stiffens. "You don't think she's going into labor today, do you?"

"Of course not." I frown. "She's fine. I'm just saying . . ." I don't finish my sentence because what *am* I saying? My thoughts are flying in so many directions these days that it's amazing I can produce a single coherent sentence. Mom and Dad are a mess, I've bitten off more than I can chew with the new business, and then there's the issue with my pregnant daughter about to pop out a baby. A child having a child.

Oscar strokes my back for a moment, just holding me. And it feels so good. Just standing there in the middle of our kitchen, in his arms, makes me not feel quite so desperate. Quite so crazy.

"Liv," Oscar says. "Do you think — now I'm just asking." He lets go of me with one hand so he can raise it high. "Should I . . . should I call the school and see what she needs to do? What they need from us to enroll her in whatever homeschool program is available? She told me it would be online, that she didn't even need someone to come to the house or whatever."

"You should not call the school." I look up at him, surprised he's made the offer. Not resentful, for once, just pleasantly surprised.

I've been the parent who always handled anything that had to do with the children's education. Oscar has never been involved. He never went to PTA meetings, never volunteered in a classroom, never did playground duty or made twenty-eight cupcakes for a bake sale. In fact, I'm in charge of Oscar's education, as well. Any continuing education credits he needs to retain or renew his physician's assistant license, I arrange for, whether it's an online course or a weekend trip to Boston.

"I don't think you should call," I say, wording it so I'm not giving a command. Hazel tells me I never make suggestions, I just order everyone in the family around. "Hazel said she would make the arrangements and I agreed she should do it."

For once, it seems like he's listening to me. Hearing me.

"She got herself into this mess," I reason aloud. "She's about to have a baby. She needs to become more mature, more responsible, not less. And honestly, I don't want to do it." I look into his eyes. "This was supposed to be my time. This was supposed to be an easy year, with Sean away at school, and Hazel being as independent as she is, always was, she was supposed to be taking care of herself more."

He thinks for a minute. "You're right. I agree a hundred percent."

"You do?" I'm surprised he's actually agreeing with me about something. Particularly when it means disagreeing with Hazel.

"I do." He gives me a gentle kiss on the lips, still holding me. "What did you argue about?"

I exhale loudly. "About her making the arrangements for homeschooling. And now it's even more important that she get everything worked out, now that Cricket says she won't keep the baby at all —"

"Wait, Cricket isn't going to babysit? I thought that was the plan so Hazel could go back to school and Tyler could work."

"And go to a community college. They were talking about him getting some kind of mechanics certification. Right." I'm looking up at him again. "That's all a no-go now that they've broken up. And Amanda What's-her-name is in the picture."

"Peterson," he offers. "I got an earful driving home with Hazel from your parents' last night."

I'm drawing a blank. "Why were the two of you at my parents'?"

I close my eyes for a second. "That's right. Honey, I completely forgot." I immediately feel terrible. I got stuck in Rockland with an interior designer who had some fabrics for me to look at and my mom called me four times in five minutes. I texted Hazel and she said she would take care of their latest catastrophe. "Thank you for picking up the prescription, and fixing the toilet. I know that's not usually your forte."

"Being Plunger Man?" He raises his arm high, an imaginary scepter in his hand.

I laugh. "It's working okay? I didn't want to call the plumber again if I didn't have to."

"Working great once I removed the bedroom slipper. Didn't even have to plunge. It was right there."

"Dad tried to flush a slipper?" I start to ask why he put his slipper in the toilet and flushed, but then I know there's no reason to ask. Either there is no explanation, or worse, the explanation will be so bizarre, I'll have one more thing to worry about today.

Oscar's looking down at me. Chuckling. And I realize how much I miss these little exchanges with him. And it makes me sad because I've allowed these moments to go unrealized. Because I've been too pre-occupied in the morning to say more than a perfunctory "Have a good day" as I go out the door. Because I've been making this household a war zone of me against them and I've shut him out. My Oscar, my husband, my lover, the man who was once my best friend.

I shake my head, carrying my thoughts back to the conversation at hand. "So the babysitting. Hazel spoke with Cricket about watching the baby and Cricket told her she had to support her son and her son didn't want them to have anything to do with the baby."

"You've got to be kidding me. This is the same woman we visited a few months ago?" He makes a face as if what she's saying sounds crazy. "She was the one all excited about his baby, buying clothes when Hazel was only three months pregnant. Talking about buying him a four-wheeler when he was old enough and crap like that."

"I know." I let go of him. "I know." I walk to the stove. Luckily I'd turned the flame off under the eggs. They might be a little cool by now but at least I didn't burn them. Cold eggs we can eat. "You need to get to the hospital, hon. I have a sandwich almost made for you. I'll wrap it so you can eat it on the way." I grab the muffins out of the toaster. "You may as well have Hazel's, too. She's not coming back for it."

He checks his watch. "I don't have to go yet. I've still got a few minutes."

I begin to assemble his sandwich. The sausage patties I made first are still warm on a back burner. "You like to be there before morning meeting."

"They can wait on me a few minutes." He sounds annoyed but not with me, for once.

"Really?" I pick up his travel mug and take it to him, feeling an unfamiliar sense of unity with him. "I already poured your coffee. Creamer went in first."

He takes the cup from my hand. Smiles at me. "Thanks."

I return the smile, suddenly feeling almost shy with him. It's been that long since we've had a conversation like this. Touched each other except while having sex. I watch him take a sip of his coffee, glad I had made it for him. We used to do little things like that for each other. I'd make his morning coffee. He'd take my car to run an errand and fill it up with gas for me. I wonder how we got out of the habit. And I wonder how much it has to do with our distance now. Are those niceties in life — pouring a cup of coffee, moving clothes from the washer to the dryer without being asked, starting dinner when you get home early even though it's not your night to make dinner — are they what make the difference between a happy marriage and a sad one? A marriage of emotional intimacy instead of distance?

I go back to making the breakfast sandwiches: English muffins, fried eggs with cheese, and a sausage patty. "No cheese on Hazel's. Sorry. So you get one with cheese and one without. Or you can have mine," I offer.

"That's okay. I don't need the calories in the cheese anyway." He pats his belly. "I've been thinking about counting calories again. Downloaded an app that looks decent. Might pull the treadmill out of the downstairs bedroom. Put it in the family room so I could walk while I watch something in the evenings."

"Sounds like a plan." I dare a hint of a smile, sniff, and start wrapping the sandwiches. Without Hazel here, I don't bother with the beeswax wrap. I go with the foil because I like foil. It wraps better. And I'm tired of being dictated to by my teenage daughter.

Oscar leans against the kitchen counter and sips his coffee. "If Tyler's mother's not watching the baby . . ." He lets his sentence go unfinished.

"What's the plan?" I pop a third muffin into the toaster, and wrap the sandwich made without cheese in foil and wait for the "lids" for the other two to come out of the toaster.

"Hazel says she's just going to stay home next year, too."

"Sounds like a terrible idea." He smooths his beard. "I cannot believe that little piss-ant bailed on her. Bailed on his kid."

"Believe." My tone is dry.

We're both quiet for a minute as I wait on the toaster to pop. But it's not the uncomfortable silence we've been sharing as of late. It's a solicitous silence.

"Hazel told you she hated you?"

"She sure did."

"She shouldn't speak to you that way," Oscar says. "No matter how angry she is with you."

"I agree." I sip my coffee from my fancy stainless-steel thermal mug Sean gave me for Christmas. A brand all the house contractors use, he told me. "But . . ." I sigh. "We probably need to cut her a break. She's pretty hormonal. You remember how batty I would get in my last trimester?"

"Still not an excuse. She's old enough to be thankful for everything you do for her, Liv. And if not that, she needs to at least be respectful. You want me to talk to her?" He meets my gaze. "Or we could sit down together and talk with her. Things are only going to get crazier when the baby is born."

I stand there wondering who stole my husband and where they took him. Where has this man been for the last five months? Was he here all along and I just didn't see him? Is this all about having our seventeen-year-old responsible daughter pregnant and about to be a mother? Or is this all on me? I'd like to blame everything on Hazel, or at least on the circumstances, but in my heart of hearts, I'm afraid it started before the day she passed me the pregnancy test through the crack in the bathroom door.

The toaster clicks and Oscar tops the sandwiches and begins wrapping them. I dig in the refrigerator for something to pack for myself for lunch. I have to hit both job sites today. I've got a beautiful I beam being delivered to the new project that I plan to use as a divider between their kitchen and living room and I also have an appointment with a stonemason. I'll be lucky if I even make it home in time for dinner. Which I just threw in the Crock-Pot: pot roast with carrots and potatoes.

Oscar looks up from his post at the counter. "This is nice, Liv."

"What?" I glance at him. I found cold pesto pasta in the back of the fridge that can't be more than four or five days old. I feel like I've hit the lotto.

"Being here with you like this. Without the kids." He pauses. "I think they make us both a little crazy."

We both stand there looking at each other, me still holding the refrigerator open. He comes to me and puts his arms around my waist and I let go of the fridge door. I wrap my arms around his neck and hold him tightly, surprised by the tears that spring to my eyes. "We have to figure this out, Liv. You and me." His breath is warm in my ear. "I miss you. I don't want to fight."

"I miss you, too," I breathe.

"Maybe we need to get away. Just you and me? A B&B or something. Vermont?"

He's still murmuring in my ear. "I think we need to take a little focus off baby mama and put more on ourselves. On our marriage. Because . . . because I love you, babe." His voice crackles with emotion. "And I don't like this. I don't like how we are anymore."

A lump rises in my throat and it takes me a moment to find my voice. "I love you, too," I manage.

"So . . . a weekend away?"

Before I can rattle off all the things I have to do besides look for a decent price on a weekend getaway at a B&B, he says, "I'll look into it. Next weekend? Or is that the baby shower?"

"No baby shower now."

"No baby shower? What happened?"

I take a breath, step out of his arms, and go back into the refrigerator for my cold pasta. "Cancelled. She doesn't want it. She said none of her friends were coming. I think she had an argument about it with Katy."

"No baby shower? So, what? You and I are going to be buying baby crap? That pissant doesn't plan to contribute anything financially toward this?"

I decide not to address the baby stuff right now because I'm a little concerned that Hazel isn't making plans as far as what she'll need. When she first found out she was pregnant, she had lists, what kind of equipment, what kind or organic sleeper, pacifiers, all highly researched. But I haven't heard a word about any of it in weeks. It's almost as if she's forgotten she's having the baby.

Maybe trying to forget.

"Next week. Let's shoot for that." I stand there holding my bowl of pasta. "You really do need to get to work."

He checks his watch. Sighs. "I'd love to call in sick. You and I could just . . . I don't know. Hang out. I could light a fire in the fireplace." He says it as if trying to entice.

"I can't. I wish I could." I shake my head. "Appointments out the wazoo."

"I know. I can't, either." He goes back to the counter and takes two of the wrapped sandwiches. "But I'll see you tonight?" He comes back to me, his lips puckered for a kiss. "Let me make that fire for us? We'll send the kid to her room. Kids."

I kiss him. "It's a date."

He kisses me again, this time his lips lingering over mine. And then he heads for the laundry room. "Can you let Willie Nelson out one more time before you leave?"

I look at the clock on the stove. Now I'm running late, too. "Sure."

"And my suit that's still at the dry cleaners? Could you run by and pick it up? I've got that meeting next week. Apparently we can't wear our pjs." He tugs on his scrubs top.

"Tomorrow, if not today."

"Love you, babe," he calls over his shoulder.

"Love you," I echo softly.

363

# 24
## HAZEL

I walk up to Katy's locker and lean against the one next to hers. My back is killing me. And my feet hurt. Thank goodness I wore my Ugg boots. My feet are already swollen and it isn't even lunchtime yet.

"Hey," I say.

"Hey." Katy's digging around in her locker so I can't see her face. I know she's still mad at me about the shower. She really wanted to have a baby shower for me. And order a cake that looked like an old-school baby rattle and play dumb games like guessing the baby's due date and weight. But I don't want a baby shower. She said she'd already made plans. Bought invitations with elephants on them. I told her I didn't care. Return the invitations. I don't want my friends sitting around playing games and eating cake. I don't want their presents. I doubt many people would have come, anyway. And those who did come would only have done so because Katy or maybe their moms guilted them into it.

"How'd you do on your quiz?"

"Ninety-one."

I peek around the corner of her locker door. "You did better than I did." *For once,* I almost say. But if I'm trying to suck up to her, that's probably not the way to do it. To rub her nose in the fact that I'm the better student. Always.

Or was. Before I started slacking off. Before Charlie.

The baby moves inside me.

He's head down already, Dr. Gallagher says. Which is supposed to be good, but now I feel like I have a bowling ball between my legs. I put both of my hands on my belly to feel him. It's like he knows I'm thinking about him. Like he's saying he doesn't care that he's ripped a big hole in my life.

Charlie settles down and I lean against the lockers again. Kids are passing by in the hall. Some people I know say hi. But some don't even make eye contact. I watch them, trying to remember what it felt like when I wasn't pregnant. When I didn't feel the responsibility of another human being weighing down on me.

"I talked to Ms. Esposito this morning," I say. "About finishing out the year at home.

It took me all week to get in. Did you know you have to make an appointment with a guidance counselor now? You can't just walk in?"

"What did she say?"

I shrug and lower my backpack to the floor. All of a sudden, just in the last week, it's started to feel heavier. I think it's because I'm so fat. I've gained twenty-three pounds! When I got on the scale at Dr. Gallagher's office the other day, I actually started bawling.

"She said I can definitely do it. Nobody wants me here, not with my titties leaking milk."

"Ewww," Katy says. "Do you have to keep talking about that?"

I'm just as weirded out by the whole idea of a baby sucking on my nips as Katy is, but I don't say so. All the research stresses how important breast-feeding is, so I have to do it for Charlie. I'm going to do it for him. "I can definitely do the online school thing. I just . . ." I groan and rest the back of my head against the locker behind me. "There's, like, a lot of paperwork and . . ." I groan again. "There's just a lot of stuff I have to do."

"Guess you better start doing it, then."

"Hey, Katy," this girl Marissa we know

calls as she walks by.

"Hey," Katy calls back.

"Hi." I wave at Marissa.

She smiles at me, but she doesn't say anything. I want to say she's acting like a total bitch. But she's not. Not really. She's one of the girls who still actually talks to me. And doesn't talk about me behind my back, like some of the other girls do.

I grab Katy's locker door and pull it back farther so I can see her. "You going to Kelsey Wright's party Friday night?"

She's flipping through a spiral notebook and glances at me. "I was thinking about it, but — Oh crap. Incoming. My three o'clock." She rolls her eyes dramatically in the direction behind my back. "Coming up on you."

I don't look. I know who she's talking about. Tyler. He's walking down the hall. Right toward us. I shrug like to say, "So?"

Actually, this is the first week I've been able to see him without having to hide so he won't see me crying. I'm so over him now. Completely. "He still coming this way?"

Katy cuts her eyes in his direction and then sticks her head back in her locker.

A bunch of freshman boys walk by, being loud and shoving one another. Tyler is walking behind them.

With Amanda.

Holding her hand.

I feel like I'm going to throw up. I swallow hard and look down. Then I look up, bringing my hand to my enormous stomach. I rub it; making it obvious I'm trying to call attention to my baby. His baby.

"Hey, Ty," I say loud enough for one of the freshman boys to look back over his shoulder.

Tyler acts like he didn't even hear me.

"Amanda." I nod my head when she meets my gaze.

She looks away fast. "Hey, Hazel. I like your . . . your sweatshirt," she says.

It's one of Dad's hoodies because I'm a whale and I can only wear his shirts now. Nothing I own, even my big stuff, fits. And nothing of Mom's fits me anymore, either. The sweatshirt I'm wearing has a beach and a sunset on it and says *Key West.* Mom and Dad took us to Key West for Easter when I was in the eighth grade. We had so much fun that it makes me sad to think about it because I won't be going on vacations like that anymore. You can't take a baby on a WaveRunner.

I force a smile. "Thanks."

Tyler and Amanda walk past me. Still

holding hands.

I wait until they get all the way to the water fountain before I whisper to Katy, "He didn't even speak to me."

"Doesn't matter." She slams her locker door shut. "You don't need him. You don't even want him." She stands beside me and leans against her locker, her books in her arms. "You said you wouldn't take him back, even if he begged you."

I rub my belly and breathe deep to keep back the tears. Tears that are his fault. Which really doesn't mean much — the fact that I would cry because the dickwad didn't say hello. I didn't used to be a crier, but I cry over everything now. Mom says it's hormonal. That it will get better after the baby is born. I sure as tarnation hope so. This week I've cried because Gran bought me a cupcake with an elephant on it. An Indian elephant. She remembered that you can tell if they are Indian elephants or African elephants because their ears are shaped like the continent they originate from. I also cried watching a cell phone commercial on TV. Then there was the breakdown in the doctor's office when I re-alized what a cow I was. The nurse actually had to tell me to sit down and she got a bottle of water for me.

"The party Friday night," I say to Katy. "You definitely going?"

"Why?"

I look at her. She's frowning so hard that her eyebrows almost go together. She has the best eyebrows. She uses some kind of plastic stencil to pluck them perfectly. I used to pluck mine; right now, they look like two azalea bushes on my forehead. Some of the hairs are almost as long as Granddad's.

"You wanna go to the party?" she asks me.

I chew on my bottom lip. "I think maybe I do."

She doesn't seem to be all that psyched about the idea. "Her parents aren't going to be there. There's going to be beer. You allowed to go?"

I look at her like that's the dumbest question I've ever heard. "Can I spend the night with you?"

She shrugs. "Sure."

"You wanna stop at Gran and Granddad's with me after school first? Then to your house? I was going to make them this chicken-and-rice casserole. Gran is supposed to pick up all the ingredients when she gets her groceries. I gave her a list."

"I didn't know you knew how to make stuff like that. From scratch."

"It's easy. Mom's recipe, but I add some

370

veggies because Gran and Granddad aren't eating as many as they should."

She nods. The hall is starting to clear out. We need to go to class or we're going to be late and I've already been late to class twice this week. Line in the girls' bathroom. I have to go between practically every class.

"I thought she wasn't going to take your granddad to Hannaford anymore because she embarrassed him at the bakery when the lady wouldn't give him a free sugar cookie because he was over six and he took a bunch of them."

I laugh. "Granddad likes cookies with sprinkles." I lean down and grab my back-pack and heave it onto my shoulder. "So no, she's not going to Hannaford's with him anymore. She's doing one of those pickup deals. She calls in the order or does it on her computer and they have the groceries ready for her when she gets there. She just pulls up and someone loads them in the car."

Katy steps back. "I gotta go. So plan for Friday — after school, we're going to make dinner for your grands, then to my house to get ready?"

I nod.

Katy starts backing up down the hall in the direction of her class. I have to go the

other way. "You sure you want to go?"
"Definitely." I grin. Lower my voice so no one else can hear me. "Because Jack told me he was going to be there."

# 25
## LIV

My mother is waiting for me at the back door and she opens it before I'm all the way up the snowy walk.

"Sorry to call you so late. I cut the water off, but the bedroom was already flooded."

"It's fine, Mom," I say tiredly.

When she called me, I had just changed into plaid flannel pajama pants, a T-shirt, and my favorite hoodie, sans bra. I had sat down with a glass of wine in my hand, yet untouched, and a blanket on my lap. I was cold and sleepy and had big plans to sit beside Oscar on the couch and watch a PBS documentary on Hitler's bunker. The scary thing is, I'm so worn-out from the week that I was actually looking forward to curling up with Oscar and watching the horrors of World War II be recounted.

"You look good, Mom." I nudge her into the laundry room and close the door behind me. Her health seems to have taken a turn

373

for the better. Her doctor isn't sure why, but he's hoping her new medication is what's giving her more movement and less pain.

"Feeling pretty chipper." She tightens the tie of her fuzzy red bathrobe; she's dressed for bed, too. "Or was, before I heard what sounded like splashing coming from the back of the house. It was your dad wading out of his bedroom to tell me there was a pipe leaking." She tries to smooth down her short white hair; it's sticking out in every direction like porcupine quills. "Had to take off my slippers, roll up my pajama legs, and wade in to shut the valve off under the sink. It's a wonder I was able to get down and reach it without going swimming."

I slip out of my coat that's covered with a dusting of snow, shake it, and hang it on a hook. Next, I step out of my boots and into the sheepskin slippers I leave at my parents' for just these occasions.

"Still coming down, the snow." Mom nods in the direction of the back door.

"Expecting six to eight inches overnight." I follow her into the kitchen. I'm in my jammies. After Mom called, I considered running back upstairs to put on jeans and a bra but decided there was no reason to change. I was just running to my parents'.

"Where is he?" I ask.

"Sitting on his bed. Won't come out." She puckers up her lips as if she's just tasted something particularly sour. "He's declared it an island in a moat. Told him he could stay there until hell or his bedroom floor froze over, for all I care."

I try to think of a response, but I'm just too tired. I understand her frustration with my dad, but I don't see any reason to be mean to him. Instead of starting what will inevitably turn into an argument with her, I head down the hall. It's dry. Maybe the "flood" isn't as bad as Mom said. Hope springs eternal.

"By the way, he's not wearing pants!" my mother calls after me. "Or skivvies."

I stop and look back. She's standing at the end of the hallway in her red robe, her spiky hair backlit by the kitchen light. She somehow reminds me of Jack Nicholson in *The Shining;* all she needs is an axe.

"Dad's naked, sitting on his bed in the flooded bedroom?" I ask as if it's an everyday occurrence.

"No. He's wearing his pajama top and wool cap. We were going to bed when he decided to install a new faucet in his bathroom."

I close my eyes for a second. I had a bad

day at the Anselins'. They were unhappy with the latest version of the layout of their bedroom suite, even though I'd been clear as to what could and couldn't be done while still keeping the exposed ceiling beams that they wanted. "Replace the faucet?" I squint, trying to process. "What was wrong with his bathroom faucet? Weren't all the fixtures just replaced last year?"

She crosses her arms over her chest. She's a small woman, but she looks pretty formidable. Even without the axe.

"Let me guess." I press my thumb and index finger to my temples, feeling a headache coming on. "There is no new faucet."

"Nope. He thinks he's a retired plumber. I told him he was a retired physician. He said I was crazy and that he was going to tell his wife on me and that she was going to put me in the loony bin." She turns away. "I'm making tea. Mint or chamomile?"

"Mint." I walk slowly down the hallway. "Dad? It's Liv. I'm going to come in so . . . so maybe throw a blanket over your lap?"

I get no response. "Dad? Is it okay if I come in?"

"Held my finger in the dike as long as I could," I hear him say from his room. Followed by a chuckle.

"You decent, Dad?" I hesitate. It's not so

much that I care if I see my dad's genitalia. It's just the idea of it. If he were himself, he'd be mortified. When he doesn't answer, I step into the doorway to his room, averting my eyes at first, then shifting my gaze.

I find my father, indeed, sitting in the middle of his bed, in a room flooded with water. But at least he's dressed. He's wearing his old tuxedo shirt and jacket, what appears to be track pants, slippers, and a gray watch cap. He's pulled the whole ensemble together with a plaid navy scarf tied jauntily around his neck. I don't know whether to laugh or cry. I want to do both. I feel as if the more my father loses his identity, the more I lose mine. My whole life I've been Dr. Edward Cosset's daughter. Who will I be when he's gone?

"Why wouldn't I be decent?" he harrumphs. "Know where the story of the little Dutch boy who sticks his finger in the dike comes from? *Hans Brinker; or, The Silver Skates*. Mary Mapes Dodge. The Dutch boy story" — he gestures with a twirl of his bony finger — "is within the story."

*How the hell does he remember that and not remember that he went to medical school?*

I look down at the shallow layer of water on his floor. Not as bad as Mom suggested on the phone; I'm not going to have to get

377

a dingy to rescue him. But definitely not good. The transition on the floor in the doorway is what's keeping the water from spilling into the hall. I kick off my slippers and roll up the hems of my plaid pajama pants. "I'm coming in, Dad."

"Careful, it's wet," he warns.

I meet his gaze. "I hear you had a little problem with your bathroom faucet."

He shakes his head slowly. Thoughtfully. "Nope."

I step into his room. The water is cold. "Then what's this?"

He looks over the edge of his bed. "Water. Once it freezes, I thought I'd take you girls ice-skating. You always loved to ice-skate."

I walk into the bathroom, trying not to splash any water onto the walls or furniture and make the situation worse. The floors are hardwood. If I get the water up fast enough with a shop vac, set up a fan or two, maybe the floors can be saved.

"Dad, you're not supposed to be messing with the —" My phone in my back pocket rings. "You're not supposed to do any plumbing in the house. You call the plumber if you need a repair. Or me." I grab my phone and look at the screen. It's Hazel's friend Katy. Which means it's Hazel. Which means she either left her phone somewhere

378

or broke it again. "Hazel?"

There's quiet on the other end of the line long enough for me to wonder if it was a butt dial. Then I hear a small voice: "Um, no it's . . . it's Katy, Miss Liv."

"Katy?" My mom alarm goes off in my head. My daughter is thirty-six weeks pregnant. Too early to be in labor. I feel a flutter in my chest. What if she has gone into labor? Why else would Katy be calling me? But I don't want to sound like a panicked mother, and I don't want to scare Katy or Hazel if she has gone into labor.

"You girls okay?" I ask carefully.

Hazel and Katy left school together. I got the full itinerary from my mother on the phone on my way home from work. The girls stopped at my parents' and made a chicken rice casserole, which my mother called to tell me was better than the one I made. Then they went home to Katy's house to watch *Titanic* and have a sleepover.

"Miss Liv, I'm sorry to bother you, but . . ."

Once she starts to speak, I realize Katy — sweet, kind, silly Katy — is drunk off her ass. My second thought is that there's something wrong. Seriously wrong, if she's calling me in this state, risking her parents finding out. "What's going on, Katy?"

"Hazel." She sounds like she's about to burst into tears. "Something's wrong with her. She . . . Oh, God, she's going to kill me when she finds out I called you. But I didn't know what else to do."

"Katy," I say sharply. "What's wrong with Hazel? Is she —" I don't want to say "in labor" because how would either of them know, if it's just the early stage? First-time mothers rarely do; I know I didn't. "She okay? The baby all right?"

"She's fine. The baby's fine, but . . . I think you better come here, Miss Liv," she says in a rush of words.

I splash my way out of my father's bedroom. "Katy, let me speak to Hazel."

"That's the thing, Miss Liv, Hazel, she —" Now Katy is crying. "She locked herself in this bathroom and she won't come out."

*This bathroom?* "What bathroom?" I demand, getting the impression Katy doesn't mean *her* bathroom, at *her* house where they're supposed to be. Where they're supposed to be eating popcorn and watching Leonardo DiCaprio and Kate Winslet lock lips.

"We're at this girl's house. Kelsey." She sniffs. "We know her from school. Actually it's her brother's house," she mumbles.

I hear my father splashing toward me.

380

He's gotten out of bed. "Dad, get out of the water. You're going to ruin your slippers." I point at his feet. "Katy, are you two at a party?" I ask suspiciously into the phone.

"Yes," she blubbers. "I'm sorry. I knew it was a bad idea. But, Hazel, she — She made me bring her," she wails.

I can't believe Hazel is at a party. An underage drinking party. Thirty-six weeks pregnant and she's partying. "Why did she lock herself in the bathroom?"

"I don't know. I . . ."

Katy's voice fades.

"Katy," I say loudly into the phone. "Why did Hazel lock herself in the bathroom?"

"She . . . Tyler was here with Amanda and . . . and this guy Jack was supposed to be here, but he didn't show, and —" She takes a blubbering, shaky breath. "Marissa is afraid Hazel is going to kill herself."

"What?" I say sharply. Suddenly *I* can barely catch my breath. "Did Hazel threaten to kill herself, Katy, because if she did —" I try not to hyperventilate. "Because if you seriously think she might hurt herself, you need to get off this phone and call 911."

"I don't think she said it." Katy burps loudly in my ear. And then she's back to crying. "Marissa exaggerates. But I still thought I should call you. Because I didn't

381

know what else to do. She won't come out, Miss Liv."

I catch my breath. "No, you did the right thing. Absolutely." I force my brain to move away from my inherent fear into logic mode. "Katy, listen to me. I want you to text me the address where you are. I'm going to hang up and call Hazel."

"She won't answer," Katy wails. "I tried. I knocked on the door. She just keeps telling me to go away."

My dad walks past me, his scarf trailing behind him. "I'm getting pretzels. You want pretzels, Bethie?"

"Text me the address," I say into the phone.

"I will."

I disconnect and call Hazel. Twice. She doesn't answer. Then I text her. You okay?

No response.

I stand there for a minute, trying to decide what to do. I can hear my parents in the kitchen arguing. Mom is telling Dad he can't have pretzels this close to bedtime. My phone dings. It's a text message from Katy with an address about twenty minutes away, maybe farther because of the snow. I look up at the water lying on the floor of my dad's bedroom. Then I dial Oscar, who was asleep on the couch. I give him the rundown on the flooded bathroom, followed by the phone call from Katy.

"Locked herself in a bathroom?" Oscar says. "What's wrong?"

"I don't know. Katy doesn't know. But Hazel won't come out of the bathroom and the door is locked. I need to go see what's going on." I hesitate. "Hon, could you come over to my parents' and run the wet vac?"

"Of course," he says.

"I'm sorry." I head toward the kitchen, pressing my hand to my forehead. I just want to get to Hazel. To my baby. "I know it's late. And I know we were going to watch TV together, but —"

"Liv," he interrupts. "Let me clean up the water. I'll get some fans set up. You go see what's wrong with Hazel. You think it's the baby? You don't think she's bleeding, do you? Placenta previa can be life-threatening. If —"

"I don't think she's bleeding," I assure him, trying to reassure myself. Hazel's made some dumb mistakes, but she's not dumb. I'm certain she's smart enough to go directly to the hospital if she has any sort of serious condition. Or call 911. "She's at a party. It has something to do with dumbass."

"Hazel's at a party? Like a birthday party?

383

I thought she was going to Katy's."

"Like a drinking party," I tell him. I find my parents in the kitchen still arguing over the pretzels. Only now Dad's got the bag in his hand and Mom is demanding he put them back in the cabinet. "Oscar, I'm going to go get Hazel. I'll call you in a little while."

"You coming back home, or to your parents' house? Should I wait for you there?"

"I'll call you," I repeat.

"I have to go," I tell Mom and Dad as I rush through the kitchen. "Oscar is on his way over to clean up the water." In the laundry room, I kick off my slippers. "Mom, Dad's going to have to sleep in the spare room. He won't be able to sleep in his room tonight with —"

"I'm not letting him mess up the spare room." Mom comes to the laundry room door. "Lynette just cleaned it, top to bottom."

I step into my boots. "Then he'll have to sleep with you." I throw up my arms. "Or on the couch in the family room. I honestly don't care where he sleeps, Mom. He can sleep at my house if that's what you want. Send him home with Oscar. He can sleep in the downstairs bedroom." I grab my coat. "I have to go. Hazel needs me."

She follows me to the door. "She's in

384

labor? It's too soon for her to be in labor."

"She's not in labor. I have to go." I slip into my coat. "Bye, Dad. Stay out of the water, Dad." I open the back door and the frigid air and snow rushes in. "Oscar will be here as quick as he can."

Mom starts to respond, but I walk out into the snow and close the door behind me.

# 26
## HAZEL

Someone knocks on the bathroom door and from the toilet, I scream, "I said go away!"

I'm not actually on the toilet, as in using it. I put the lid down. I *was* sitting on the floor, my back against the door, but the linoleum was so grotty, I was worried it might have bacteria that could be harmful to a baby. The whole house is disgusting: dirty dishes in the sink, trash on the floor, dog hair everywhere. When Kelsey said we were invited to her party, I thought she meant at her house. This is her older brother's place that he shares with a bunch of guys. They all work the lobster boats and the whole house stinks of rotten seafood. I've been in houses where lobstermen live and it never smelled like this.

Whoever is on the other side of the door knocks again and I say, "I told you —"

"Hazel!"

My mom's voice startles me and I jump

up. "Mom?" I walk to the door. "What are you doing here?" I'm beyond embarrassed. I'm mortified. What's everyone at school going to say when they hear my mother showed up at Kelsey's party? "Mom! You can't be here."

She turns the doorknob, but the door won't open because I locked it. It's a miracle the door even locks. I tried to hide in a bedroom, but this girl and guy were in one; they both had their shirts off. The other two bedrooms didn't even have doors.

"Hazel, open the door," Mom says, rattling the doorknob. I know that tone. She's pretending she's not angry, but she is.

"Go home, Mom." I cross my arms over my boobs, looking around, trying to figure out how to get out of here. But I'm trapped because it's a bathroom and it only has one door. Duh.

"Hazel, you need to let me in." She softens her voice, though she's still speaking loud enough to be heard over the music. Angry Mom is sounding like worried Mom now.

I put my hands on my head and squeeze my eyes shut. I don't want to be here. I don't know where I want to be, but I know I want to be anywhere but here. I want to be anyone but Hazel Ridgely. Pregnant Hazel Ridgely. Tears sting my eyes. "Please,

Mom," I beg.

"I called you and texted you. You didn't answer."

*"Because I didn't want to talk to you,"* I holler. She doesn't answer and I lean against the door, the side of my head to it. "Can you go, Mom? *Please?"*

"I can't." Her voice comes from only inches from mine. "I can't leave you here, not locked in a bathroom. I don't know what's going on with you, Hazel, but you need to come home."

"I'm not going home!" I mean to scream it at her, but my voice cracks.

I start pacing the dark, dirty bathroom that smells like piss. Boys are so gross. They can never pee in the toilet. They can pee on the seat, on the floor in front of it, they can even hit the wall behind, but they can never get their pee in the water. Mom makes Dad and Sean sit to pee, just so she won't have to clean it up. When I potty train Charlie, I'm going to teach him to sit when he pees; standing isn't even going to be an option.

I get to a wall with a poster with snakes on it and turn and go the other way. Who puts a snake poster on a bathroom wall? It's seven steps from one wall to the other. Eight from the door to the window. This is all Katy's fault. If she hadn't been flirting with some guy named Reds she doesn't even know, we could have gone home an hour ago. But then she got drunk and couldn't drive. I just had one beer. I could have driven us home. But she wouldn't give me her keys because she didn't want to go home. She wanted to make out with Reds. That's when I locked myself in the bathroom. When she said we weren't going home. Which was stupid because now I don't know how to get out of here. Everyone at the whole party knows. I'm sure they're all talking about it. How am I going to walk out now, with everyone staring at me, knowing I'm the crazy, pregnant girl who locked herself in the bathroom?

"Hazel, honey." Mom rattles the doorknob again. "Please let me in. I just want to see if you're okay."

"Mom," I groan. "I'm fine. Go *a-way!*"

She pushes on the old door. Kind of hard. "Hazel, I'm not kidding! Let me in." She stands there for a minute, I can tell by the light blocked under the door. Then she walks away.

I stare at the door. Music is blasting from the living room; it's so loud the old floorboards are practically vibrating.

Maybe it blew out Mom's eardrums and she went home. Either that, or she went out to the car to call Dad, where she could hear. Or call the cops.

God, if she calls the cops, everyone will hate me.

Tears run down my cheeks; I can't stop them. My eyes are stinging from the mascara I know is running down my face. I go back to sit on the toilet seat again. I'm tired and my back hurts and I hate this stupid party. I hate my stupid life. I hate this stupid alien living inside me.

Jack was supposed to be here. I curled my hair and put on makeup and I put on one of Katy's button-up shirts over Dad's Guns N' Roses T-shirt. Real vintage, right out of his drawer.

Jack didn't come.

I waited and waited for him and then, after drinking the beer, I texted him. He put his number in my phone yesterday. I don't even know why. He just took my phone out of my hand and put in his number under the name Jack Sparrow. A joke because I told him his name reminded me of the Johnny Depp character in the *Pirates of the Caribbean* movies. He's got the black hair that's kind of long. I didn't tell him I liked the movies because I know how cheesy they are. But then he told me he liked them. That's when he gave me his number.

The minute I texted him tonight, I wished I could suck the text back into my phone. Or suck myself into a vortex and disappear from Earth. Neither happened. Jack texted me back to say he couldn't come because his grandma fell and broke her hip and he was on his way to a hospital in Portland with his mom. I don't know if he was telling the truth or not. Probably not, although that seems like a weird lie for a guy to make up. What high school guy wants to admit he's hanging out with his mom and grandmother?

I wanted to go back to Katy's then, but she kept saying no. That was when Tyler and Amanda showed up. That's when things went from bad to catastrophic. They kissed right in front of me, tongues and everything. I thought I was going to throw up the beer and Doritos I just had.

A sound at the bathroom window startles me and I jerk my head around to look at it. There isn't a curtain or even a towel on it. This is one of those old houses where it has a big window in the bathroom like the room was something else a long time ago like another bedroom. Back in the day when there wasn't any running water, there were no bathrooms in houses. You had to use an outhouse. Which I can't imagine with the temperatures below zero at night and the snow up to my butt cheeks.

I come off the toilet, squinting at the window. It's snowing hard now and dark out. The wind is blowing. Maybe a branch hit the glass. I can't see anything. It's all fogged up.

Then the window begins to rise and it scares me. Is someone trying to break into the — My mom's coat appears in the open window, then she leans over and sticks her head in.

"Mom!" I take a step back, feeling like this must be a nightmare. This can't be happening. "What are you doing?"

"I want to talk to you."

She's got Dad's knit cap pulled down over her head and it looks stupid. She's also wearing her old, ugly glasses that make her look bug-eyed. She never wears her glasses out. Not where people can see her.

*"Mom,"* I say again. Someone has finally turned the music down. I don't have to shout.

She throws one leg over the window; she's wearing plaid pajama pants. Pajama pants! Snow is blowing in and falling on the floor.

I glance over my shoulder, seriously considering running out the door. Running outside and down the street. But where am

I going to go? Especially with no coat. It's on a chair in the kitchen.

"How did you even know I was here?" I'm tempted to push her out the window and slam it shut and lock it. I know the answer as soon as it comes out of my mouth. "Katy. She called you, didn't she?" I turn away, shaking my head. I groan out loud. "I can't believe she called you. I'm gonna kill her."

Mom half steps, half falls through the window, onto the bathroom floor, making a loud thump. I'm petrified someone in the house has heard her.

"I can't believe you just climbed through some guy's window." I gesture at it.

"Katy was worried about you." Mom steadies herself with her hand on the windowsill as she gets to her feet.

"Will you keep it down?" I beg, looking at the door again.

"Katy was afraid you might hurt yourself. That's why she called me. And I hope you'd do the same thing for her." She pulls off her cap and snow and droplets of water fall on the floor. She's making such a mess I'm going to have to mop it up. Which might not be a bad thing, as dirty as the floor is. I just don't know what I'll use. I couldn't find any towels when I washed my hands after I peed. I had to wipe them on my yoga pants.

"*Hurt* myself? What are you talking about?" Then I realize what she means. Not hurt myself. She means *kill* myself.

"Mom!" Now I'm pissed. More pissed at her than I was at Tyler when I locked myself in here. "I would never do that. I can't believe Katy would say that. What would make her think I wanted to commit suicide? Mom, you know me. I would never . . ."

She unzips her coat. "Somebody told her you said you were going to kill yourself." She's wearing her paint-splattered, stained hoodie that I hate. I can't believe she walked into this house wearing that. I'll never be able to go back to school. I'll have to move out of state. Out of the country.

I back up, trying to get as far away from my mother as I can, which isn't far because the bathroom isn't all that big. "Someone told her —" I roll my eyes. Had to be Marissa. She's such a drama queen. Her Snapchats are beyond ridiculous. Always sad-face photos of herself. She's always saying someone is going to kill themselves, usually about stupid things like failing a test or getting caught by their mom masturbating. Marissa is always saying she's going to kill herself. "Mom," I say. "I can't believe you would think I would do that." I just stand there, my eyes closed, trying to will her away.

She walks up to me. I can hear her dripping on the linoleum floor. "You shouldn't be here." She pauses. "And you shouldn't be drinking. Not just because you're underage, but because —"

"I wasn't drinking," I interrupt. A lie.

"I can smell it on your breath, Hazel."

I'm so sick to death of her always being right. "One beer," I tell her. I bite down on my lower lip, trying not to start crying again. I can't believe tonight has turned out like this. All I wanted to do was see Jack.

"What happened to upset you?" Mom says. She rubs my arm.

I pull away. "Nothing."

"Katy said that Tyler and his new girlfriend were here."

"I swear I'm going to kill her," I say under my breath.

Mom waits. Which is worse than her talking.

I tear up and wipe at my eyes, which make them sting more. I bet I look like a raccoon. "He . . ." My lower lip trembles. "He and Amanda were making out right in front of me. I know it was just to show off. To hurt me. Then he wouldn't even talk to me, Mom. At school, he acts like I don't even exist. He's being so mean." I close my eyes because I don't want her to see that that dickwad can make me cry like this. "It makes me mad because he can pretend he never loved me, but I've got this." I lay my hand on my big, fat belly. "And I can't make it go away."

"Oh, Hazel." Mom sounds like *she's* going to cry.

She tries to hug me and, at first, I don't want her to, but then . . . Then I realize I really need a hug.

"Mom," I blubber, laying my head on her wet coat.

"Sweetie," she whispers, holding me tight. "Why didn't you tell me Tyler was acting like this?"

"And what were you going to do about it? *Tell his mom?*"

"No. I'd run him over with my new truck."

I can't help it, I laugh. And then take in a deep breath and let it out, sniffling. "I didn't tell you," I say, "because it's all my fault. You didn't think I should have gone out with him to start with. You knew he was a jerk."

"He's not a jerk, sweetie. He's a teenage boy."

"You know what I mean," I say miserably. "It's all my fault. I was stupid. Stupid.

Stupid. Stupid."

"We all make mistakes, Hazel."

"Not you. You never do stupid things," I blubber, getting snot on her coat that's cold and wet against my face.

She hugs me really tight and then leans back, taking me by the shoulders, making me look at her. My eyes are really stinging; I knew I was allergic to Katy's eyeliner. I just wanted to look pretty for Jack, but now I know that's stupid, too. He doesn't like me. I'm going to have a baby. He could have any girl in the school. He doesn't want one stupid enough not to use a condom.

"I have made mistakes. Some bad ones."

"Mom, getting the kind of orange juice with pulp instead of without pulp is not a bad mistake." I run my hand between us, my head still on her shoulder, and touch my belly. "I screwed up. I really screwed up." I hesitate. "I know that's why you've been so mad at me. Because you never screw up."

She laughs but the kind of laugh where what's been said is so ridiculous that you're half crying. "Hazel, do you really think I never screw up? Would you like the list of things I've screwed up? Big things? Like getting a useless degree, even after my parents warned me it would be hard to get a job.

How about marrying your dad right out of college when I should have waited, should have been on my own for a while? And my parenting? I've done so many things wrong. How I've handled your pregnancy being one of them."

"You're right to be mad. This is a screw-up of epic proportion."

"Hazel . . ." she says quietly. "I made the same mistake."

"What?"

She smooths my hair. "I made the same mistake that you made, sweetie. I thought I was in love. I thought this guy I was dating in high school loved me and I had sex with him. And I got pregnant. I was sixteen. Just like you."

I pull back, as shocked as I would be if she said it had been proven that climate change isn't real. Or that Dad wasn't biologically my father, even though I look like a female version of him. "You? You got pregnant in high school?" I whisper.

She meets my gaze. Nods. She looks so sad.

"Mom —"

There's a knock on the bathroom door. "You comin' out today?" some guy shouts.

I turn around and holler at the door, "No. Go piss in the snow!" I look back at Mom, lowering my volume. Adjusting my tone. "You had a baby. What happened to it?"

When she looks at me, I see that her eyes have tears in them.

The guy knocks again. No, pounds on the door. "Hey! You got a medical problem in there?"

I turn away from Mom, drop my hands to my sides, and scream, "I said, go piss in the snow, you ass—"

"Hazel," Mom says, definitely not approving of my behavior.

I turn back to her, making a face. "What? He's a guy. He can pee anywhere."

We're both quiet for a minute then. Standing face-to-face, her in her wet coat, gross sweatshirt, and ugly glasses. Me with my big belly where an alien is growing.

"I can't believe you got pregnant, Mom. No, I can't believe Gran and Granddad let you have an abortion."

"I didn't have an abortion."

I stare at her. "Jeez, I don't have a secret sister, do I? Please, Mom, tell me you didn't put my sister up for adoption." I'm staring at her, trying to read her face. "I always thought I had a sister, you know, somewhere out there. I thought you guys were going to have another baby. It didn't occur to me that you could have *had* another baby."

She walks over to the toilet, unzips her coat the rest of the way, and plops down. "Your grandparents don't know I got pregnant in high school. I'd prefer they never know."

I walk toward her. I can't believe we have a family scandal. We never have scandals like other families. Well, we didn't until I got knocked up. Turns out, Mom beat me to it. Just no one ever knew it. "Does Dad know?"

She nods. "But no one else. I never told anyone. Not Aunt Beth, not my friends . . ." She hangs her head and wipes her face with her hands. Then she looks up at me again. "Because I didn't have the courage to tell my parents. I didn't have the courage that you had to tell me, Hazel."

I chew on my bottom lip, looking at her. I think about what Mom is saying. I didn't feel brave when I asked her to help me with the pregnancy test. I'd bought it at work at the drugstore days before, but I was too scared to do it by myself, or even with Katy.

"What happened to your baby?" I ask.

She puts her hands together and looks down at her feet. At the dirty floor. "When I was about eight weeks, I got lucky. I had a miscarriage."

"And you didn't tell anyone about that, either?"

She shakes her head. "Never, not until I told your dad, and that was after we were married."

I think for a minute. "What were you going to do? What was your plan? When you *did* have the baby?" I'm staring at her, thinking this isn't the mom I know. The mom I know would never have been dumb enough to think she could get pregnant and then just never tell *anyone.*

"I don't know." She shrugs. "I didn't have a plan."

"Wow. How did you —" I cross my arms over my chest, resting them on my belly. "Wow," is all I can think to say.

She looks up at me. "I know you don't want to hear this, but I'm going to say it anyway. You don't have to keep this baby, Hazel."

I roll my eyes and groan. "Mom —"

"Hazel." She raises her hand, interrupting me. "Let me say this and then I'll shut up. We'll go home and I won't say another word tonight."

I open my mouth to argue but close it. Because right now, going home, getting in my own bed, sounds really good.

"I know I've said this before, but you're in

401

a different place now. And honestly, even if you don't want to hear it, as your mother, I need to say it. So, just be quiet and listen to me." She takes a breath, seeming to think about what she wants to say. "Somewhere, there's a couple that desperately wants a child. The way Gran and Granddad wanted a child before they adopted me. After they were told Gran would never conceive. You could give a family a gift that might be the best thing you ever do for someone else, in your whole life, sweetie."

"Mom, I'm not —"

"Hazel, I'm not done." She pushes the hair out of her eyes. "I'm not saying you can't raise a child. I'm saying I don't want you to because it's going to be so hard. So damned hard. Because it's not easy when you're married and you have good jobs and a decent house. It's not easy then. But, sweetie, if you have a baby, you're going to miss out on so much of life. You're going to miss your senior prom, you're going to miss spring breaks in college, and chances are, you're never going to make it to medical school."

I cross my arms, thinking that's a mean thing to say. Especially if you're a mom who has told her daughter she can do anything.

"You're going to sacrifice all that, and so

much more. So many things I can't begin to tell you about. And . . ." She sighs. "I'm afraid you're going to lose a part of yourself, Hazel."

"But you hated being adopted," I snap, mostly so I won't start crying again. Because the tone of her voice makes me want to cry. I point at her. "You *told* me you always hated the fact that you were adopted. It bothered you that your mother gave you away." Tears are in my eyes again. "Mom, how could I even consider such a thing?" I beg, feeling terrible that even the idea of giving away Charlie would cross my mind.

She stands up, taking both my hands in hers. "I was a kid. A lot of kids choose something to blame their unhappiness on, to blame their parents for. Not every adopted child feels the way I did. And now that I'm an adult, now that I'm a mother, I know my birth mother, whoever she was, did the right thing."

I stand there trying to imagine what it must have been like for Mom's mother to hand her over to a stranger. To give her away to a stranger. Then I imagine handing my little baby boy over to some lady I don't know. Some lady who would become Charlie's mother.

Tears run down my cheeks.

403

I can't do it.

This is my fault. Not Charlie's. I can't punish him like that for my mistake.

"I'm not doing it," I say. "I'm not giving him away. I told you, Mom, I'm going to make this work. Even without a dad for him. I'm going to figure it out."

Mom just sits there, looking at me. Then she gets up. "Okay," she says. She zips up her coat.

I stare at her, suspicious that she's given in so easily. "Okay, what?"

"Okay." She puts up her hands. "I told you, I had to say it. I said it. You're going to keep the baby. You're going to make it work. And I guess . . . I'm going to try to figure out how to accept that."

I just stand there, staring at her.

"Let's go home," she says.

I look at the door. "I don't know if I can go out there, Mom. Everyone out there thinks I'm in here trying to kill myself." I chew on my thumb cuticle that's so raw now that I can taste blood. "And my coat's in the kitchen. Everyone's going to see me. They're going to see *you.*"

She stands there for a minute, thinking, and then unzips her coat and takes it off. "Here." She holds it out to me. "Put it on."

"What —" I watch her walk over to the

window. Open it. Then I realize what's she doing. What she wants me to do. "Mom, I'm not — I can't . . ."

"Sure you can. It's not far down. Look, the window goes to the floor. I just stepped in. Come on." She holds out her hand. "I'll help you."

I look at the window. At my mom climbing out of it. I look behind me at the door. Then back at the window, debating.

I put on Mom's coat and pull out my phone and text Katy.

Went home. Will pick up my car tomorrow. Get my coat.

Then I unlock the bathroom door, take Mom's hand and climb out the window, big belly and all.

# 27
## LIV

I roll over onto my side, under the quilt, and rest my head on Oscar's shoulder. "Thank you for doing this," I whisper, kissing him lightly on his bare chest.

He rubs my bare back and kisses the top of my head. "You're welcome. Glad you like the place. Carol at work said it was one of Bar Harbor's hidden gems. Perfect for a romantic weekend."

"Carol was right." I rest my cheek on his chest, gazing at the crackling fire on the hearth. "Not many places where you can have a room with a fireplace you're actually allowed to have a fire in."

"I'm sure the fire marshal will eventually get wind of it and close the place down."

I smile, still basking in the afterglow of our lovemaking. "This has been so nice," I say. "I hate to go home tomorrow." I close my eyes. "I don't want to go back to my life." I groan. "Our lives."

"We talking your crazy dad, your crazy clients, or your crazy seventeen-year-old pregnant daughter?" he teases.

I groan and roll onto my back, my head on the pillow. I push my hair out of my eyes and stare at the ceiling. "She actually hasn't been too bad this week. Hazel," I say thoughtfully.

"*Our* daughter? Because I'm pretty sure I saw her head spinning around last week."

I turn to meet his gaze in the semidarkness of the room and smile, glad we can laugh about this. Glad I'm laughing instead of crying because all the tears I've shed haven't changed the fact that our teenage daughter will become a mother in less than a month. "I know. Right?" I'm quiet for a minute, thinking. "No, she's definitely been calmer since the party intervention."

"More interest in the baby?" He kisses my bare shoulder. "I saw the box with the Pack 'n Play in the barn and baby clothes in the dryer."

"I think she's over the hump with the Tyler thing. In fact . . ." I hesitate, debating whether or not to say anything. But then I do because Oscar and I don't keep things from each other. Even with our problems over the last year or so, that was one mistake we haven't made. "I suspect she might be 'talking' to another boy." I do air quotes around *talking.*

"What?" He pushes up on his elbow to look down at me. "What high school boy is interested in a girl who's about to have some other guy's baby?"

I chuckle. "Teenagers are strange creatures. Thursday night before dinner she was texting with someone. She left her phone on the counter when she was setting the table and a text popped up on her phone from a Jack. Jack isn't usually female."

"You read the text?"

"No." I give him a nudge and he flops back on the bed. "I didn't *read* her text. I don't do that." I look at him. "Do you think I've become that person, Oscar? A person who reads other people's texts?"

"Of course not." He gives me a quick kiss. "I wouldn't blame you if you did, though. She's not *other people,* she's our daughter. She's still underage. And we know for a fact that she makes poor choices because she had unprotected sex."

"Well, she can't get pregnant now." I raise my finger in the air. "But as soon as Charlie is born, she's going on some form of birth control, I can promise you that."

"Hm, you're calling him Charlie. Sounds like maybe you're . . . resigned to the fact

408

that we're going to have a baby in the house. A grandson."

"We don't know if it's a boy." I roll over to rest my head on him again, wrapping my arm around his waist.

It's been a good weekend. Oscar and I haven't just called a truce, we seem to have mended some of the wounds of the past months. We've talked a lot, and not about my parents, or our work, or Hazel. We've talked about us. And it's been good. So good, that we ended up canceling our restaurant reservations tonight and having wine and cheese and crackers in bed together for dinner. Living on love, as Oscar called it.

But a two-hundred-dollar-a-night room in a B&B isn't the real world. And we can't stay here. No matter how much either of us would like to.

"I know we don't know." Oscar strokes my arm. "But I'm with Hazel. I think it's a boy." I can hear his smile in his voice. "I think we're going to have a grandson."

His tone worries me a little. I still feel he's overly attached to this baby as if he's ours and not our daughter's. It sounds like he's talking about a son and not a grandson. But maybe that's not a bad thing. Considering the indifference I still feel, even now that I am resigned to the fact that Hazel is going to be a mother. That we're going to have a baby in the house again. Probably for a few years because, once Hazel graduates high school, she's going to have to go to community college. She's going to have to learn to do something she can make enough money at to support this baby because what are the chances his father is ever going to support him financially in any way?

"Speaking of sons," I say, deciding to change the subject. Because if we talk about Hazel for too long, we invariably get into a disagreement. "Yours texted earlier. When you were in the shower. He was checking in."

"Checking to see if his allowance had been deposited, I imagine."

I smile. "It's his money. For the most part. I'm just doling it out. Anyway, he said he and *Kyo* went to a concert last night."

"Kyo." He raises his eyebrows. "He actually used her name. You think that's his way of telling us he has a girlfriend?"

"That's my guess. I'd heard mention of a girl, but this is a new one. I wanted to text back and ask him if —"

My phone, on the nightstand, vibrates. I glance at it. It's after ten. Calls after ten are never good.

410

"My mom?" I ask. The phone is closest to him.

"Nope." He picks it up. "Your sister." He answers it. "Beth."

He listens. I can hear my sister's voice, but not what she says.

"Shit," Oscar says. "But they're okay?" He pauses again. I'm gesturing for him to give me the phone. "No, no, we're in Bar Harbor. Our weekend getaway. Liv told you we were going, Beth. I was standing next to you when she told you." He catches my eye. "Beth . . . Beth. Let me give you Liv. I'm going to get dressed and get us packed up."

I sit up in bed, scared.

"They're okay. They both got out."

I meet his gaze. *Both got out?* I grab the phone. "Beth?"

"Jesus Christ, Liv. I go away for a few days and they set the house on fire?"

Oscar turns on the light and starts putting his clothes on.

"Mom and Dad set the house on fire?"

"Who do you think?" Beth says.

I scramble out of bed. "But they're okay? How bad is it?"

"I don't know." She sounds pissed. And a little drunk. "I'm in Cancun."

"*Cancun?* What are you doing in Cancun?"

411

In boxers and a T-shirt, Oscar lays my jeans on the bed. "I'll get you some underwear," he says quietly. "Start getting dressed."

"I told you I was going to Cancun with Jason."

"No, you did not tell me —"

Oscar hands me a pair of pink panties.

"Those are dirty," I tell him, my tone short. Then into the phone, "You did not tell me you were going to Cancun, Beth. I talked to you a week ago. I told you that Oscar and I were going to be out of town for the weekend. If you'd told me you were going to be in *another country,* we wouldn't have gone!"

"Hon, they're okay," Oscar says from behind me. "I can't find any clean underwear in your bag."

I walk naked to my duffel bag and start digging through the clothes. "What happened, Beth? Is it bad? Were they hurt?"

"How the hell do I know how bad it is? Mom called me. They were at the neighbor's."

I hear music in the background. It sounds like disco. "I'm two hours away. I don't —" I give up on the underwear and go back to the bed to sit down and pull on my jeans. I'll just go commando.

"We'll call Hazel," Oscar says, laying my bra on the bed beside me. He's in jeans now, but hasn't buttoned them up yet.

I stand back up, pulling up my jeans. "I'll call Hazel," I say into the phone. "She stayed with Mom and Dad Friday night, but she and Katy were —" I press my hand to my forehead. "Dad set the house on fire? How did he —"

"I don't know the details, Liv. Mom was pretty pissed when she called. The firemen couldn't find the cat. It had something to do with popcorn. Mom had already gone to bed when the fire started."

"Putting you on speaker," I say, setting my phone on the bed so I can put on my bra.

Oscar has added a cami and sweater to my pile.

"Look, I can't change my flight. I'll be home Wednesday."

"You're not coming?" Tears fill my eyes. I don't know why I care. It's not as if Beth is going to be any help.

"Liv," Oscar says gently, buttoning up a flannel shirt. "They're okay. Everything's going to be okay. I'm calling Hazel now. Beth, are they at Jessop and Lori's?" he says louder.

"I don't know. Yes . . . I guess."

413

"Look, I'm going to try to call Mom," I say to Beth. "Did she call you from her cell or one of Jessop and Lori's numbers?"

"She called from her cell," Beth huffs at me.

"I'm on it," Oscar tells me. "I'll send Hazel over now."

"I'll call you back after I get there, okay, Beth?"

"Sure. Okay. Talk to you later. Tomorrow if you can't get me tonight. Tell them I love them," my sister adds cheerfully.

I hang up without saying good-bye, à la Mom.

# 28
## HAZEL

"Nope. You asked for cereal, Granddad." I plop the bowl down in front of him at our dining room table and tighten the tie on Dad's robe that I'm wearing. My prego jeans and one of Dad's flannel shirts are tumbling in the dryer because I forgot to put them in last night before I went to bed. "Cereal is what you're getting."

"Don't want cereal." My grandfather swipes at a piece of candy on the screen of his new iPad.

Dad got it for him yesterday. His burned up in the fire. Pretty much everything they owned burned in the fire. Gran's cat died. She cried. Not about the house and all of her pretty furniture and all her photos and stuff. She cried about her old cat, which made me cry. But Gran and Granddad didn't get hurt. Which is a miracle, Dad says. And what matters. Granddad just had a small burn on his hand that's almost already healed.

The night the fire happened, I was at Katy's. Jack and Katy's new boyfriend had come over and we were watching one of the old *Saw* movies. Jack was super sweet about me having to leave to rescue my grand-parents from the neighbors. He wanted to come with me, but I didn't think that was a great idea. He kissed me good-bye, which I think surprised both of us. Then he texted me, like, six times to make sure I was okay and my grandparents were okay after I left Katy's.

That night, Mom and Dad drove home from Bar Harbor and met me at the hospital where Gran and Granddad were getting evaluated. They crawled out the window in Granddad's bedroom. We all got home at three o'clock in the morning. I think that's why I'm still so tired. Even though that was almost a week ago.

No one talked about Gran and Granddad moving in with us. Everyone just assumed that's what would happen, at least until we know how long it's going to take to rebuild their house. It's pretty bad. And even if the house does get fixed, I wonder if they're go-ing to be able to move back anyway. I mean, Granddad set the house on fire. Gran can't watch him every minute. One of them could

416

have gotten seriously hurt, or even died of smoke inhalation like the poor cat. But if anyone else has considered that, they haven't said so. Not even Aunt Beth, who told me she was relieved they were staying with us instead of her. So I'm keeping my mouth shut.

The problem is that I was going to move into the downstairs bedroom with Charlie after he's born. So if he cried, he'd just wake me up and not Mom and Dad. That was the plan. Now my grandparents have taken over the spare bedroom *and* the family room where Dad used to lie on the couch every night and watch TV. Dad's squeezed into the tiny sitting room with a great big TV he bought when he bought Granddad the iPad. I don't think Mom was happy about a second TV in the house, but she didn't come out and say so. Not in front of me. How could she say anything to Dad? Both of her parents have moved in and one is wearing a bib and a nighttime diaper.

"I want crepes," Granddad tells me.

He was already awake and playing Candy Crush when I came downstairs half an hour ago. I told Mom she could go ahead and take her shower and I'd get Granddad his coffee. She's still not down, so we're having Rice Krispies.

"Crepes with Nutella," Granddad tells me. "We had them at the Eiffel Tower, my girlfriend and I."

"I don't know how to make crepes. And if I did, I couldn't make them for you because I have to go to school. And that was Gran, your wife, Granddad. Her name is Bernice. You and Bernice went to France for your fiftieth wedding anniversary. You saw the Eiffel Tower and you went to Normandy to see where the allies landed on D-day."

"I don't have a wife."

"Ever been married?" I ask.

"Cripes, no."

"Children?"

"Negative," he responds.

"Then no grandchildren, either?"

He shakes his head without looking up from the bright screen. I turned the sound off yesterday and he doesn't seem to have noticed. Or he doesn't care if he hears the candies explode.

"Hmm. Interesting," I say, wondering exactly who he thinks I am. He called me by my name when I came into the kitchen this morning. Which was nice because yesterday he kept calling me by his dead sister's name. I don't know why, but that creeps me out.

I set his spoon down on his cloth napkin

and go back to the counter for a second napkin to tie around his neck. Otherwise, he'll dribble milk all over his pajamas. I move slow because I'm tired, even though I went to bed at seven last night. And slept eleven hours. My belly is so big now that it's a wonder I can walk at all. Actually I don't walk. I waddle. That's what Sean said. He borrowed his roommate's car and came home for a night, last week after the fire.

Turns out Granddad started it. No surprise there. He was making popcorn and the oil caught on fire. Then he tried to put it out with kitchen towels. Then when the towels caught on fire, he went to bed. After he took the battery out of the smoke detector in the kitchen. So it wouldn't wake up Gran. By the time the smoke detector in the hallway went off, the kitchen was what the fire marshal referred to as "fully engulfed." Apparently he spilled vegetable oil all over the stove and the floor.

I still don't know how Gran and Granddad got out of the house, except that they did. Gran doesn't want to talk about it and Granddad keeps making up stories. They're good stories but aren't really relatable to what actually happened. And they usually involve his girlfriend. Or the guys he was in Vietnam with during the war. He's been talking a lot about Vietnam. So much that Dad started reading a history of the Vietnam War and he and I plan to watch the whole Ken Burns Vietnam documentary after the baby is born. He's going to take a few days off to hang out with me, which is cool.

I lean over Granddad from behind, turning sideways so I fit.

"I said I don't want cereal," Granddad tells me. "I ordered crepes. And *pain au chocolat,*" he says, his French accent pretty good.

"Too bad." I don't say it mean, just giving him the facts. "No chocolate croissants in the house. Come on, Granddad, let's eat now. Put away the game."

"I'm winning."

"Pause it."

"Don't know how."

I finally get the knot tied on the napkin around his neck and walk around to sit next to him. "Then you can start another game." Sitting beside him, I slide the iPad away from him. "Hungry?"

He grunts and picks up his spoon.

I pour almond milk over his cereal, then mine. I watch him shovel it into his mouth like he doesn't even taste it and wonder what's going on inside his head. I wonder if he knows he's crazy. Well, *crazy* isn't exactly the right word. Dad says it's dementia. No matter what the neurologist says, he says Granddad has dementia either because he has hardening of the arteries or Alzheimer's. Doesn't really matter which.

I take a bite of my cereal and think how weird it is that I'm putting a bib on my grandfather and pretty soon I'll be putting a bib on my baby. I don't know exactly how old they are when they sit in a high chair and eat cereal. Mom gave me a book about a baby's first year. I told her I was reading it, but I lied. I know I should read it. I'm thinking maybe when I'm at the hospital in labor. Like, between contractions. I keep opening it to read it at night, but I'm also reading *The Scarlet Letter* for English class and I'm so tired by the time I open the baby book that I can't read more than a few words and I fall asleep. Last night I fell asleep with the light still on. Dad came in and turned it off.

I take another bite of cereal and check the clock in the kitchen. Jack and I have kind of been meeting in the parking lot every morning and walking into school together. He hasn't tried to kiss me again and I haven't had the nerve to kiss him first. I keep wondering if he kissed me the other night when I was leaving because I was upset about Granddad and Gran. But what if he hasn't kissed me again because he didn't like how I kissed? Or he doesn't wanna kiss a girl with a baby in her uterus? A girl who let a dickwad like Tyler get her pregnant. Because he knows Tyler's the dad. Everyone in school knows.

Granddad grabs the box of cereal and adds more to his bowl.

"I thought you didn't want cereal."

He keeps pouring until I put my hand on the box and stop him. He's filled up his bowl. Like, to the top.

The dryer buzzes and I jump up. If I hurry, I have time to get dressed, to do something with my hair, and put on some makeup. The baby is due in two weeks. My cervix isn't doing anything yet. That's like the door to let the baby out. I know that sounds juvenile, but I liked the analogy Dr. Gallagher gave. Mom says most first babies are late. So I'm thinking I still have three weeks. Three weeks to get Jack to kiss me again.

# 29
## LIV

My dad squints through his Clark Kent reading glasses at the faded black-and-white photo on my laptop screen. "Hee hee hee." He chuckles and points. "That's John Lark. We called him Johnny Cake." He shakes his head, staring at the black-and-white photo of a tall, skinny African American kid in a uniform and bucket hat. "Medic from some little town outside of Atlanta. Best one I had."

I type the man's name on the photo and add *medic*. Dad and I have been doing this almost every night since they moved in. Looking at the photos that I scanned last winter after buying a fancy photo scanner. Some nights he hasn't had much to say, but a couple of times, like tonight, his recall has been amazing. He can't remember that Mom is his wife, but he remembers a teenage soldier from six decades ago. The human mind is an amazing organ.

"You were in Saigon, right, Dad?"

He stares at the photo. "Ran a little clinic there for six months, before they sent me to A Shau Valley." He shakes his head. "Bad place, that valley. A lot of men died. Had both hands tied behind my back. No sutures, no scalpels, nothing for me to work on them with but IVs and drugs. I don't know why they even sent docs there."

"This you?" I ask, pulling up the next photo. I barely recognize the man in uniform, wearing a helmet. But I see his eyes. I know his eyes.

"That's me. In A Shau Valley. Longest six months of my life. Never thought I'd see my girlfriend again."

I hope he means Mom. They were married just before he went to Vietnam for a year, after medical school, after his internship, before he decided to study ophthalmology. "The photo says 1967," I muse.

My father is sitting on the couch beside me. We decided to let Mom and Dad have the family room and we would take the little room we call the sitting room. This way everyone could have some privacy and Mom and Dad can watch what they like on TV. Oscar agreed it was the best thing to do, especially with our spare bedroom suite being off the family room. But he didn't

424

seem to be thrilled with giving up the family room. He went out and bought a huge TV for the sitting room. One even bigger than the one in the family room. Maybe to establish his dominance over the older male now in the household. Like marking his territory with urine, but instead with a big TV?

Dad stares at the photo of himself in front of the building that looks as if it's been abandoned a long time. "Did my training at Fort Sam Houston. Commitment to Uncle Sam was a year. Took that picture right after I got to Saigon." Now he's shaking his head. "I was so scared those first few weeks. *Sard.* Didn't think I'd make it."

His use of a creative swearword makes me smile and then I tear up and have to look away. It's been a while since I've heard him use one of his archaic curses. He told me many years ago that he started researching old curse words so he could curse and no one would know he was being inappropriate. That was so like my father, so proper, but he never crossed into snooty. Or *bougie,* as Hazel would say.

I type out Dad's full name and add *Saigon.* The date is already printed along the bottom of the four-by-four-inch black-and-white photo.

"Where'd you get these pictures?" he asks.

425

"I had some of me in the war, but they burned up. My house caught on fire. Bad wiring."

I smile, but it's a sad smile. I'm still trying to process the fact that my father set his house on fire. That he and Mom are living here now. Probably permanently. Oscar and I haven't talked about it, but I know he knows they can't go into their own home again. And that I can't put them in an assisted living facility because they'd hate it. I just don't have it in me. I couldn't do that to the two people who took a child not of their body — me — and made her their own. They loved me and cared for me at the beginning of my life and now it's my turn to do the same for them at the end of their lives. How we're going to manage two old folks and a newborn baby in the house, I have no idea. I guess I'm going to try to do what Hazel plans to do. Figure it out.

"I scanned the photos on to my computer last year, Dad. I made an album for you for your birthday. We had a big party." I've removed "remember?" from my vocabulary with him because it makes both of us feel bad. He doesn't remember.

"And you've got my pictures on there?" He taps my laptop screen as if he's not entirely sure what it is.

"I sure do." I look up at him.

He's dressed in spanking-new pjs and a robe because none of their clothes, except what he was wearing, survived the fire. What wasn't damaged by fire or water was beyond rescue because of the smoke. I took Mom to Freeport yesterday while Dad stayed home with Oscar and Hazel. Mom had a field day at the L.L.Bean store. I haven't seen her that chipper in weeks. The woman loves her Bean clothing, which I find interesting because she's also a pearls woman.

"You said you ran a dispensary in Saigon?" I ask Dad, hoping to get him to tell me more.

He nods slowly, his gaze not focusing on the laptop screen. His mind seems far away. Back in Saigon, maybe. "Medicine came in, we kept track of it. Guarded it. Stored it, shipped it out. Had a little clinic there, too. For GIs." He sits back on the couch. "Know what affliction I treated the most?"

"No, what?"

These evening hours spent with my father, looking at photos, has been an amazing gift. Over the last few months, I've felt as if I was losing him. Losing my connection with him because he can't remember any of the things that once connected us. But looking at his old photos, they have, in a way, brought my father back to me. Photos from his childhood, medical school days and Vietnam, and then the ones before he and Mom had me and then Beth, they've allowed me to relate to him, through them, through his memories. They've reminded him of who he was before he was my dad. I think they remind him of who he used to be, too.

"What did you treat most of the GIs for in Saigon?" I prod when he seems to have lost his train of thought.

"Gonorrhea."

I blink. Of all the things he might have said, that was not an answer I had anticipated. I guess I was expecting him to say gunshot wounds. Which wouldn't have made sense because there wasn't fighting going on in Saigon when he was there. *Gonorrhea?* I echo.

"A sexually transmitted disease. Treat it with penicillin."

I want to tell him I know what gonorrhea is, but I don't want to interrupt his train of thought. I do it too many times, and he'll want his iPad so he can play Candy Crush.

"Houses of ill repute," he goes on. "Couldn't keep the boys out of 'em. The soldiers. Not even after they came in for treatment. Be right back the next month. Knew when they'd gotten paid by the number of boys in my clinic with pain when they urinated. Or discharge." He shakes his head. "They always came in to see the doc when they were pissing green."

I hear Oscar snigger and look up to see him standing in the family room doorway.

We make eye contact and share a moment of amusement. Dad would never have said "piss" in front of me if he was himself. Oscar keeps teasing me that he likes this new version of my dad.

"I'm making popcorn," Oscar announces to the room. "Anyone want some?"

I look to my father. "Dad, you want popcorn?"

He shakes his head. He's studying the photo of himself as if he's trying to figure out something.

"Mom, popcorn?" I call over the sound of the TV. They listen to it so loud that Oscar ordered wireless headphones and paid eight dollars for overnight delivery so he could hear his new TV and not my parents' in the family room. "Mom?"

"No thank you." She doesn't look up. She's watching something on BBC. A British mystery, I think.

I look back at Oscar. "No popcorn for us, but I'd like some tea. Peppermint."

He points at me. "I can do that."

I return my attention to my computer screen and bring up the next photo. It's another from Vietnam. A group of young men standing outside a tent in what appears to be a field camp. One corner of the photo has a jagged line; it was probably torn and I taped it before scanning it. The only man I recognize is my father. He looks thin, and his eyes, beneath the helmet, look dark. Empty. "Who's in this photo, Dad?"

He squints. "Don't know anyone there."

"Sure you do. That's you, isn't it?" I point to the officer I know is him.

He leans closer, studying the photo. He pushes the bridge of his glasses back onto his nose and sits up again. "No. That's not me."

"I think it is."

He picks up his iPad off the coffee table. Turns it on.

I've been dismissed. I consider bringing up another photo, trying to engage him again. I decide against it. I can tell he's tired. He and Mom will probably go to bed soon. Mom wasn't happy about having to sleep with him, but we have a king-sized bed in the room, so I know very well she's comfortable. And someone needs to keep an eye on him at night so he doesn't burn my house down, too.

I close my computer and get up, leaving my dad to crush brightly colored candies on the iPad screen. I kiss him on top of his bald head as I walk away, absently wondering what he's done with his knit cap. He was wearing it earlier. I hope it's not in the toilet. He's taken to flushing things. I think he likes to see them disappear.

I find Oscar in the kitchen pouring avocado oil into a pot on the stove. Even though we have microwave popcorn in the pantry, he likes to make it "old school." He's turned on the electric water kettle for me. I get a mug and then retrieve a peppermint teabag from a mason jar on the counter. While I wait for my water to boil, I go over to stand near the stove. "How was your day?" I ask, leaning against the counter, crossing my arms over my cozy flannel shirt. It's been bitterly cold for days now, below zero at night.

"Okay. Pretty light day. A couple of fender benders. Two cases of flu. A broken arm. An old lady with DTs. She ran out of her *medicine.*" He smiles. "Easy peasy."

I look up at him, making eye contact. Our weekend away wasn't even two weeks ago, but it seems like two years. The house fire, my parents moving in, it's been pretty overwhelming. For all of us. And Oscar has been a good sport. Even if he did, on impulse, go out and buy a forty-six-inch TV.

Oscar nods in the general direction of the family room. "Sounded like you and your dad were having a good time in there."

"We were. I'm so glad you thought of his photos. Of looking at them with him. It's been —" My voice catches in my throat. "Nice," I finish weakly.

Oscar takes my hand, squeezes it, and then lets go to add the popcorn kernels to the hot oil in the pan. "The ones from Vietnam are pretty amazing. I know I've seen them before, but I guess I didn't really look at them. I started reading about the area where he was posted his last six months. That's the general area the movie *Hamburger Hill* was supposed to take place."

The water whistles and clicks off. I just stand there. "Hazel go to bed?"

"I think so. She watched a little TV with me while you were sorting your parents' clothes, but she was drifting off to sleep. Dropped her cell phone on the floor." He grins. "She moved the fastest I've seen her in weeks, trying to get to it before I did. Didn't want me to see that the mysterious Jack was texting her, I suspect."

A popcorn kernel pops in the pot and I hear my mother telling my father something.

432

I can't make out what over the blast of the TV.

I shrug. The entire pregnancy I've been caught between truly feeling for her when it's come to the changes in her body and wanting to say she should have thought about the havoc pregnancy would wreak on her one-hundred-and-thirty-pound body before she had unprotected sex. "She's thirty-nine weeks. She probably *is* tired. I'll go up and check on her after I make my tea."

He rattles the pot on the stove and more kernels of popcorn burst. "You know I'm proud of you, Liv."

"How so?" I look at him, suddenly realizing how tired I am. After I finish my tea, I'm heading to bed. I hope I can convince Oscar to come with me. Not for sex. I'm definitely too tired for that, but it would be nice to rest my head on his chest and talk for a few minutes in the quiet darkness of our bedroom.

"I know this isn't what you . . . what we wanted for Hazel. For our first grand, but you've really been there for her." He reaches out to me and wraps one arm around my waist. "I see the little things you do: rub her feet, buy the kind of sorbet she likes, run upstairs to get her coat so she doesn't have to take the stairs again." He pulls me to him and kisses my temple.

I lean against him. "I feel like a chapter in my life is ending. I'm not going to have a little girl anymore. Our daughter is going to be a mother."

"And we're going to be grandparents." He sounds hopeful and excited. All the things I'm not.

"You know," I say softly, "I haven't changed my mind. I still think she should put the baby up for adoption."

He sighs and strokes my back. "I know. But you'll feel different after he's born."

I lay my head on his shoulder, feeling as worn-out as I imagine I would be if I were the one thirty-nine weeks pregnant. "I don't think you understand what —"

A crash comes from the living room.

"Ed!" my mother cries.

I let go of Oscar. We both run for the living room. As I round the corner, the smell of freshly popped popcorn fills my nostrils. And then this chapter of my life ends sooner than I expected.

# 30
# HAZEL

I take a deep breath and sink under the surface of the warm bathwater. I close my eyes and try to imagine the weightlessness Charlie must feel tumbling around in my amniotic fluid. I'm hiding here in the bathroom from Gran and Mom and Dad because all they do is watch me. Like they think any minute Charlie is just going to fall out of my V. I need a break from all of them. I just need some time to wrap my head around Granddad kicking the bucket like that.

I knew it would happen someday. Because we all die. We get old before it happens if we're lucky, but we all die. But this isn't how I expected it to end.

I was just drifting off to sleep, still in my clothes, when I heard the sound of the coffee table crash over. I was holding my cell phone, waiting for Jack to text me back about Saturday. Turns out I couldn't meet him at the movies Saturday because I had to go to a funeral.

I didn't have a dress to wear. Black or otherwise. Mom said I could just wear my yoga pants and her navy-blue sweater, but I wanted to wear black. I threw such a fit that Aunt Beth took me all the way down to Brunswick to Target because I found they had black maternity dresses and tights. I end up having to wear ankle boots instead of my knee-high boots because my calves are too swollen to zip them up.

I come out of the bathwater gasping for air. As I come up, it occurs to me that maybe it wasn't such a good idea to hold my breath that long. What if it was depriving Charlie of oxygen? What if he'll be born brain-dead now?

It doesn't sound like a thing, but I decide not to do it again, just to be on the safe side.

I run my hand over my belly that's way bigger than a basketball now. It's a beach ball. I run my finger down the weird little line that runs from my belly button to my pubes.

Which I can't see anymore.

I lie back with my head on a rolled-up towel and close my eyes again. The whole week has been surreal.

I like that word. It means to have the qualities of surrealism, which was an art that was supposed to demonstrate things that were going on in the subconscious mind. Bizarre stuff. Like the paintings Dalí and Magritte did with the melty watches and stuff. But my favorite surrealistic artist is Frida Kahlo. I have a T-shirt in my Amazon cart that has one of her paintings on it with her sitting at a dining room table with a skeleton and a deer. I also have disposable boob pads and this cute baby onesie with elephants on it in my cart. Without a job, I don't know how I'll buy either. If Granddad was alive, I bet he would buy the T-shirt and the onesie for me. He and Gran have an Amazon account. He used to let me put things in the cart when Gran wasn't paying attention and he'd hit "Place your order" for me. When boxes arrived, Gran would complain and say she was going to return the stuff, but she never did.

Guess you can't have an Amazon account if you're dead.

I sniff and try not to cry. Because all I do is cry.

I can't believe Granddad died. Of a stroke, of all things. He didn't die crossing the street in his boxer shorts, he didn't die mowing his lawn, even the time his bathrobe tie got caught in the mower blades. He didn't even die when he set his house on fire.

He died of a stroke. He stood up in our family room and then he fell onto the coffee table and upended it. Landed right on his iPad. Candy Crush was still playing when I ran downstairs to see what happened. Granddad had a blood clot in his brain and oxygen got cut off, which kills your brain. They tried to save him anyway, which I don't get because I know he didn't want to come back to life paralyzed or a vegetable or whatever. I don't even think he wanted to be alive the last six months, because a lot of his brain seemed dead already. And he knew it. I could see it in his eyes when he'd ask me for a fork to eat his eggs, but the word *rake* would come out of his mouth.

When I came downstairs, Dad was laying him out on the floor in front of the couch. Granddad's robe was pulled up and he was missing the beanie he likes to wear in the house to keep his bald head warm. His glasses were lying halfway across the room.

Dad started CPR.

Mom called 911.

Gran stood there in her bathrobe just staring at Granddad. Her face was red, but she wasn't crying. I was crying hard enough for both of us.

Charlie does the weird turn thing he does in my belly and I hold on to him with both my hands. He's getting ready to come out. Today, at Dr. Gallagher's, I had to let her examine me. I was two centimeters dilated. Yesterday was my due date. She said I could go into labor any day now, but not to be worried if it's another week.

I try not to think about labor. About how much I know it's going to hurt. I try not to think about what it's going to be like trying to take care of another human being that's totally dependent on you. I just think about how cute Charlie is going to be. About how much he's going to love me.

Jack and I were talking about that last night. Texting. Things are heating up with Jack. Just thinking about him makes my face feel hot. He's been so nice to me. Way nicer than Tyler ever was and I haven't even had sex with Jack. Not that I think he'd even want to have sex with me like this. But we have kissed. Real kissing and just thinking about it makes my face warm. I like him. Like, *really* like him. And we have so much more in common than Ty and I did.

There's a knock on the bathroom door and I close my eyes. "Yes?"

The door opens and I open my eyes as Mom sticks her head in the door.

"Mom!" I say, covered my naked boobs that are *waay* bigger than they were before I got pregnant. "I'm trying to take a bath."

"I'm not looking." She *was* looking, but now she turns her head and looks toward the sink. "I hate to tell you, dear, but your modesty is going to go out the window once you go into labor. After a while you won't care if the birth center janitor wants to have a peek at your cervix."

"Mom," I groan. "Is that what you busted into the bathroom to tell me? That I should let a janitor see my V?"

She laughs, which makes me mad.

"It was not. I came to tell you that Aunt Beth is coming for dinner, but we're going to eat as soon as your dad gets home because Beth can't stay. She has a hot date." She looks at me and raises her eyebrows in a totally exaggerated way.

"Mom!" I cover my boobs with my hands. "Get out."

"May as well get over that, too," she tells me as she backs out the door. "Everyone in town is going to see those in one place or another."

"I'm not going to breast-feed in public."

"No? That baby cries, you'll stick your

440

nipple in his mouth in line at the grocery store just to shut him up."

She closes the door before I can say anything. I take a big breath and slip under the water.

# 31
## LIV

I stand outside Hazel's room at the birth center, holding a vanilla milkshake in one hand, and a bag with a banana, a cookie, and a salad in it in the other. The nurse midwife is doing a postpartum check. I took the opportunity to step out and catch my breath. I'm tired and sad and happy. The last hours are a blur.

I've always found it interesting how a woman going into labor is depicted in movies. Often the scenes are played comically, with the expectant father running around the house frantically looking for his keys, while the mother-to-be stands patiently, looking gorgeous, at the front door, car keys dangling from her finger. I haven't seen any movies with teenagers in labor, although I think about the movie *Juno* that I watched with Hazel and the scene that follows the character Juno giving birth. I thought the actress did a good job depicting what a woman feels and looks like after twelve to eighteen hours of labor.

I didn't expect any of the comical nor the frantic behavior when Hazel went into labor, and there wasn't any. She woke me up at about four in the morning, trying not to cry, telling me she'd been having regular contractions since midnight. We were careful not to wake up the household. I didn't want the added confusion that would come from my husband and mother. Hazel didn't want their advice. So I made tea and walked around the house with Hazel. I rubbed her feet. I brought her a cold, wet washcloth when she felt nauseated. In the morning, I convinced Oscar to go to work, at least for a few hours. Hazel had already decided I would be in the room when she delivered, but she didn't want her father or her grandmother, which I completely agreed with. My mother kept herself busy sorting through my father's clothes and other belongings to donate them. Hazel's water broke at noon and I calmly drove her to the birth center and left my mother in the waiting room with my dad's iPad.

At three forty-seven, Charlie was born. Without a penis. With a vulva. When the nurse midwife held her up in the air, still wet, Hazel was crying. Then she laughed.

443

"A girl? Charlie's a girl?"

I kissed my daughter's cheek. "Guess she needs a new name," I whispered, choking up.

The nurse midwife walks out of Hazel's room. Dr. Gallagher was off today, so Lacey, from her office, was here for the birth. Lacey is a cheerful young thing who has probably had several more cups of coffee than I have.

"She did great." She pats my arm. "Congratulations, Grandma."

*Grandma.* I groan silently. I'm not ready to be a grandmother any more than Hazel's ready to be a mother. And I'm certainly not ready to be called Grandma by anyone.

I wait until bubbly Lacey is gone, then knock on the door frame. "Okay if I come in?"

"Only if you brought food. They're supposed to be delivering a tray, but I bet it will be full of additives and food dyes."

Hazel's sitting up in a bed that doesn't look like a hospital bed. Because she had no complications during labor and the delivery, she was able to stay right here in the birthing room that looks like a hotel room. Except for the baby in the bassinet on wheels on the far side of the bed.

"What did you bring me?" Hazel asks,

holding out her hands to receive the bag and shake.

I hand them over. "You said milkshake, so I got a milkshake. It's dairy. You're not going to find a dairy-free shake around here. And a salad and a banana. I just went across the street to that little deli."

"Thank you, Mom!" She looks into the bag.

I cross my arms over my chest, feeling awkward, and I don't know why. I've just shared with my daughter one of the most intimate events a woman experiences in her life. During the labor and delivery, none of the distance I've felt with Hazel, none of the anger, was there. I didn't even feel as if we were mother and daughter by the time she got to the point that she was ready to push. I was just one woman trying to support another as she brought a life into the world.

I clear my throat, hoping I'm not coming down with something. I think I'm just tired, though. It's been an intense day. "Your dad is on his way. He's feeling really guilty that he didn't get here sooner. They had a bad car accident on Route 1 involving a tractor-trailer and several cars. Someone ended up being airlifted out."

"Straw?" Hazel asks me.

I pull it out of my back pocket.

She rips the paper off the straw, stuffs it into the lid, and sucks on it. "Oh my God, that's good. Is this what vanilla shakes made from cow's milk always taste like?"

I laugh and come to stand beside her bed. I'm purposely not looking at the baby. I don't know why. It's not her fault her parents were foolish.

"How are you feeling?" I ask.

She's wearing her red hair piled on top of her head in a tangled bird's nest, but little wisps have fallen and frame her face and trail down the back of her neck. When she was in labor the bits of hair were damp with sweat and stuck to her face. Several times I pressed a cool washcloth to her face and brushed the hair back.

"My V still feels like it's on fire," my daughter tells me, sucking so hard on the straw that her cheeks are concave.

The baby fusses.

"That will ease up," I say. "Not even any stitches. That's amazing. You were amazing. I was so proud of you, Hazel."

The baby is squirming now. Making the mewing sounds a newborn makes.

Hazel holds up her hand to me. "Please don't tell me you're going to give me details on how many stitches you had to get in your

446

V after you had me. Criminy, two different nurses had to give me their stories in agonizing detail." She begins peeling the banana. "No thank you."

I smile. At her sassiness. At the fact that she said *criminy*. It was something my dad used to say. In the last two weeks since he died, she's been using a lot of his silly words. I'm surprised that she remembers so many. Pleasantly surprised.

As Hazel takes a big bite of banana, the baby wails. Chomping, Hazel glances her way. "You want to hold Charlie? I've got to eat."

"Charlie? You're still going with that name?"

"Not Edward, obviously, but I kind of like Charlie for a girl." She smiles at me and takes another bite of banana. "I haven't decided what her middle name will be. Or even if she'll have one. She might just be Charlie Ridgely." She makes a face. "But that's kind of singsongy, isn't it?"

"You don't have to decide today," I hem. All the while I'm thinking, *My granddaughter's name is* Charlie? This is why seventeen-year-old girls shouldn't have babies.

Charlie is really squawking now. And pumping her little fists.

"Mom, she's crying. Get her. I'll eat and

then I'll try feeding her again. The boob nurse said to just keep putting her to my nip and she'll latch eventually. She told me not to get all worried or anything if it takes a few tries. She said no baby will starve itself to death with mother's milk right there."

I glance at the baby and then back at Hazel. "Boob nurse?" I'm just stalling now. I don't know why. Even though I've made it clear to Hazel, and to my husband, that I'm not taking care of this baby when she and Hazel get home, I'll still hold her, of course. She's still my granddaughter. I just . . .

"Mom," Hazel whines. "Get her."

I take my time walking around the end of the bed. I don't know why I'm so apprehensive. Maybe all the old anxieties I felt when we first gave birth to Sean are coming back. At the bassinet, I look down. She was wet when she was delivered; then, when Hazel was holding her, she was wearing a cotton cap to keep her body heat in. But she's not wearing a cap now and her head is covered in red fuzz. Red, just like my babies.

A lump rises in my throat as I reach out for the squawking little thing. She was seven pounds, seven ounces, and twenty inches long. A perfect-sized baby, round cheeks and so precious that . . . Tears slide down my cheeks as I reach for her, and draw her close.

I try to resist the surge of emotion I feel rising in my chest. An overwhelming feeling of what can only be love for this tiny little creature who I didn't want to keep.

"Oh, sweetie," I coo.

Charlie is still fussing, but not so loudly. Holding her in one arm against me, I reach into her bassinet and retrieve a pacifier. I jiggle her, making soothing sounds. "How about this? Would you like this? Oh, I know, you're hungry, aren't you?" I whisper, trying to get her to take the Binky. "Shh, you're okay, you're okay. Your mama's going to feed you in just a minute." I turn and walk toward the window. When Hazel was a newborn, she wanted to be walked constantly. I walked her by the hour. It was the only way to soothe her. "That's right," I say softly. "Mama just needs a little something to eat first, that's all."

The baby takes the pacifier in her rosebud lips. "That's right, thatta girl," I murmur. "That's my girl, that's my Charlie."

My back to Hazel, I hold the baby tightly to my breast and sniff her. I take in her newborn baby scent that resembles newborn creatures of every species on earth. What is it about a newborn that makes you want to protect it, at the risk of your own life? A chick, a kitten, an elephant calf, it doesn't matter.

A tear falls from my cheek to Charlie's. I give a little laugh and brush it off, feeling silly. And completely overwhelmed. Overwhelmed by the events of the day and overwhelmed by the powerful love I unexpectedly have for this baby.

# 32
## HAZEL

"What? What do you want?" I don't yell at Charlie, but I say it kind of loud.

She won't stop crying. So now I'm crying. I flop down on my bed beside her, which makes her bounce a little bit. It's not like she's on the edge of the bed and is going to fall off or anything, but I think it scares her because she cries louder. Now her face is turning red, she's screaming so hard. And I feel bad because I think I scared her.

"Charlie," I say, lowering my voice, because I don't want Mom and Dad to hear me. If they hear her crying, one will get up to help, but no matter who it is, there will inevitably be an argument between them tomorrow about it. Or even tonight in the hall. Dad says Mom isn't helping me enough. Mom says Dad is helping me too much. I think Mom used the word *enable* at dinner last night. She thinks Dad and Gran are both enabling me. I think Mom and Dad are both right.

I close my eyes and Charlie's cries wash over me like a tide of water. Of lava. This is sooo much harder than I thought it would be. I mean, I love her. I love her like I never thought I would. And my love for her is different than it was when she was just floating around in my belly. Now that she's here, it's the kind of love that makes you know that if something happens where one of you has to die and I have a choice, it would be me every time.

But Charlie doesn't know that. And she won't listen even if I try to tell her. She just keeps screaming. And kicking her legs and shaking her little fists.

I cover my ears with my hands. I know it's juvenile. Not something a mother does, but if she'd just cut me a break. Would she stop screaming for five minutes? Just five minutes. That would give me enough time to pee because I've had to pee for an hour. It would give me enough time to go downstairs and make another bottle just in case now she's hungry even though she wasn't half an hour ago. It would give me enough time to text Jack and tell him I'm sorry I didn't text him back tonight, but my BABY won't stop crying.

"Dagnabbit!" I tell her, turning my head

so I can look at her. She's dressed in a little lavender snuggly thing that's so cute. Mom bought it for her and brought it to me in the birthing center after I had her. Because I didn't have any girl things, just boy things. Because I thought she was a he.

"Look, buster. You don't want my boob so I gave you a bottle of formula," I tell my baby. "I changed your diaper. I put that gross butt paste on your ass in case it was sore. I burped you. I rocked you. I carried you around in the stupid kangaroo-pouch thing you're supposed to like. I even changed your whole outfit in case something was pinching you." I take a shuddering breath. "What do you want from me?"

She just keeps screaming.

I get up, wiping at my eyes because I feel stupid that a two-week-old baby is making me cry. "You have to do what I say, Charlie, I'm your mother." I stand there looking down at her, my arms crossed over my sore boobs. I've been in my yoga pants, nursing bra, milk-stained T-shirt, and Mom's old terry bathrobe since yesterday. I look like Aunt Beth after she's been drinking at home for a couple of days. My hair is dirty and I can smell my armpits because I haven't had time for a shower.

I start pacing my bedroom with its Save

the Rain Forest and recycling posters on the walls. Where my Science Olympiad medals hang on a shelf Mom made for my American Girl doll clothes when I was little. I'm a nostalgic person. I still have the same blue-and-green quilt I've had since I was a baby.

But everything is different now. The room's not really mine. It's Charlie's. For one thing, half the room is taken up with baby crap: the crib, her bouncy seat, the gigantic empty box of diapers, the pile of poopy baby clothes. Charlie has changed everything. Her fuzzy fleece snowsuit hangs over my first-place medals. She's barfed on my pretty bedspread. And the room smells like baby poop because I forgot to empty the trash can again.

"I'm your mother, Charlie," I tell her again. "You're supposed to be nice to me."

She doesn't hear me because she's CRYING SO LOUD.

Then I start to get angry. Not at her, but at Tyler. What a dickwad. Why am I the one up every night, all night, with our baby? Why isn't he taking *his* turn? Why is he sleeping eight or nine hours a night when I figure I've gotten nine hours of sleep in the last three days?

I actually had this stupid idea that when

Charlie was born, he'd have a change of heart and want to be a part of her life. That Cricket would want to babysit her granddaughter. That even though Ty and I weren't together anymore, we'd find a way to parent together. To share the responsibilities. How naïve was I? How right was Mom?

*As always.*

I look down at Charlie. Her face is all red and she's not even kicking and waving her hands anymore. But she's still crying. I'm so desperate to shut her up that I pick her up, even though I know it won't help. I snuggle her inside my robe. I smell gross. It's the milk leaking out of my boobs. Milk she doesn't want. Even though it's good for her.

I walk to my closed door that leads to the hallway, turn, and walk to the other side of the room. It's exactly nine steps to the Recycle Earth poster and nine steps back to the door. I jiggle Charlie, one hand on her back, the other under her little butt. I pull back my milk-stained T-shirt so her face can be against my skin. The lactation nurse at the birthing center told me skin to skin was good for new babies. It makes them bond with their mother. Of course, maybe she lied about that because she sure lied about how easy breast-feeding was going to be.

Charlie doesn't want my milk and she isn't bonding to me. She doesn't even act like she likes me. She likes everyone else in the house: Mom, Dad, Gran. Any one of them can pick her up and she stops crying.

As I walk past the bed again, jiggling her, I scoop up a pacifier from half a dozen lying on the bed and the floor. She took one in the hospital. Now she won't. I've tried at least six different kinds. She doesn't like any of them. I think she doesn't like them because when one is in her mouth, she can't cry as loud.

She's still screaming in my ear. She won't take the pacifier. I throw it into her crib.

"Charlie," I whisper. "Please? Can we just sleep for a few hours?" I keep jiggling her the way Mom does, hoping it will chill her out. "I'll make a deal with you." I stop at my nightstand, pick up my phone, and check the time. A pic of her is my screen saver. It's one forty in the morning. "Here's the deal," I tell her, walking her again. I kiss her little head. She has the prettiest red curls. They look like someone drew them on her little noggin with a red Sharpie. And she smells so good. I like to sniff her when she's sleeping. Well, I like to sniff her for a minute, and then jump in my bed and take a quick nap before she wakes up again.

"Are you listening to your mama?" I ask her. "You want to hear my deal?" I keep talking because that's how Gran gets her to stop crying. She talks to her. Mostly about Granddad and how much he would have liked meeting her, but sometimes about her gardening club or the Miss Marple episode she watched on TV. "You stop crying, Charlie, and go to sleep. I put you in your crib and then I get in my bed and go to sleep. And in two hours, you can wake up and scream as much as you want." I reach the door and turn around to go the other way.

I think maybe she isn't screaming quite so loud. I think she might be listening to me. "What do you think?" I ask her. "That a deal?" I snuggle her in both my arms, holding her "football style" the way the nurse showed me. "How about if I sweeten the pot?" I ask her. "You let me sleep for two hours and I don't care how much my boobs hurt because you won't drink my milk, I won't try to make you take my nip. I'll make you a big, fat bottle of nasty formula and you can be a lazy girl and drink it." Mom says she thinks that's the problem, that some babies are lazy. That Charlie's lazy and doesn't want to work at breast-feeding. She'd rather just let milk practically drip out of the bottle into her mouth.

"What do you say to that?" I ask my daughter. "Do we have a deal?"

I look down at her in my arms. She's cried so much that now she's actually crying real tears. "Please, Charlie?" I beg. Now I'm crying again.

I hear a knock at my door. "Yeah?" I call, swiping my face with the sleeve of my robe to wipe away my tears.

"Okay if I come in?" It's my dad.

I don't even make an attempt to tie my robe over my wet T-shirt. I'm too tired. "Sure," I say, trying not to sound too pitiful.

He opens the door. He's wearing his robe and slippers. He just stands there for a minute looking at me, looking at what a mess I am. "How about I take her for a couple of minutes?"

I hand her over to him. "Dad, she won't stop," I whine and blubber at the same time. "I did everything you guys told me. And she *wooon't* stop." I push a dirty hank of hair out of my face and then hug myself. "What am I supposed to do?"

Dad holds my daughter to his chest and starts to bounce her just a little. She's still crying, but she's definitely calming down. "She wet?"

I shake my head. "I changed her for the

tenth time. I'm almost out of diapers again," I groan.

"We'll get some more."

"Dad, do you know how much they cost a box?" I'm trying not to cry. "I called Tyler today to see if he could buy some diapers. To see if he wanted to see Charlie." I press my lips together. I don't tell Dad how stupid I was to think maybe Tyler would want to get back together with me after Charlie was born. Not that I would have wanted to, but blimey, he doesn't want to see his own little girl? "Tyler doesn't want to see her. I offered to take her over so Cricket could see her. Maybe watch her for a couple of hours, but she doesn't want to see her, either." I sniff. "Because she wants to *support* her son in his choice."

Charlie starts to fuss a little again.

"She hungry?" Dad asks. I know he's purposely not making any comment about Tyler because he gets angry when we talk about him now. Which upsets me because I'm the one who made this whole mess in the first place. And Dad doesn't want to upset me any more than I already am.

"I don't think she's hungry. I don't know! She won't take my —" I start crying again.

I don't even care about talking about my boobs with my dad. I'm so over that. He's seen so much of them in the last two weeks, I think he's over it, too. At first, he tried to give me space whenever I was feeding her. *Trying* to feed her. He kept his eyes somewhere else when he was talking to me. But it's gotten to a point that neither of us cares.

"Ah, Daisy." Dad switches Charlie to his left hand. Charlie, who now is barely crying. Just making little sniffly sounds. He wraps his arm around me and pulls me tight. He smells good. Like shampoo and popcorn. Like my dad. "It's going to be all right," he whispers, kissing the top of my head.

"It's not," I say, trying to get ahold of myself. "Dad, she *haaates* me."

He laughs and I pull away from him.

"It's not funny," I tell him.

"I know, it's not. At least not right now at — whatever time of the night it is?"

"Two o'clock," I tell him, wiping my snotty nose on the sleeve of Mom's bathrobe.

"You get any sleep at all?" Dad's still bouncing Charlie. He takes a pacifier from the end of my bed and puts it in my daughter's mouth.

She takes it, the little punk.

"Tonight?" I have to think for a minute. I grab a hunk of hair on the top of my head and pull it back. "Not yet. I had a nap this afternoon while Gran watched her. I think they watched TV together. I told her not to let her sit in her bouncy seat too close to the TV, but I was so tired, I didn't even care."

Charlie is quiet now, sucking on her pacifier and making cute little baby noises.

"How about a shower? Had one this week, Daisy?" He smiles. I know he's trying to get me to smile.

"A couple days ago. I feel bad leaving her when she's awake and . . . Dad, if she sleeps for ten minutes, I'd rather sleep for ten minutes than shower."

He smiles the kind of smile your parents do when they think they know how you feel. When they think they know everything. "I know you don't want to believe me when I say this, but it gets easier. How about schoolwork? Get any done today?"

I shake my head no.

Charlie's eyes are closed now. She's stopped thrashing.

My dad runs his big hand over her tiny little red head. She has hair the same color as his. As mine. "I think maybe you need a little break."

"You're right. I need a shower," I admit.

"Done. She and I will go downstairs and

see what's on the History Channel."

"You sure?" I make a face, hoping he really does mean it. "You have to go to work in the morning."

"I'll give you half an hour. But what I meant is that you could use a break from here, from her. You haven't been out with your friends since she was born. You haven't been away from her since she was born."

I look at her in his arms. She looks so sweet. So quiet. "I don't know if I *can* leave her," I say, unable to take my eyes off her. She has the prettiest eyelashes. I swear, they're longer than mine.

"Sure you can. And you should. I'll watch her for a couple of hours tomorrow when I get home from work. Go have some dinner with Katy. Catch up with the gossip at school." He rests one hand on the doorknob. "What do you say, Daisy?"

I look up at him. "I don't think Mom will be very happy if I go out."

"I'll handle your mom." He opens the door. "Now get a move on. Chop chop. Get a shower. I'll bring her back up in a little while. Then maybe we can all get some sleep."

"Thanks, Dad." I lift up on my toes to give him a kiss on the cheek and duck out of the room and down the hall toward the

bathroom, pretty sure this shower is going
to feel like heaven on earth.

# 33
## LIV

I carry two bags of groceries into the house. Willie Nelson greets me at the door. No one seems to be home. Oscar went to help his brother carry an old couch out of the house and bring in a new one. I think they were going to do something with a water heater, too.

Hazel's car is gone, so she and my mom must have gone somewhere. Probably to buy more diapers or formula. I'm a little upset that Hazel's given up breast-feeding. She was so gung ho before Charlie was born. I don't think she understood that every baby is different and some need a little time to figure out how to take to the breast. Hazel was so worried Charlie wasn't getting enough food. She said she was going to try the breast pump, but she ended up using the formula samples, and the next thing I know, my mother is calling me on my way home from one of my job sites to ask me to stop for formula. And now the dishwasher is full of baby bottles.

I go back out to my truck for the other two bags of groceries. I'm dead tired. Shingles were delivered this morning at the new site, and then I got a call from the client, Terri, saying that they were the wrong shade of brown. I drove all the way to Lincolnville, after being there yesterday, after planning to take an entire Saturday off and go with Oscar to his brother's. Maybe even sit with my sister-in-law and have a glass of wine. I get to Lincolnville thinking I'm just going to talk Terri down because the shingles don't look like what she thought they would look like. But she was right: The supply company sent the wrong color. On a special-order item.

I start unloading groceries from the cloth bags. Oscar texted me a half an hour ago to say he was headed home and should he pick up takeout for dinner. I was tempted, but we've had takeout three times this week, guaranteeing I won't win awards for wife, mother, or daughter of the year. And if Charlie could vote, I don't think she'd vote for me, either, just out of principle. In light of that, I pulled a Bernice and picked up a roasted chicken at Hannaford. I plan to boil some red-skinned potatoes for garlic mashed potatoes; steam some prewashed, precut broccoli; and call it a day. A night. I'm hoping to be in my jammies, in my bed by seven thirty with my laptop, searching the Internet for a nineteenth-century porcelain farm sink to appease Terri.

I'm just putting almond milk, soy milk, and coconut milk in the refrigerator when I hear the distinct sound of Charlie cooing. I recognize the sound in a second because she just started making noises other than crying two days ago.

I close the refrigerator door. "Hazel? Where's your —" Before I can ask her where her car is, I hear my mother's voice. She's talking to Charlie, trying to get her to talk back. I walk into the family room to find her sitting on the couch; Charlie's in her baby seat on the coffee table. My granddaughter is waving her little hands and trying her hardest to respond to her great-grandmother.

I break into a grin. For a baby I didn't want, I've become awfully attached to her. It's all I can do not to take her from Hazel's arms every time Hazel struggles to get her to eat, to change her diaper, to soothe her when she's fussy. But I told Hazel and Oscar that I would not be the baby's parent and I have to keep reminding myself of that vow because I don't want to be a mother to a baby again. I *don't*. I love my job, even though it can be stressful at times. I love just getting up in the morning and doing what I want to do, even if it is just to work.

"Is that you talking, Charlie?" I say in the voice adults use with infants. "Can you talk to Gigi? Can you?"

Charlie slowly shifts her gaze from my mother to me. "There she is," I coo. "That's my girl. Can you tell your grandma all about it?"

Charlie pumps her fists and lets out a string of nonsense.

"She's smart, this one," my mother tells me. "You were three months old before you did this."

I can't help but smile at the fact that my mother has to criticize me, or the infant version of me, to compliment her great-granddaughter. I sit down on the couch beside her and pick up a brightly colored baby toy Hazel had insisted we order for Charlie before she was even born. I found it, apparently forgotten, in a bag in the linen closet while looking for the extra crib sheets I knew I'd bought. Hazel's been struggling to keep up with the laundry. I don't want to start doing it for her, but also don't want my granddaughter sleeping in spit-up.

"You here all by yourself?" I ask my mom, holding the toy in front of Charlie's face.

"You think I can't handle a baby? I feel great. I'm on the upswing. Been thinking about going to water aerobics again with the girls if I keep improving."

My mother *has* been doing well physically. She hasn't needed her wheelchair, even for a few hours, in the two-plus months she's been living with us. But not requiring assistance to get around is not the same thing as being able to care for a newborn.

"Hazel go to the store?"

Mom sits back and reaches for her mug of tea. I can tell she's stalling.

"She'll be home after a while," she says.

"Okay." I nod. "How long's she been gone?"

She shrugs. "A few hours."

"A few *hours*?" I echo.

Mom slurps her tea. "Four or five. That roast chicken I smell?"

"Five hours?" I repeat. "Hazel's been gone since I left this morning?"

"She got invited to go shopping. Prom dresses."

I lower the baby toy to my lap. "She's not going to the prom."

"She went with friends who are going, I guess." Mom gives a dismissive wave. "A

468

group of girls went shopping. It's what teenage girls do."

But is it what teenage girls do with a baby that's only five weeks old? "Is Hazel going to the prom at her school?" I ask. "She's not even a student there anymore."

"I don't know anything about that." My mother takes another slurp of berry tea. I can smell it.

I stand back up, setting Charlie's toy on the couch. She's animated this afternoon. Her eyes are bright, and she seems to be watching everything. She starts cooing again, and I have the urge to pick her up. But I have cold things to put away still. And I have potatoes to wash, and I need to start a load of towels, or Oscar won't have one to shower with when he gets home. If I start playing with Charlie now, no one will eat until eight tonight.

"I think I should call Hazel." I take my phone out of the back pocket of my jeans.

"No, no. Let her have some fun," my mother insists. She's waving me away with her hand again.

"Mom, you watched Charlie yesterday. Hazel went for diapers at one, and she still wasn't home when I got home from work." I think for a minute. "And didn't she go to Katy's Wednesday night to help her with

469

her math? You went to bed and Oscar was in the sitting room asleep with the TV on with Charlie asleep in her chair." After my father died, my mother suggested we could all sit together in the family room at night, that Oscar didn't have to be exiled to the smaller sitting room, but he declared he liked the room and he liked the bigger TV.

"The child's worn out with this baby." She points at Charlie.

I close my eyes, shaking my head. *Which is why children shouldn't have children,* I want to say. But then I feel terrible because now that Charlie is here, she's indisputably loved. I love her more than I thought possible.

"Let her have a little fun, Liv," Mom says, gentling her tone. "I don't mind a few hours here and there. It gives me something to do. Something to think about besides the fact that your father is gone."

I sigh and slide my phone back into my pocket. "Roasted chicken, garlic mashed potatoes, steamed broccoli, and baking powder biscuits if I get motivated. Oscar is on his way home. We'll eat at six thirty."

"Excellent." Mom reaches for the remote control to the TV. "Charlie and I are going to watch an episode of *Poirot.* Unless you need our help in the kitchen." She leans forward and joggles Charlie's seat. "Because we'll help if Gigi needs us, won't we?" she coos.

As upset as I am that I think Hazel is taking advantage of her grandmother, as I walk out of the family room I can't help but smile at the joy Charlie has brought to my mother. To all of us.

# 34
# HAZEL

"So . . . tomorrow night," Jack says to me as we walk hand in hand across some guy's lawn.

We each have a beer in our hands. It's Friday night, and we're teenagers; teenagers have a beer once in a while, I tell myself. And I'm not breast-feeding anymore, so it's not like it's going to hurt Charlie. It might even help her if I actually get some sleep tonight. Maybe I won't be so cranky with her then.

We both stop to sip our beers. It's cold as crap outside, even though it's the first weekend of May. At least all of the snow has finally melted. We both shift from one boot to the other, trying to stay warm.

"You think you can go to the movie?" he asks me.

I chew on my lower lip. For days, I've been thinking Jack's going to ask me to prom. He's a senior. He has to go to prom, and

472

it's in two weeks. I can't believe he hasn't asked me. I know he wants to. The other night he even started telling me who was having parties afterward and stuff.

Katy thinks he's afraid to ask because he thinks I'll say no because that would pretty much mean we're going out. Like, boyfriend and girlfriend going out, and she thinks he thinks I think I can't date right now. Because of Charlie. Because I'm a mother. But that doesn't make any sense because anytime he asks me out, I go. Gran's been babysitting for me so I can do some stuff and if I'm going to be out late, Dad's been putting Charlie to bed. Mom's been complaining about it, but what does she care as long as it's not her putting Charlie to bed?

Charlie doesn't need me. My milk's all dried up now. She likes the formula better anyway. And Dad is better at putting her to bed than I am. He can lay her in her crib on her back awake, give her her Binky, and she'll go to sleep. I have to rock her and walk her and beg her to go to sleep. I've gotten better at it, but some nights Dad still walks her for me. A couple of nights ago, Charlie was a little stuffy and Mom even walked her because Dad had to be at work earlier than usual the next morning. Mom used this bulb thing they gave me at the birthing center to suck snot out of Charlie's nose. It looked gross, but it worked, and my daughter slept four and a half hours before she woke up wanting a bottle. Four and a half hours is the most extended block I've gotten of sleep since she was born two months ago.

"You said you wanted to see the movie." He catches a piece of my hair that's fallen forward on my face. It took me half an hour at Katy's house to get my hair just right with my wool beanie. He smiles at me. Plays with my hair.

"I . . ." I twist my mouth one way and then the other, thinking. That will be four nights in a row I've been out. Not at parties, but stuff: at Katy's, at an end-of-the-year school concert, at Amanda Peterson's. She invited me over to her house for taco night with her family. She and I have kind of become friends since she dumped Tyler. We talk smack about him and make fun of his truck. He's dating her friend Christina now. I *knew* he liked Christina back when we were still together. He liked Amanda *and* Christina.

"If you can't go," Jack says, letting go of my hair and sipping his beer, "I understand. I know you can't leave Charlie with your parents every night. Maybe we can —"

474

"Yeah, I can go." I look up at him. He's so cute. And so nice. He graduates in a month and he's going to UMass to study engineering. That was where I wanted to go. Not to Mom and Dad's alma mater, but to UMass to study premed. Or maybe biology. Back when I was researching colleges when I was getting ready to apply, I read some things that said medical schools were looking for more diverse students. That you didn't have to follow a strict premed program, not as long as you took all the required classes to get into med school. "What time is the movie tomorrow night? Seven? I can meet you there."

*"Ayuh,"* he says.

*"Ayuh,"* I repeat.

And we both laugh because we talk about the fact that we're both Mainers and that's one of the reasons we get along so well. We just *get* each other.

Jack leans toward me and when he touches his lips to mine, I close my eyes. This feels so different than when Tyler and I were dating. When we kissed. Jack's definitely a better kisser. He's —

"Hey, that your phone?" Jack whispers in my ear. "I think whoever is texting you wants you to respond. That was three texts right in a row."

"What?" I laugh and slip my hand into the pocket of my winter coat that now fits me again. Yay. I'm also in my own jeans again. Not my skinny ones. And I had to lie down on the bed to zip these up over my squishy belly. But I look like myself again. I almost feel like myself. At least I do when I'm out of the house.

I fumble with my phone because I'm wearing gloves.

It's my mother. I groan, closing my eyes for a second. Then I read her text.

Where are you?
You need to call me
Now!

I glance at Jack and text back, Something wrong?

Call me now

I exhale, annoyed. I'll be home soon, I respond, my fingers flying over the keyboard. I want to add a mean emoji face, but I don't.

Now! she texts back.

I'm standing there debating if I should get Jack to take me back to my car that's parked at his house and go home. But before I can decide what to do, my phone rings. Of course I know who it is. And I can't even stick my phone in my pocket and pretend she's not calling because Jack is looking right at my phone.

"Yeah?" I answer.

"Where are you, Hazel?" my mother says. I can tell she's pissed.

I turn my back to Jack, letting him block the wind. And hopefully keep him from hearing what I'm saying. I don't want him to think I'm a bad mom or anything. I taste his ChapStick on my lips. "Is Charlie okay?"

"Charlie is fine, except that it's nine thirty at night and she should be in bed."

"Dad can —"

"No, Hazel," my mother interrupts. She's almost shouting at me. "We talked about this last week when you were out late."

She's been so bitchy to me for weeks. Just because I want to get out of the house a couple of times a week. Dad was the one who said I needed a break from Charlie.

"It's not late. It's nine thirty," I say, being just as bitchy back.

"Your father needs to go to bed. He's not getting enough sleep. He's almost fifty years old. He needs his sleep. Otherwise, he's going to make a mistake at work. You want to be responsible for that? And she's not his baby," she adds.

I groan. "Can't you just get Gran to —"

*"Come home now,"* she repeats, saying each word slowly.

"Fine."

I hang up on her.

"Everything okay?" Jack asks me.

I turn around and smile up at him. "Yup."

"Need to go home?"

I think for a minute. I weigh the good against the bad. Mom's going to be pissed when I get home no matter what I do. If I go home or stay here. If I stay here with Jack for another hour or so, he might ask me to the prom.

"Nope. Everything's fine." I step closer to him, and then I get really brave, or maybe it's because I'm a little drunk. And I kiss him on the lips.

# 35
## LIV

I glance in the rearview mirror at the car approaching fast. The headlights are still on high beam. It's late. Later than I like to be out because of idiots like this. There's a high rate of alcohol-related accidents at this time of night.

I almost laugh out loud. A caustic laugh. I sound like Hazel.

Keeping my eye on the car behind me, I grip the steering wheel of my truck, trying not to cry. The whole evening started off nice enough. Even if Hazel wasn't there. Even if my mother was watching the baby *again.* This time because Hazel had to go to a "friend's" to do something for graduation, I think my mom said. Last week, every night was about prom, because it turned out, she *was* going to prom. With her new boyfriend, Jack. Who she tells me right to my face isn't her boyfriend. How does a seventeen-year-old girl get a boyfriend when she's got a ten-week-old baby? By a different boy? It boggles my mind.

I kept the peace over dinner tonight. Oscar and Mom and I talked about the summer internship Sean landed in Portland. He was so excited when he called just before dinner that he had me put him on speakerphone. Working so close to home this summer, he said he'd be able to come up to the cottage on weekends.

During our meal, we also talked about redoing Mom's bathroom. Because over the last couple of weeks, we all came to a conclusion, separately and then together, that Mom would be staying with us here at our house. Ironic, considering the turn of events following dinner.

When dinner was over, Mom took Charlie into the family room to change her and feed her. Instead of carrying her everywhere, Mom has been pushing her around in her stroller, which is actually quite ingenious. Of course, I made the point to Oscar, when he said it was resourceful while handing me a dirty plate for the dishwasher, that my mother shouldn't have to figure out how to move the baby around, Hazel should be here to do it.

That was how we got into the discussion. That's how I ended up in my truck with

480

two bags, my computer, my iPad, and a photo of Charlie that I took off my dresser as I walked out of our bedroom.

"Liv, really?" Oscar handed me another plate. He was rinsing, I was loading. We've gotten into the habit of doing the dishes together because it's a good way to spend a few minutes together alone, without my mom, or Hazel, or the baby.

"She's a teenage girl," he defends. "Teenage girls like to hang out with their friends."

"I understand that," I say, trying to keep my tone civil. "But she's a teenager with a baby. She should be taking her baby with her when she goes to a friend's house."

He walks back to the table and grabs the three water glasses. "It's almost Charlie's bedtime. She'll be fussy if she's out late."

"Which means her mother should come home." I take the glasses from him, one at a time, and load them in the top shelf of the dishwasher. "You know how many nights she's been out this week?"

"Liv."

"Do you know how many?" I repeat. "It's Thursday night. Do you know how many nights she's been out? Let's see. Saturday and Sunday —"

"Saturday night was prom. You encouraged her to go. You bought her a prom

481

gown, for Pete's sake. A hundred-and-forty-dollar prom gown."

"You're right, I did," I agreed. "Because she's seventeen and seventeen-year-olds should get to go to the prom if they're asked. One night was perfectly reasonable. But then she was gone all day Sunday, then Monday night." I dropped one dirty utensil after another into the basket in the dishwasher as I ticked off the days. "She was home Tuesday all day, but mostly because Mom had appointments. And I don't know when she left yesterday because she wasn't here when I got home. And she wasn't here when I got home tonight."

Oscar was standing at the sink, scrubbing a pot with more vigor than necessary. I could tell he was getting angry with me, but I felt like the conversation had been coming for weeks. The tension had been building between the two of us for weeks, and we've both been just trying to get by, trying not to fight. Hoping the situation would improve.

The car with the bright headlights finally passes me and I speed up a little. I'll be at the cottage in ten minutes. I just hope I can get the pilot light lit because if I can't, it's going to be a chilly night.

I remember taking the pot that Oscar had rinsed three times and began to dry it.

"Hon, this isn't working."

He found a wooden spoon to scrub.

"Hazel," I said. "The baby. She's neglecting Charlie."

"Charlie's not *neglected,*" he insisted. "Someone is practically holding her every minute of the day."

"That's true, but it's my mother during the day and you or I at night. Charlie is sleeping through the night now. Hazel can't use the excuse that she needs to get away because the baby is keeping her up all night. Your daughter is getting more sleep than you are, Oscar. Because after you and I leave for work, Hazel goes back to bed. My mother is watching Charlie until noon when Hazel gets up. Then while she takes a shower. And plays on the computer. The only time Mom is not watching Charlie when she's not asleep is when your daughter is dressing her and posing her for photographs."

"Hazel loves Charlie," Oscar said, emotion filling his voice.

"I don't disagree." I took the spoon from him, the last item in the sink, shut off the water, and left the spoon in the dish rack. I crossed my arms over my chest, facing my husband. "She loves her, but she's not taking care of her. She doesn't *want* to take care of her."

We were both quiet for a moment. He just stood there, leaning against the sink, looking out over my shoulder. Not looking at me.

"Oscar, I know you don't want to consider this. . . ." I took a breath. Tears clouded my eyes because I didn't want to say it. But I had to say it. Not because I don't love Charlie, but because I love her *so* much. Not because I don't love my daughter, but because I do.

I reached out and rested my hand on his arm. I looked at him. I made him meet my gaze. "We need to talk to Hazel about putting Charlie up for adoption."

Tears filled his eyes at once and he pulled away from me. "We could adopt her."

I hesitated because that thought had crossed my mind. The person I am today, I could be a better mother in some ways to Charlie than I was to Sean and Hazel. But I also know myself. I've learned a lot about myself in the last ten months. And I know that if I agree to take Charlie, I'll regret it later. I'll care for her, I'll love her as my own, but I'll regret it. Because grandparents shouldn't raise babies.

"I told you, Oscar, I'm not agreeing to that. I'm not adopting her." I was quiet for a moment and then I repeated, "I told you, we were not adopting her."

I saw the pain on his face. "I thought you'd change your mind. I thought you'd fall in love with her."

I pressed my lips together, trying not to start crying because that would delay the conversation. It wouldn't solve it. "I *do* love her." I shook my head. "But I'm not adopting her. Because that's not what's best for Charlie. It's not what's best for you or me. It's not even what's best for Hazel. Because if we adopt her, she'll be ours. We'll become her parents and Hazel will see the mistake every time she sees you and me or Charlie for the rest of her life."

That's when Oscar's pain turned to anger. Not anger at the situation or at Hazel for getting pregnant, or that little shit Tyler for not taking responsibility for his child. That's when he got angry with me. The lines on his face deepened, and when he met my gaze, his blue eyes were filled with rage. Directed at me. It had been building for months. I saw it at that moment.

"You won't take your granddaughter, even if your daughter can't take care of her?"

I noted at once that he didn't argue that Hazel was capable of caring for Charlie, or even that she genuinely wanted to. And I agree because while I think Hazel truly does love her daughter, I don't think she's equipped to care for her. And I think she knows it. I think that's why she's hiding from Charlie, from all of us.

"We can't do it, Oscar." I wrapped my arms around my waist, feeling as distant as I had felt from my husband in a very long time. "I won't do it."

Oscar looked at me as if I disgusted him. "Who are you, Liv? Who are you that you would give away Charlie?"

"That's not fair. *I'm* a child who was adopted. I, of all people, know what it means. It wouldn't be giving her away. It would be giving her the best life we could give her." Tears slipped down my cheeks.

He took a step away from me. "I don't even know you anymore." He shook his head. "I'm not even sure I want to be married to you anymore."

That was the worst thing Oscar had ever said to me, in all the years we had been together. In all the disagreements, the all-out fights. Never once had he suggested he wanted a divorce.

I don't know what kept me from crumpling to the floor right there in the kitchen. His words cut me so deeply, so . . . permanently.

I backed away from him. Without looking at him, I said, "I'm going to pack some stuff and go to the cottage."

He didn't ask for how long. He didn't ask me to stay. And when I came downstairs and told my mother, bawling by then that I needed to get away and think for a few days, Oscar didn't come into the family room.

I lifted a sleeping Charlie from her bouncy seat and hugged her warm, sweet little body to mine. She smells so much like my babies that I had to choke back tears.

And I almost gave in at that moment.

I almost committed to make her mine. But I knew . . . I *knew* it wasn't the right thing for Charlie.

I returned her to her baby seat and told my mother that she was welcome to come with me to the cottage. She looked as tired as the rest of us. She declined. I told her I would call her in the morning and then I left. Oscar never came to speak to me and he didn't call on the ride here.

I put on my signal and turn into the cottage driveway. The motion detector light comes on at the back door. I don't miss the irony in the fact that I would run away from my husband, from my marriage, to my husband's family home.

In the driveway, I check my cell phone,

which has a photo of Charlie as my wallpaper. I update it every couple of days because she's changing so quickly right now. No message from Oscar. No texts.

*What if he doesn't call?* I wonder. What if he actually does want a divorce? What if this is the end of our marriage? What will that look like? Mom living with me? We'll have to get a place. Hazel and Charlie will live with Oscar.

A part of me is devastated by the thought that my marriage might be over. But things have been so hard these last months, with the pregnancy, with my new job, with losing Dad, who I miss so, so much. A part of me wonders if I'd be happier alone. At this moment, I can't honestly say how I feel. Our lives have gotten so off track that I agree with Oscar. I don't know who I am anymore, either.

# 36
## HAZEL

"Monkey bread? I can't believe you made me garlic monkey bread, Mom." I stand up to grab the basket of warm bread before Aunt Beth gets it. I'm on my third piece. I'm cutting myself off after this. I'm almost back to the weight I was BC. Before Charlie. BTTN. Before the Tyler Nightmare. That's what Katy and I call last year. She says I should just pretend Tyler was a bad dream.

We're all sitting around the kitchen table at the cottage. The Cosset girls, Gran calls us: Gran, Mom, Aunt Beth, me, and Charlie. Charlie is sitting in her bouncy seat on the floor near Mom so Mom can see her. Mom says she's grown a bunch in the last week and a half. That's how long Mom's been gone. It seems like it's been longer. The house is weird without her. And I think Charlie misses her, if that's possible. I don't know how much babies this young know about what's going on, but she looks at me sometimes and I think she wants to know where her Gigi is.

I know Mom leaving is my fault, even though neither Mom nor Dad will come out and say so. It's about Dad helping me too much. Mom not helping enough. It's about me keeping Charlie. Mom saying I wouldn't be able to handle taking care of a baby and her being pretty close to being right. I'm not going to admit that to anyone, of course. I can barely admit it to myself. I keep thinking if I try harder, I'll get better at this mom thing. I just have to try harder.

I feel bad. I feel bad because I caused the fight between Mom and Dad. I feel bad because now she's moved out and Charlie misses her. I also feel bad because Gran misses her.

"There's still sauce on the back of the stove if anyone wants more," Mom says, leaning down to put Charlie's pacifier in her mouth.

Charlie smiles at Mom and I'm so proud because she's so smart. I use my phone to take a pic of her. I try to take at least one picture of her every day because she's so beautiful and so perfect and I don't ever want to forget what she looked like yesterday. Today.

Secretly I'm glad Charlie's on the other end of the table with Mom. The kid stresses me out. I've been trying hard to spend more time with her, to be home more with her, but it's hard. It's so much work to take care of her. So much to do and I never know what she wants and I feel like a loser every time she cries. Also, I'm busy. I'm finishing up my schoolwork for the year. And there's a lot going on at school that I'm allowed to participate in, even if I'm not officially attending. I haven't said anything to Mom or Dad or Gran yet, but I've been talking to my guidance counselor about going back to school next year for my senior year. I really miss school and I think, academically, I'm better off going there than being home-schooled. I figure I can find a babysitter to watch Charlie.

Dad's started saying I need to stay home more, which is getting on my nerves. Jack is getting ready to graduate so there are lots of parties. And we're officially boyfriend and girlfriend, which I can't believe because I never thought a guy would like me again. And Charlie is fine. Anyone who looks at her can tell she's fine. She likes hanging out with Dad and Gran. And she and I always sleep together every night. Except for a couple of nights ago when Jack came over to visit, and we fell asleep on the couch in the family room watching TV. Dad had already taken Charlie upstairs and put her to bed in her crib. After Jack left, I was going to go upstairs, but the next thing I knew it was morning and Dad was waking me up. He was kind of cranky because it was only five.

"Feed her," he grumbled, handing a squawking Charlie over to me, and then he went back upstairs to bed.

I take a bite of Mom's spaghetti with spicy marinara sauce. Aunt Beth is telling us all about Paris. I don't know what this guy she's dating does for a living, but he seems to have the bucks. He took her to Mexico when they first started dating. Then to Paris last weekend and they're making plans for some kind of river cruise in Europe. I wonder if he is in the Mafia or something because he apparently doesn't have a nine-to-five job. So either he's in the Mafia or he's like Aunt Beth and calls out sick a lot. Of course, how could he afford the trips if he doesn't work? And I don't know if there's such a thing as the Mafia in Maine.

"The Louvre was better than you see on TV," Aunt Beth is telling Gran. "And you can get right up to the paintings. And the restaurant we went to" — she puts a big forkful of salad into her mouth — "was a five-star restaurant, even though they called it a café." She shrugs. "Or would be one here."

As Aunt Beth is talking, I keep glancing at Mom. She looks good. She's gotten a little bit of sun on her face. I guess from working outside and because spring has finally, *finally* come to Maine. I also think she looks skinnier.

Dad, on the other hand, looks terrible. We've been eating mostly takeout. He'd been losing weight, but I think he's gaining again. Last weekend he just lay around all weekend and watched TV. We never did watch that documentary series about Vietnam together. The one we'd planned to watch after Charlie was born. I offered to stay home from bowling and watch an episode or two with him. But he didn't want to. He just wanted to eat Doritos and change channels. I ended up taking Charlie to Katy's. Then Jack invited us all for pizza and I ran Charlie home and Gran put her to bed. Gran can't climb the stairs well, but I got a Pack 'n Play and Charlie sleeps in that in the family room sometimes, now. Not just for naps, but at night, if I come home late. I always hear her when she wakes up. Or Gran just yells up the stairs to me.

Charlie starts fussing. I ignore her. Aunt Beth is still going on. Now she's telling us about Nutella crepes she had from a street vendor, which makes me sad because I remember the morning Granddad wanted me to make him crepes. Now I kind of wish I had Googled a recipe and tried it. It wasn't like he asked me to do a lot of things for him.

Charlie is still squawking and Mom tries to put her pacifier in her mouth again. "She hungry?" Mom asks me.

I keep eating. "She can't be. She ate when we got here."

"Maybe she's wet." Mom takes a sip of wine. "You want to change her?"

"Not while I'm eating." I reach for another piece of bread. They're small but this is definitely my last piece. "Where's this river cruise?"

"The Rhine," Aunt Beth tells me.

She only had salad and bread for dinner. No pasta. She's trying to lose weight. When she told us that was why she wasn't eating the spaghetti, Mom suggested she cut back on her alcohol consumption. She stuck her tongue out at her.

"What countries?" I ask Aunt Beth.

"Germany, Austria, and France. The boat stops in lots of towns and cities, and you can get off and just walk around, eat, go shopping."

"Hazel, I think she's poopy." Mom talks over Aunt Beth.

Aunt Beth turns to me, going on with her story about all of the excursions available on the river cruise.

"Have you talked to him?" I hear Gran say to Mom.

"Just about logistics. There's a leak in the roof here." Mom is still trying to get Charlie to take her Binky. "About Sean's plans right after school gets out. He's going to California to meet Kyo's parents and her little brother."

"I mean *talk* to him." Gran touches Mom's hand, something I don't see her do often. She's not a physical person, not like Granddad was. Before he got dementia. Before he had a stroke and died. I still can't believe he's dead. I loved him so much. And I liked him, too. Even when he got crazy.

Aunt Beth is still going on about the trip her boyfriend is going to take her on. I want to ask her how she can afford to take off so much time from her job, but I'm also trying to listen in on Mom and Gran's conversation, so I just let Aunt Beth go on.

"He really misses you, Liv," Gran says. "He wishes he could take back what he said to you."

I have to read Gran's lips to get this part. "How do you know what he said to me?" Mom says kind of loud.

Charlie is really starting to fuss now so I don't hear Gran's response.

"If he's sorry, I think he'd have said so, Mother." My mom's voice sounds weird. Higher pitched than normal. Like she's trying not to cry. I don't want her to cry. I don't want her to divorce Dad because he said something dumb. I wonder what he said. I doubt Gran will tell me. I know Mom and Dad won't. They've never done that, even when they were really mad at each other — get Sean or me involved.

"You know how men are," Gran goes on. "You need to be the one to offer the olive branch."

Mom is bouncing Charlie's seat with her foot and making soothing sounds. Charlie isn't having it and now she's squirming and fussing louder. She's about to go ballistic. I can see it in her little squinched-up face.

"Maybe I don't want to offer an olive branch."

"Oh, baloney," Gran says, sounding a lot like Granddad.

". . . Thinking about the Greek islands," Aunt Beth is going on. "But Jason's always wanted to try a Viking river cruise. He says . . ."

Charlie's fussing that has now escalated to crying is drowning out Aunt Beth. Which is kind of a good thing because I don't care that much about her rich boyfriend or her river cruise. It's not that I'm not happy for her, but she always gets like this with a new guy. And then he always turns out to be a dickwad and she ends up back in her bathrobe, drinking wine out of a box and watching *Little Women: Atlanta,* or *Real Housewives* of somewhere. She has terrible taste in men. We all think so.

"Mother," my mom says loudly. "I'm not discussing my marriage difficulties with you. It's not your business."

"It's my business if I'm living in your house, listening to him every day," Gran says, her voice louder than Mom's.

Aunt Beth stops talking mid-sentence to look at Mom and Gran. Charlie never takes a breath.

"Hazel?" Mom speaks sharply, turning to me. "Are you going to —" She stops and starts again, getting out of her chair. "Never mind," she says, unbuckling Charlie and taking her out of the seat. "I'll do it. You finish your dinner."

All three of us watch Mom walk out of

the kitchen, holding Charlie, who is still giving it her best. She cries so loud sometimes that, at home, I put Dad's noise-canceling headphones on.

Mom disappears down the hall and I turn back to look at Aunt Beth and Gran. Aunt Beth is eating the little pieces of bread that have fallen out of the basket onto the tablecloth. According to her, things like that don't count calorie-wise. Also whatever she eats off other people's plates.

"I'm sorry," I say to the table. I don't even know why I say it.

Gran looks at me. "It's not your fault."

Aunt Beth picks up a glass of wine. "I beg to differ." She turns to me. "You know why she left, right?"

I can faintly hear Charlie crying. Mom has taken her upstairs.

"Because of me," I mumble, looking down at my plate. I haven't finished eating my spaghetti, but all of a sudden I'm not hungry anymore.

"Because of that." She points in the direction my mom has just taken my screaming daughter. "You're not taking care of her properly."

"Beth," Gran says sharply.

"What?" She looks at her mother and then at me again.

"I am taking care of her," I say. "I'm doing my best." My voice quivers.

"Well, your best isn't good enough. And where's Baby Daddy in all of this?" my aunt asks, opening her arms and looking around. "Huh? Why isn't he walking her? Buying her diapers and shit?"

Gran gets up and takes her dirty plate with her.

Aunt Beth has another drink of wine. "Honey, I'm not trying to pick on you. You know I love you, but you've got to step up. Because leaving your baby with your grandmother all the time?" She waggles her finger at me. "Not cool."

I stare at my plate, not sure what to say. Mostly because I know she's right.

"It's time you take on your own responsibilities, Hazel." She gets out of her chair. "You wanted to be an adult and have sex with your boyfriend? Too dumb to use a condom? Well, it's time to put your big girl panties on and be a mother to the byproduct of that stupidity."

I hear Aunt Beth walk out of the room. Go up the stairs. Charlie isn't crying anymore.

But I am.

Gran walks over and stands beside my chair. We're both quiet for what seems like a long time. I can hear Aunt Beth talking to Mom upstairs. She's pretty loud.

"You can't let what she says hurt your feelings," Gran says gently. "She's had too much to drink."

I sigh and pick up my fork, pushing some noodles around my plate. "But what if Mom and Dad get a divorce because of me?" I'm trying not to cry. I feel like this all the time now. Except when I'm with Jack. He's the only one who makes me feel better about myself. Makes me feel like I'm not such a loser. Such a crappy mom.

Gran pulls out Aunt Beth's chair and takes her time sitting down. I think she's in pain today. She seems to be moving slowly. "Couples who have been together as long as your mom and dad have issues to work through sometimes. I can't tell you how many times I threatened to divorce your grandfather."

I stare at my plate. "But they're fighting about me. About Charlie."

"I think they're *disagreeing* about you and Charlie. But this is not just about you, I can promise you that."

I look up at her. "Then what's it about? Why's Mom living here and Dad's in Judith?"

Gran sighs. "My daughter refuses to talk

to me about it, but I think it's just growing pains."

"Growing pains?" I think for a minute. "Isn't that's something little kids have? When Sean's legs used to hurt at night, Dad said they were growing pains."

Gran runs her hand over the back of my head and down over my hair. Which worries me a little because first she touched Mom, now she's touching me. I hope she doesn't think she's going to die or something.

"Your mother's life has changed. Sean's gone off to college. You've made her a grandmother. She has a job now." She shrugs. "Different times in your life, you have to go through things. Not just when you're seventeen." She picks up Aunt Beth's plate. "I don't think you should worry. Your mom and dad love each other. They'll work it out." She sets the plate down again. "That said, I have to tell you, I think your mom's right about you not being home enough with Charlie."

I press my lips together, staring at my plate.

"I'm old, Hazel. I helped you out in the beginning because I knew how hard this was, but . . . you need to be home more. I'm not going to watch her as much as I have been watching her. One night a week.

Maybe two, that's all I'm going to give you. And no more going back to sleep in the morning after your dad goes to work." She pauses and goes on. "My friend Anne called me this week and asked me to come back to mah-jongg. Monday, Wednesday, and Friday mornings. They've got an open seat at the table. I had to stop playing when your grandfather couldn't be left alone anymore. I want to play again." She picks up the plate and this time gets up, taking it with her to the sink.

I sit there staring at my stupid plate, trying not to cry anymore. She's right. I know she's right. I know they're all right. I just . . . don't know if I can do it anymore. And what's the alternative? Charlie's almost three months old.

Tears drip onto my spaghetti plate.

When I first found out I was pregnant, I overheard a conversation with Mom and Dad. Dad was talking. About him and Mom adopting my baby. At the time, it sounded so crazy. It still does. But not as crazy now as it did then.

# 37

## LIV

It takes longer for Oscar to make the phone call than I expected. In fact, I'd nearly given up on him making the call at all. And I wasn't sure if I could make it.

When my phone rings, I'm sitting behind the cottage in his favorite Adirondack chair, trying to read a book I picked up at the grocery store on the way home from Lincolnville. I'm not reading, though, I'm worrying. I'm worrying about my mom, who's not feeling well this week. About my project in Lincolnville, about the bid on the store project, and my upcoming meeting with the owners. And then there's Hazel. And Charlie. I miss Charlie so much that it hurts.

It's a beautiful evening, warm for May, and the view from the cliff top is astounding. I can hear the waves crashing as the tide comes in and the faint call of the female loon as she hunts. Calling to her partner.

When I answer my cell, the first thing out

of Oscar's mouth is, "I'm sorry, Liv. I'm so damned sorry."

It takes me a few seconds to respond, long enough for him to say, "Liv? Are you there, hon?"

"I'm here," I say softly.

He exhales. "I miss you, baby."

"I do not miss the baby," I joke. "Well, I do *miss* her."

"But not the crying," he puts in.

We both chuckle. It's not a laugh. Neither of us is at the point of laughing, but at least we're at the point of joking. There's been no joking on the phone since I left. Just brief, curt exchanges involving the who, what, and where of our lives.

"I want you to come home," he says.

I set my book down on the red chair and make my way to the edge of the bluff where the house sits. There's a path that leads down to the beach. It's a steep walk so there's a rope attached to a pinion at the top, to use if you need it. I don't go down to the beach. I just stand there looking out at the water, at the jagged black rocks protruding from the white surf.

"I'm sorry for what I said. I don't want a divorce," he goes on. "You know I don't. I was angry, and tired, and . . . hon, I don't want to sleep another night without you. I

504

miss you. I need you, Liv."

I press my hand to my forehead. "I miss you, too," I confess. "But I have to admit, I don't miss the chaos, Oscar. I don't miss the arguing. I don't miss . . . being at odds with you about Hazel and the baby."

"You were completely right. I've been babysitting too much, covering for her too often. Making it too easy for her to come and go as she pleases. I'm working on that. Your mom and I. We both agreed to limit our babysitting time. Hazel has been home every night but one since she and your mom came back from visiting you. And the one night, I watched Charlie and I told her she had to be home by ten or I wasn't watching her again."

I smile to myself. I know that had to be hard for Oscar to do. I'm touched he would do it for me. But he's skirting the issue of what the argument was actually about. I decide not to bring that up right now.

"How's our daughter making out?" I ask.

"Terrible. A lot of whining. A lot of time on the phone talking to her friends, whining. We got a baby swing that plays classical music so she puts Charlie in that a lot. Charlie likes it."

We're both quiet for a minute.

"Liv, I've been thinking," he says. "When

505

you come back . . . if you'll come back, I want to focus on our marriage. On what we used to have because I want that again. And I think you do, too. I'm going to put you first. Ahead of work, ahead of Hazel and Charlie. Like the old days. Remember when the kids were little?"

"Oscar first," I say, feeling nostalgic.

"Liv first," he says into the phone.

It was a silly thing we used to say each night before we went to sleep. It went with "I love you." In those days, it was a reminder that no matter how crazy things got with work, our families, a house sadly in need of repair, two toddlers, we'd always put each other first. It was a reminder that we married because we loved each other. That we had children to deepen our relationship. We didn't marry so we could have children.

"Tell me what you're thinking," he says.

I can't help thinking how sexy he sounds. His voice and that he would want to know my feelings on all this. But I don't say that. "I don't know, Oscar. I can't come back to the way things have been. And Hazel and Charlie aren't the only problems." A seagull soars over my head, making that mournful sound they make. "I mean, they are. Hazel is, but . . . Oscar, we weren't connecting well before Hazel got pregnant."

"I know," he says quickly. "I know, but I don't think it was because we don't love each other anymore. I've been thinking a lot about this since you left. After I got done being angry. And feeling sorry for myself."

I smile. One of the things I always loved about Oscar was that he could take a good snapshot of himself. It might take him a while, he might fight it, but in the end, he's always been able to analyze his behavior accurately.

"I think we just . . . I think we got lazy, Liv. Like a lot of couples who have been together as long as we have."

"You're probably right," I agree. "We were distant, too. I know I was. And I was apprehensive about my new company. I didn't know if I could make it fly. I didn't know if I could do the work."

"I knew you could do it, Liv."

"But — Oscar, you never said that to me." I turn and walk back toward the house. "You made me feel like I was inconveniencing you by doing something for myself. Something I really wanted to do. I thought . . . I thought you didn't think I could succeed."

"Really? You thought that?" He groans. "I'm sorry, then, because that was never my intention. To make you feel that way. I knew you could do it. I was just wrapped up in what was going on at work. All the changes in policy, the new medical records system. Then after we found out that Hazel was pregnant and you told me the whole thing about wishing you had worked when the kids were little." He exhales, seeming to be looking for the right words to express himself. "You were so angry about staying home to work. Resentful. Liv, it pissed me off that you held that against me for all those years and I didn't know it. I've been thinking back and you never told me you were unhappy."

I look at the sky, running my hand over my head, tugging at my ponytail. "I wasn't *unhappy.* I just felt . . . trapped. Unfulfilled. I loved being a mother but —" I hesitate. We're having a good conversation here, the best we've had in months. I wonder how honest I should be, though. Well, *forthcoming.* I decide I have to be completely honest with him and speak my mind. Because that's at least partially why we're here where we are now, because I haven't always told him everything I was thinking or feeling. "If I had it to do over again, I wouldn't have been a stay-at-home mom. I don't know that I would have wanted to work full-time when the kids were little, but I should have worked. I would have felt better about myself, which I think might have made me a better mother. Maybe a better wife."

"You should have told me at the time that's how you felt." His tone isn't accusatory. It's only honest.

And we're both quiet again. Both thinking.

He's the first to speak again. "Will you at least consider coming home? So we can talk? If you come home tomorrow after work, we could go out to eat dinner. Just you and me."

I hesitate. Truthfully, I don't know if I want to go home or not. Things have gotten so turned around since Hazel became pregnant. Who I am has changed. My roles have changed. And not just with Hazel, but with my parents, too. With Mom now. And I'm still reeling from Dad's death. Subsequently, my expectations of myself and of what other people want from me have changed. It feels overwhelming. And I've enjoyed my time alone here at the cottage. Enjoyed not having so many people need me. Not risking disappointing them. Not risking disappointing Oscar.

Tears spring to my eyes. We've had such a good life together; the idea that our marriage could be over breaks my heart. But I truly don't know if I can go home to him. To the life we had.

"Please, Liv," my husband says. "Will you come home? Or . . . at least think about it?"

I walk back toward the sea. I hear the female loon calling again and the sounds make me shiver. A female loon out hunting calls to the male loon in the nest caring for their young. It's the way they keep in touch while she's out fishing. It's their communication.

"I'll think about it, Oscar."

"Okay." I can tell by his tone of voice that he's hurt. And disappointed. But he's also not defeated.

It's so like him that he thinks one ten-minute conversation, even if it's a good one, and this has been a good one, can solve problems that have been building for years.

My phone beeps. I check the screen; it's my client Terri. "Oscar, I have to go. A client is calling me. They commit to a couple of hundred thousand dollars and they expect me to pick up the phone every time they call, day or night," I joke.

He chuckles. "Could I maybe call you later? Just to talk?"

That makes me smile. I almost feel as if he is wooing me. Like back in the days of dorm living. "Sure." I say good-bye and answer the incoming call. I spend the next hour on the phone with Terri. They're rethinking the choices they made in their kitchen cabinetry. While she talks and I mostly listen. I take my book inside, pour a glass of wine, and make some dinner.

I'm surprised when I hear a car pull into the driveway. Most of our neighbors are only here in the summer. It's still a lonely street in May. Dumping half a bag of sugar snap peas into my stir-fry, I peek out the window. It's Oscar.

I open the back door when he comes up the steps. "What are you doing here?"

"I own the place." He holds up a bottle of wine. "I brought your favorite. Take notice that I spared no expense; it's in a bottle and not a box."

I can't resist a smile. I hold open the door to let him pass. "I just made shrimp stir-fry. You eat yet?"

"Nope."

I follow him into the kitchen.

"You want a glass now?" He holds up the bottle. I can tell he's showered and shaved and put on clean jeans and a collared shirt. For me. "I don't know if it goes with stir-fry."

I smile at him, taking two shallow bowls from the cabinet. "Malbec goes with everything. Yes, I'll have a glass."

We end up carrying our dinner out onto the deck and even after it gets chilly enough that we need sweatshirts, we stay outside. We drink the bottle of wine Oscar brought and then we start on my box of wine. I'm a little tipsy when he puts out his hand to me. "How about a walk on the beach?" he asks.

I can't remember the last time we went for a walk on the beach alone at night. It occurs to me that he should head home. He has work in the morning. But I'm not sure how many glasses of wine he's had. He's a lot bigger than I am, but I know he'd never drive impaired. I know there's no way *I'm* going anywhere tonight behind the wheel of a car.

I accept his hand and he pulls me out of my chair. We stand nose to nose for a minute and then my husband kisses me. He kisses me the way he used to. The kind of kiss that makes your heart skip a beat. The kind that makes you tingly to your toes. Then, before I can say anything, he leads me across the lawn toward the edge of the bluff.

"You going to be okay to drive home?" I ask him.

"Nope," he says. He slips his arm around me. "Luckily I brought my scrubs and a clean pair of undies."

I laugh. Hazel used to call her father's underwear undies and no matter how many times I told her that the word *undies* describes female underwear, she insisted on using the term. "Brought clean undies, did you? Were you hoping to get lucky?"

"Maybe."

We laugh and he pulls me tighter to him and we walk arm in arm. The half-moon is rising in the east and it's big and bright.

"Liv, we've talked about a lot of things tonight, but we haven't talked about our fundamental disagreement about Charlie. About Hazel . . . you know, us adopting Charlie when she was born."

I stop and turn to him. There's enough light from the moon for me to see his face but not his eyes. "Actually, what we argued about was that I thought it was time Hazel consider putting Charlie up for adoption. And you got angry about me wanting to *give her away.*"

He looks down and then back up at me. I hear the loon still calling to her mate. She's still out fishing.

"If Hazel can't do this, I think we should consider taking the baby. Because, honestly, I don't think I could stand to see her go to strangers. If we took her, Liv, I could have a

513

do-over."

"A do-over?"

He puts his arms around my waist. I slide my hands over his shoulders and look up at him.

"I had this idea that if we took Charlie . . . our grandchild and . . . made her our own, it would be like a second chance for me. Third, I suppose. Technically. Liv, I made a lot of mistakes being Sean and Hazel's dad. I wasn't home enough and, when I was, I didn't take enough responsibility." His voice is filled with emotion. "What we were talking about earlier, about you staying home with kids? I wanted it that way. It made things easy for me. You made things easy for me. But if I could do it again, I wouldn't take the easy route. I'd change diapers and clean up puke and . . . and lie on the floor and play with DUPLOs. I'd do all the things I missed with Sean and Hazel."

I smooth his cheek with my hand. His beard is close-trimmed, the way I like it. The fact that he's had a haircut in the last few days doesn't go unnoticed, either. I wonder if he'd been planning all week to come here. And had finally gotten the nerve tonight.

"I'm sorry," he whispers.

"For what?" I ask, feeling sober now.

514

"For everything. For not being a better father. For not being a better husband."

"You've worked hard. Your hours were always so long at the hospital."

He shakes his head, looking down at me. "True. But work is an easy excuse. Work kept me from going to concerts and soccer games and robotic competitions. It gave me a good excuse to do what I wanted to do on weekends with my coworkers, friends, instead of being here with you."

"Oscar, you weren't a terrible dad. Sean and Hazel love you. And you're the fun parent." I shrug. "I'm the one who made them eat their vegetables and do their homework. It was my role. You got to buy video games and let them eat dessert before dinner."

He pulls me against him and I rest my head on his shoulder. "Will you come home?" he asks me. "I'll do whatever you want. Counseling. Getting down on my knees and begging you. Whatever it takes."

"I don't know if I'm ready yet," I say carefully. "I still need time to think. You and I need to talk more. Minus a bottle of wine each."

"Okay." He kisses my temple. "Can I stay over?" he says softly in my ear.

"You own the house," I whisper.

He strokes my back. "You know what I

515

mean, Liv."

I lift my head from his shoulder and smile up at him. "If you're asking me if you can seduce me, I think that would be a good idea."

My husband leans over and kisses me, mouth open, the kiss of a lover, not of a twenty-year marriage. I kiss him back and I wonder if maybe we really can save our marriage. Because there are so many good things between us. This being one of them.

Then I think of Hazel. Of my sweet grandbaby. And the trajectory they're headed in. Because no matter what Hazel says, she's not as committed to being a teen parent as she was when Charlie was born. The question becomes, What do we do as her parents to help her? Where do we go from here and what are Oscar and I willing to sacrifice for her?

# 38
## LIV

Monday morning when my phone rings, I almost don't pick it up, thinking I'll check to see who called once I'm in the truck. I'm running late because Oscar ended up staying Thursday night, then met me back here at the cottage Friday night. Our one-night assignation turned out to be a weekend of walking on the beach, talking, and making love. When he left this morning, I hadn't agreed to move home yet, but I was considering it. Because I do love Oscar and I'm not ready to give up on him or me or us.

I've got a meeting this morning with the company that bought an old house on the edge of Judith and wants to turn it into a high-end shop that sells women's clothing and handbags in the house portion and a café in the attached barn. The exciting thing about the project is: (A) it would be my first commercial job, B) it would be right in Judith so no long drive to work, and (C) it's a big job that would probably take a year to complete. Timing-wise, it would be perfect. About the time the job in Lincolnville should be done, this new project would begin. The house the company purchased is a dump, but structurally it's sound. I could bring it back to life again, I know I could.

I pull my T-shirt over my head and reach for my phone, just to see who's calling. When I see my mom's name, I pick up at once. "Good morning."

"It is not," she says, definitely miffed.

"Okay . . ." I sort of sing the word. I duck into the bathroom to throw on some makeup. I don't usually wear it when I'm working, but because this is a meeting and I'm trying to put my best foot forward, I'm amping up my game. "What's up?" I gaze into the mirror, scrutinizing the fine lines around my mouth.

"You're going to have to come home."

I step back from the mirror. "What's wrong? I have that meeting this morning. To put in my bid for the store in Judith."

"Maybe you could postpone."

"Mom, I can't —"

"Hazel never came home last night," she interrupts stiffly.

I go to the side of my bed and sit down to pull on my work boots. After the meeting,

I'm headed to Lincolnville to oversee the installation of the barn doors that will serve as garage doors. "Hazel didn't come home? Where's Charlie?"

On cue, I hear the baby cry. "With me," Mom says into the phone. "I kept her all night, thinking your daughter would come home. She didn't. I have mah-jongg at nine, and the ladies are expecting me. You'll just have to come home and watch your grandchild. I'm not doing this, Liv. I went through this with your sister. Not coming home at night. Not knowing where she is. If she's safe. Even alive."

I grab my utility jacket and head for the stairs. "Did you call her?"

"Of course I called her. What's all this fussing? Take this Binky and shush. I'm not in the mood."

I gather my mother's last comments were not for me. "Hazel isn't picking up?"

"I also texted her. In all capital letters. She hates that. No, she didn't pick up. Or respond to my texts. That's what teenagers do when they don't come home. They don't answer the phone. I bought your sister a cell phone. They were very expensive in those days. She used it to call her friends and run up my bill because there was no such thing as unlimited data in those days.

She called friends, all right. But didn't answer when her parents called. I was thinking about giving her some rice cereal. I bought it last week."

I'm struggling to switch gears. She's talking about the baby now. Downstairs, I grab my bag and keys, checking to make sure my proposal is inside as well as my wallet. "Hazel doesn't want her having solid foods yet."

"Well, Hazel's not here, is she?" my mother says indignantly. "Baby's hungry." I hear Charlie fussing in the background. "I'm giving it to her. Just a tablespoon or two."

"I'm on my way," I tell her, going out the door.

My mother hangs up.

I call Hazel. It goes straight to voice mail. For a moment, I'm concerned for her safety, but I push that to the back of my mind because odds are, she's just fine. Odds are, she's with the new boyfriend. Next, I call Katy.

"Miss Liv? Is everything okay?" She's whispering.

"Katy, do you know where Hazel is? She didn't come home last night."

There's a beat of silence before the teen says, "I . . . I didn't see her last night."

"Is she with Jack? What's his last name?" I go through a yellow light. "Wait, he's a senior. Is he at school today?"

"Senior skip day," she says in a small voice.

"I didn't even think kids did that anymore." I shake my head. "Maybe he had enough sense not to skip on *skip day*?"

"I don't know. I don't have classes with him."

"Katy, I'm on my way home to pick up Charlie because Hazel isn't there."

"Charlie's alone?"

"No, Katy, of course she's not alone. She's with my mother, but my mother can't watch her. I'm driving from the cottage to our house, picking up Charlie, and taking her to a business meeting." I'm on a roll now. I'm angry and I'm scared for what the future is going to look like for this baby. But mostly I'm angry at my daughter right now for creating this mess.

"I'm . . . I'm sorry. I don't know where Hazel is."

"Fine. This is what I want you to do, Katy. I want you to call Hazel and I want you to tell her to get her ass home." I hang up Bernice-style. It's getting to be a habit with me.

My last call is to Oscar. I know he won't pick up this time of the morning. It's always a madhouse at the beginning of his shift, but he'll check his phone at some point. I ask him to call me. I don't tell him why.

On the ride home from the cottage, I start trying to think through how this would work. If Oscar and I take Charlie. It would have to be an adoption. Hazel would have to give full custody to us. That's the only way I will agree to it. I'm not going to take her for my own daughter, make her my own, and then ten years from now give her back. Hazel can go to Judith High School next year and graduate, but then a college far enough away that she wouldn't be coming home often would be best. For her. For Charlie. For all of us. By the time Hazel goes to college, Charlie will be eighteen months old. She might miss Hazel at first, but at that age, I think with some distance from her mother, Charlie will come to accept me as her mother. I decide here and now, while trying not to drive more than ten miles over the speed limit, that I'm not going to negotiate with Hazel. I'm not going to accept tears and apologies. We're not going to give her another chance because we don't have time to do that. The adults have all seen the writing on the wall for weeks. I think Hazel, in her heart of hearts, sees it, too. She can't care for a child. And I don't blame her a bit. Because, in a lot of ways, *she's* still a child. But we have to do what's best for Charlie.

Driving, I imagine what it will be like to be the mother of a baby again. I think about what Oscar said about a do-over. Could Charlie be my do-over? At our age, with everything we've learned, sometimes the hard way, will Oscar and I be able to be better parents to our granddaughter than we were to our children?

When I arrive at home, my mother has her coat on. She's all dolled up and walking with the aid of a cane. "I'm sorry about this, Liv." She's standing in the kitchen, putting on lipstick. "But you need to get control of her." She waggles her finger at me. "Before you've got a second baby to take care of. It happens, you know, with teenaged girls. They have one baby and the next thing you know, they're pregnant again."

I sigh. A part of me wishes my mother could have met me at the door with a hug and commiserated with me about how poorly this is working out with Hazel caring for her baby. It would have been nice for her to tell me I was right and she was wrong. When Hazel got pregnant, I said she couldn't handle caring for a newborn, but Mom thought she could. But my mother says no such thing, and honestly, were our roles reversed, I don't know that I would have behaved any differently.

"She's in the family room. Fed. Changed. Diaper bag is packed. Car seat's on the dining room table." She points. "The base thing is in the garage on the shelving next to the door. Having lunch afterward, so I don't know when I'll be home." She gives me a quick wave as she heads for the garage. "Good luck."

She gets all the way out the door and comes back in. "By the way, she liked the rice cereal. Mixed it with formula." Then she's gone again.

I stand there in the kitchen for a moment, imagining what life is going to become again: diapers, night feeds, loads of wash. And I'll have to find day care for Charlie because I'm not giving up my job. Of course, if we adopt Charlie, Oscar and I will not be getting divorced. Oscar was talking about a do-over. Maybe he wants to become a stay-at-home dad, which would be fine with me. It's not going to be me, not this time. We'll figure it out. I already love Charlie like she's my own and Oscar does, too. We'll make it work.

My thoughts then drift to the joy another child will bring me. The joy my children have brought me, the joy Charlie already brings me now. The slobbery kisses, the laughter at bath time, the little sticky hands that will hold mine. Standing in the middle of my kitchen, I clench my fists. I can do this, I tell myself. I can do this.

*I can't do this. I can't do this,* I'm telling myself an hour later.

I'm pacing a downtown parking lot, Charlie on my shoulder. Charlie is screaming bloody murder. She's been crying for half an hour. In my meeting. I took her in to meet John and Luke Morris, the brothers who are opening the store. They already have one in Portland and one in Rockland. I apologized profusely for having to bring my granddaughter, giving no explanation because I refuse to lie for my daughter. I also don't want them to think there's going to be drama if they hire me.

I start to cry, my tears matching anything Charlie has to offer. First, it's just a trickle down one cheek, but then I start to cry in earnest. Afraid John and Luke might see me, I walk to my truck. I don't want them to see me like this. Not that I have a chance of getting the bid now. I decide to go looking for Hazel. Find her car.

I'm still crying as I buckle Charlie into her car seat because I know Hazel can't take care of her. I cry even harder because I realize I can't, either.

# 39
## HAZEL

My phone dings, startling me, and I sit up on the couch. Jack and I didn't mean to fall asleep. We didn't mean to stay all night at his friend Arden's house. Arden's parents are in Aruba, and his older sister was supposed to be supervising, but she spent the weekend at her boyfriend's house. The sister said Arden could have some friends over for tacos. Friends like Jack who wouldn't wreck their place. The sister did not say we could spend the night.

I wipe my mouth with the back of my hand. I can tell it's late morning by the sun coming through the windows. I can't believe we slept in this late. I look around, wondering where Jack is. Today is senior skip day, so he and Arden are skipping school. So is Arden's girlfriend, Molly, who's only a junior and goes to another school. Plus, another guy who's friends with them, Turtle. I don't know what his real name is, but he seems nice. His girlfriend, Liza, was here last night, but she went home at eleven, just as we were starting the second *Star Wars* movie. She said her parents would kill her if she was out past curfew.

I glance around the room. Turtle is asleep on the floor, wrapped up in a pink quilt. Arden and Molly are sleeping on the other couch; she's kind of lying on top of him. The TV is still on. I think it's *The Last Jedi.* Somehow, Arden had them all cued up and we were watching them in chronological order instead of the order they were released.

I reach for the bottle of blue Gatorade Jack and I were sharing last night; my mouth tastes like spicy Doritos. I smile and sip. We had a really good time last night, making tacos with his friends. And not from a box. We made rice and beans and fresh guacamole. We had some beers, but nobody got super drunk. Nobody barfed. I like his friends. They're funny and smart and a little geeky. Kind of like Jack and me. But still cool. Last night Liza even talked to me about Charlie and said she couldn't imagine trying to take care of a baby. She never said a thing about how dumb I was to get pregnant in the first place.

Being here with Jack was really fun. He

was even cool when I told him I wasn't having sex with him last night. I kind of wanted to, but I just got the birth-control-implant thing in my arm. I went to see Dr. Gallagher without telling Mom, just because I don't want to talk to Mom about my sex life. Supposedly it should be working by now. I've had it eight days and Dr. Gallagher said no unprotected sex for a week, but I want to be sure it's working because I *cannot* have another baby. I can't do it. And in a way, it's a good excuse not to have sex with a boy this time until I'm ready.

Jack walks into the living room in his boxers and sweatshirt. He looks kind of cute, all sleepy-eyed with his hair messed up.

My phone dings again.

"Hey," Jack says.

"Hey," I answer, picking up my phone.

He kisses me on the corner of my mouth and I hope he can't taste the Doritos like I can. "Guess we fell asleep."

"Guess we did." We both keep smiling at each other.

I actually woke up at about two in the morning and thought about going home. Because Gran was watching Charlie and I knew she was going to be really mad. And not watch her anymore. And then she'd tell Dad and *he'd* get mad and say he wasn't watching her, either. And my life would be ruined because I'll be stuck sitting in my parents' house with Charlie until she goes to kindergarten. So, if my life is already going to be ruined, I decided I may as well sleep on a couch with Jack and let my parents and Gran go ballistic tomorrow.

I haven't told Jack anything about what's been going on at home, mostly because everyone there already knows what a bad mom I am. I don't want Jack to know, too, because then he'll break up with me. Of course, now he's going to break up with me because I'll never be able to go out with him again unless I take my baby. So maybe I should have gone home last night at ten.

I close my eyes for a second, thinking about what a mess my life has become. All because I stupidly thought Tyler was cute. Because I thought I was old enough, mature enough, to be a mother.

I look at my phone and fall back on the couch, closing my eyes.

*I am in sooo much trouble.*

I've missed calls from Gran, Mom, Dad, and Sean. *Sean??* And Katy. Katy's called five times in the last thirty-six minutes. And I have nineteen texts and seven voice messages. The voice messages are from Gran, Mom, and Dad. People my age don't leave messages.

*So much trouble.*

I'm going to be grounded for the rest of my life. Which is so not fair because I made one mistake. One time I had sex without a condom, and now Mom and Dad and Gran are going to punish me for the rest of my life.

I don't know what the big deal is. Charlie probably only got up once or twice last night to eat or be changed. She's a good baby. For a baby. And she was happier with Gran than she would have been with me. She cries with me.

"What's the matter?" Jack steps into his jeans. He's wearing red boxers with yellow cowboy hats on them. Which made me smile last night when I saw them. I'm not smiling now.

"I need to go." I'm still lying on the couch. I close my eyes, afraid I'll start crying and embarrass myself.

"Charlie okay?"

I open my eyes and stare at the ceiling, realizing I don't know if Charlie is all right. I can't believe I didn't think of that. What if she's sick or hurt or something?

I look at my texts from Katy first because she was the last one to call and text this morning.

Where are you? You ok??????
your mom called!!! she is really pissed

The last message from her was sent thirty-eight minutes ago. The same time as the last call.

your mom is driving around looking for you. for your car

I bring my phone to my chest and wipe my eyes with my other hand. "I have to go," I say again. I look around. "I need my shoes. Do you know where they are?"

Then the doorbell rings. And I know who it is. I just *know*. Because my car is parked out front. Jack and I drove separately, so if he wanted to stay, I could still get home on time.

The doorbell rings again. Molly sits up, looking around like she's not sure where she is.

"Here they are." Jack pulls my Converse sneakers from under the couch and hands them to me.

The doorbell rings again.

And again.

And again.

And then Arden and Turtle both sit up.

"I'll get it," I say, hurrying toward the front hall. Arden lives in a nice house. In one of the newer neighborhoods in Judith. "I'll call you," I tell Jack.

"Hazel?" comes my mom's voice from the other side of the door.

Now the doorbell is ringing nonstop. I'm so embarrassed.

"I'm coming!" I holler.

I grab my coat off the bench in the foyer and yank open the door.

Mom looks like she's going to kill me. I mean, *literally* like she's going to shoot me or knife me or however parents commit filicide. We learned that word in my honors English class when we had to pick a Pulitzer Prize–winning novel and write a paper on it. I did Toni Morrison's *Beloved* and wrote about filicide, which is when parents kill their children.

"Get in the truck," Mom says. Her teeth are clenched.

"My car's here," I murmur, not looking at her. I'm trying not to cry.

I hear Jack behind me calling my name. I walk out of the house. "I'll text you later," I holler over my shoulder and close the door behind me.

I follow Mom down the sidewalk in my socks because I'm carrying my sneakers. The sidewalk is wet and it soaks my plaid socks. I'm praying Jack doesn't decide to try to be some kind of hero and come outside.

"We're leaving your car here," Mom tells me.

I look up to see her truck parked in the driveway. Right behind my car.

"I can't leave it. It'll block everyone in." I sound belligerent. Mostly because I'm trying not to cry.

She keeps walking.

"Mom," I call after her, opening my arms wide like to say, "What the hell?" "I can't leave my car here." I'm so mad, so mortified she would come here.

"Follow me home," she barks.

As I walk between my car and the truck to get into the driver's seat, I look through Mom's windshield into her backseat. I see Charlie in her car seat. Sound asleep, her little lips sucking like she doesn't know she lost her Binky. I keep going. I get into my car and slam the door. While I wait for Mom to back out, I put my shoes on.

Jack walks out of the house and stands on the front porch. I don't make eye contact with him.

When Mom pulls onto the street, I back out and put the car into drive. But I hold my foot on the brake.

At the end of the street, I could turn left when Mom goes right, headed for home. I could get on the interstate and just go. I don't know where. Somewhere I could start a new life. I'd miss Charlie, but she's better off with Mom and Dad. If I abandon her, I think they can sue for custodial rights. Then adopt her when they never hear from me again.

I think about going to Alaska. Jobs pay well there. Or maybe I could work on an oil rig somewhere. I read an article about how more women are doing that.

Of course, that's all just a fantasy because when Mom pulls out, I roll to the stop sign, put on my signal, wait the appropriate amount of time to let her get far enough ahead of me, and then I turn right, too. I go home.

# 40
## HAZEL

When I get home, I walk straight into the house, past Mom, who's getting Charlie out of her car seat. Mom calls after me, but I don't answer her.

I think about telling her to give me Charlie. That she's *my* daughter and I want her. But I'm tired, and I just want to go to sleep. I just want to hide from everyone. From Mom and Gran and Dad and Charlie. I want to hide from myself and all the things going through my head because I don't like them. I don't want them there, and I don't know how to stop them.

About Charlie. About what a terrible mistake I made last summer when I decided to keep her. I still don't think I could have had an abortion, but Mom's argument for adoption keeps coming back to me. Proof I'm a terrible mother. And I feel so guilty even thinking about what it would be like if I didn't have Charlie anymore.

I go to my room, lock the door, and lie down on my bed. Eventually Mom comes upstairs and knocks, calls my name, but I don't answer. She has Charlie with her because I hear her talking in a quiet voice, saying things like, "You can't have Gigi's earring," and "Give me that nose."

I hear Charlie making cute baby sounds.

I roll over and close my eyes and pretend I don't hear either of them. Pretend I'm asleep. When Mom goes back downstairs and then texts me, I turn off my phone. I don't even text Jack back after he texts, you k? call me.

The sound of someone knocking on my door, much later in the day, wakes me up.

"Hazel?" It's my dad. He's home from work. He knocks again.

I sit up, leaning against the headboard, and draw my knees up. I stare at the door. I have to pee, but there's no way I'm leaving this room. At least not with him standing in the hall.

"Daisy . . . honey, we need to talk."

I stay quiet.

Enough time passes in silence that I think maybe he left, he was just quiet about it, but then I hear his voice again. "You have to come down for dinner. Nonnegotiable. We need to talk about Charlie."

537

He doesn't sound angry. He sounds really sad, which makes me start to cry, but softly so he can't hear me.

"Dinner is at six thirty," he tells me from the other side of the door. "And a family meeting. You owe it to Charlie to come down and be a part of this."

I hear him walk down the hall to his room. About twenty minutes later, I hear his footsteps again and he goes downstairs. I sneak out of the room, go to the bathroom, and run back in my room and lock the door before anyone catches me. When I'm in the hall, I hear Charlie's swing. It's playing Chopin. Not because it will make her smarter. Gran said that playing classical music to her would make her smarter, but I researched what's called the Mozart Effect. It's bullshit. There's no scientific evidence classical music will make Charlie smarter. We play it because it soothes her.

I have no intention of going downstairs at six thirty to talk about Charlie. There's nothing to talk about. She's mine. Nobody can make any decisions about her except me. Nobody has that right but me. Well, I guess, legally, *Tyler* has a right, but he's a nonissue. He couldn't care less about Charlie.

I turn my phone back on and check the

time. It's six twenty. I really don't want to go downstairs.

But I feel like I should.

Because I love Charlie.

And I'm hungry. I haven't eaten since the Doritos last night.

I wait until six thirty-five. No one comes upstairs and bangs on my door. I wonder if, because I'm still a minor, Mom and Dad can just take Charlie from me. I don't *think* they can, but I don't know.

When I smell food, I creep downstairs.

Mom, Dad, Gran, Aunt Beth, and Sean are all at the dinner table passing around containers of Korean takeout. It's from a new place in town; Mom and Dad always like to support local businesses.

"What are *you* doing here?" I ask Sean, taking my chair. Someone's put a plate and silverware and a glass of water at my place.

The swing is set up between the kitchen and the living room. Charlie's asleep. The swing is playing something classical I don't recognize. The swing plays, like, twenty songs. And it's one of the safest swings on the market; I did the research before I let Mom buy it.

"Mom asked me if I could come." Sean shrugs and uses a chopstick to push *bulgogi,* a beef dish, onto his plate. "Not leaving for

California until Wednesday. Thought about coming home anyway."

"My sister said I *had* to come," Aunt Beth puts in. She's ladling the spicy tofu stew, *soondubu,* into a bowl.

Everything looks so delicious. It smells so good. I put some rice on the corner of my plate and wait for Dad to hand me the kimchi. "You get *bibimbap*?"

"Without egg," he tells me. He smiles at me, but his smile seems tight. "Just for you."

"Here it is." Mom hands me a plastic container.

Everyone puts what they want on their plates. Aunt Beth is the first one to speak up after we've been eating for several minutes in silence. "This is going to be awkward, so let's move it along for the sake of everyone." She sets down her chopsticks and picks up a full-to-the-rim glass of wine. "And I've got somewhere to be tonight."

"Beth," Gran says, folding her cloth napkin just so. "I think we should let Liv handle this."

"Nah, I'm going to do my big sister a favor." Aunt Bethie swings around in her chair to face me, ignoring Gran. "Instead of beating around the bush for half an hour before anyone actually says what they think, I'm going to say it." She takes a big swig of red wine. "Hazel, you can't take care of that baby." She shrugs; she's wearing a black cold-shoulder T-shirt that's a size too small. "You can't take care of her and you don't even want to all that much."

"I *do* wanna take care of her," I argue. "I didn't mean to stay out all night. I fell asleep. I'm sorry." I open my arms to her. Then I look at Gran, because she's the one I owe an apology to. She was the one who took care of Charlie all night. I guess until Mom came and got her in the morning. "I'm sorry, Gran. It won't happen again."

"No, it won't, because I'm not watching her anymore," she answers stiffly. "You took advantage of me, Hazel. You've been taking advantage of me. Of your father and your mother, too" — she points at me — "when you can get away with it. Although I know Liv won't admit it because she's been playing the bad cop in this soap opera."

I look down at my plate, then back up at Gran. "I didn't mean to take advantage of anyone."

She surprises me by smiling at me. A sad smile. "I know you didn't. Apology accepted." She takes a bite of rice. She's the only one at the table not using chopsticks. "I love Charlie to death, but I'm not babysitting again. I'm too old and too cranky."

I drop some cucumber kimchi onto my plate, not as hungry as I was when I came down. I knew this is what we were going to talk about, but I didn't think we'd start right in on it. I was thinking maybe we would eat and talk about stuff that doesn't matter first.

"You have to let Charlie go, Hazel," Mom says, looking at me. "You're not ready to be a mother."

A tear somehow makes its way to my nose and drips off the end onto my plate and into my rice.

"Oh, Hazel." Mom, who is sitting beside me, takes my hand and squeezes it in hers. "You have so much to look forward to in life. But you need time on your own. You need to finish high school, and go to college, and then do whatever you want to do after that. Someday you can have more children."

I stare at my plate, tears running down my face. Because Mom's right. I know she's right. I just hate so much that she is right. That's she's *always* right. I hate that her predictions were entirely accurate. Tyler didn't stay with me and I'm too young to be anyone's mother.

I feel like my heart is breaking. I've heard that phrase a million times, but I never really understood it. I understand now.

542

"What? You think I can just have another Charlie someday?" I demand, trying hard not to cry. Not succeeding.

My dad clears his throat. When he speaks, I can tell he's trying not to cry, too. I don't think I've ever seen my dad cry. "Daisy, no one is saying you can ever replace Charlie. What your mom is saying is that you can have more children when you're older, when you're settled and have lived some. When . . . when you're able to care for and financially support not just yourself but someone else. When you have a husband or . . . whatever."

Aunt Beth chuckles. "She's not gay, Oscar."

"You know what I mean," he says to me, ignoring Aunt Beth. "When you have a committed partner. Someone to share parenting with."

Everyone is quiet for a minute. No one is really eating anymore.

"You tried," Sean says clumsily. His eyes look wet, too. "Don't keep her just to be stubborn. Because you don't want to do what Mom wants you to do. You gotta do what's best for Charlie. She's a baby. She can't decide what's best for her, but *you* can."

"Hazel, please don't think this is easy for

any of us," Mom says. She's crying, but she's keeping it together. "I think we *all* need to put our own feelings aside and do what's best for Charlie." She looks around the table. "We need to help Hazel do what's best for Charlie. Because . . ." — her voice cracks — ". . . because she's her mother."

Dad puts his arm around Mom's shoulders and whispers something in her ear.

I just sit there, staring at my plate.

Charlie keeps swinging in her swing, asleep, having no idea what we're talking about. Not knowing her life is about to change.

"Hazel," Mom says slowly. "You're not ready to be a mother. You can't keep her."

"But I love her," I say, my voice sounding like I can't get enough air.

"I love her, too." Gran pours wine into her empty water glass. She never drinks wine. "But that doesn't mean I can be her mother, either."

"Gran, you . . . you thought I should keep her. When I got pregnant you said I should keep her."

"I was wrong." She crosses her arms over her chest. No apology, no explanation. Which is so like her.

"We've all talked about it, sweetie," Mom says. "And we think you need to put Charlie up for adoption."

I chew on my bottom lip so hard that I taste blood. "You mean give her to you?"

Mom looks at Dad and then back at me. "No." It comes out as not much more than a whisper. "I mean put her up for adoption. She should go to a young family. Someone who can care for her the way she deserves to be cared for. The way she deserves to be loved."

I stare at my mother, wondering if I can die from this tightness in my chest that I know is my broken heart. I feel so betrayed by her. "I can't believe you won't take her," I whimper. I look at my dad. "I thought you wanted her."

"It's not that we don't want her, Daisy."

Mom presses her lips together and then says, "I think that would be best for Charlie."

I start to come out of my chair, my fingers laced together, my hands on top of my head. I feel like my brain is going to explode. "I don't understand . . . I thought —" I look at Dad. Then back at Mom. "I thought I came down here to — I thought we were going to talk about you and Dad adopting Charlie. Not giving her away to strangers."

Mom wipes her mouth with her cloth napkin. She meets my gaze. Exhales as if she's tired beyond exhaustion. "I can't do that, Hazel. I love Charlie. I love her *so* much." Tears trickle down her cheeks and I realize she looks like she's been crying all day. "But that's not what's best for Charlie. Not being raised by grandparents."

"I can't believe you want me to give her to a stranger!" I scream. "I can't believe you thought I would do that!" As I get up, I accidentally knock my chair over. It hits the wood floor with a bang and startles Charlie. She starts to cry. I go to her, unbuckle her from her swing, and lift her out of it. "I'm not doing it! You can't make me give her away!"

I run out of the dining room, holding my daughter in my arms. I run up the stairs and into my room and slam the door shut. Charlie screams louder. I lock the door. I put Charlie in her crib, stuff her pacifier in her mouth, and go to my closet. I come out with my suitcase.

"If they don't want you here, then they don't want me here," I tell Charlie. "We're out of here. I don't know where we're going, but somewhere far away."

I start throwing clothes into the suitcase. Anything I grab goes in: jeans, a sweater, a pile of shorts, T-shirts. I yank out my whole drawer of underwear and bras and dump everything in, into my suitcase.

There's a knock at my bedroom door. "Daisy?"

"Go away!" I scream at Dad. "Leave me alone."

"Hazel, let me in so we can talk. Your mother and I want to talk to you."

"But I don't want to talk to you!" I throw a sneaker that's in my hand and it bangs against the door and bounces off.

Dad rattles the knob. But the door is locked and he's not getting in. I turn my back on the door.

"We're not staying here," I mutter, yanking shirts off hangers and throwing them into the suitcase. I toss a tray of jewelry on top. "We're going to be fine, Charlie. We'll figure it out." I retrieve the sneaker I threw and wedge it in.

Charlie is still crying.

Dad's gone.

I add another pair of shoes and, realizing my suitcase is full, I drop to the floor on my knees. "We're packed," I tell my baby. "We're out of here!" I start zipping it up, shoving stuff in so it will close. I've almost got it zipped when I sit back, pulling my hands off the suitcase like it burned them.

I just stare at it.

I packed a suitcase. I'm ready to go.

But I didn't put a *single* thing of Charlie's inside.

My whole room is full of diapers, and blankets and onesies, and leggings and tops for Charlie. And I didn't put anything in the suitcase for her. Not *one* thing.

Crying so hard, I can hardly get up, I go to the crib. I pick Charlie up so gently, and I hold her against me, rocking her. I breathe deep, trying to imprint on my brain the feel of her in my arms. "I'm sorry," I whisper in her little ear that looks like a lima bean.

I slide to the floor and lean against the crib. And miracle of miracles, she starts to calm down. "I can't do it," I tell her.

I kiss her chubby cheek.

"I'm sorry, Charlie," I sob. "But I can't take care of you."

I nuzzle the little red curls at the back of her neck.

"You deserve a mom and a dad. Adults. Adults with jobs and a way to take care of you."

Charlie looks up at me and makes sounds like she's talking to me.

I pull her against me and hug her, smelling her baby smell that's a combination of Mrs. Meyer's lavender fabric softener, diaper rash butt paste, and formula.

And I sob. I cry like I've never cried before.

Eventually, like Charlie, I stop crying. I look down to see that she's fallen asleep, sucking her Binky that I gave her. And she's so beautiful.

Being careful not to wake her, I stand up. I walk to my door and unlock it. I open it and then I lean against the wall and wait.

Only a few minutes pass before Mom is standing in my doorway. "May I come in?" she asks.

I nod, not trusting my voice yet.

She looks at the suitcase, then back at me.

It feels like a long time passes before I find my voice. But when I speak, I'm surprised by how loud it sounds. Like I'm not crumbling to pieces inside. "You're right," I say, holding Charlie against me. "I can't take care of her." I take a breath, my whole body shaking. "I want . . . I want to put her up for adoption. If . . . if you and Dad don't want —"

I look at Mom to see her crying. "We can't. I can't." She mouths the words.

I take another breath. "If you don't think you can take her, then I want to put her up for adoption. I want someone to adopt her. Someone who can't have babies."

"Oh, Hazel," Mom says in what sounds

like a sigh.

She comes to me and wraps her arms around me and it's like the two of us are holding Charlie.

"I'm so proud of you, Hazel," she murmurs. "So very proud of you."

I nod, still crying. I squeeze my eyes shut because I can't imagine handing Charlie to someone she doesn't know.

"So proud of you," Mom says again. "For being smart enough, brave enough to do this. Because you know what?"

"What?" I ask, not taking my head off her shoulder.

"I wasn't mature enough to have a baby when I had Sean. I shouldn't have gotten pregnant. But your dad wanted a baby and I wasn't brave enough to admit I wasn't ready. I wasn't as brave as you are, Hazel."

For a long time I just stand there, letting Mom hold me and Charlie in her arms. And then she carefully takes Charlie from me and puts her in her crib while I just stand there watching her. And then she takes my hand and she leads me past my suitcase to my bed.

"You need to sleep. We can make plans in the morning," she whispers.

I climb into bed in my clothes and lay my head on my pillow. Mom pulls up the sheet and kisses the top of my head the way she used to when I was little. Then she starts stroking my hair and I drift off to sleep.

# 41
## LIV

I wait until Hazel falls asleep; it doesn't take long. Then I get up from her bed, careful not to jostle her, and tuck the sheet around her. I stand over her bed, watching her sleep, remembering the tiny redhead that once rested on a pillow in this same room, in the same bed. Fighting the tears that I'm afraid will never end if they start again, I check on Charlie in her crib. Indian elephants dance on the sheet. She should probably have a diaper change, but she's so deeply asleep that I decide to let it go for now. I'll leave our bedroom doors open and when she wakes, I'll hear her. I'll change her and feed her and let Hazel rest.

Kissing my granddaughter good night, I turn off the light and walk out of the bedroom. The hallway is dark. I can hear the faint sound of the TV downstairs. My mom and Sean are watching a movie. Beth left. She had a date.

I put my hand on the wall to steady myself, a little dizzy. I feel as if I'm being crushed inside. It's not just my heart is being destroyed, but my internal organs. They're shattering and piling up at my feet.

I truly believe that adoption is what's best for Charlie, but now that Hazel has agreed to it, I don't know if I can do it. I just don't know if I have it in me.

I sit down on the floor in the dark hall, draw up my knees, and hug them to my chest. I take one shuddering breath after another as the memories of what it felt like to be an adopted child wash over me. All those insecurities, the fear Mom and Dad would "send me back" if I was bad, the fear that I would never be good enough for them, for anyone, come over me in waves.

"Liv?"

I hear Oscar. I don't look up.

"Oh, honey." He sits down beside me on the floor and pulls me to him.

I sob. "I don't know if I can do it. I don't know if I can let Charlie go," I say, gasping for breath. "I love her so much."

Oscar wraps his arms around me and holds me tightly. "I love her, too. We all do."

He lets me cry myself out as he strokes my back, whispering in my ear that he loves me. That we're doing the right thing.

"She's better off to be adopted. To be raised by younger parents," I say into his neck.

"I agree with you," he murmurs. "I know I said I want to keep Charlie, but you were right. She's better off placed in a home with parents desperate for a baby. Not old folks our age." He kisses my wet cheek. "And the truth is, Liv, that I love Charlie, but I love you more."

His voice cracks and it breaks my heart.

"I know this sounds selfish," he goes on. "But the simple truth is that I want you more than I want her."

I open my eyes and look into his and realize that I should have let this last year of our life bring us closer together, not force us farther apart. I kiss him on his mouth. "It's the right thing," I murmur. "Even if we thought we *could* care for her, it would be too hard for Hazel to see her with us. To hear Charlie call me Mom."

He nods and pulls me against him, embarrassed by his tears, I think. "You're right."

We hug each other tightly. "It's the right thing to do for Hazel, too," I tell him. "For our daughter. But —" My voice catches in my throat again. "It hurts so much. The thought of saying good-bye."

Oscar tightens his arms around me and I

cling to him. I allow myself to be vulnerable, to feel my pain. To let my husband see my pain. We sit there in the hall on the floor for a very long time, in the dark, just holding each other. And then Oscar suggests we should go to bed because the next few days are going to be long and hard. He helps me to my feet and, hand in hand, we go into Hazel's bedroom. By the glow of the elephant nightlight, we gaze into the crib at Charlie, who reminds me so much of Hazel at that age that my tears come again. But this time, they're not just tears of sadness but of relief too.

And then, together, Oscar and I stand over Hazel's bed. I don't dare touch her, for fear of waking her, but arm in arm we watch our daughter sleep and know we're doing what's best for her. Which, as her parents, is really who we need to put first.

# 42
## LIV

"Dad, what are you getting?" Hazel asks. Then she shoots out of her chair. "Amanda! Amanda!" she shouts across the old-fashioned ice cream parlor that is packed with graduation day celebrations like ours. She waves vigorously and the girl who was once her nemesis grins and waves back. "See you at Katy's later?"

Hazel looks gorgeous in the thrifted white dress and sandals we found in Amherst while visiting UMass where she'll attend in the fall as a premed/health major. I wasn't sure how I felt about the dress when she first tried it on. It seemed so old-fashioned and the color had yellowed with time and wear. But against her pale, freckled skin and long hair she styled in curls, she was the prettiest girl on the stage at graduation.

"See you at Katy's," the friend calls.

Hazel drops back into her chair, next to her boyfriend, Jack, who just finished his freshman year at UMass. "I'm thinking banana split," she tells her father. "With strawberry, pistachio, and mint-chocolate-chip ice cream, and butterscotch, hot fudge, and marshmallow cream on top. Oh, and pistachio nuts and whipped cream. And a cherry."

Oscar makes a face at her. "You eat that and you won't make it to Katy's for the graduation party. You'll be in the ED having your stomach pumped."

"Jack's going to share it with me, right?"

Jack is dressed in khakis and a teal polo shirt, seated next to her, shakes his head. "There's no way you can get me to eat that." He puts his menu in the middle of the table. "I'm having a black-and-white shake."

"What about you, Aunt Bethie?" Hazel calls across the table.

It's good to see Hazel so happy, so animated. A year ago, right after Charlie left us, was a dark time for Hazel. For all of us. Even after we donated all of the toys, the clothes, the car seat, all the trappings of a newborn, the house still smelled of Charlie. And when we closed our eyes we could still hear her. Sometimes crying, sometimes cooing.

But Hazel was a trouper. She stuck with

her decision to put her daughter up for adoption, never once wavering, once it was made. Even when it was time to hand her over to Tesha Crawford, at the adoption agency, Hazel stood her ground, insisting she was doing the right thing. And we supported her, emotionally, sometimes physically, like when she had to walk out of the building after Tesha passed Charlie on to the parents waiting in another room.

That was the hardest part for me. Handing her over to people we never met. When we started the process of looking for an agency to place Charlie, I assumed it would be an open adoption. That Hazel would get updates and photos of Charlie, maybe see her a couple of times a year. That we could send gifts for holidays. I assumed Oscar and I would get to see her. When Hazel broke the news to us that she wanted a closed adoption, I almost caved. I almost told her that her dad and I would take Charlie. But in my heart that only another mother can truly understand, I knew the adoption was the right thing. For Charlie and for Hazel.

Beth, seated across the table from us, between our mother and her fiancé, Jason, takes a sip of water. "I'm thinking I'll have a peanut-butter-chocolate sundae. Jason's going to get a hot-fudge sundae so I can have some of his. Right?" She looks at him and he looks back at her with a devotion most women would be jealous of. I still can't believe after all the losers my sister has dated over the years, she's finally found a winner. Oscar and I both like Jason and our mother seems almost as smitten with him as Beth is. Which is funny, to see my mother, at her age, all giggly with a man.

"Oooh, that sounds good." Hazel reaches for the menu. "Maybe I don't want the banana split."

I look at Oscar. "What are *you* having?"

He shrugs. "Whatever you want, honey." He leans over and kisses my shoulder that's bare in my sleeveless blue sundress. "I thought we'd share."

I turn to him and smile and we meet each other halfway between our seats to kiss.

"Hey, you two," my mother says from across the table. Her comment is directed at Oscar and me. "Knock it off. No one else is doing that at this table." She waggles her finger.

Oscar laughs, steals another kiss, and picks up one of the ice cream menus. I watch him, smiling. After the night we sat on the floor in the hall coming to terms with losing Charlie, our relationship took a turn for the better. I've learned to rely on him more, and he's gotten better at listening to me, even when I just need him to hear me and not necessarily solve my problem. Our marriage certainly isn't perfect, but I feel like it might be stronger now than it's ever been.

Sean, seated at the end of the table beside his latest girlfriend, Sarina, starts telling us a story about some kid climbing into his dorm window, confused as to not only which dorm he's in, but at which college.

As I listen to Sean talk and to my family around the table laughing, I have to struggle not to cry. It was one of several decrees Hazel made this morning: no crying, no bragging about her being salutatorian of her senior class, and no mention of Charlie.

It's been almost two years since Hazel passed the positive pregnancy test through the opening of the bathroom door to me. And our family has been through hell, with the pregnancy, my dad's death, losing Charlie. But I feel as if we've come out the other side with just a few smoking embers. Hazel is off to college. Beth is getting married. Sean has a girlfriend and loves school. My mom, still living with us, is in pretty good health and is actually enjoying life again. Oscar just started a new job training PAs at the hospital, which means less stress. My business is going well. So well since I was awarded the contract to restore the house for the shop here in Judith that I just hired my first part-time employee. For all those good things, I need to be grateful. I am grateful.

"Can you take a pic of us, Aunt Bethie?" Hazel asks, passing her phone across the table.

Jack puts his arm around Hazel's shoulders and they grin.

Watching my sister take the photo brings up a lump in my throat. After Charlie was placed, Hazel removed all of her daughter's framed photos from around the house. She went around to each of us, took our phones, and removed all the photos of Charlie. I assumed she was just storing them on her computer so she wouldn't have to see daily reminders of her daughter. Come to find out, she *had* put them on a computer, but she'd had her brother put them in some sort of digital vault. I didn't even know such a thing existed. So now, none of the photos can be viewed for ten years.

Hazel and I got into a terrible argument when she told me what she'd done. Maybe the worst we'd ever had. I was so angry because, in a way, I felt as if I was losing Charlie again. Because at least, after she was gone, I had the photos and videos. Then

561

suddenly I had nothing of her but what was in my mind and the memories Oscar and I shared alone in bed at night. Hazel's argument was that Charlie was no longer ours. She belonged to her new family, whose names we would never know. She said people don't keep photos of strangers' children.

"Thanks, Aunt Beth." As Hazel stands to retrieve her phone, a waitress stops at the table.

"I'll be right back to take your order." The girl in shorts and a T-shirt with the ice cream shop logo on it rests her hands on the back of the high chair at the head of the table. "Okay if I take this?"

"Sure, we're not using it," Jason says.

"No." Hazel's hand shoots out and she keeps the waitress from picking up the high chair. "We need that."

"Okay. Sorry." The waitress flashes a cautious smile and walks away. "Be right back."

"Who's the high chair for?" Jason asks innocently.

Beth grabs his hand as if she can somehow take back the words he's spoken.

We all look at one another: Oscar, Mom, Sean, Beth, and Jack. Only Sean's girlfriend and Jason don't know.

Hazel, still standing, shifts her gaze until

it meets mine. Tears fill her eyes but she has the tiniest smile on her lips. And at that moment, I know my daughter will be just fine. In fact, my dream is coming true, the dream every mother has for her daughter. That she'll be a happier and more emotionally stable woman than I will ever be.

I hold my daughter's gaze and I speak the words she can't bring herself to say. "The chair is for Charlie."

■ ■ ■ ■

# READING GROUP GUIDE: OUR NEW NORMAL

## COLLEEN FAULKNER

■ ■ ■ ■

## ABOUT THIS GUIDE

The suggested questions are included to enhance your group's reading of Colleen Faulkner's *Our New Normal*!

# DISCUSSION QUESTIONS

1. What was your response when Liv saw the results of her daughter's pregnancy test? Did you sympathize more with Liv or Hazel? Why?

2. Did you think Liv's suggestion that the baby be put up for adoption was a good one? What did you think about Hazel's plan?

3. Do you believe Oscar really wanted to keep the baby? Was his desire realistic? Why or why not?

4. What are your experiences with adoption? How was your response to Liv's desire to put her grandchild up for adoption affected by your own experience?

5. Do you think, with more support from

their parents, that Tyler and Hazel could have raised the baby?

6. If Liv hadn't had the stress of dealing with her own parents, could she have been more available emotionally and physically to help Hazel?

7. Could Liv and Oscar have prevented Hazel's pregnancy from causing a divide between them? How?

8. Was Hazel a good mother? Why or why not? Was Liv?

9. Do you think Liv was being selfish in wanting to put the baby up for adoption? Was Oscar being selfish in wanting to keep her? Did your opinion change after Charlie's birth?

10. Had you written the book, how would you have ended it? Why?

# ABOUT THE AUTHOR

**Colleen Faulkner** lives in Delaware, where her family settled more than three hundred years ago. She comes from a long line of storytellers and spends her days, when she's not writing, running the family farm, reading, and traveling the world. She has four children and six grandchildren. Look for Colleen on Facebook or visit her website at: www.colleenfaulknernovels.com.